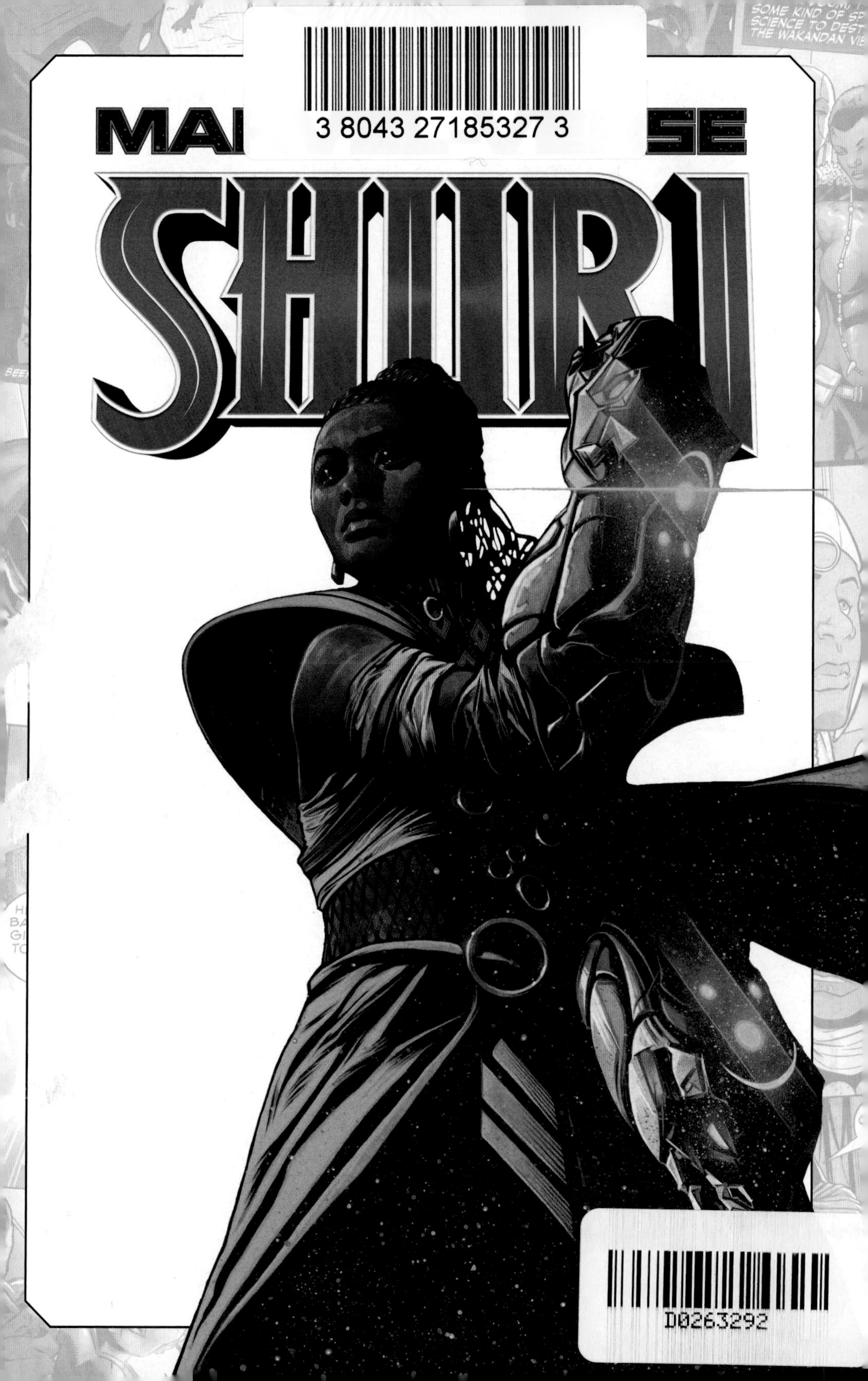
SHURI

MARVEL-VERSE
SHURI

SHURI #1

WRITER: **NNEDI OKORAFOR**
ARTIST: **LEONARDO ROMERO**
COLOR ARTIST: **JORDIE BELLAIRE**
LETTERER: VC's **JOE SABINO**
COVER ART: **SAM SPRATT**
ASSOCIATE EDITOR: **SARAH BRUNSTAD**
EDITOR: **WIL MOSS**
EXECUTIVE EDITOR: **TOM BREVOORT**

SHURI #6-7

WRITER: **VITA AYALA**
ARTIST: **PAUL DAVIDSON**
COLOR ARTIST: **TRÍONA FARRELL**
LETTERER: VC's **JOE SABINO**
COVER ART: **KIRBI FAGAN**
ASSOCIATE EDITOR: **SARAH BRUNSTAD**
EDITOR: **WIL MOSS**
EXECUTIVE EDITOR: **TOM BREVOORT**

MARVEL'S VOICES #1

WRITER: VITA AYALA
ARTIST: BERNARD CHANG
COLOR ARTIST: MARCELO MAIOLO
LETTERER: VC's TRAVIS LANHAM
COVER ART: RYAN BENJAMIN & ANTHONY WASHINGTON
EDITOR: CHRIS ROBINSON

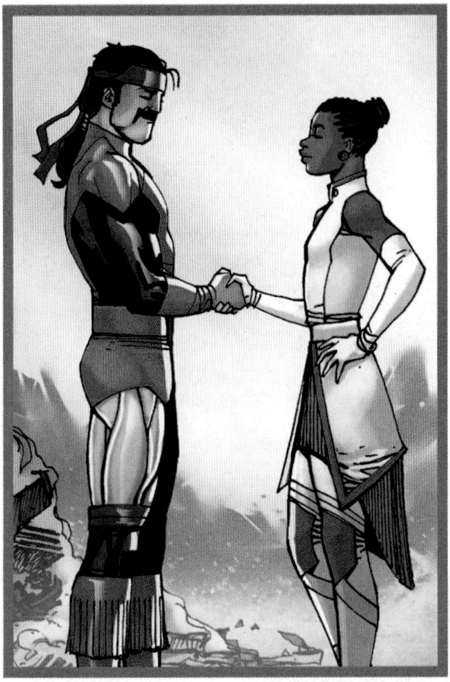

MARVEL ACTION: BLACK PANTHER #5-6

WRITER: VITA AYALA
ARTIST: ARIANNA FLOREAN
COLOR ARTIST: MATTIA IACONO
ART ASSISTANT: MARIO DEL PENNINO
COLOR ASSISTANT: SARA MARTINELLI
LETTERER: SHAWN LEE
COVER ART: ARIANNA FLOREAN
ASSISTANT EDITOR: ANNI PERHEENTUPA
ASSOCIATE EDITORS: ELIZABETH BREI & CHASE MAROTZ
EDITOR: DENTON J. TIPTON
SPECIAL THANKS TO WIL MOSS
ASSOCIATE EDITOR, MARVEL: CAITLIN O'CONNELL

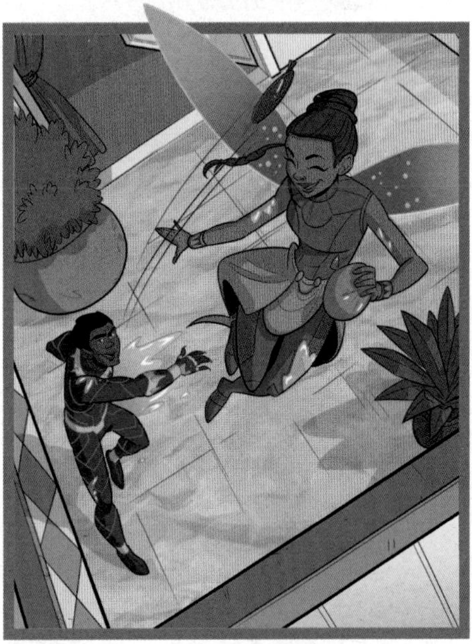

COLLECTION EDITOR: JENNIFER GRÜNWALD ASSISTANT EDITOR: DANIEL KIRCHHOFFER
ASSISTANT MANAGING EDITOR: MAIA LOY ASSOCIATE MANAGER, TALENT RELATIONS: LISA MONTALBANO
ASSOCIATE MANAGER, DIGITAL ASSETS: JOE HOCHSTEIN VP PRODUCTION & SPECIAL PROJECTS: JEFF YOUNGQUIST
RESEARCH: JESS HARROLD BOOK DESIGNER: ANTHONY GAMBINO SENIOR DESIGNER: ADAM DEL RE
SVP PRINT, SALES & MARKETING: DAVID GABRIEL EDITOR IN CHIEF: C.B. CEBULSKI

MARVEL-VERSE: SHURI GN-TPB. Contains material originally published in magazine form as SHURI (2018) #1 and #6-7, MARVEL'S VOICES (2020) #1, and MARVEL ACTION: BLACK PANTHER (2019) #5-6. First printing 2022. ISBN 978-1-302-94599-2. Published by MARVEL WORLDWIDE, INC., a subsidiary of MARVEL ENTERTAINMENT, LLC. OFFICE OF PUBLICATION: 1290 Avenue of the Americas, New York, NY 10104. © 2022 MARVEL No similarity between any of the names, characters, persons, and/or institutions in this book with those of any living or dead person or institution is intended, and any such similarity which may exist is purely coincidental. **Printed in Canada.** KEVIN FEIGE, Chief Creative Officer; DAN BUCKLEY, President, Marvel Entertainment; DAVID BOGART, Associate Publisher & SVP of Talent Affairs; TOM BREVOORT, VP, Executive Editor; NICK LOWE, Executive Editor, VP of Content, Digital Publishing; DAVID GABRIEL, VP of Print & Digital Publishing; SVEN LARSEN, VP of Licensed Publishing; MARK ANNUNZIATO, VP of Planning & Forecasting; JEFF YOUNGQUIST, VP of Production & Special Projects; ALEX MORALES, Director of Publishing Operations; DAN EDINGTON, Director of Editorial Operations; RICKEY PURDIN, Director of Talent Relations; JENNIFER GRÜNWALD, Director of Production & Special Projects; SUSAN CRESPI, Production Manager; STAN LEE, Chairman Emeritus. For information regarding advertising in Marvel Comics or on Marvel.com, please contact Vit DeBellis, Custom Solutions & Integrated Advertising Manager, at vdebellis@marvel.com. For Marvel subscription inquiries, please call 888-511-5480. **Manufactured between 7/29/2022 and 8/30/2022 by SOLISCO PRINTERS, SCOTT, QC, CANADA.**

10 9 8 7 6 5 4 3 2 1

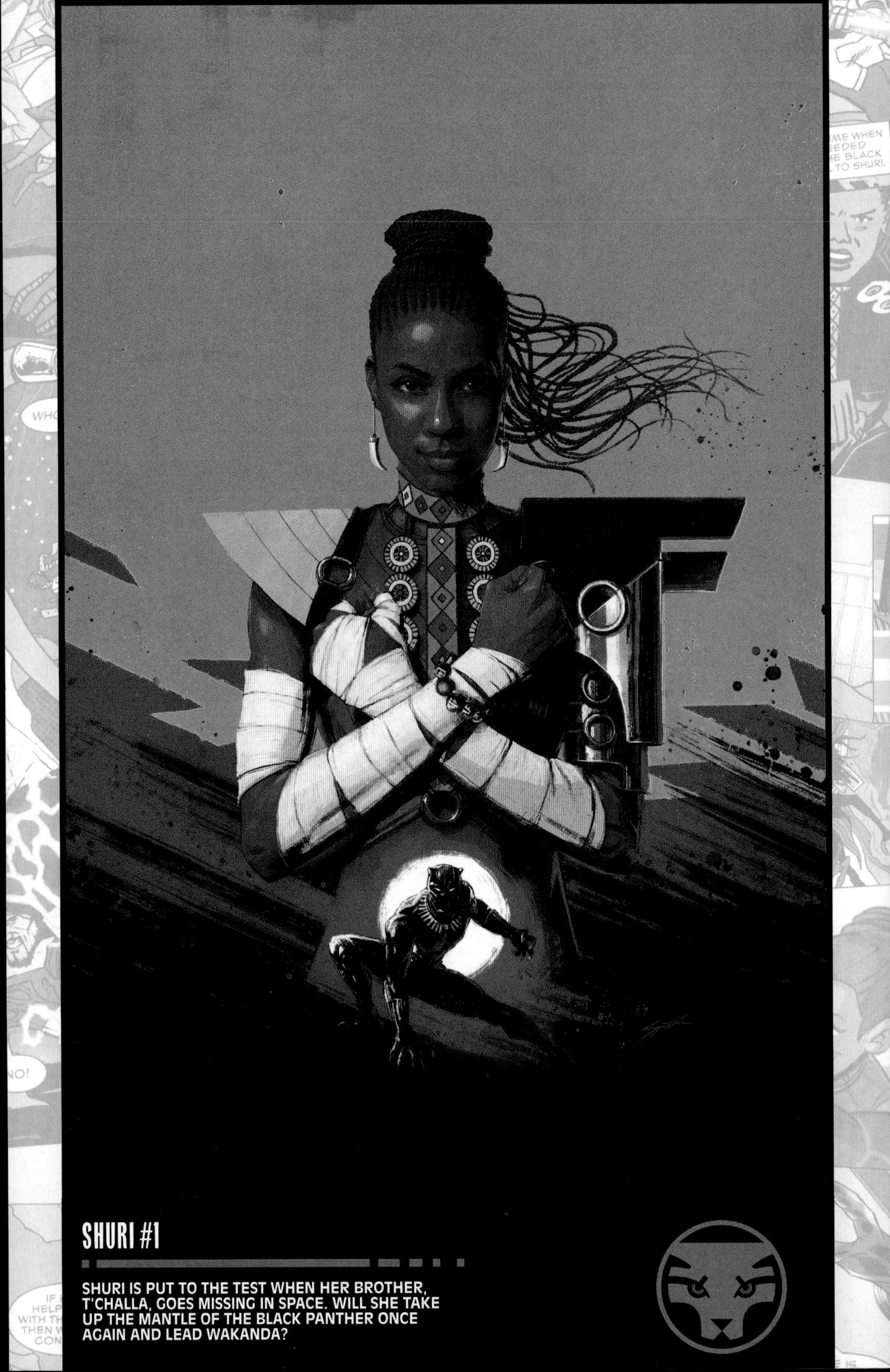

SHURI #1

SHURI IS PUT TO THE TEST WHEN HER BROTHER, T'CHALLA, GOES MISSING IN SPACE. WILL SHE TAKE UP THE MANTLE OF THE BLACK PANTHER ONCE AGAIN AND LEAD WAKANDA?

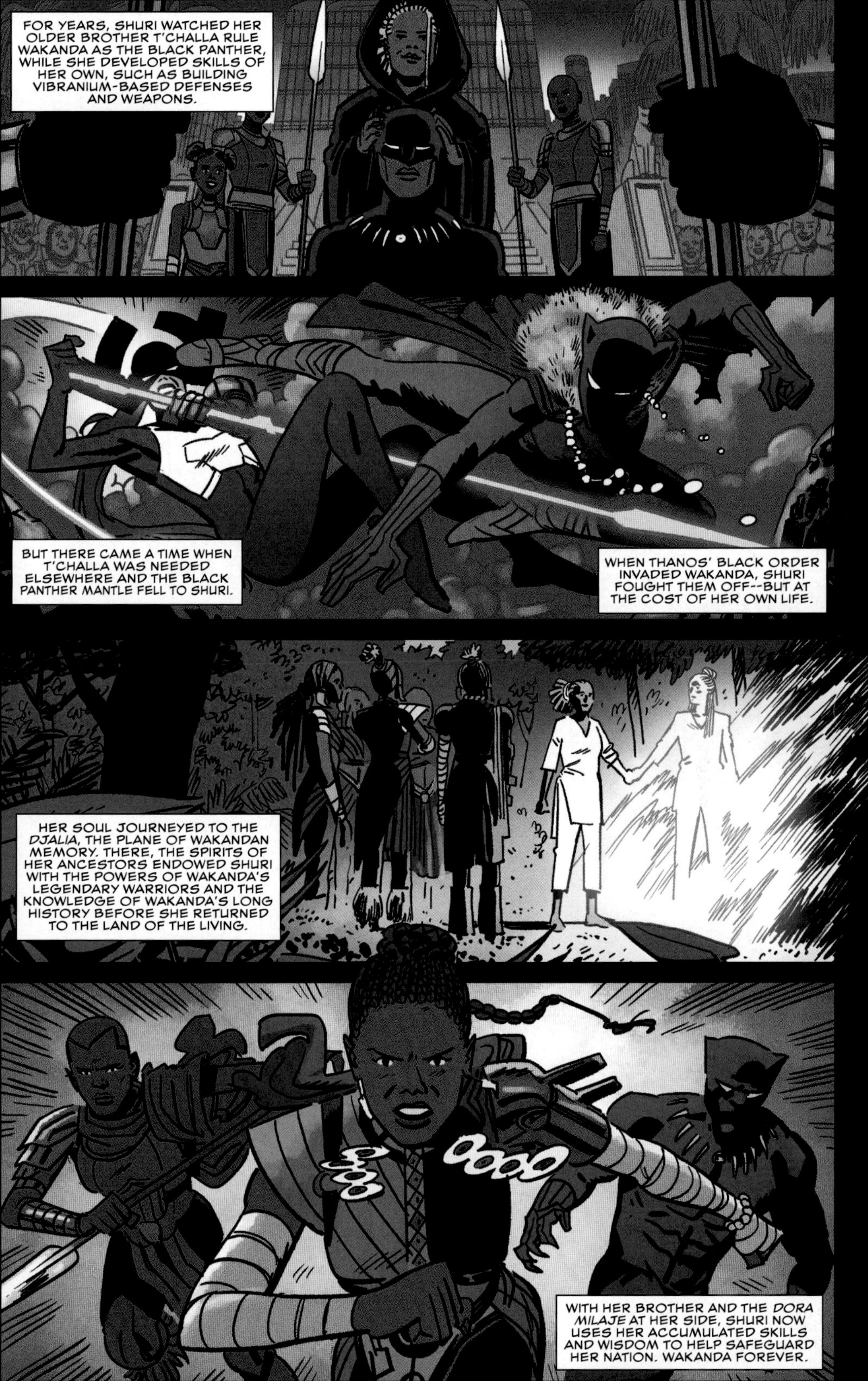
FOR YEARS, SHURI WATCHED HER OLDER BROTHER T'CHALLA RULE WAKANDA AS THE BLACK PANTHER, WHILE SHE DEVELOPED SKILLS OF HER OWN, SUCH AS BUILDING VIBRANIUM-BASED DEFENSES AND WEAPONS.
BUT THERE CAME A TIME WHEN T'CHALLA WAS NEEDED ELSEWHERE AND THE BLACK PANTHER MANTLE FELL TO SHURI.
WHEN THANOS' BLACK ORDER INVADED WAKANDA, SHURI FOUGHT THEM OFF--BUT AT THE COST OF HER OWN LIFE.
HER SOUL JOURNEYED TO THE *DJALIA*, THE PLANE OF WAKANDAN MEMORY. THERE, THE SPIRITS OF HER ANCESTORS ENDOWED SHURI WITH THE POWERS OF WAKANDA'S LEGENDARY WARRIORS AND THE KNOWLEDGE OF WAKANDA'S LONG HISTORY BEFORE SHE RETURNED TO THE LAND OF THE LIVING.
WITH HER BROTHER AND THE *DORA MILAJE* AT HER SIDE, SHURI NOW USES HER ACCUMULATED SKILLS AND WISDOM TO HELP SAFEGUARD HER NATION. WAKANDA FOREVER.

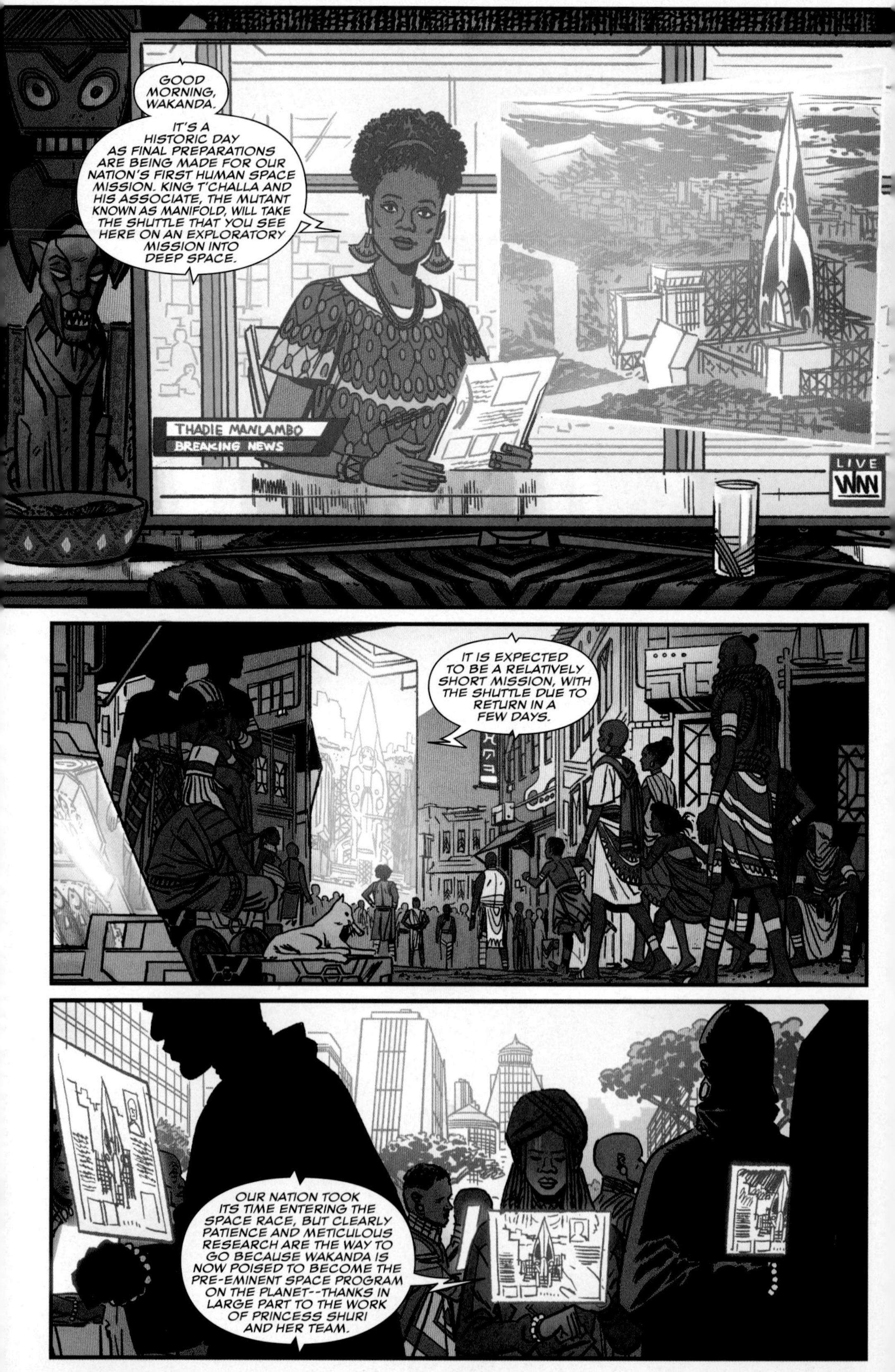
GOOD MORNING, WAKANDA.
IT'S A HISTORIC DAY AS FINAL PREPARATIONS ARE BEING MADE FOR OUR NATION'S FIRST HUMAN SPACE MISSION. KING T'CHALLA AND HIS ASSOCIATE, THE MUTANT KNOWN AS MANIFOLD, WILL TAKE THE SHUTTLE THAT YOU SEE HERE ON AN EXPLORATORY MISSION INTO DEEP SPACE.
THADIE MANLAMBO
BREAKING NEWS
LIVE
WNN
IT IS EXPECTED TO BE A RELATIVELY SHORT MISSION, WITH THE SHUTTLE DUE TO RETURN IN A FEW DAYS.
OUR NATION TOOK ITS TIME ENTERING THE SPACE RACE, BUT CLEARLY PATIENCE AND METICULOUS RESEARCH ARE THE WAY TO GO BECAUSE WAKANDA IS NOW POISED TO BECOME THE PRE-EMINENT SPACE PROGRAM ON THE PLANET--THANKS IN LARGE PART TO THE WORK OF PRINCESS SHURI AND HER TEAM.

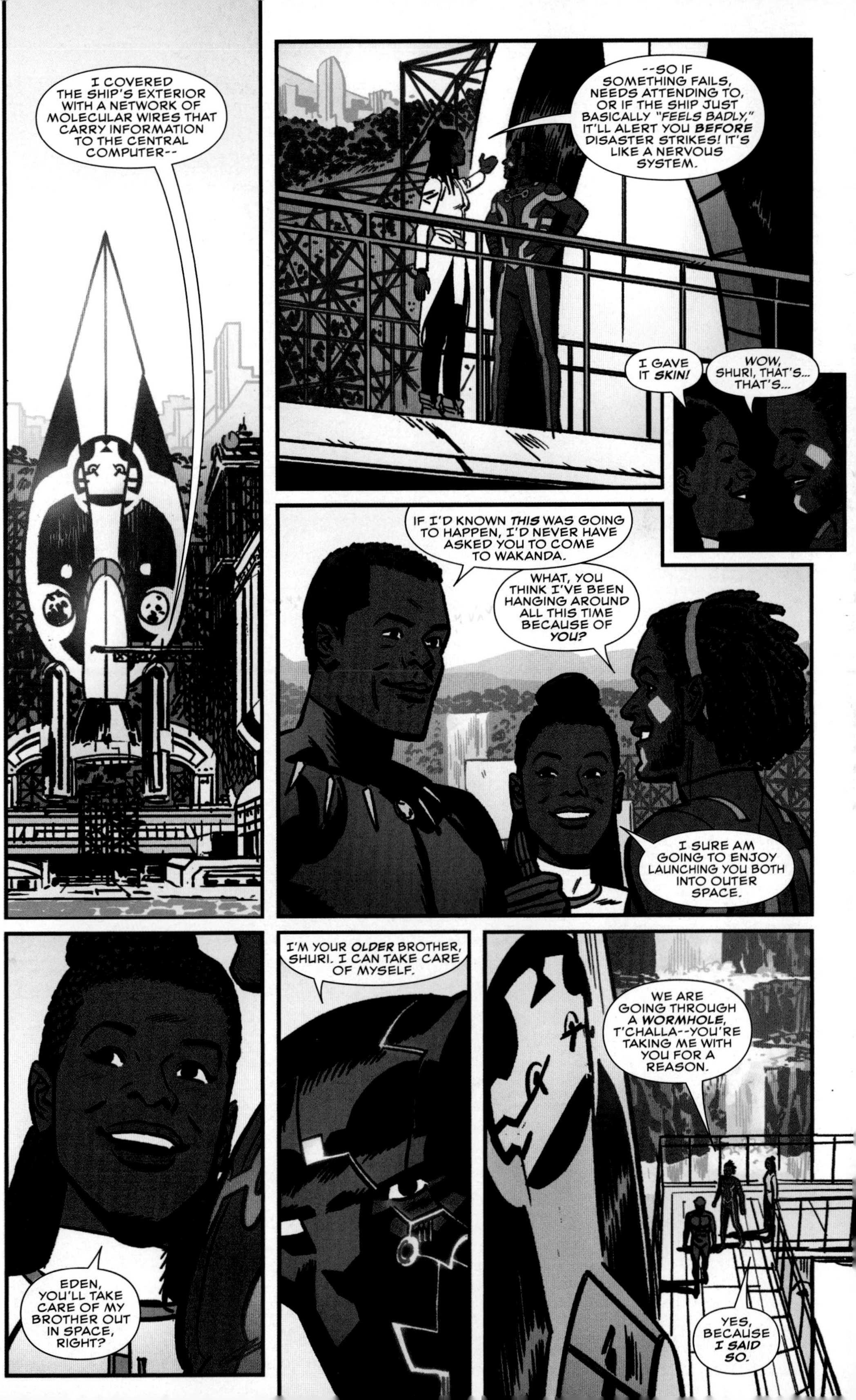
I COVERED THE SHIP'S EXTERIOR WITH A NETWORK OF MOLECULAR WIRES THAT CARRY INFORMATION TO THE CENTRAL COMPUTER--
--SO IF SOMETHING FAILS, NEEDS ATTENDING TO, OR IF THE SHIP JUST BASICALLY "FEELS BADLY," IT'LL ALERT YOU BEFORE DISASTER STRIKES! IT'S LIKE A NERVOUS SYSTEM.
I GAVE IT SKIN!
WOW, SHURI, THAT'S... THAT'S...
IF I'D KNOWN THIS WAS GOING TO HAPPEN, I'D NEVER HAVE ASKED YOU TO COME TO WAKANDA.
WHAT, YOU THINK I'VE BEEN HANGING AROUND ALL THIS TIME BECAUSE OF YOU?
I SURE AM GOING TO ENJOY LAUNCHING YOU BOTH INTO OUTER SPACE.
EDEN, YOU'LL TAKE CARE OF MY BROTHER OUT IN SPACE, RIGHT?
I'M YOUR OLDER BROTHER, SHURI. I CAN TAKE CARE OF MYSELF.
WE ARE GOING THROUGH A WORMHOLE, T'CHALLA--YOU'RE TAKING ME WITH YOU FOR A REASON.
YES, BECAUSE I SAID SO.

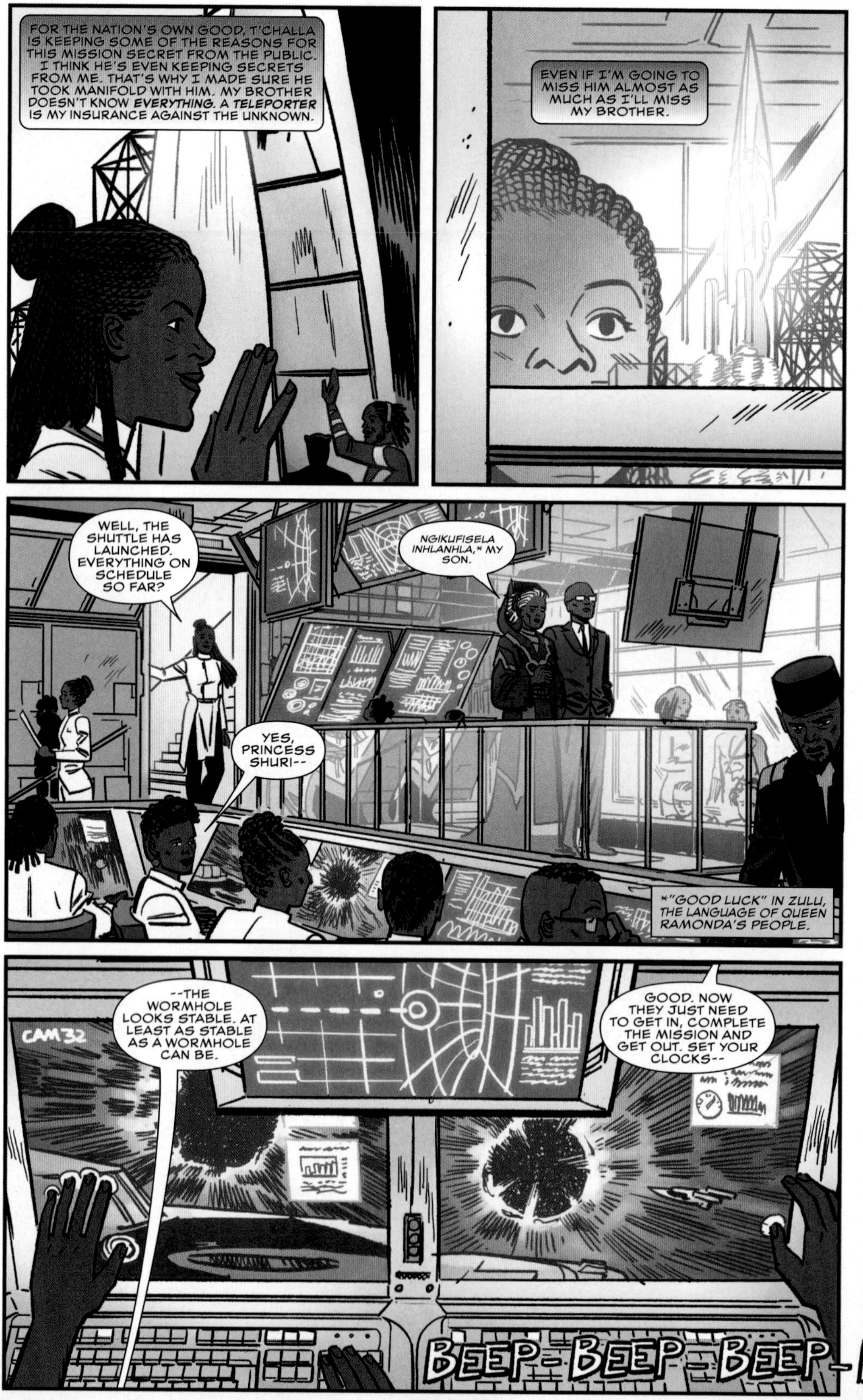
FOR THE NATION'S OWN GOOD, T'CHALLA IS KEEPING SOME OF THE REASONS FOR THIS MISSION SECRET FROM THE PUBLIC. I THINK HE'S EVEN KEEPING SECRETS FROM ME. THAT'S WHY I MADE SURE HE TOOK MANIFOLD WITH HIM. MY BROTHER DOESN'T KNOW *EVERYTHING*. A *TELEPORTER* IS MY INSURANCE AGAINST THE UNKNOWN.
EVEN IF I'M GOING TO MISS HIM ALMOST AS MUCH AS I'LL MISS MY BROTHER.
WELL, THE SHUTTLE HAS LAUNCHED. EVERYTHING ON SCHEDULE SO FAR?
NGIKUFISELA INHLANHLA,* MY SON.
YES, PRINCESS SHURI--
*"GOOD LUCK" IN ZULU, THE LANGUAGE OF QUEEN RAMONDA'S PEOPLE.
CAM 32
--THE WORMHOLE LOOKS STABLE. AT LEAST AS STABLE AS A WORMHOLE CAN BE.
GOOD. NOW THEY JUST NEED TO GET IN, COMPLETE THE MISSION AND GET OUT. SET YOUR CLOCKS--
BEEP-BEEP-BEEP-

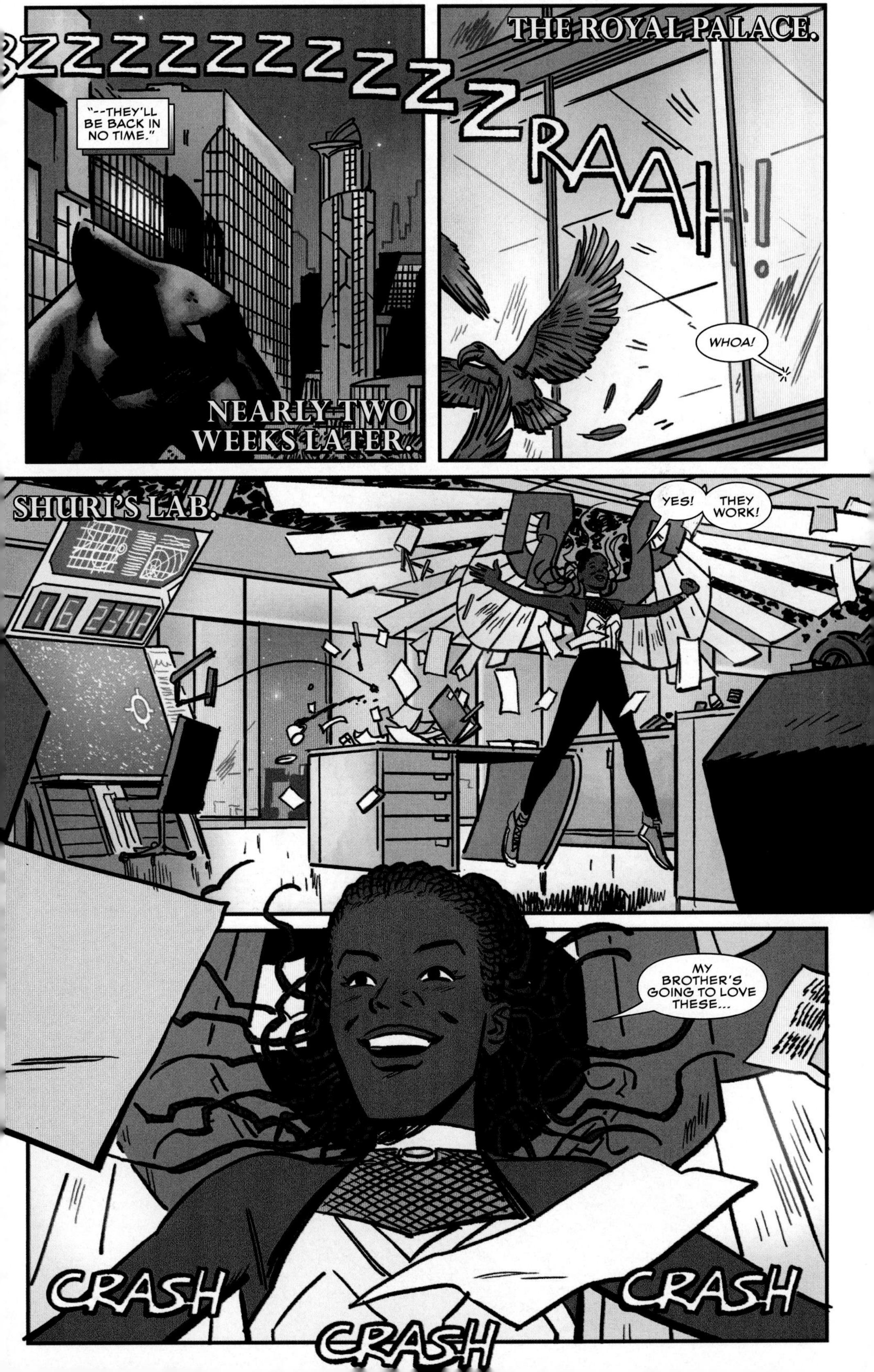
BZZZZZZZZZZZZ
"--THEY'LL BE BACK IN NO TIME."
NEARLY TWO WEEKS LATER.
THE ROYAL PALACE.
ZRAAAH!
WHOA!
SHURI'S LAB.
YES!
THEY WORK!
MY BROTHER'S GOING TO LOVE THESE...
CRASH
CRASH
CRASH

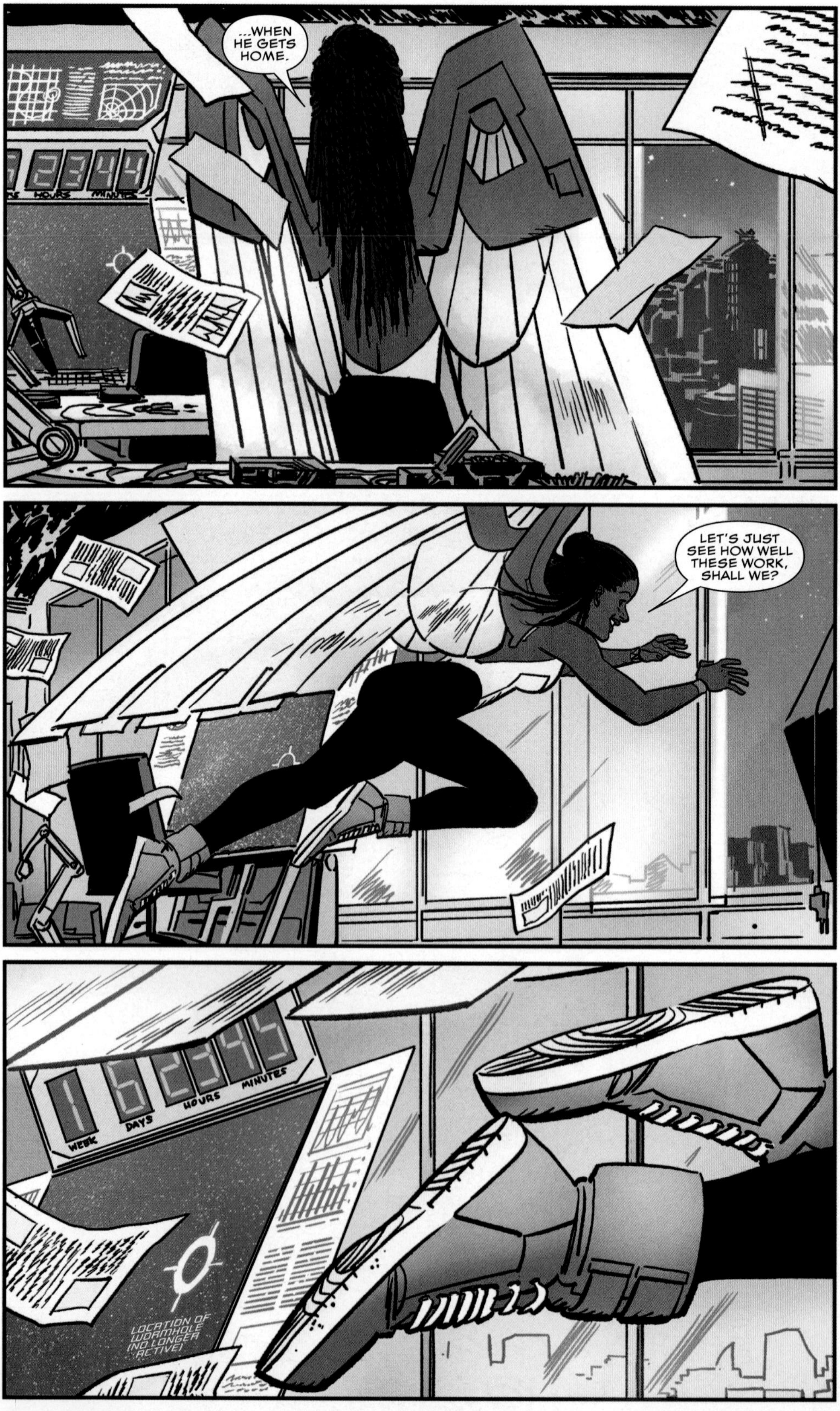
...WHEN HE GETS HOME.
HOURS
MINUTES
LET'S JUST SEE HOW WELL THESE WORK, SHALL WE?
WEEK
DAYS
HOURS
MINUTES
LOCATION OF WORMHOLE (NO LONGER ACTIVE)

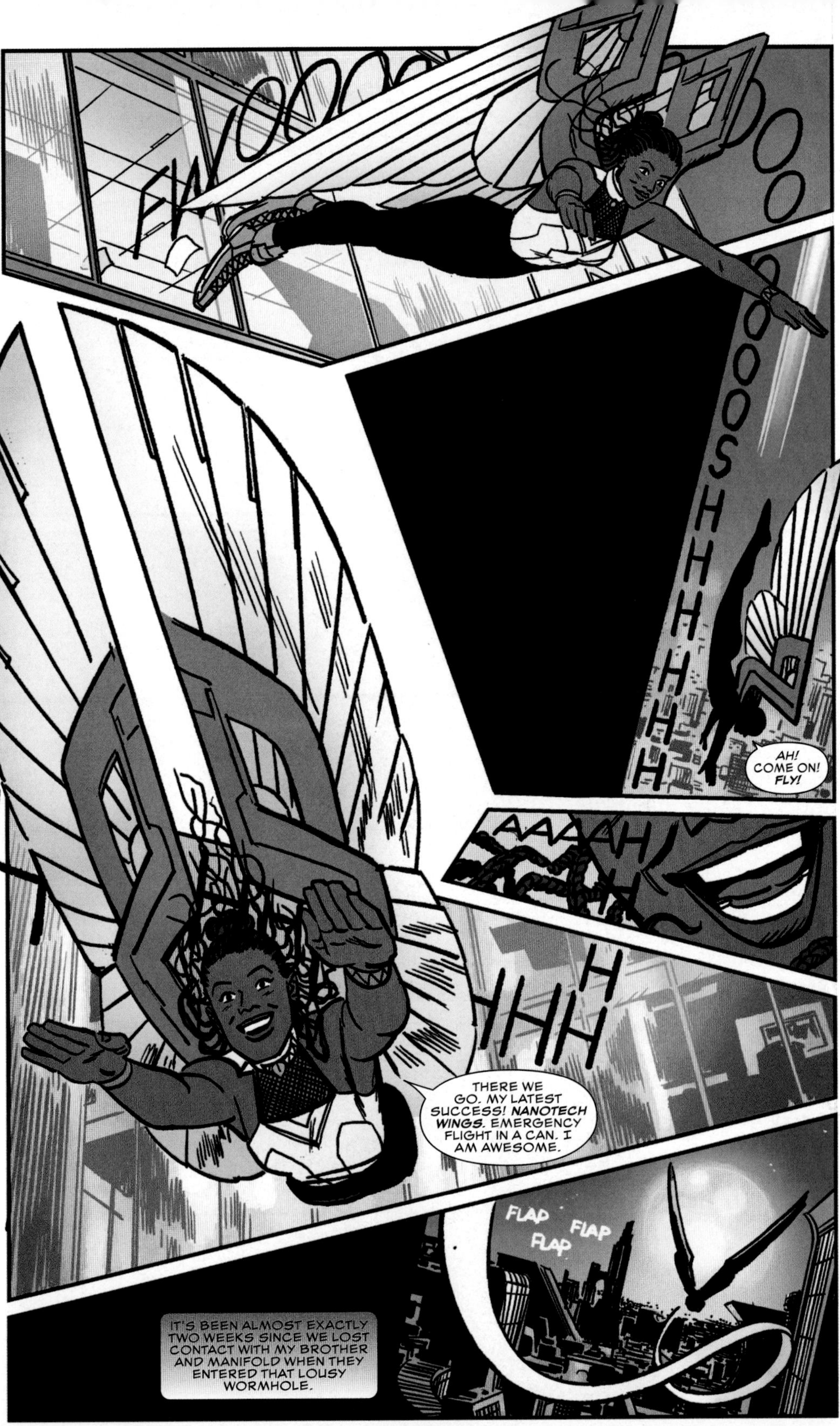
FWOOOOOOOOOOOOOOOOOSHHHHHHHHHH
AH! COME ON! FLY!
AAAAHHHHHHHHH
THERE WE GO. MY LATEST SUCCESS! NANOTECH WINGS. EMERGENCY FLIGHT IN A CAN. I AM AWESOME.
FLAP FLAP FLAP
IT'S BEEN ALMOST EXACTLY TWO WEEKS SINCE WE LOST CONTACT WITH MY BROTHER AND MANIFOLD WHEN THEY ENTERED THAT LOUSY WORMHOLE.

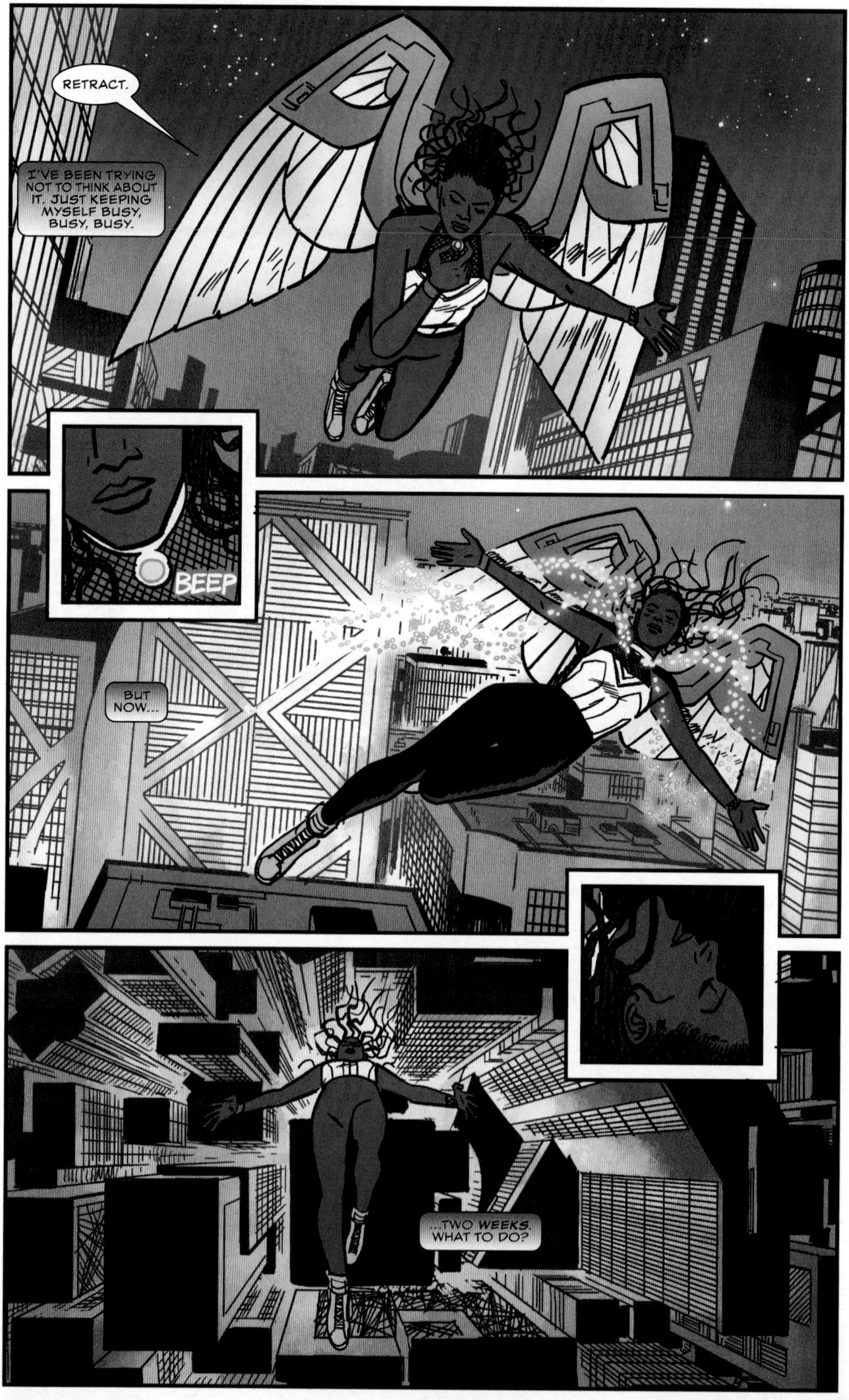
RETRACT.
I'VE BEEN TRYING NOT TO THINK ABOUT IT. JUST KEEPING MYSELF BUSY, BUSY, BUSY.
BEEP
BUT NOW...
...TWO WEEKS. WHAT TO DO?

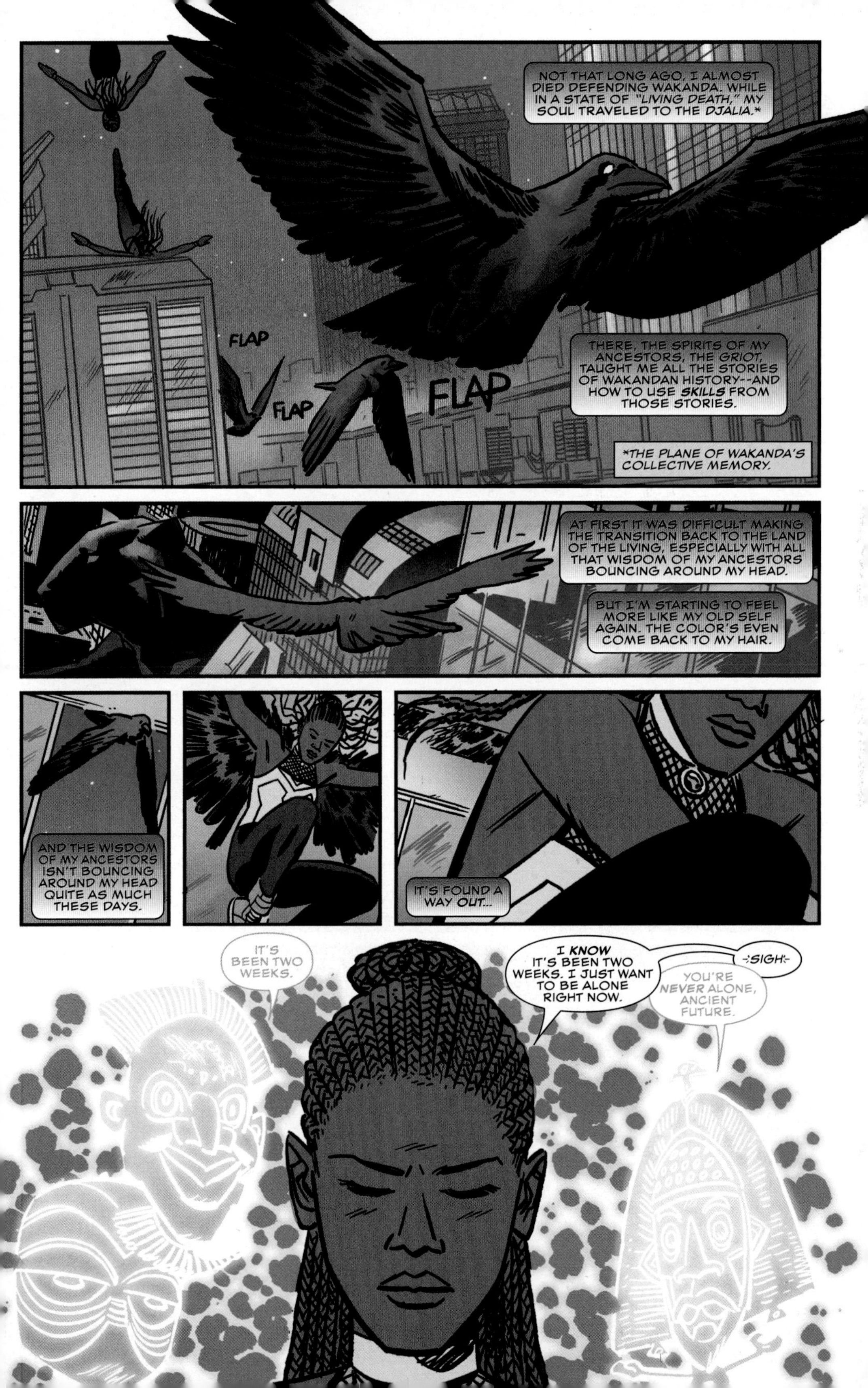
NOT THAT LONG AGO, I ALMOST DIED DEFENDING WAKANDA. WHILE IN A STATE OF "LIVING DEATH," MY SOUL TRAVELED TO THE DJALIA.*
FLAP
FLAP
FLAP
THERE, THE SPIRITS OF MY ANCESTORS, THE GRIOT, TAUGHT ME ALL THE STORIES OF WAKANDAN HISTORY--AND HOW TO USE SKILLS FROM THOSE STORIES.
*THE PLANE OF WAKANDA'S COLLECTIVE MEMORY.
AT FIRST IT WAS DIFFICULT MAKING THE TRANSITION BACK TO THE LAND OF THE LIVING, ESPECIALLY WITH ALL THAT WISDOM OF MY ANCESTORS BOUNCING AROUND MY HEAD.
BUT I'M STARTING TO FEEL MORE LIKE MY OLD SELF AGAIN. THE COLOR'S EVEN COME BACK TO MY HAIR.
AND THE WISDOM OF MY ANCESTORS ISN'T BOUNCING AROUND MY HEAD QUITE AS MUCH THESE DAYS.
IT'S FOUND A WAY OUT...
IT'S BEEN TWO WEEKS.
I KNOW IT'S BEEN TWO WEEKS. I JUST WANT TO BE ALONE RIGHT NOW.
-SIGH-
YOU'RE NEVER ALONE, ANCIENT FUTURE.

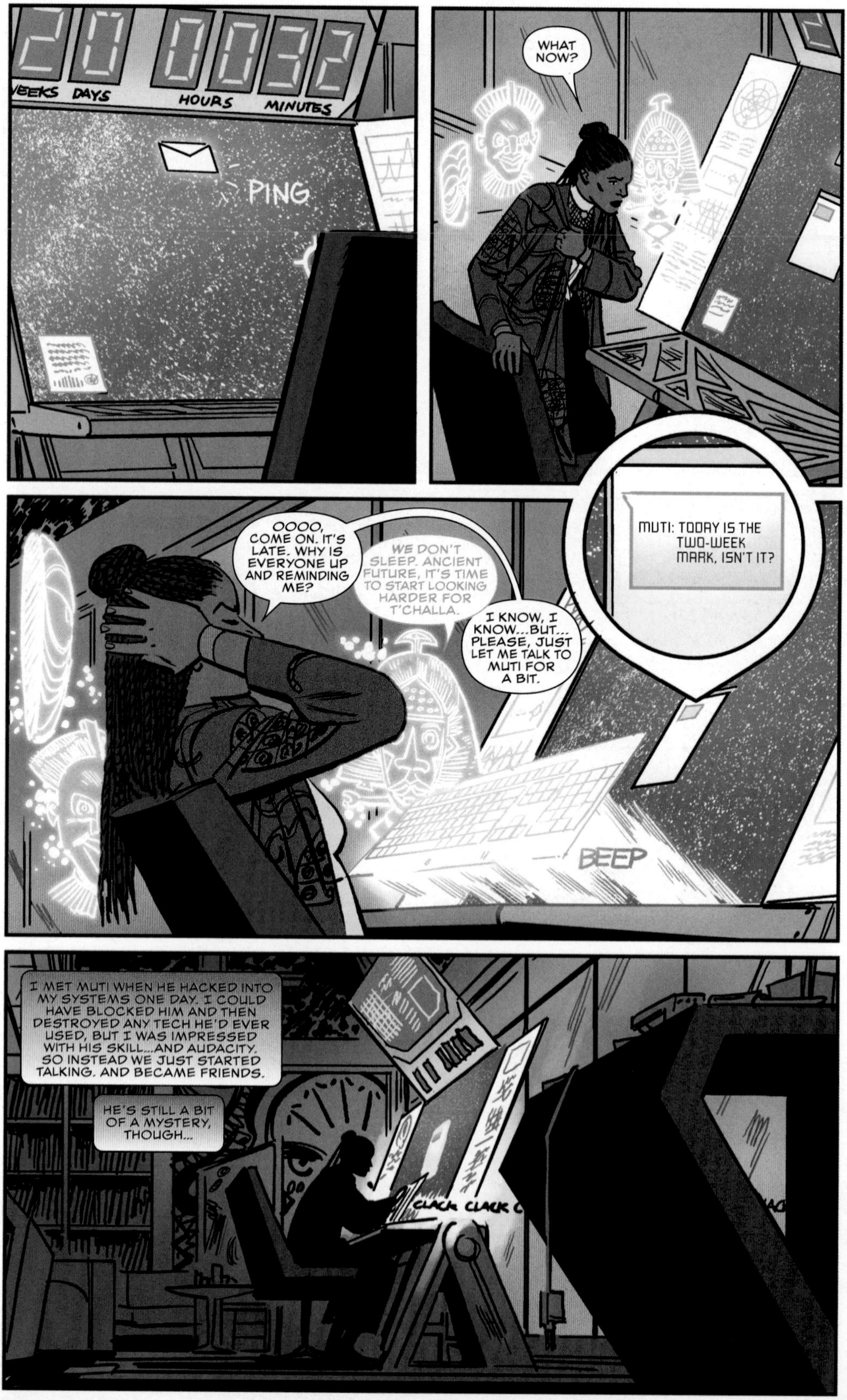
20 00 03 2
WEEKS DAYS HOURS MINUTES
PING
WHAT NOW?
MUTI: TODAY IS THE TWO-WEEK MARK, ISN'T IT?
OOOO, COME ON. IT'S LATE. WHY IS EVERYONE UP AND REMINDING ME?
WE DON'T SLEEP. ANCIENT FUTURE, IT'S TIME TO START LOOKING HARDER FOR T'CHALLA.
I KNOW, I KNOW...BUT... PLEASE, JUST LET ME TALK TO MUTI FOR A BIT.
BEEP
I MET MUTI WHEN HE HACKED INTO MY SYSTEMS ONE DAY. I COULD HAVE BLOCKED HIM AND THEN DESTROYED ANY TECH HE'D EVER USED, BUT I WAS IMPRESSED WITH HIS SKILL...AND AUDACITY. SO INSTEAD WE JUST STARTED TALKING. AND BECAME FRIENDS.
HE'S STILL A BIT OF A MYSTERY, THOUGH...
CLACK CLACK

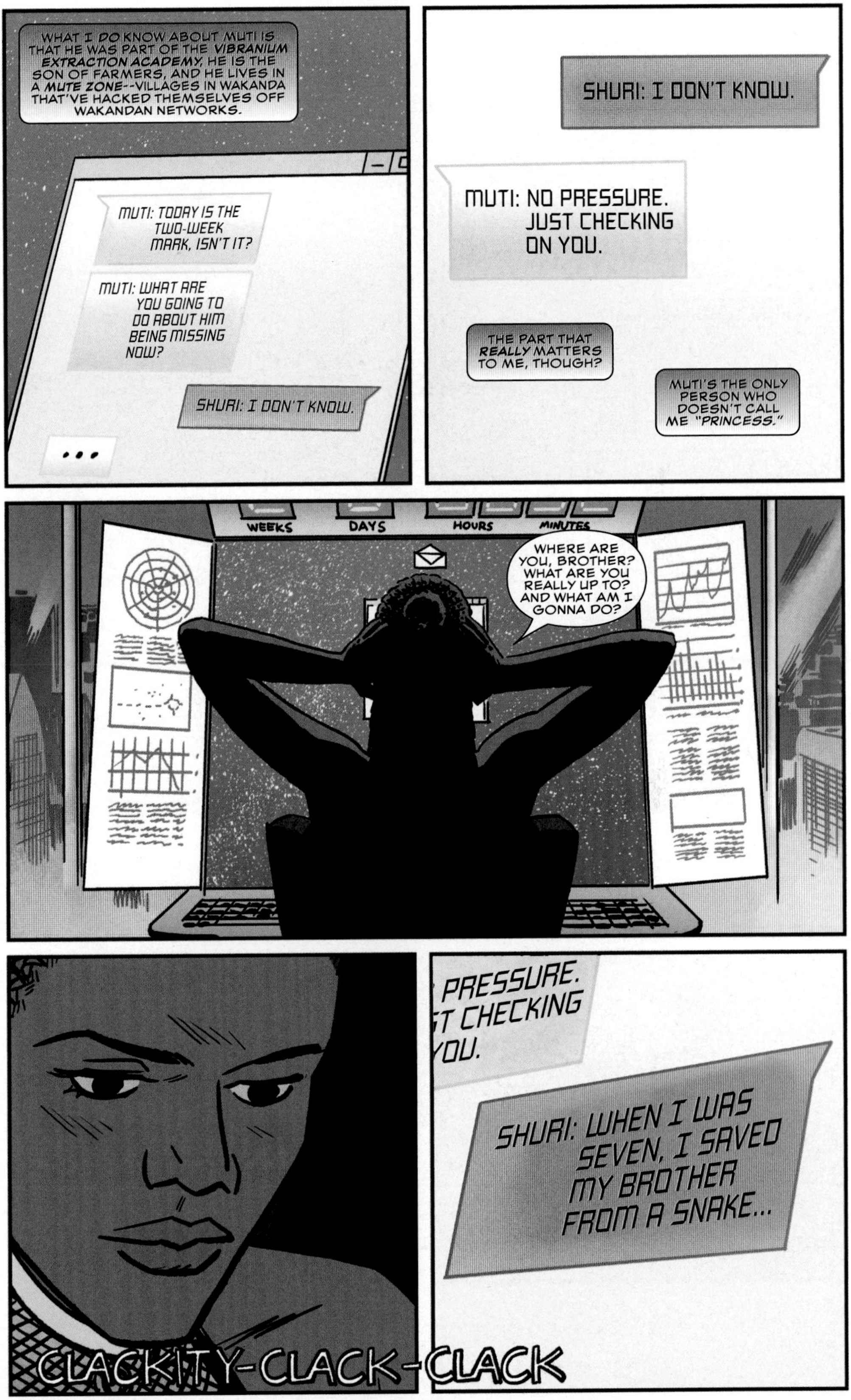

WHAT I *DO* KNOW ABOUT MUTI IS THAT HE WAS PART OF THE *VIBRANIUM EXTRACTION ACADEMY,* HE IS THE SON OF FARMERS, AND HE LIVES IN A *MUTE ZONE*--VILLAGES IN WAKANDA THAT'VE HACKED THEMSELVES OFF WAKANDAN NETWORKS.
MUTI: TODAY IS THE TWO-WEEK MARK, ISN'T IT?
MUTI: WHAT ARE YOU GOING TO DO ABOUT HIM BEING MISSING NOW?
SHURI: I DON'T KNOW.
...
SHURI: I DON'T KNOW.
MUTI: NO PRESSURE. JUST CHECKING ON YOU.
THE PART THAT *REALLY* MATTERS TO ME, THOUGH?
MUTI'S THE ONLY PERSON WHO DOESN'T CALL ME *"PRINCESS."*
WEEKS
DAYS
HOURS
MINUTES
WHERE ARE YOU, BROTHER? WHAT ARE YOU REALLY UP TO? AND WHAT AM I GONNA DO?
SHURI: WHEN I WAS SEVEN, I SAVED MY BROTHER FROM A SNAKE...
CLACKITY-CLACK-CLACK

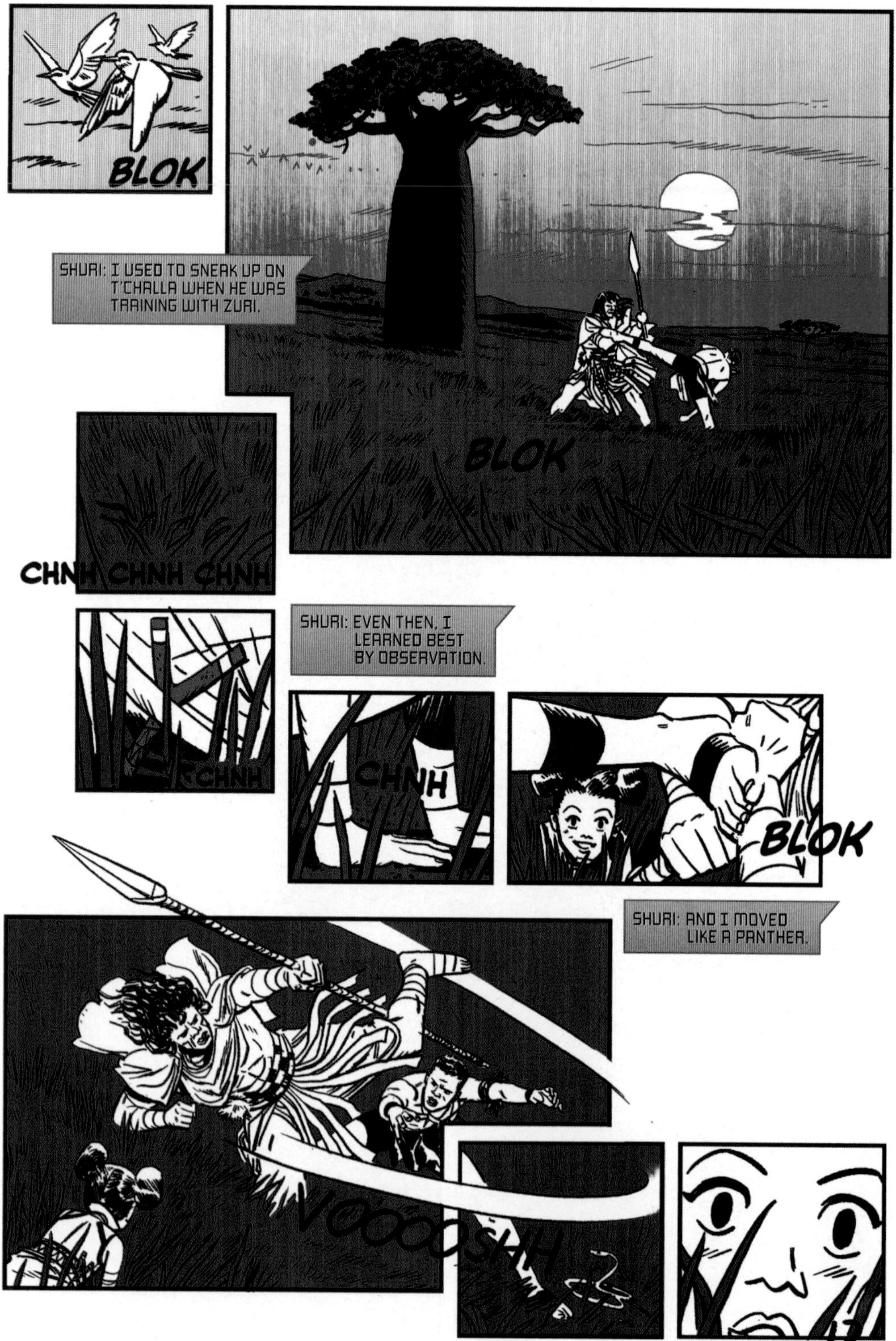
BLOK
SHURI: I USED TO SNEAK UP ON T'CHALLA WHEN HE WAS TRAINING WITH ZURI.
BLOK
CHNH CHNH CHNH
SHURI: EVEN THEN, I LEARNED BEST BY OBSERVATION.
CHNH
CHNH
BLOK
SHURI: AND I MOVED LIKE A PANTHER.
VOOOOSHH
!!

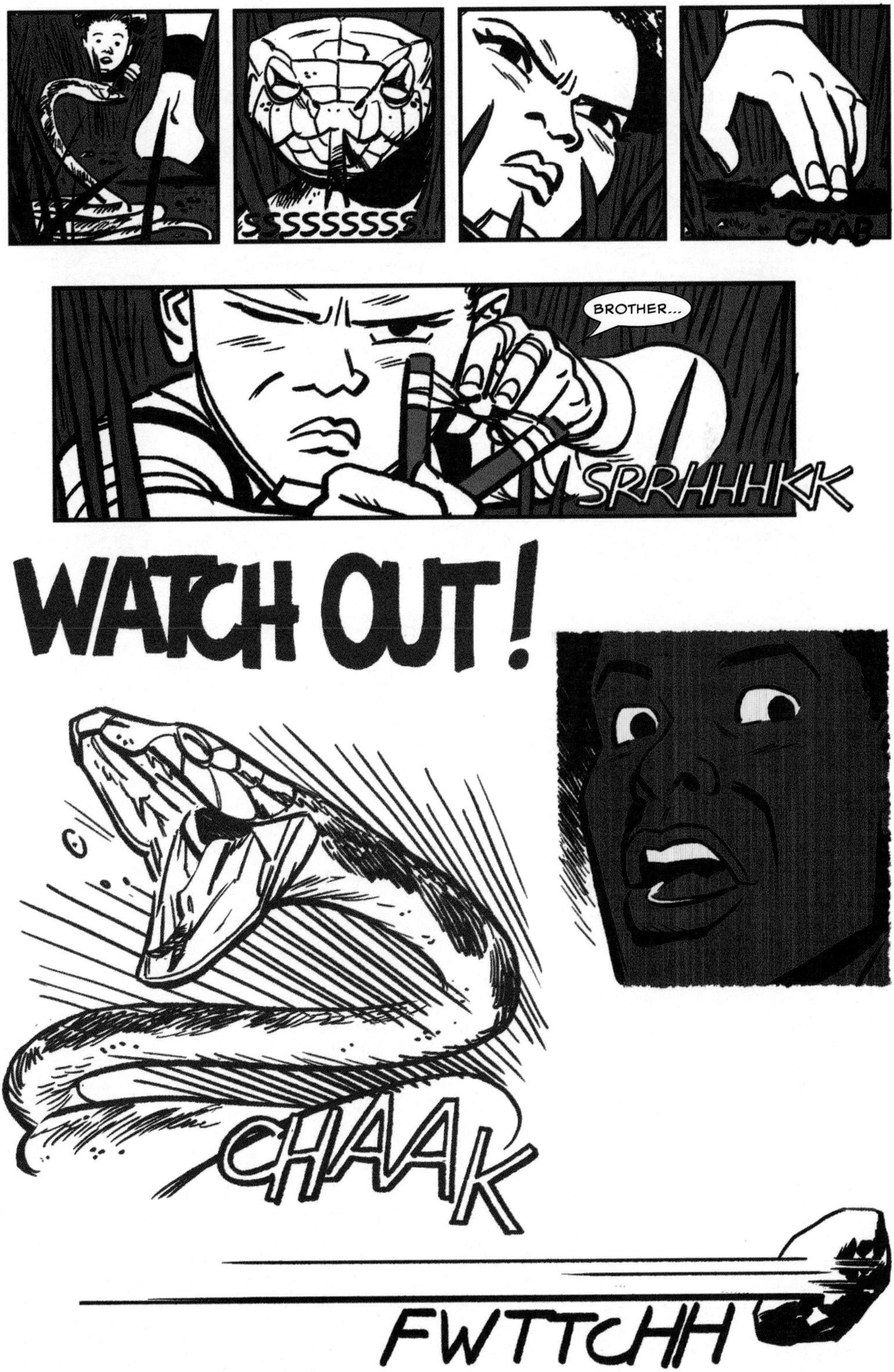
SSSSSSSSS...
GRAB
BROTHER...
SRRHHHKK
WATCH OUT!
CHAAK
FWTTCHH

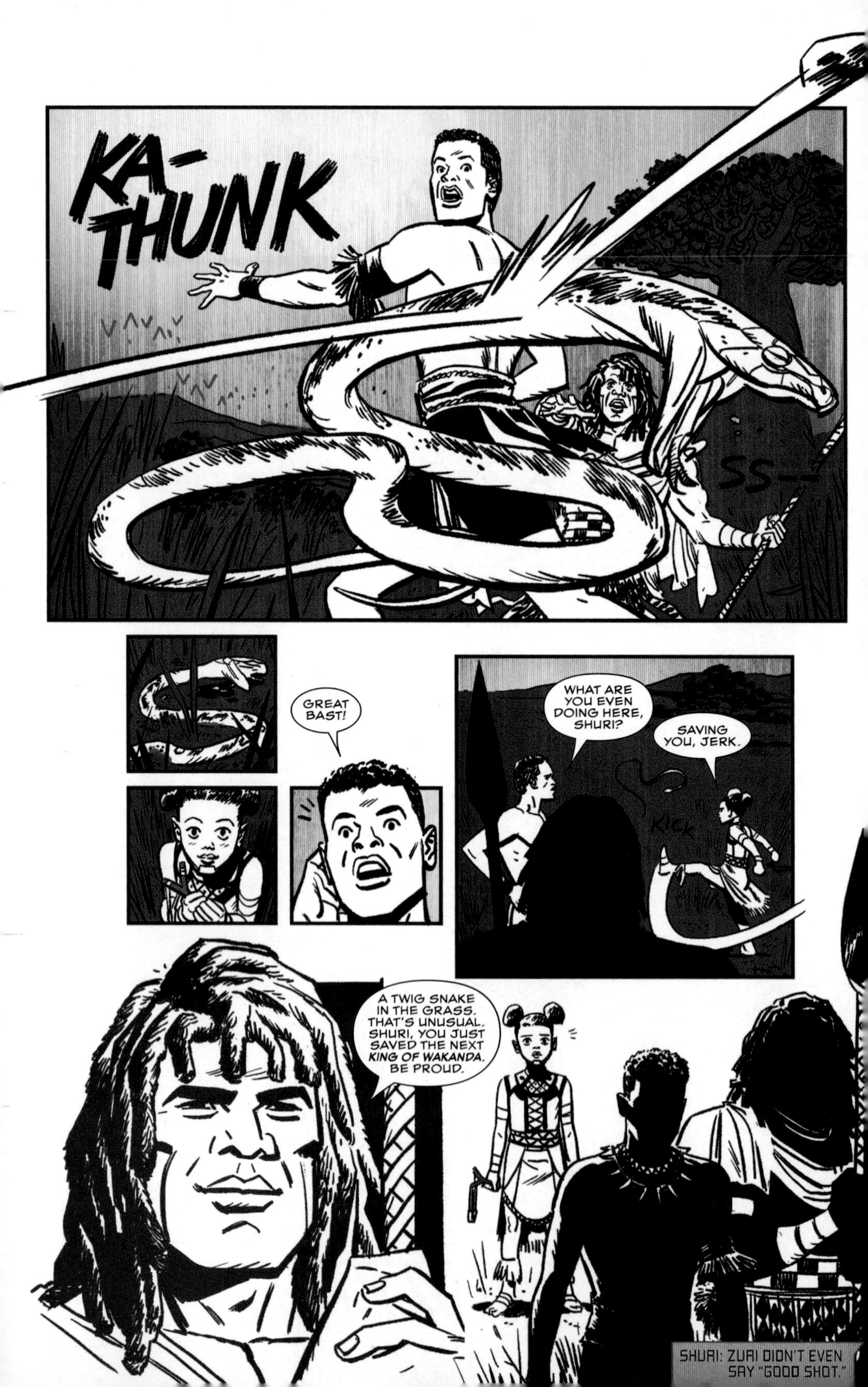
KA-THUNK
SS--
GREAT BAST!
WHAT ARE YOU EVEN DOING HERE, SHURI?
SAVING YOU, JERK.
KICK
A TWIG SNAKE IN THE GRASS. THAT'S UNUSUAL. SHURI, YOU JUST SAVED THE NEXT *KING OF WAKANDA.* BE PROUD.
SHURI: ZURI DIDN'T EVEN SAY "GOOD SHOT."

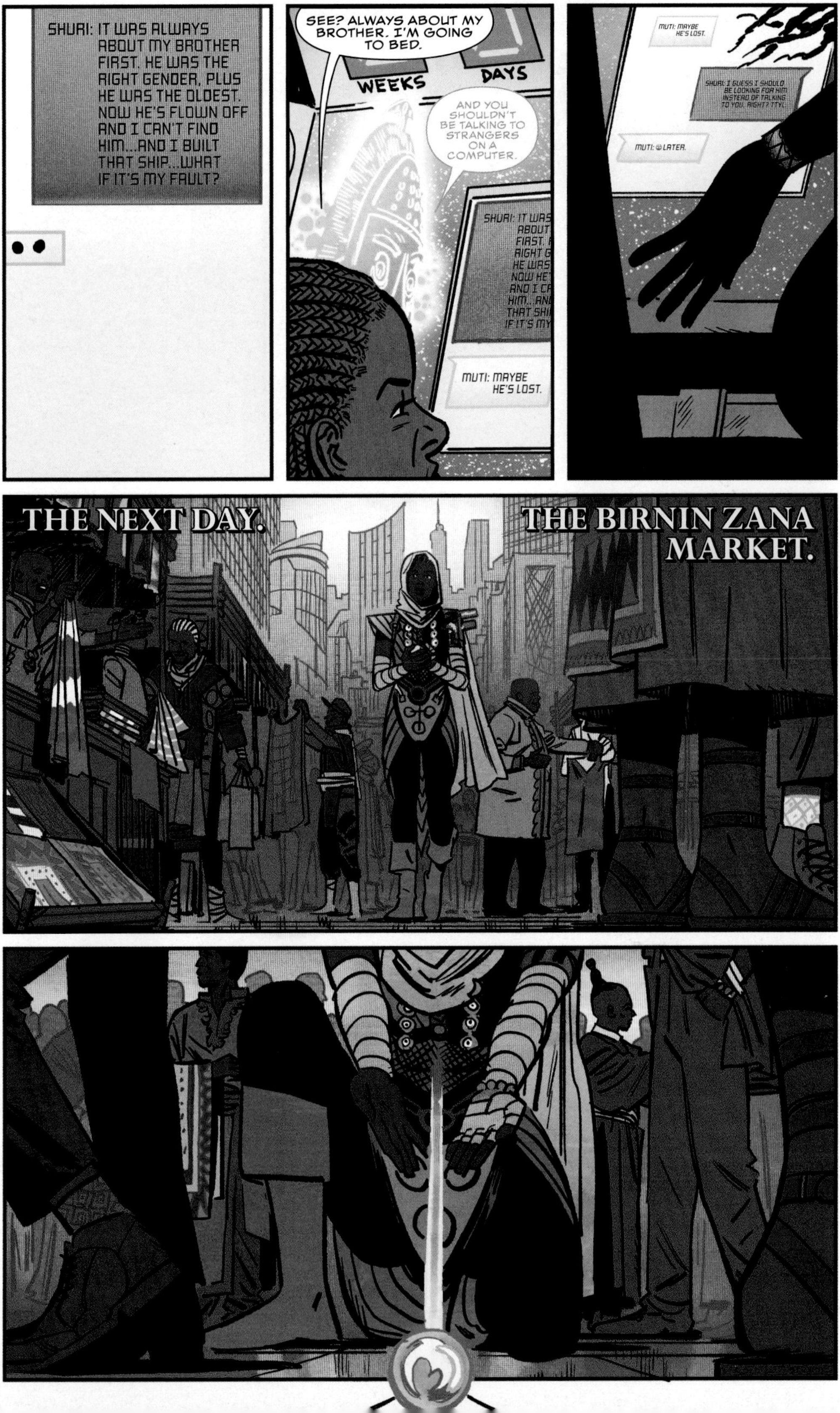
SHURI: IT WAS ALWAYS ABOUT MY BROTHER FIRST. HE WAS THE RIGHT GENDER, PLUS HE WAS THE OLDEST. NOW HE'S FLOWN OFF AND I CAN'T FIND HIM...AND I BUILT THAT SHIP...WHAT IF IT'S MY FAULT?
SEE? ALWAYS ABOUT MY BROTHER. I'M GOING TO BED.
WEEKS
DAYS
AND YOU SHOULDN'T BE TALKING TO STRANGERS ON A COMPUTER.
MUTI: MAYBE HE'S LOST.
MUTI: MAYBE HE'S LOST.
SHURI: I GUESS I SHOULD BE LOOKING FOR HIM INSTEAD OF TALKING TO YOU, RIGHT? TTYL.
MUTI: LATER.
THE NEXT DAY.
THE BIRNIN ZANA MARKET.

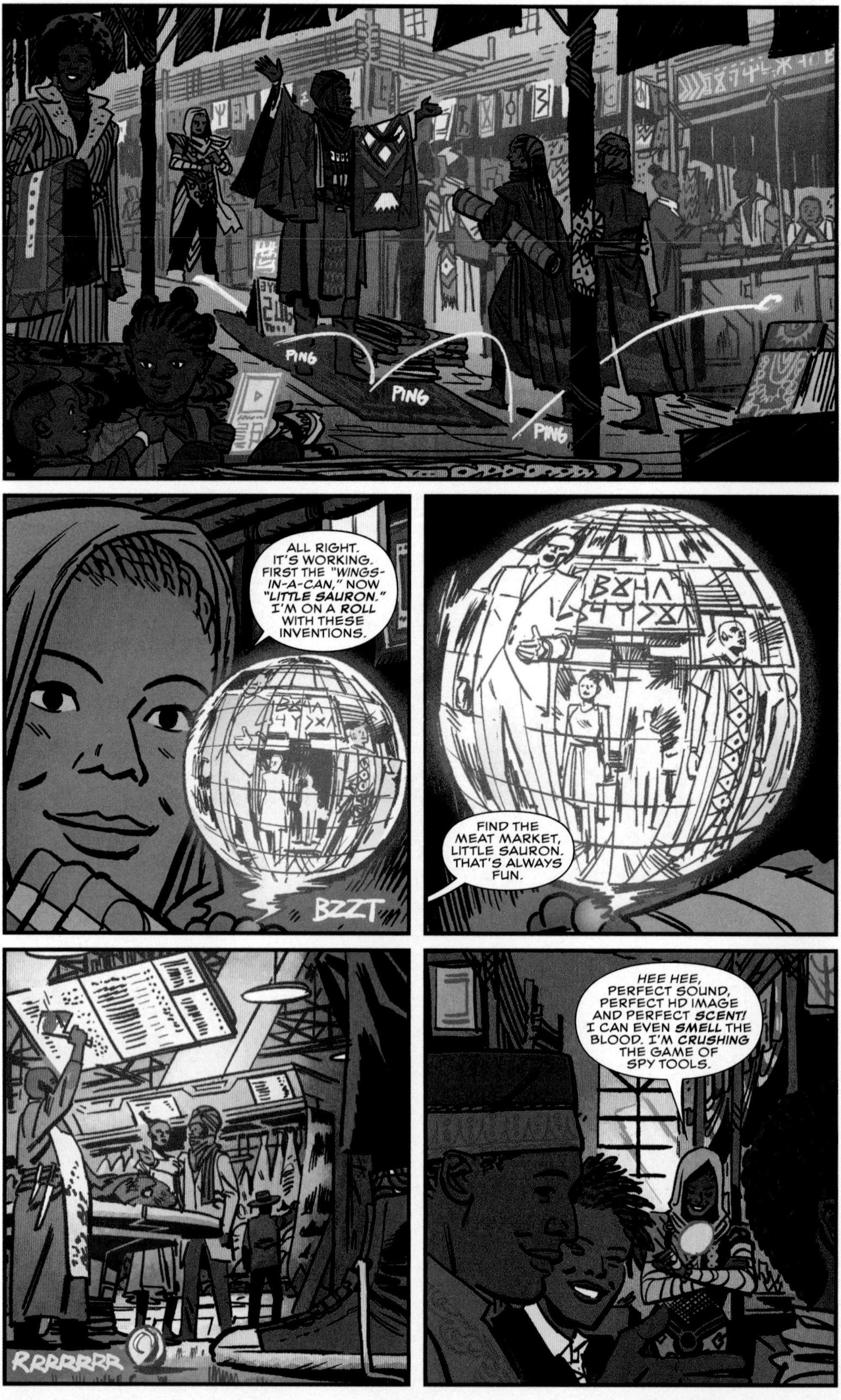
PING
PING
PING
ALL RIGHT. IT'S WORKING. FIRST THE "WINGS-IN-A-CAN," NOW "LITTLE SAURON." I'M ON A ROLL WITH THESE INVENTIONS.
BZZT
FIND THE MEAT MARKET, LITTLE SAURON. THAT'S ALWAYS FUN.
RRRRRRR
HEE HEE, PERFECT SOUND, PERFECT HD IMAGE AND PERFECT SCENT! I CAN EVEN SMELL THE BLOOD. I'M CRUSHING THE GAME OF SPY TOOLS.

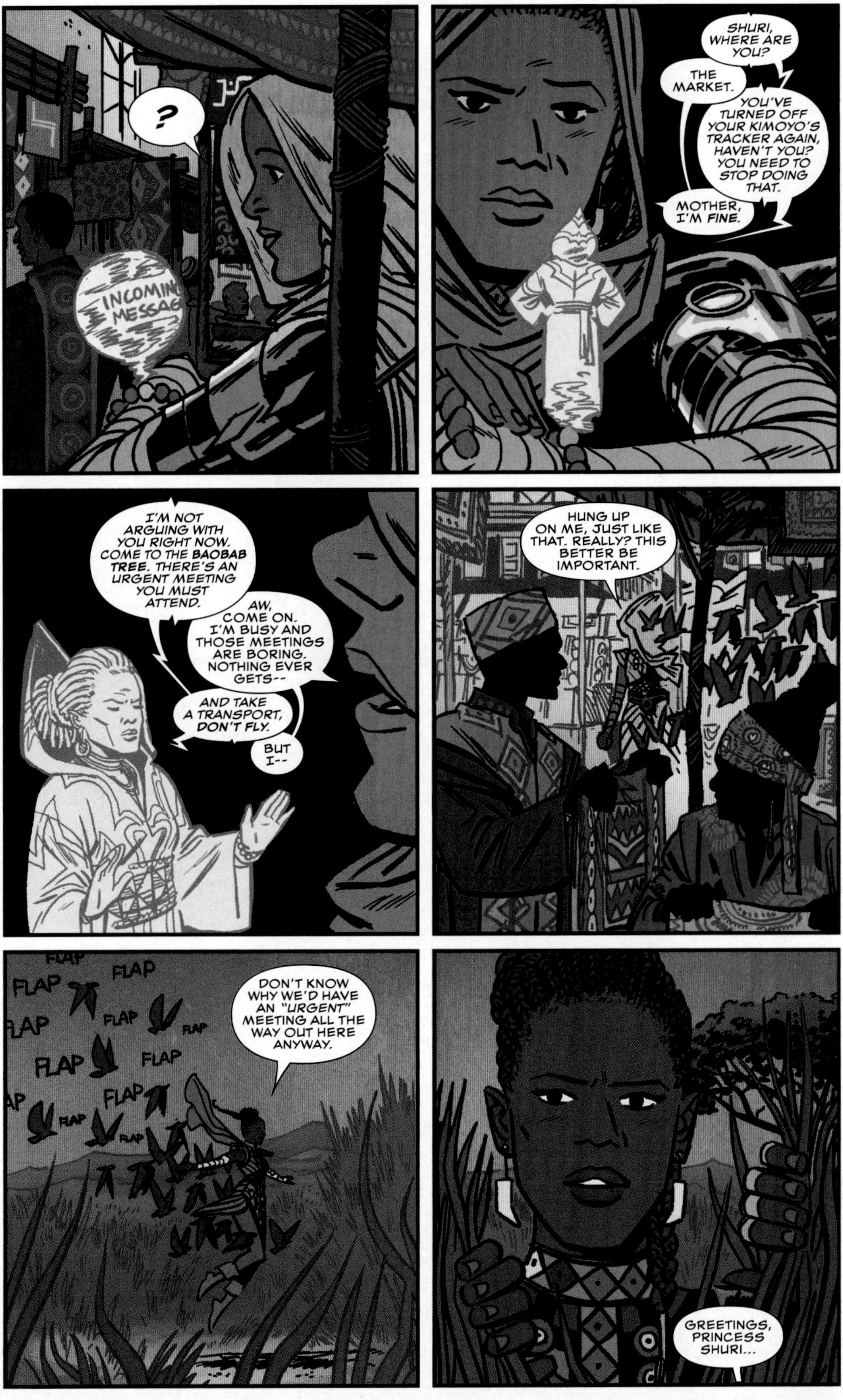
?
INCOMING MESSAGE
SHURI, WHERE ARE YOU?
THE MARKET.
YOU'VE TURNED OFF YOUR KIMOYO'S TRACKER AGAIN, HAVEN'T YOU? YOU NEED TO STOP DOING THAT.
MOTHER, I'M FINE.
I'M NOT ARGUING WITH YOU RIGHT NOW. COME TO THE BAOBAB TREE. THERE'S AN URGENT MEETING YOU MUST ATTEND.
AW, COME ON. I'M BUSY AND THOSE MEETINGS ARE BORING. NOTHING EVER GETS--
AND TAKE A TRANSPORT, DON'T FLY.
BUT I--
HUNG UP ON ME, JUST LIKE THAT. REALLY? THIS BETTER BE IMPORTANT.
FLAP FLAP FLAP FLAP FLAP FLAP FLAP FLAP FLAP FLAP FLAP FLAP
DON'T KNOW WHY WE'D HAVE AN "URGENT" MEETING ALL THE WAY OUT HERE ANYWAY.
GREETINGS, PRINCESS SHURI...

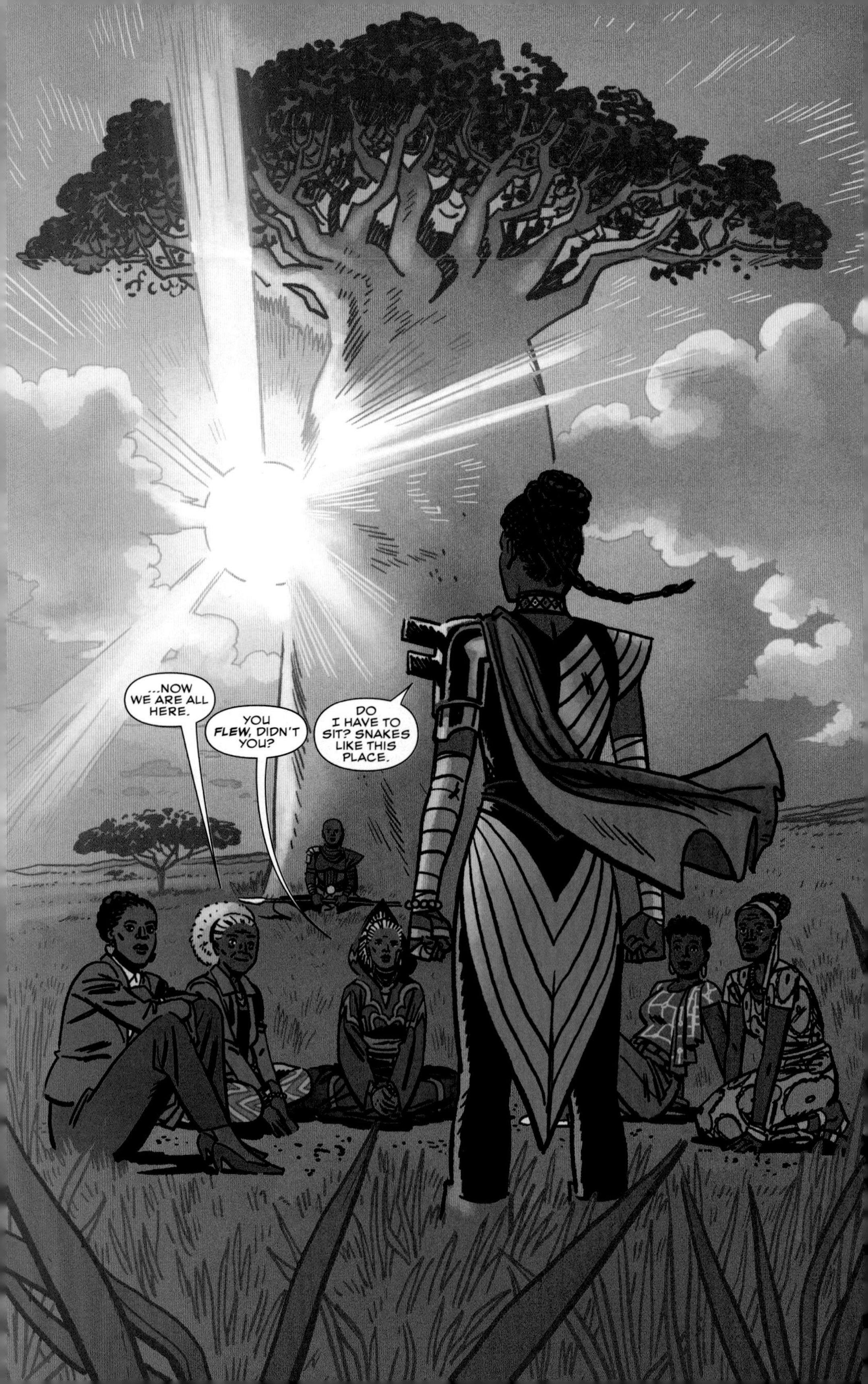
...NOW WE ARE ALL HERE.
YOU FLEW, DIDN'T YOU?
DO I HAVE TO SIT? SNAKES LIKE THIS PLACE.

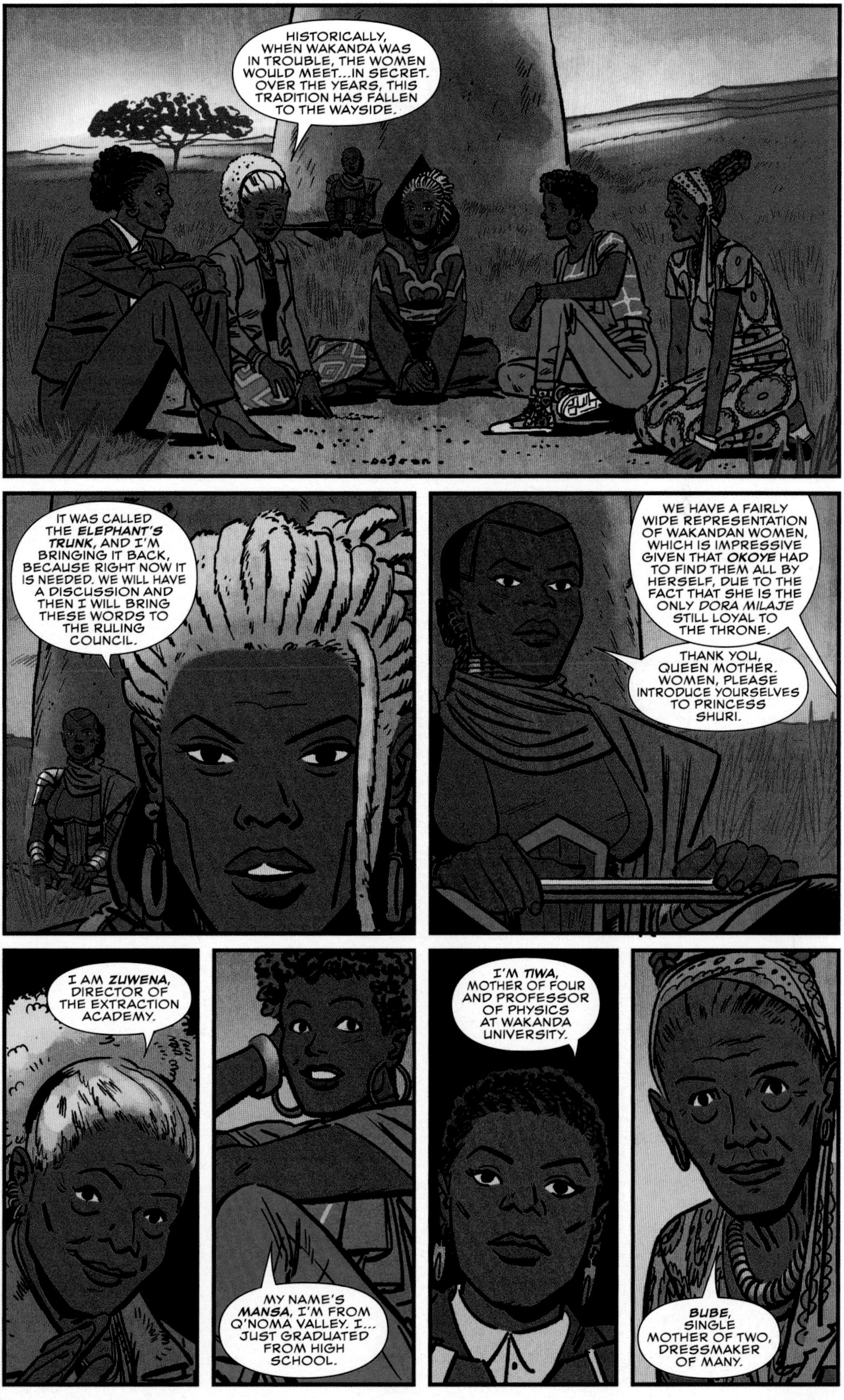
HISTORICALLY, WHEN WAKANDA WAS IN TROUBLE, THE WOMEN WOULD MEET...IN SECRET. OVER THE YEARS, THIS TRADITION HAS FALLEN TO THE WAYSIDE.
IT WAS CALLED THE ELEPHANT'S TRUNK, AND I'M BRINGING IT BACK, BECAUSE RIGHT NOW IT IS NEEDED. WE WILL HAVE A DISCUSSION AND THEN I WILL BRING THESE WORDS TO THE RULING COUNCIL.
WE HAVE A FAIRLY WIDE REPRESENTATION OF WAKANDAN WOMEN, WHICH IS IMPRESSIVE GIVEN THAT OKOYE HAD TO FIND THEM ALL BY HERSELF, DUE TO THE FACT THAT SHE IS THE ONLY DORA MILAJE STILL LOYAL TO THE THRONE.
THANK YOU, QUEEN MOTHER. WOMEN, PLEASE INTRODUCE YOURSELVES TO PRINCESS SHURI.
I AM ZUWENA, DIRECTOR OF THE EXTRACTION ACADEMY.
MY NAME'S MANSA, I'M FROM Q'NOMA VALLEY. I... JUST GRADUATED FROM HIGH SCHOOL.
I'M TIWA, MOTHER OF FOUR AND PROFESSOR OF PHYSICS AT WAKANDA UNIVERSITY.
BUBE, SINGLE MOTHER OF TWO, DRESSMAKER OF MANY.

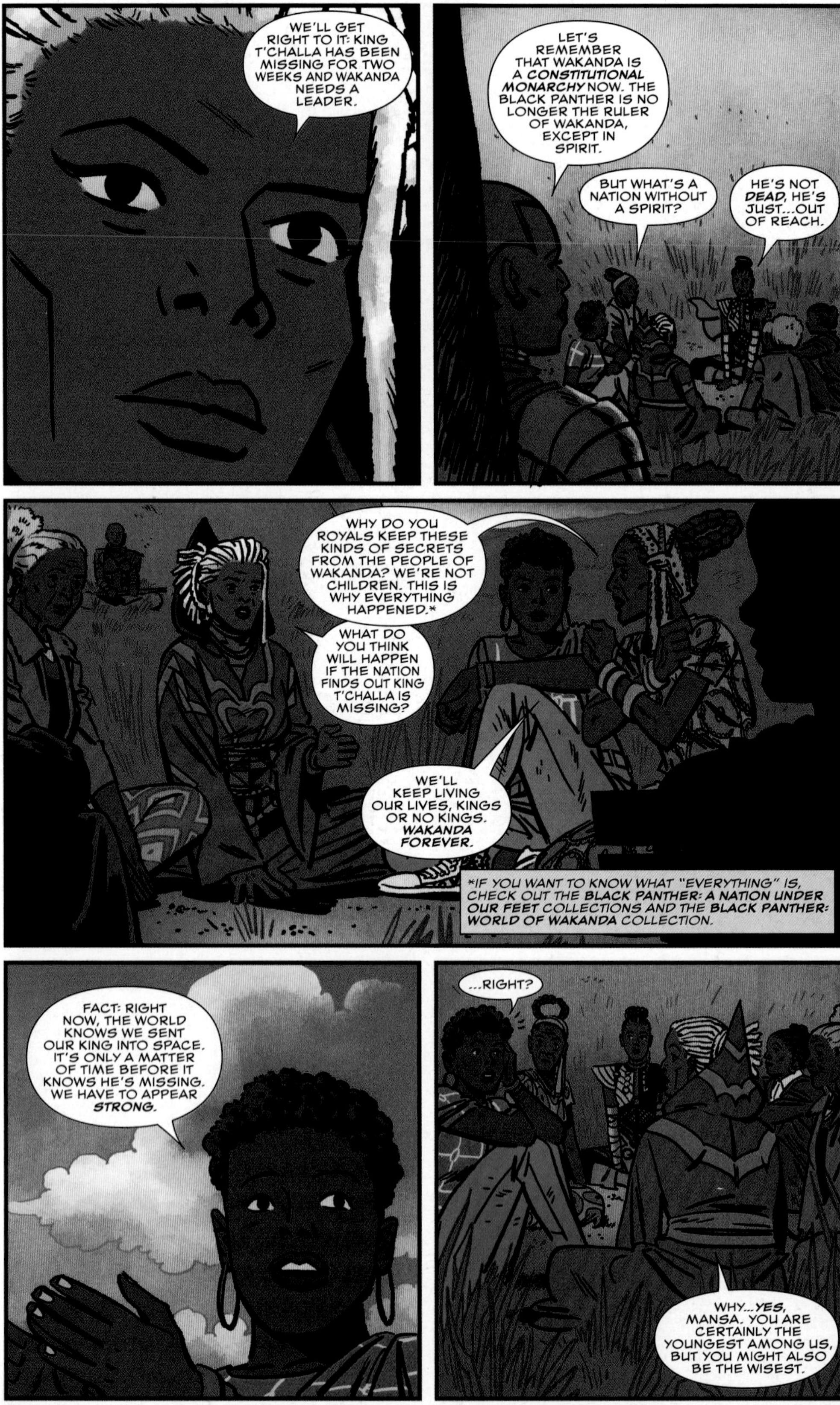
WE'LL GET RIGHT TO IT: KING T'CHALLA HAS BEEN MISSING FOR TWO WEEKS AND WAKANDA NEEDS A LEADER.
LET'S REMEMBER THAT WAKANDA IS A **CONSTITUTIONAL MONARCHY** NOW. THE BLACK PANTHER IS NO LONGER THE RULER OF WAKANDA, EXCEPT IN SPIRIT.
BUT WHAT'S A NATION WITHOUT A SPIRIT?
HE'S NOT **DEAD**, HE'S JUST...OUT OF REACH.
WHY DO YOU ROYALS KEEP THESE KINDS OF SECRETS FROM THE PEOPLE OF WAKANDA? WE'RE NOT CHILDREN. THIS IS WHY EVERYTHING HAPPENED.*
WHAT DO YOU THINK WILL HAPPEN IF THE NATION FINDS OUT KING T'CHALLA IS MISSING?
WE'LL KEEP LIVING OUR LIVES, KINGS OR NO KINGS. ***WAKANDA FOREVER.***
*IF YOU WANT TO KNOW WHAT "EVERYTHING" IS, CHECK OUT THE **BLACK PANTHER: A NATION UNDER OUR FEET** COLLECTIONS AND THE **BLACK PANTHER: WORLD OF WAKANDA** COLLECTION.
FACT: RIGHT NOW, THE WORLD KNOWS WE SENT OUR KING INTO SPACE. IT'S ONLY A MATTER OF TIME BEFORE IT KNOWS HE'S MISSING. WE HAVE TO APPEAR ***STRONG.***
...RIGHT?
WHY...***YES***, MANSA. YOU ARE CERTAINLY THE YOUNGEST AMONG US, BUT YOU MIGHT ALSO BE THE WISEST.

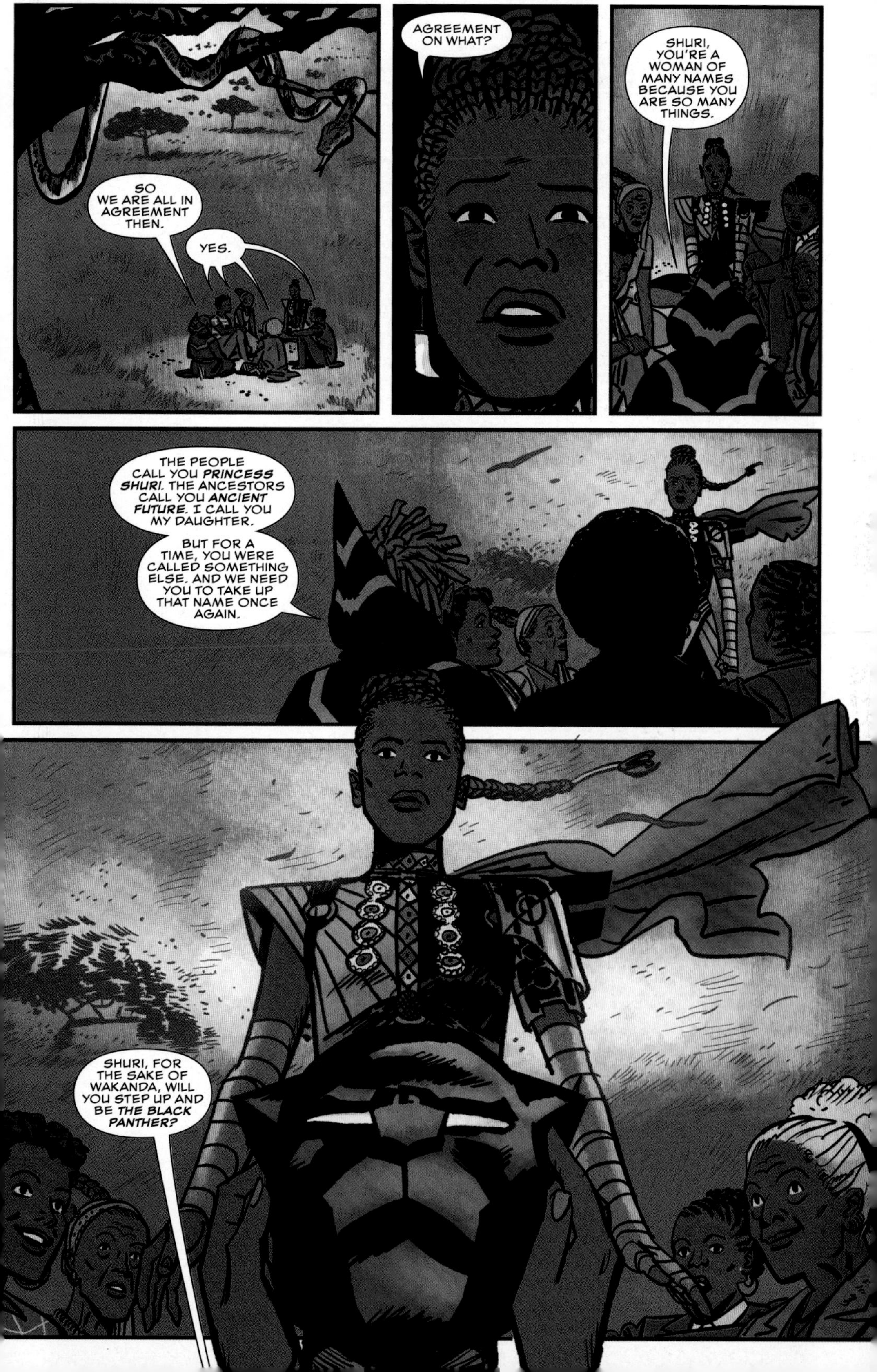
SO WE ARE ALL IN AGREEMENT THEN.
YES.
AGREEMENT ON WHAT?
SHURI, YOU'RE A WOMAN OF MANY NAMES BECAUSE YOU ARE SO MANY THINGS.
THE PEOPLE CALL YOU PRINCESS SHURI. THE ANCESTORS CALL YOU ANCIENT FUTURE. I CALL YOU MY DAUGHTER.
BUT FOR A TIME, YOU WERE CALLED SOMETHING ELSE. AND WE NEED YOU TO TAKE UP THAT NAME ONCE AGAIN.
SHURI, FOR THE SAKE OF WAKANDA, WILL YOU STEP UP AND BE THE BLACK PANTHER?

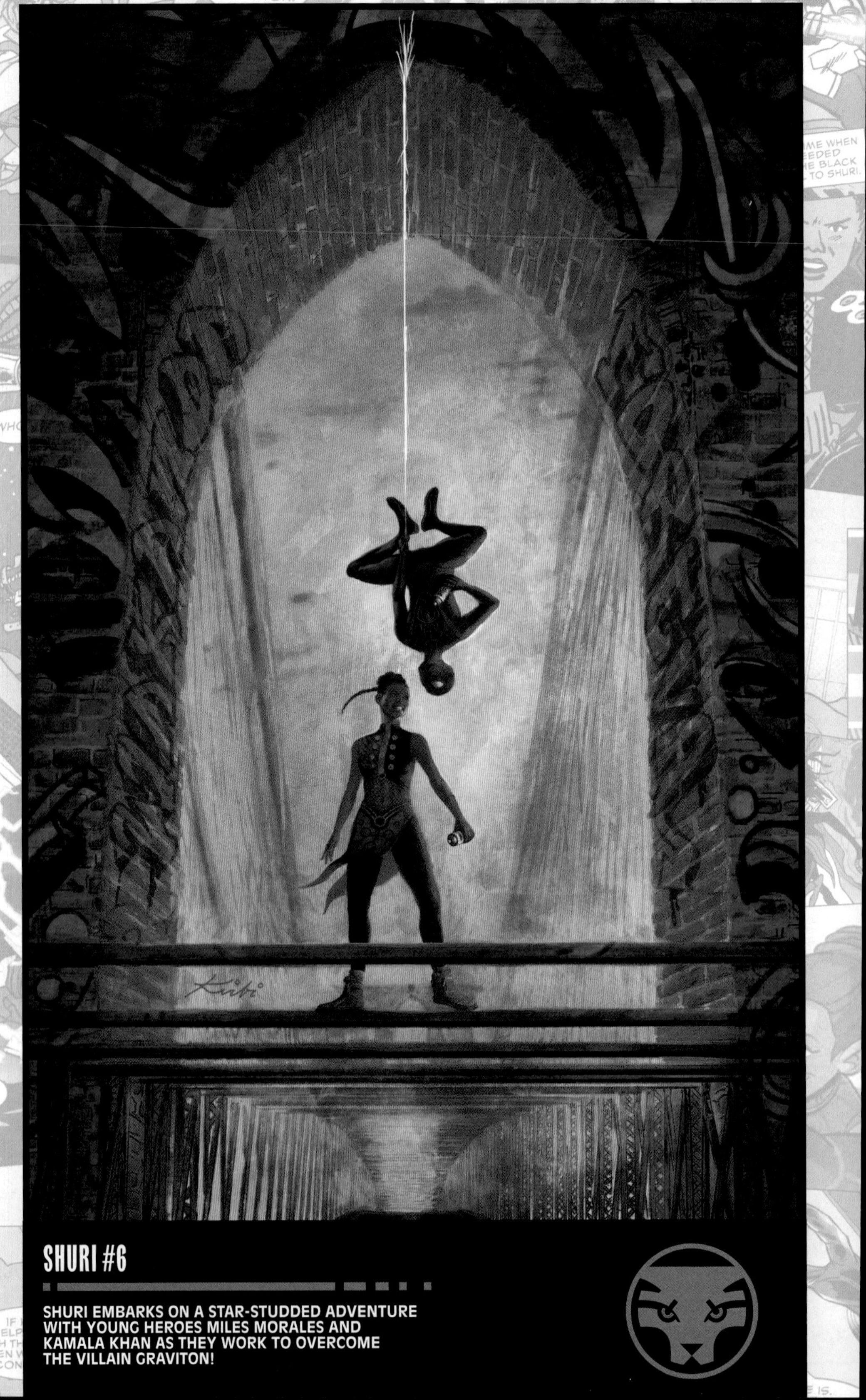

SHURI #6

SHURI EMBARKS ON A STAR-STUDDED ADVENTURE WITH YOUNG HEROES MILES MORALES AND KAMALA KHAN AS THEY WORK TO OVERCOME THE VILLAIN GRAVITON!

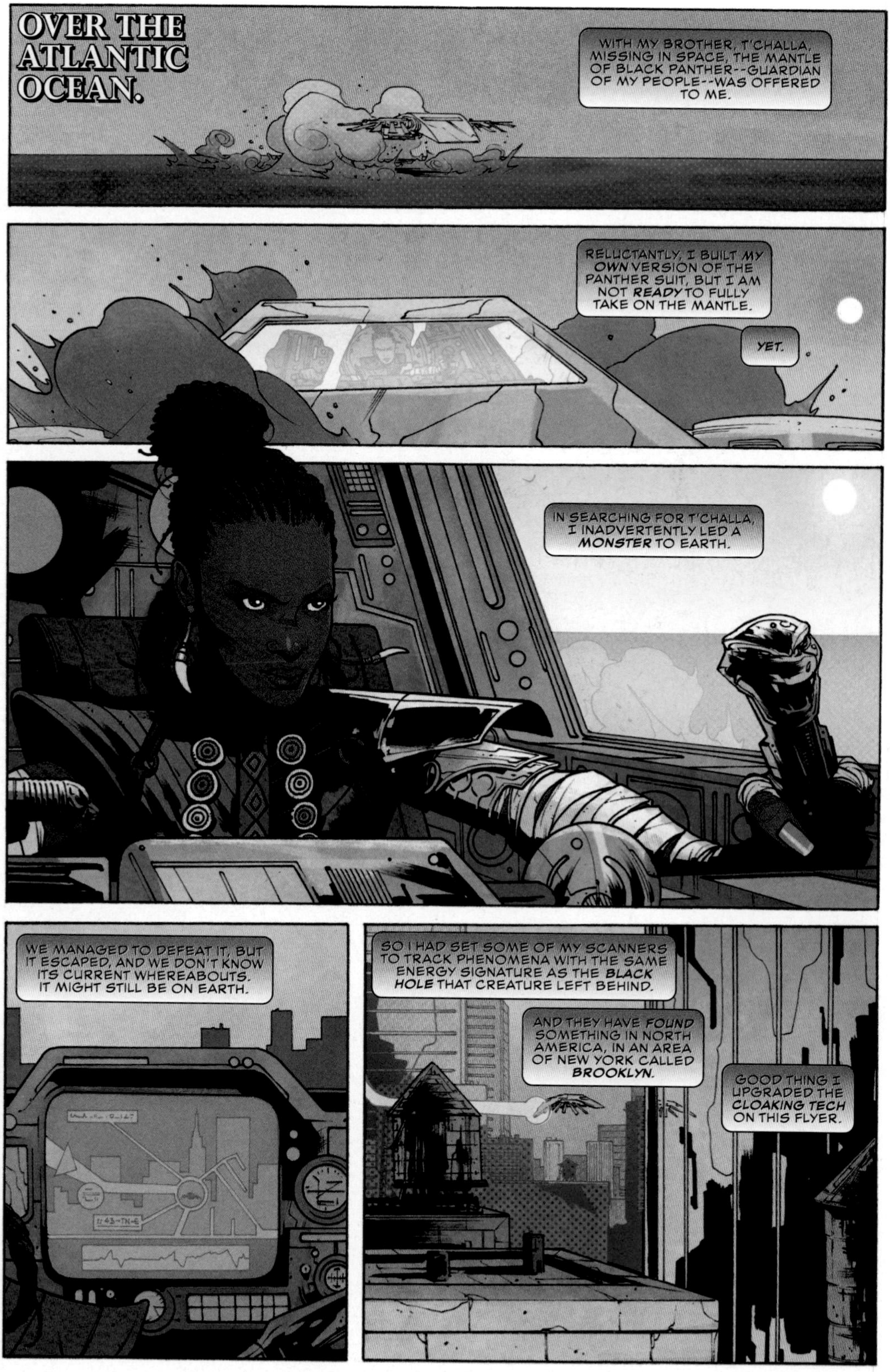
OVER THE ATLANTIC OCEAN.
WITH MY BROTHER, T'CHALLA, MISSING IN SPACE, THE MANTLE OF BLACK PANTHER--GUARDIAN OF MY PEOPLE--WAS OFFERED TO ME.
RELUCTANTLY, I BUILT MY OWN VERSION OF THE PANTHER SUIT, BUT I AM NOT READY TO FULLY TAKE ON THE MANTLE.
YET.
IN SEARCHING FOR T'CHALLA, I INADVERTENTLY LED A MONSTER TO EARTH.
WE MANAGED TO DEFEAT IT, BUT IT ESCAPED, AND WE DON'T KNOW ITS CURRENT WHEREABOUTS. IT MIGHT STILL BE ON EARTH.
SO I HAD SET SOME OF MY SCANNERS TO TRACK PHENOMENA WITH THE SAME ENERGY SIGNATURE AS THE BLACK HOLE THAT CREATURE LEFT BEHIND.
AND THEY HAVE FOUND SOMETHING IN NORTH AMERICA, IN AN AREA OF NEW YORK CALLED BROOKLYN.
GOOD THING I UPGRADED THE CLOAKING TECH ON THIS FLYER.

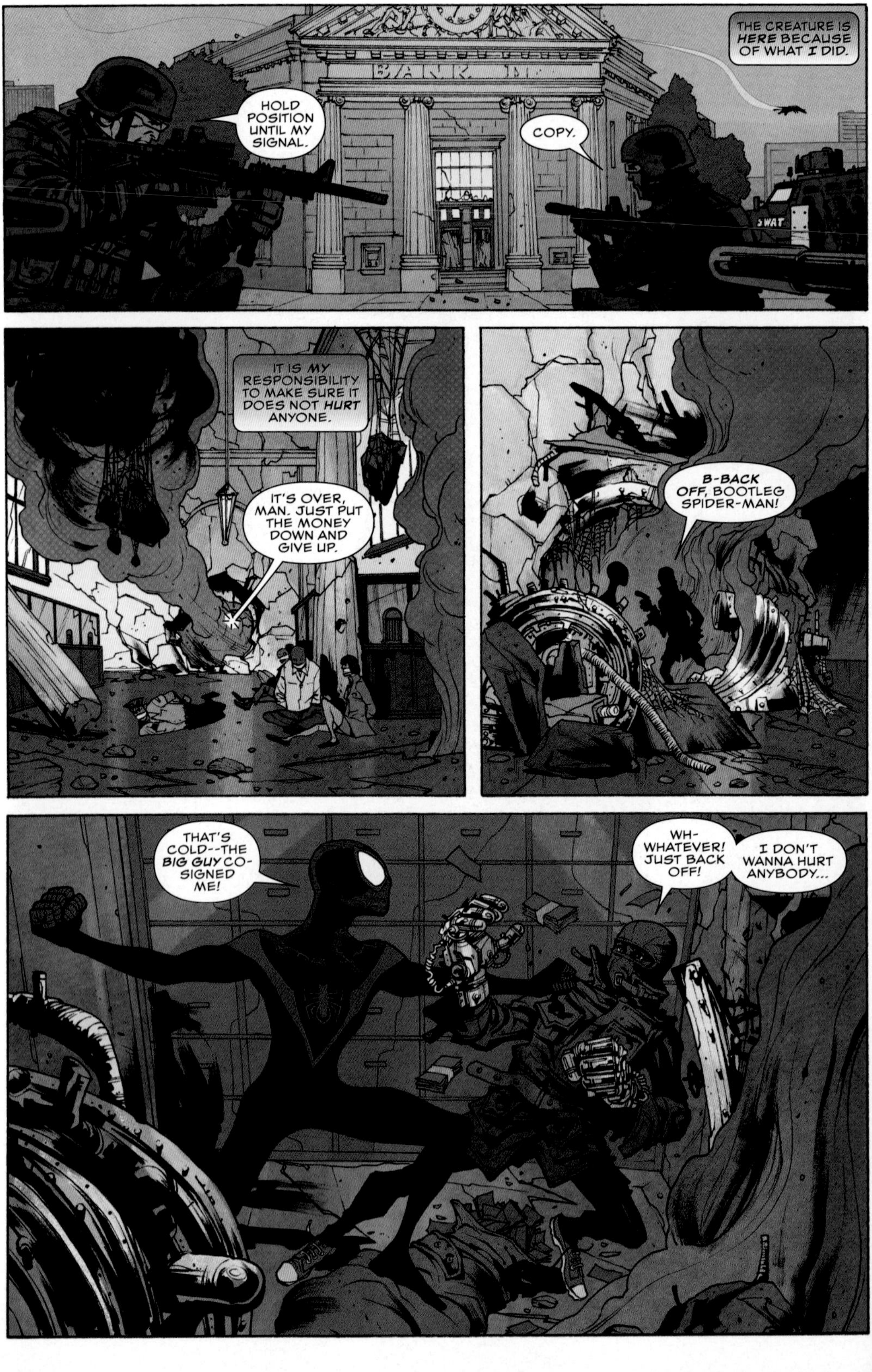
THE CREATURE IS HERE BECAUSE OF WHAT I DID.
HOLD POSITION UNTIL MY SIGNAL.
COPY.
IT IS MY RESPONSIBILITY TO MAKE SURE IT DOES NOT HURT ANYONE.
IT'S OVER, MAN. JUST PUT THE MONEY DOWN AND GIVE UP.
B-BACK OFF, BOOTLEG SPIDER-MAN!
THAT'S COLD--THE BIG GUY CO-SIGNED ME!
WH-WHATEVER! JUST BACK OFF!
I DON'T WANNA HURT ANYBODY...

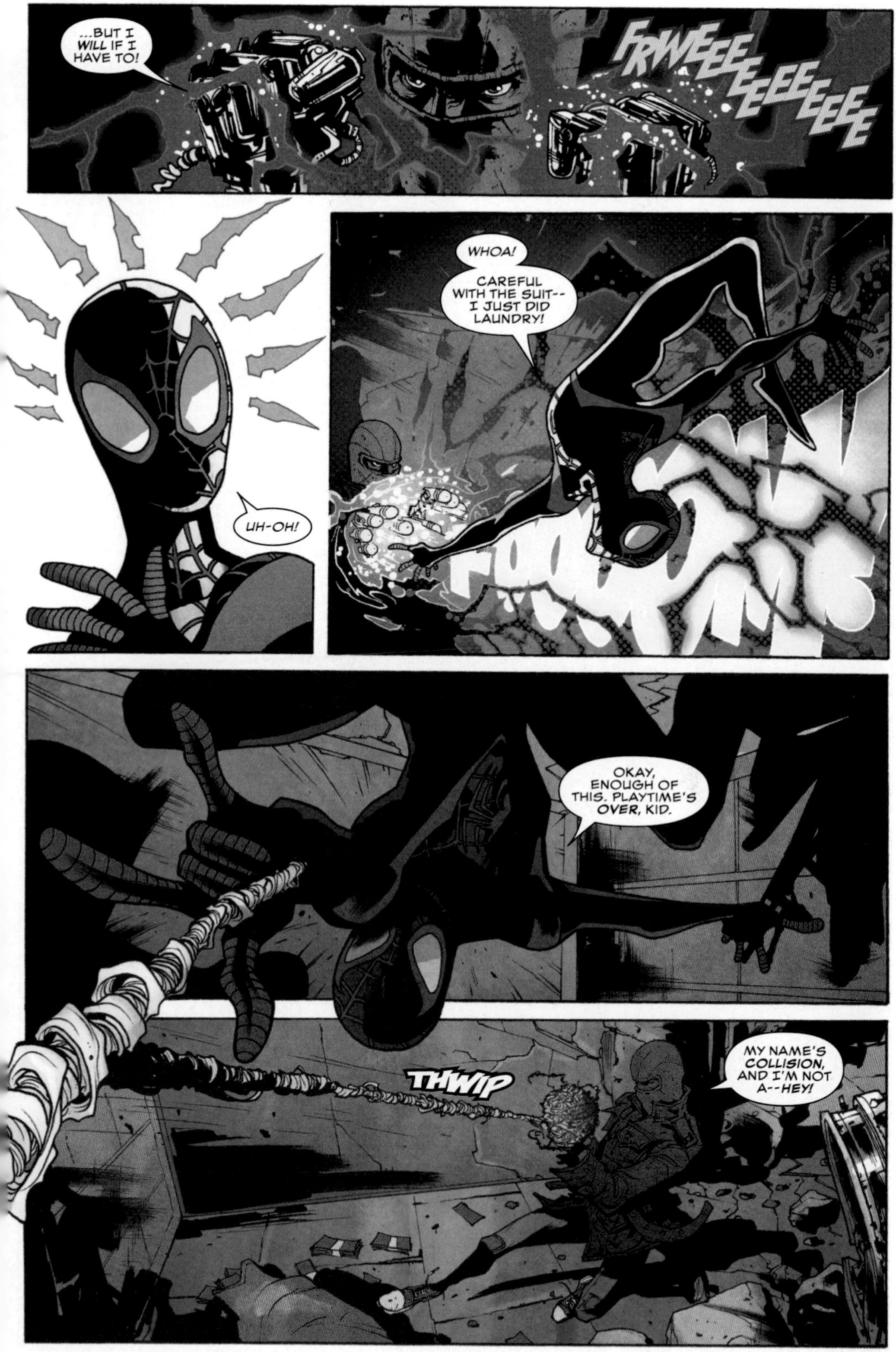
...BUT I WILL IF I HAVE TO!
FRWEEEEEEEEEEEE
UH-OH!
WHOA!
CAREFUL WITH THE SUIT-- I JUST DID LAUNDRY!
OKAY, ENOUGH OF THIS. PLAYTIME'S OVER, KID.
THWIP
MY NAME'S COLLISION, AND I'M NOT A--HEY!

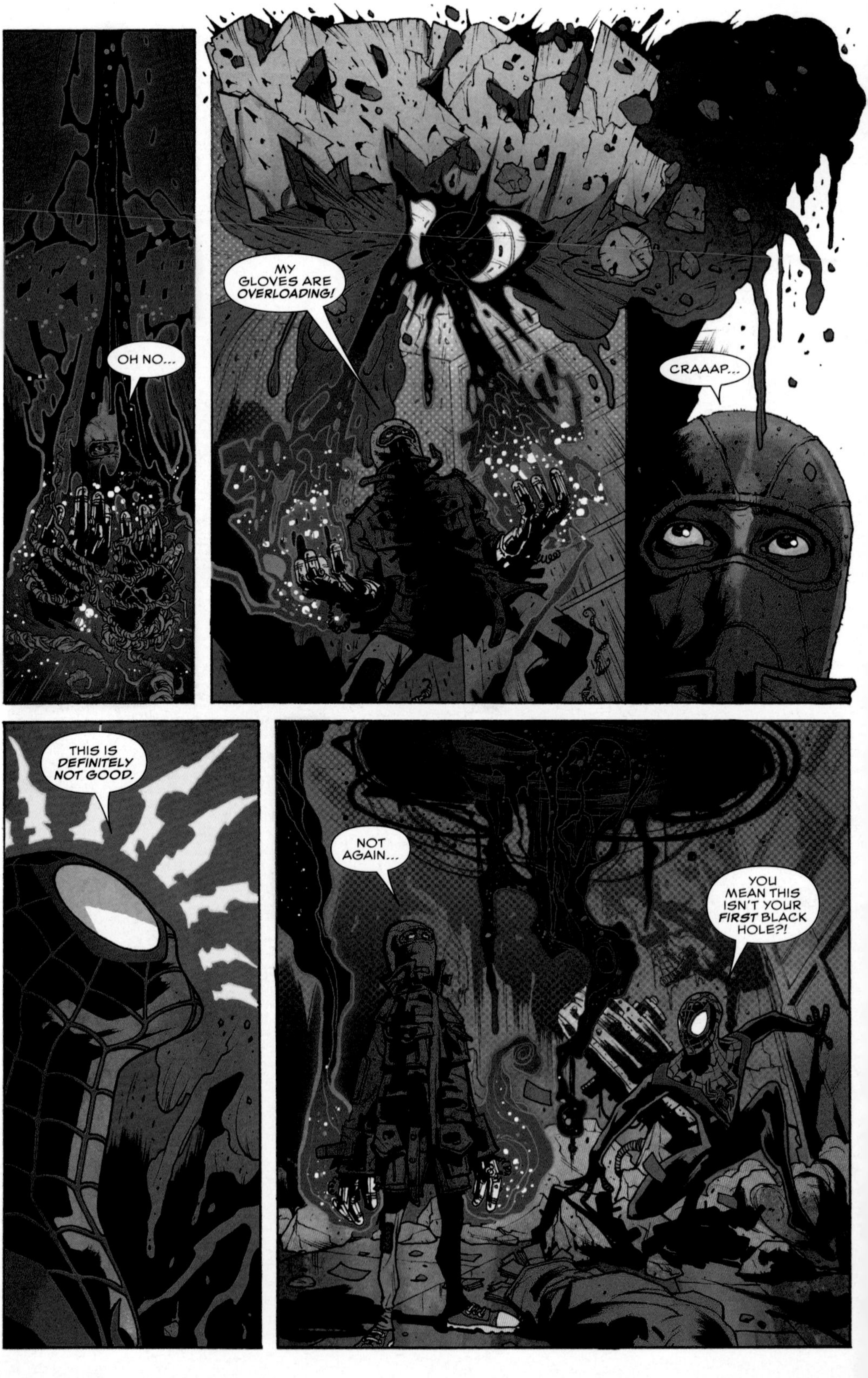
OH NO...
MY GLOVES ARE OVERLOADING!
CRAAAP...
THIS IS DEFINITELY NOT GOOD.
NOT AGAIN...
YOU MEAN THIS ISN'T YOUR FIRST BLACK HOLE?!

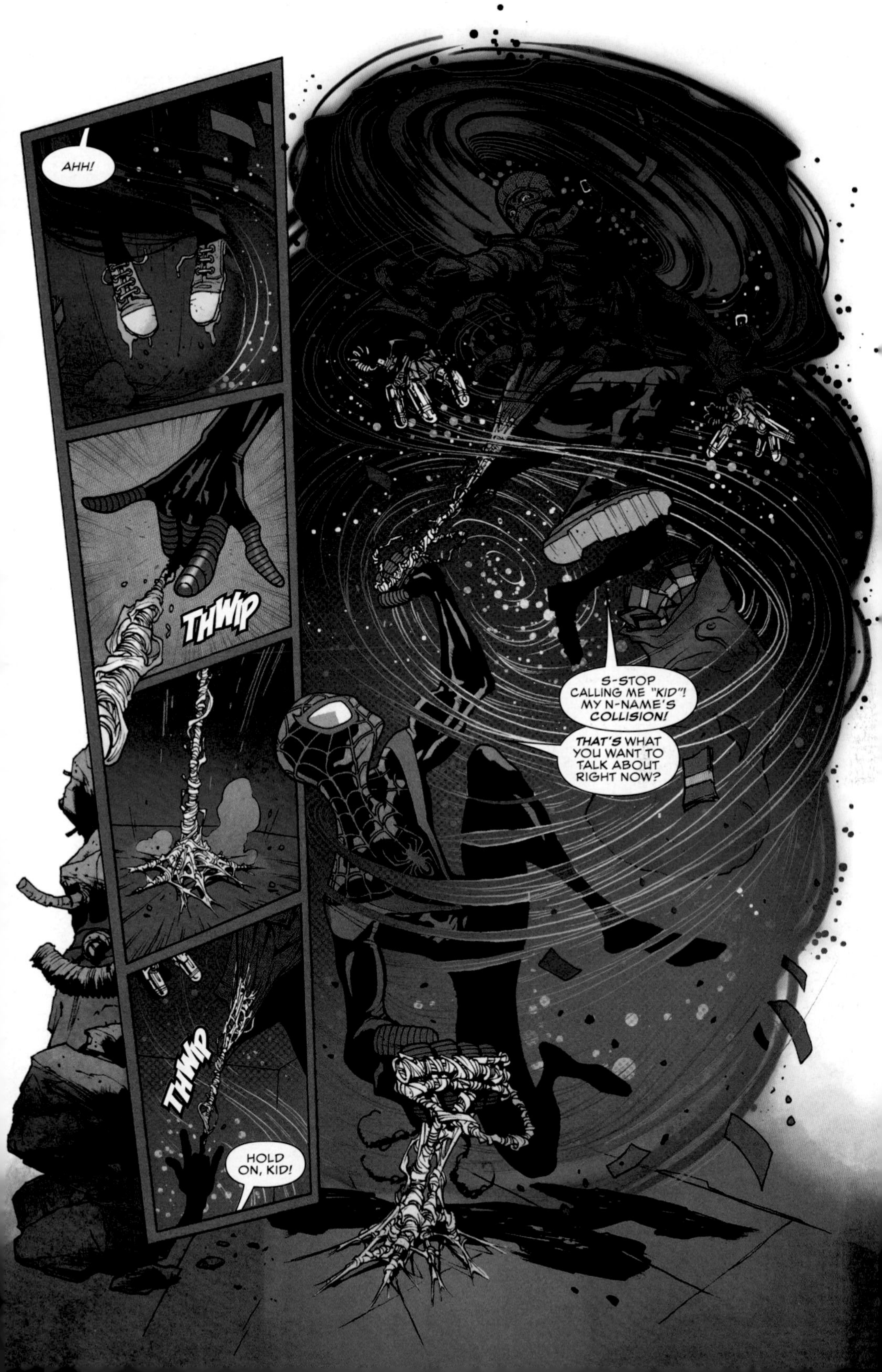
AHH!
THWIP
THWIP
HOLD ON, KID!
THAT'S WHAT YOU WANT TO TALK ABOUT RIGHT NOW?
S-STOP CALLING ME "KID"! MY N-NAME'S COLLISION!

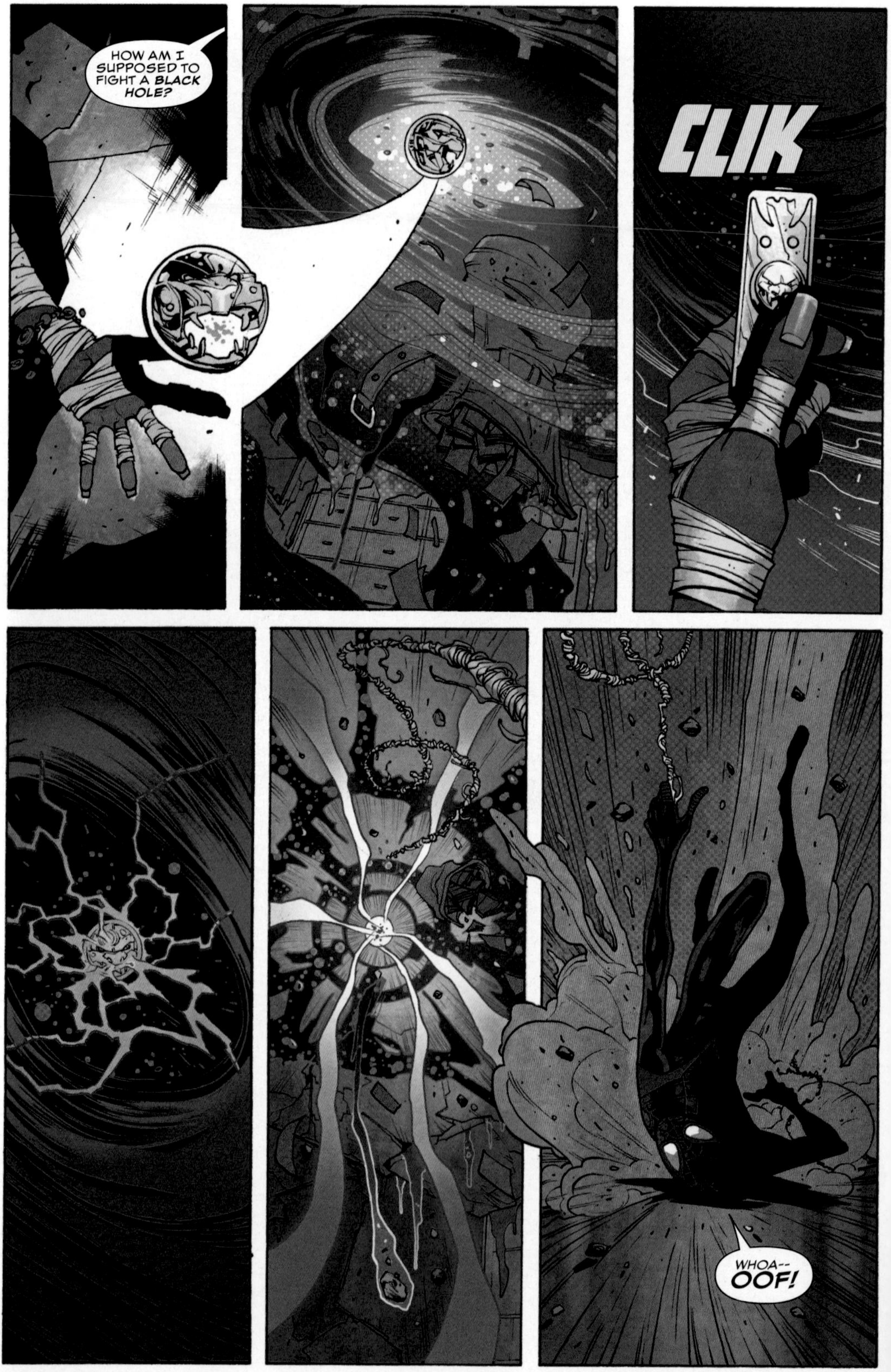
HOW AM I SUPPOSED TO FIGHT A BLACK HOLE?
CLIK
WHOA-- OOF!

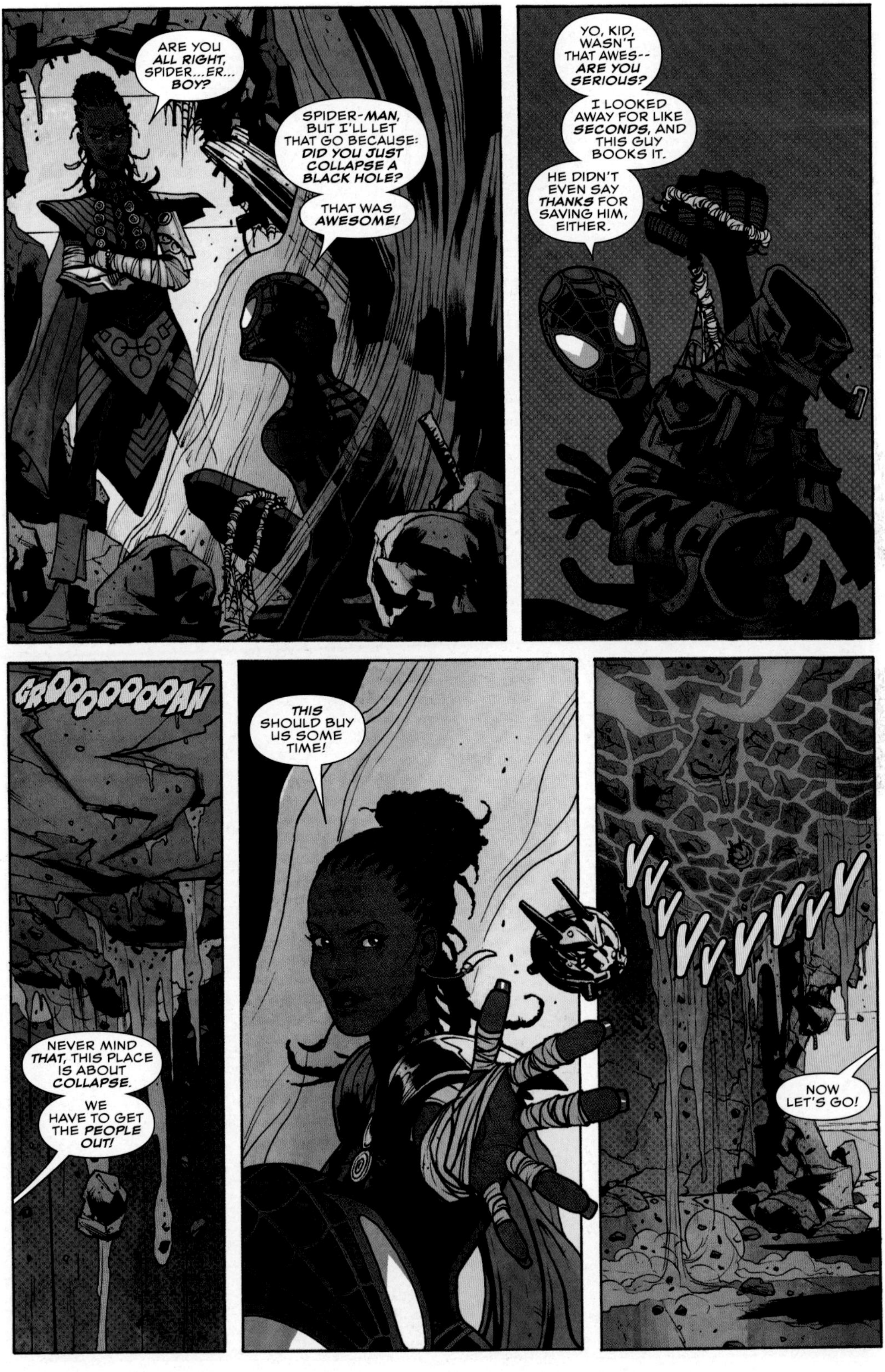

ARE YOU ALL RIGHT, SPIDER...ER... BOY?
SPIDER-MAN, BUT I'LL LET THAT GO BECAUSE: DID YOU JUST COLLAPSE A BLACK HOLE?
THAT WAS AWESOME!
YO, KID, WASN'T THAT AWES-- ARE YOU SERIOUS?
I LOOKED AWAY FOR LIKE SECONDS, AND THIS GUY BOOKS IT.
HE DIDN'T EVEN SAY THANKS FOR SAVING HIM, EITHER.
GROOOOOOOOAN
NEVER MIND THAT, THIS PLACE IS ABOUT COLLAPSE.
WE HAVE TO GET THE PEOPLE OUT!
THIS SHOULD BUY US SOME TIME!
NOW LET'S GO!

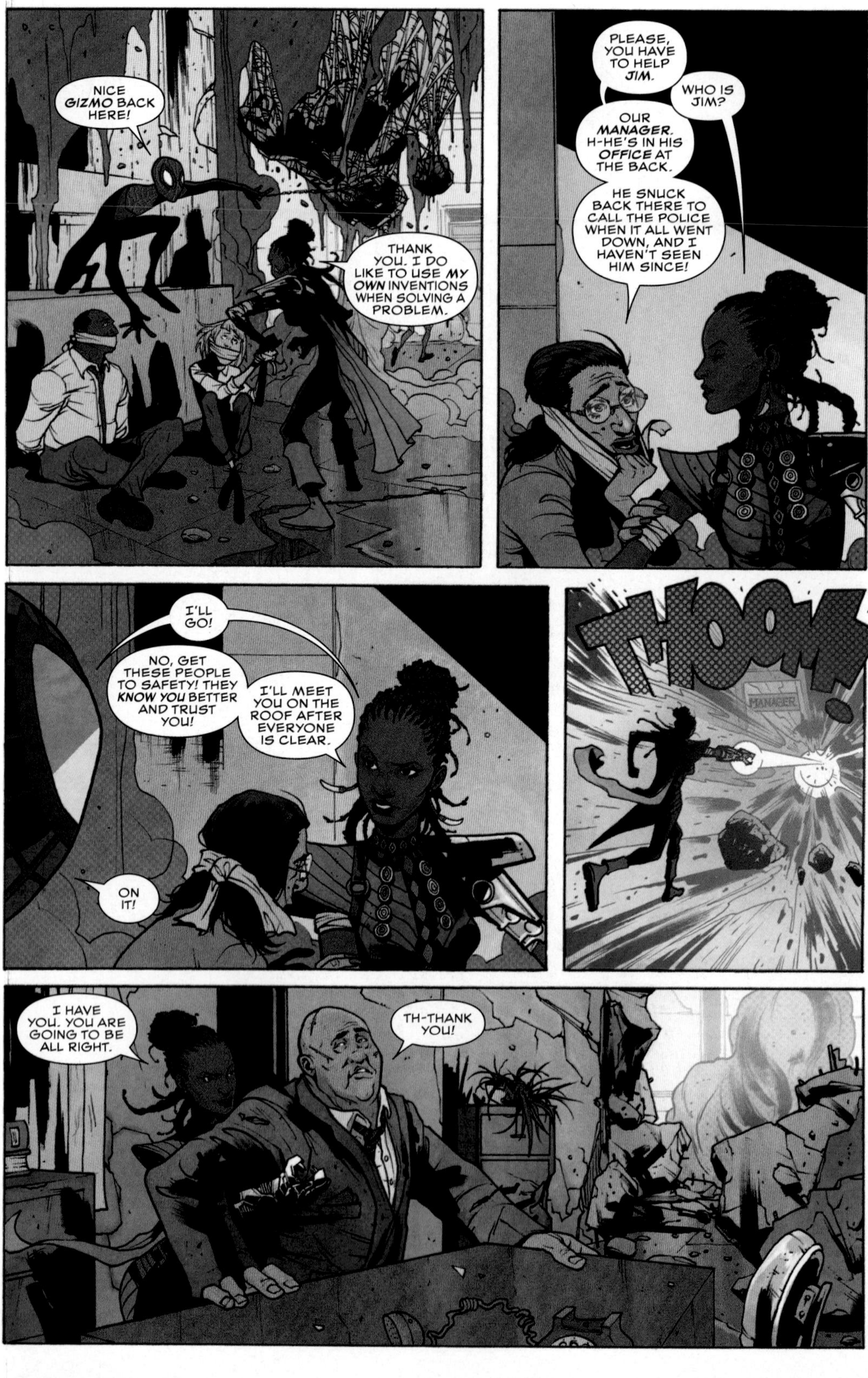
NICE GIZMO BACK HERE!
THANK YOU. I DO LIKE TO USE MY OWN INVENTIONS WHEN SOLVING A PROBLEM.
PLEASE, YOU HAVE TO HELP JIM.
WHO IS JIM?
OUR MANAGER. H-HE'S IN HIS OFFICE AT THE BACK.
HE SNUCK BACK THERE TO CALL THE POLICE WHEN IT ALL WENT DOWN, AND I HAVEN'T SEEN HIM SINCE!
I'LL GO!
NO, GET THESE PEOPLE TO SAFETY! THEY KNOW YOU BETTER AND TRUST YOU!
I'LL MEET YOU ON THE ROOF AFTER EVERYONE IS CLEAR.
ON IT!
THOOM!
MANAGER
I HAVE YOU. YOU ARE GOING TO BE ALL RIGHT.
TH-THANK YOU!

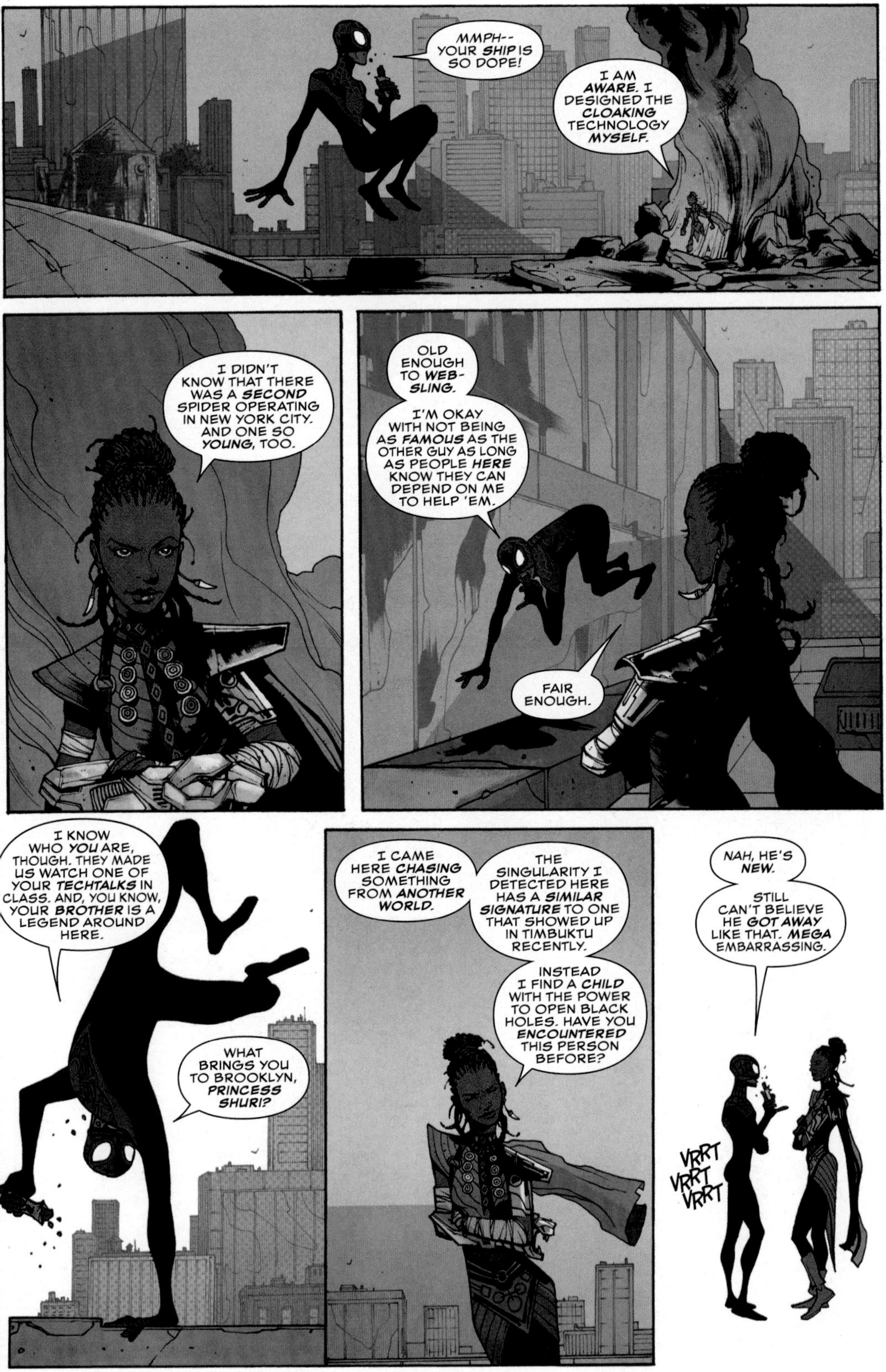
MMPH-- YOUR SHIP IS SO DOPE!
I AM AWARE. I DESIGNED THE CLOAKING TECHNOLOGY MYSELF.
I DIDN'T KNOW THAT THERE WAS A SECOND SPIDER OPERATING IN NEW YORK CITY. AND ONE SO YOUNG, TOO.
OLD ENOUGH TO WEB-SLING.
I'M OKAY WITH NOT BEING AS FAMOUS AS THE OTHER GUY AS LONG AS PEOPLE HERE KNOW THEY CAN DEPEND ON ME TO HELP 'EM.
FAIR ENOUGH.
I KNOW WHO YOU ARE, THOUGH. THEY MADE US WATCH ONE OF YOUR TECHTALKS IN CLASS. AND, YOU KNOW, YOUR BROTHER IS A LEGEND AROUND HERE.
WHAT BRINGS YOU TO BROOKLYN, PRINCESS SHURI?
I CAME HERE CHASING SOMETHING FROM ANOTHER WORLD.
THE SINGULARITY I DETECTED HERE HAS A SIMILAR SIGNATURE TO ONE THAT SHOWED UP IN TIMBUKTU RECENTLY.
INSTEAD I FIND A CHILD WITH THE POWER TO OPEN BLACK HOLES. HAVE YOU ENCOUNTERED THIS PERSON BEFORE?
NAH, HE'S NEW.
STILL CAN'T BELIEVE HE GOT AWAY LIKE THAT. MEGA EMBARRASSING.
VRRT VRRT VRRT

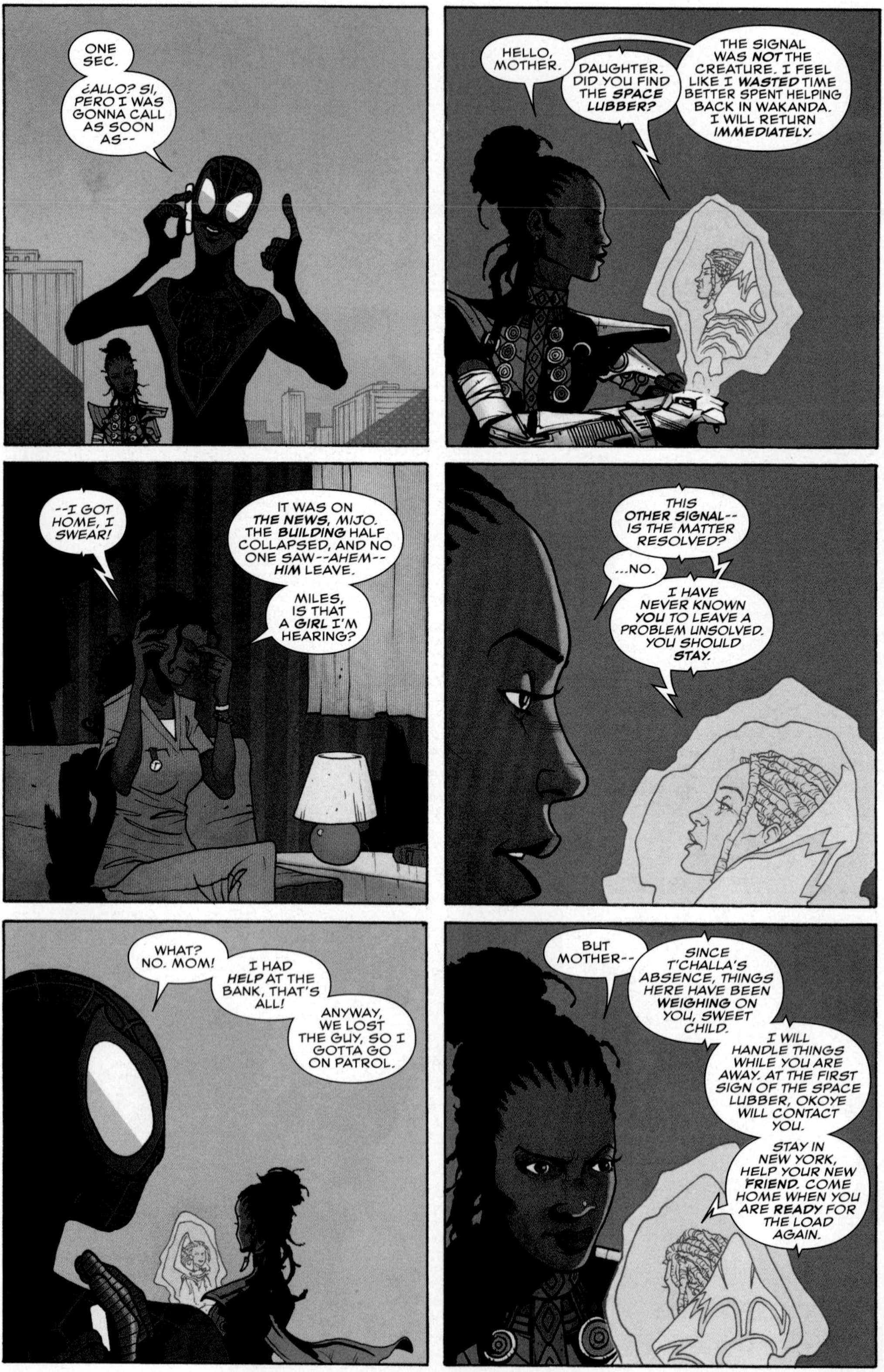
ONE SEC.
¿ALLO? SI, PERO I WAS GONNA CALL AS SOON AS--
HELLO, MOTHER.
DAUGHTER. DID YOU FIND THE SPACE LUBBER?
THE SIGNAL WAS NOT THE CREATURE. I FEEL LIKE I WASTED TIME BETTER SPENT HELPING BACK IN WAKANDA. I WILL RETURN IMMEDIATELY.
--I GOT HOME, I SWEAR!
IT WAS ON THE NEWS, MIJO. THE BUILDING HALF COLLAPSED, AND NO ONE SAW--AHEM--HIM LEAVE.
MILES, IS THAT A GIRL I'M HEARING?
THIS OTHER SIGNAL--IS THE MATTER RESOLVED?
...NO.
I HAVE NEVER KNOWN YOU TO LEAVE A PROBLEM UNSOLVED. YOU SHOULD STAY.
WHAT? NO. MOM!
I HAD HELP AT THE BANK, THAT'S ALL!
ANYWAY, WE LOST THE GUY, SO I GOTTA GO ON PATROL.
BUT MOTHER--
SINCE T'CHALLA'S ABSENCE, THINGS HERE HAVE BEEN WEIGHING ON YOU, SWEET CHILD.
I WILL HANDLE THINGS WHILE YOU ARE AWAY. AT THE FIRST SIGN OF THE SPACE LUBBER, OKOYE WILL CONTACT YOU.
STAY IN NEW YORK, HELP YOUR NEW FRIEND. COME HOME WHEN YOU ARE READY FOR THE LOAD AGAIN.

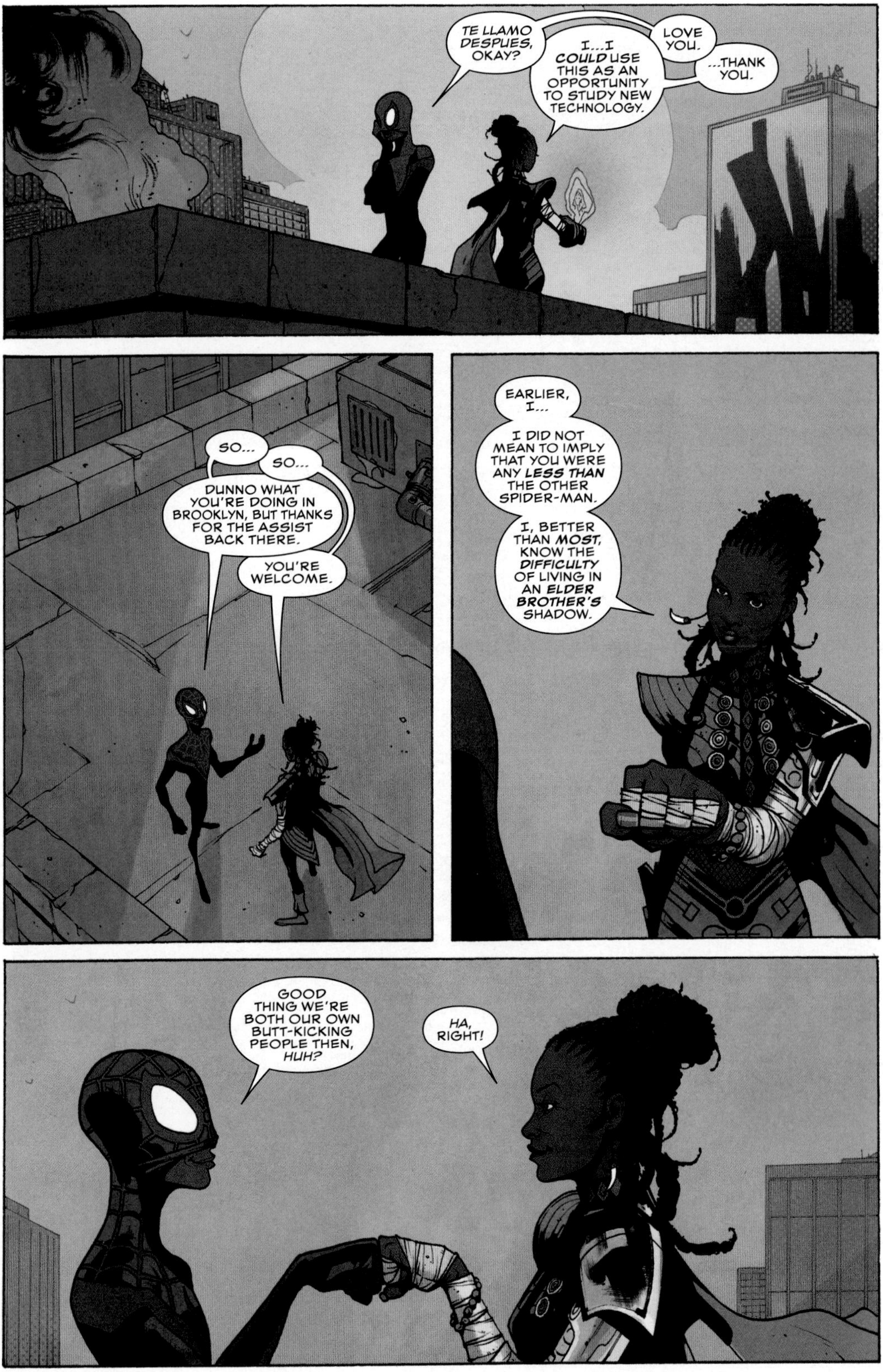
TE LLAMO DESPUES, OKAY?
LOVE YOU.
I...I COULD USE THIS AS AN OPPORTUNITY TO STUDY NEW TECHNOLOGY.
...THANK YOU.
SO...
SO...
DUNNO WHAT YOU'RE DOING IN BROOKLYN, BUT THANKS FOR THE ASSIST BACK THERE.
YOU'RE WELCOME.
EARLIER, I...
I DID NOT MEAN TO IMPLY THAT YOU WERE ANY LESS THAN THE OTHER SPIDER-MAN.
I, BETTER THAN MOST, KNOW THE DIFFICULTY OF LIVING IN AN ELDER BROTHER'S SHADOW.
GOOD THING WE'RE BOTH OUR OWN BUTT-KICKING PEOPLE THEN, HUH?
HA, RIGHT!

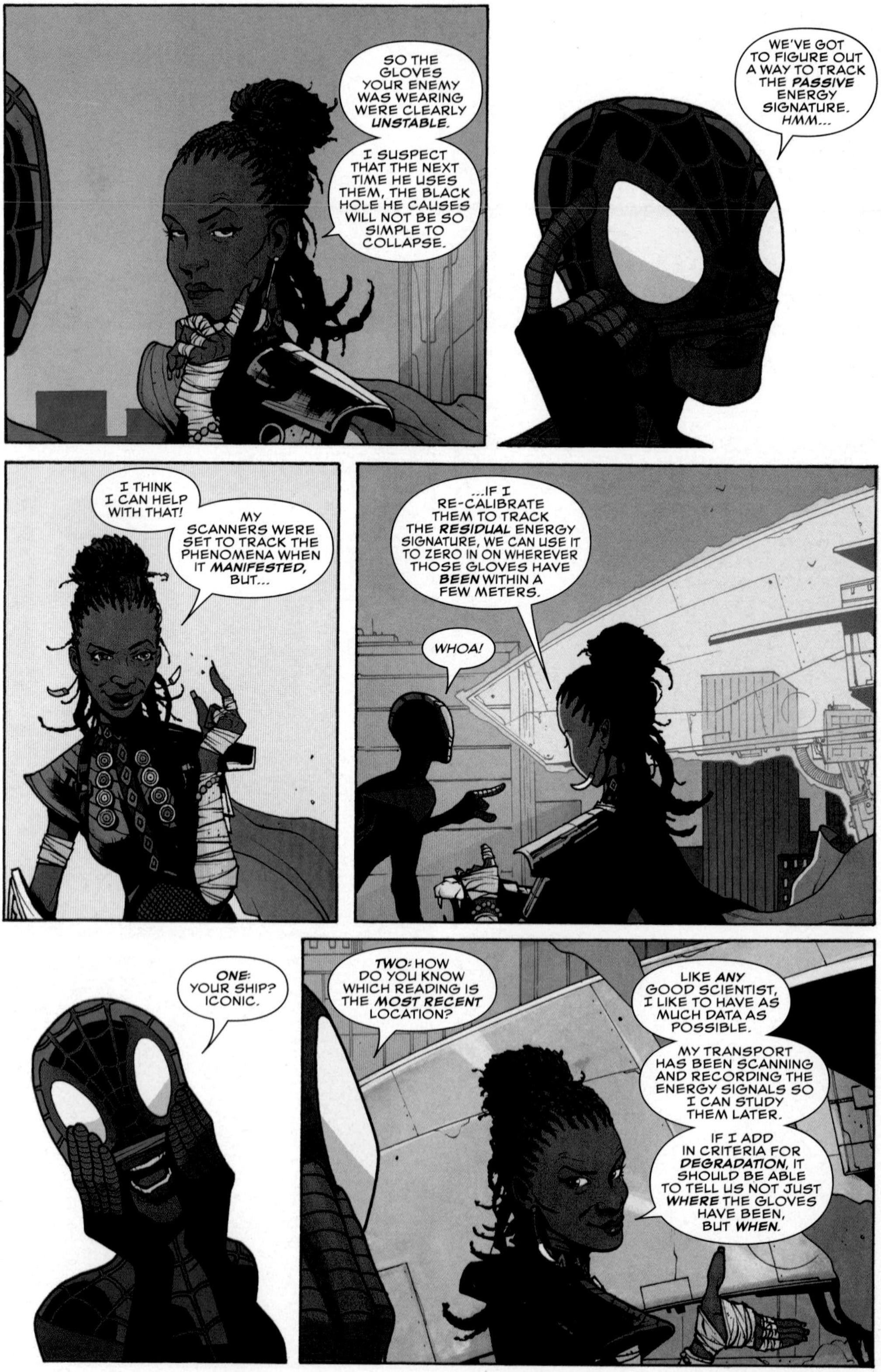
SO THE GLOVES YOUR ENEMY WAS WEARING WERE CLEARLY UNSTABLE.
I SUSPECT THAT THE NEXT TIME HE USES THEM, THE BLACK HOLE HE CAUSES WILL NOT BE SO SIMPLE TO COLLAPSE.
WE'VE GOT TO FIGURE OUT A WAY TO TRACK THE PASSIVE ENERGY SIGNATURE. HMM...
I THINK I CAN HELP WITH THAT!
MY SCANNERS WERE SET TO TRACK THE PHENOMENA WHEN IT MANIFESTED, BUT...
...IF I RE-CALIBRATE THEM TO TRACK THE RESIDUAL ENERGY SIGNATURE, WE CAN USE IT TO ZERO IN ON WHEREVER THOSE GLOVES HAVE BEEN WITHIN A FEW METERS.
WHOA!
ONE: YOUR SHIP? ICONIC.
TWO: HOW DO YOU KNOW WHICH READING IS THE MOST RECENT LOCATION?
LIKE ANY GOOD SCIENTIST, I LIKE TO HAVE AS MUCH DATA AS POSSIBLE.
MY TRANSPORT HAS BEEN SCANNING AND RECORDING THE ENERGY SIGNALS SO I CAN STUDY THEM LATER.
IF I ADD IN CRITERIA FOR DEGRADATION, IT SHOULD BE ABLE TO TELL US NOT JUST WHERE THE GLOVES HAVE BEEN, BUT WHEN.

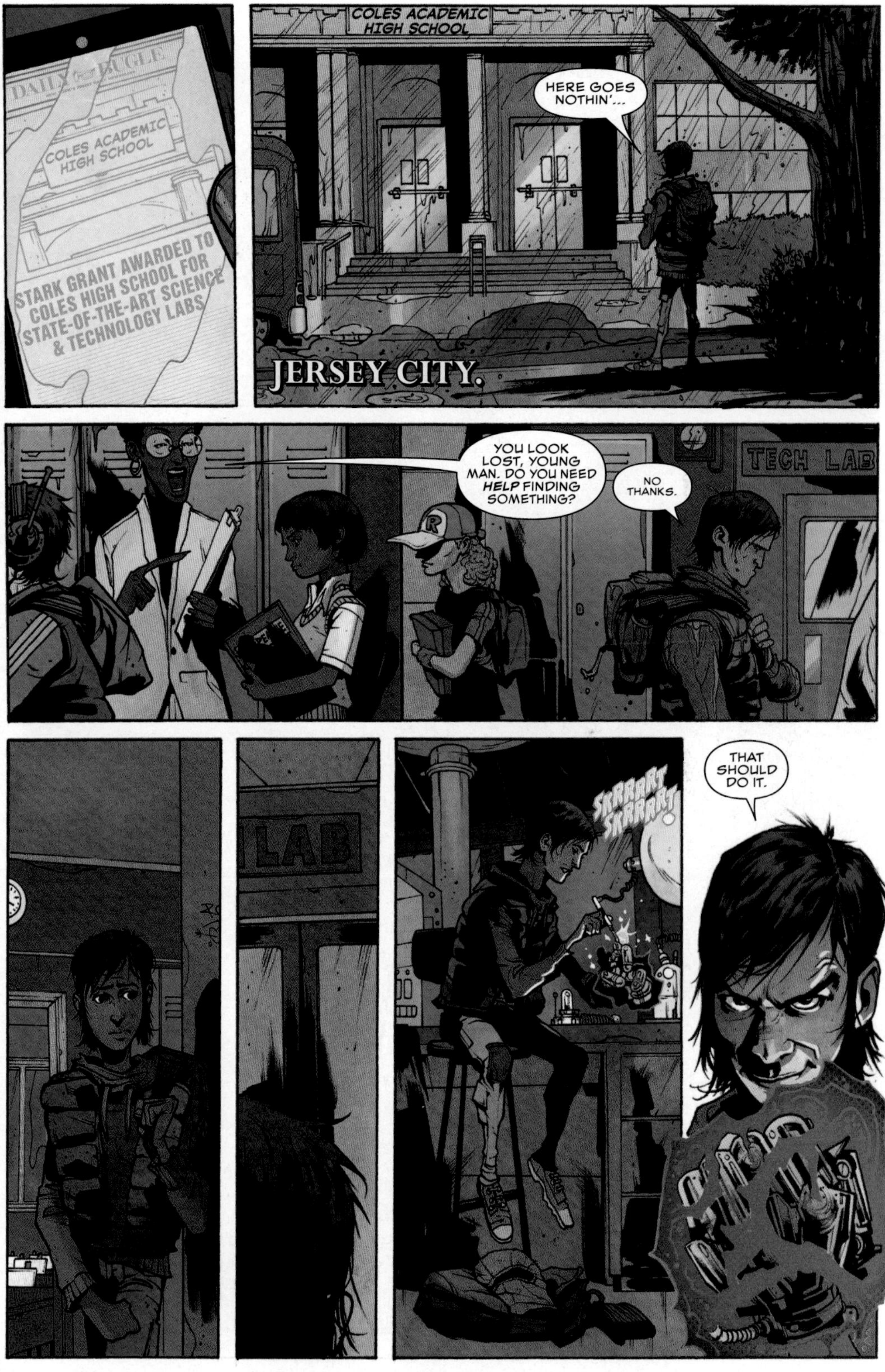
DAILY BUGLE
COLES ACADEMIC HIGH SCHOOL
STARK GRANT AWARDED TO COLES HIGH SCHOOL FOR STATE-OF-THE-ART SCIENCE & TECHNOLOGY LABS
COLES ACADEMIC HIGH SCHOOL
JERSEY CITY.
HERE GOES NOTHIN'...
TECH LAB
YOU LOOK LOST, YOUNG MAN. DO YOU NEED HELP FINDING SOMETHING?
NO THANKS.
LAB
SKRRRRT SKRRRRT!
THAT SHOULD DO IT.

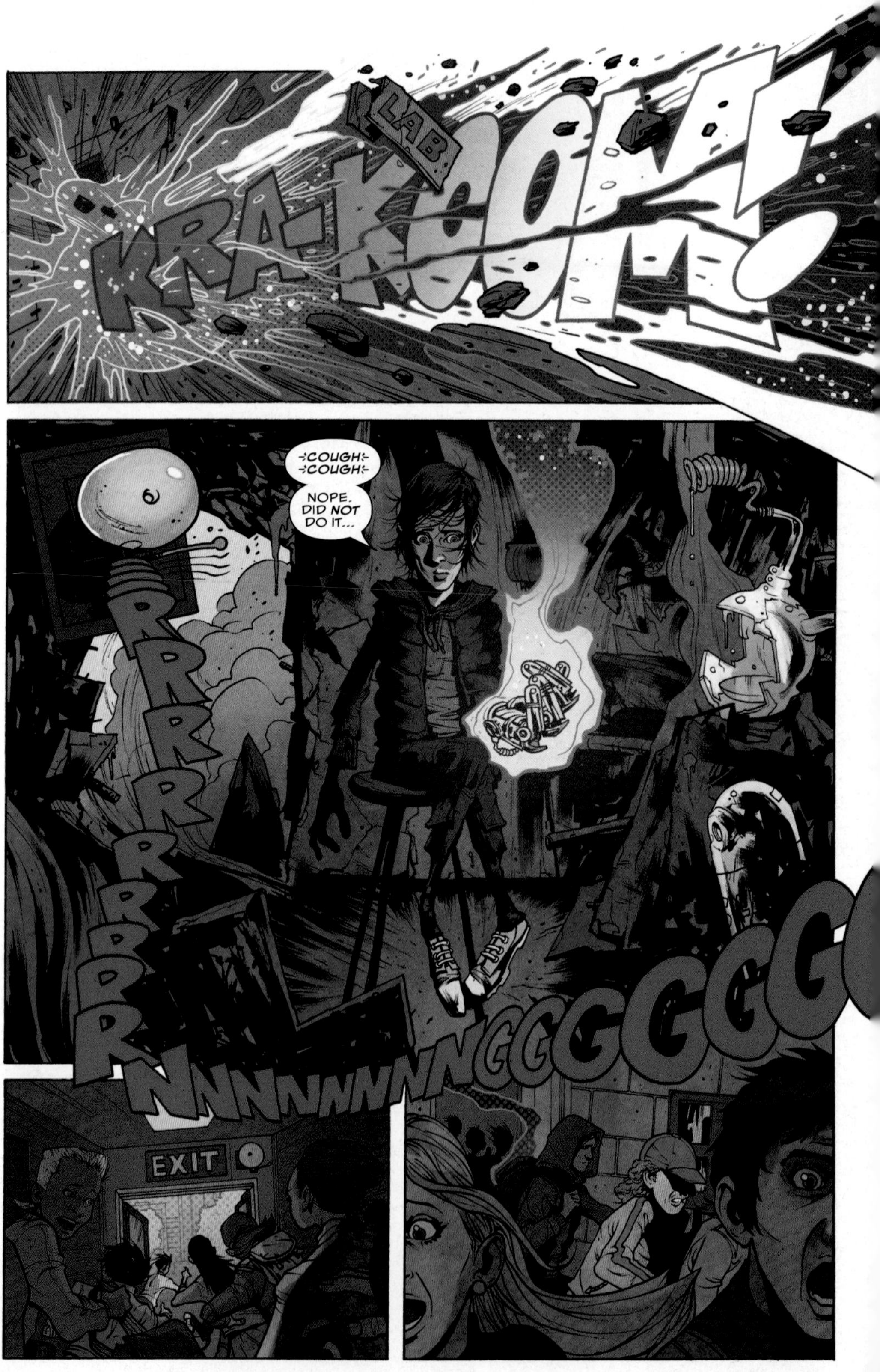
LAB
KRA-KOOM!
COUGH
COUGH
NOPE. DID NOT DO IT...
RRRRRRRRRRNNNNNNNNGGGGGGG
EXIT

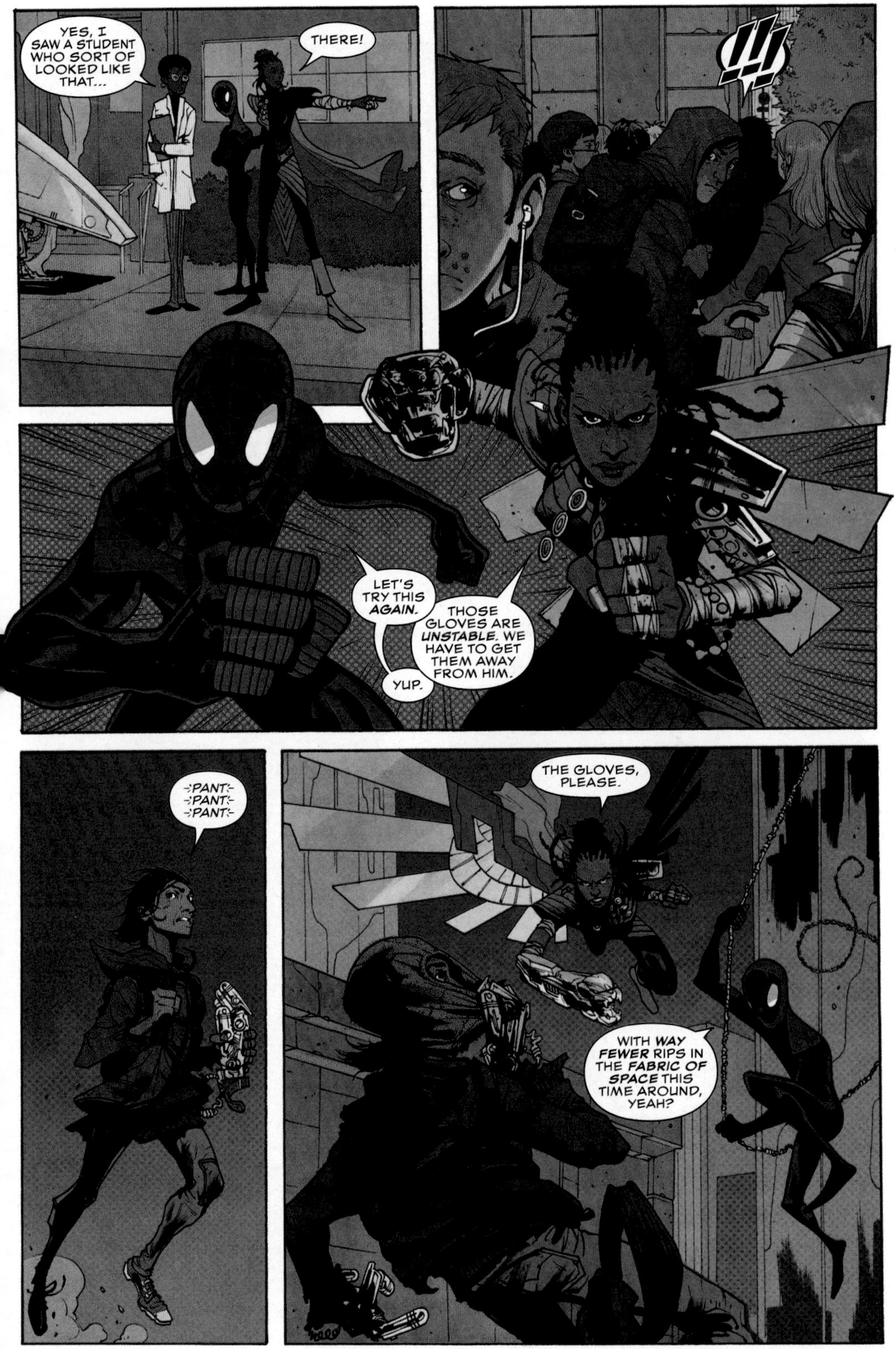
YES, I SAW A STUDENT WHO SORT OF LOOKED LIKE THAT...
THERE!
!!!
LET'S TRY THIS AGAIN.
THOSE GLOVES ARE UNSTABLE. WE HAVE TO GET THEM AWAY FROM HIM.
YUP.
-PANT- -PANT- -PANT-
THE GLOVES, PLEASE.
WITH WAY FEWER RIPS IN THE FABRIC OF SPACE THIS TIME AROUND, YEAH?

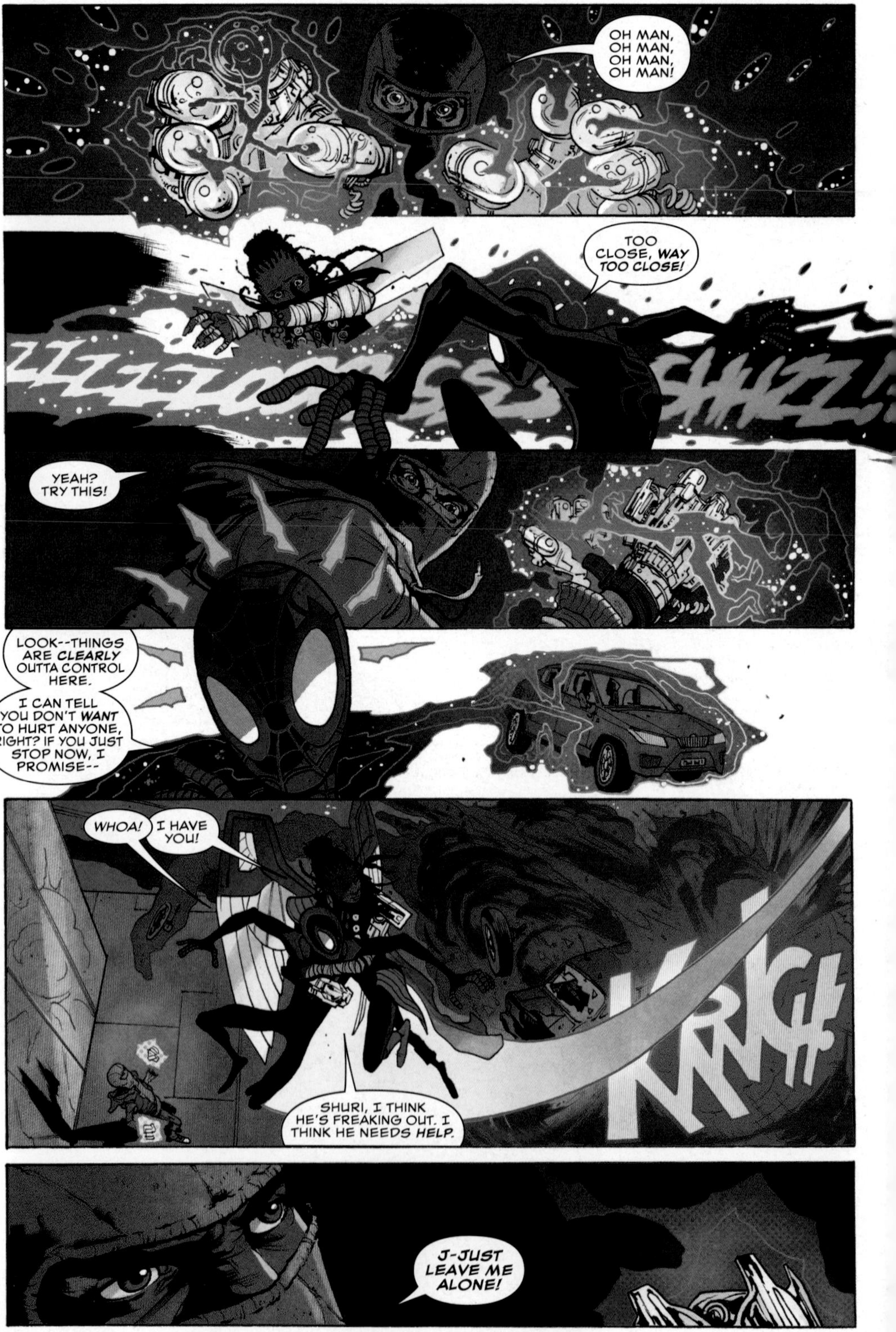
OH MAN, OH MAN, OH MAN, OH MAN!
TOO CLOSE, WAY TOO CLOSE!
ZZZZOOSSS
SHHZZZ
YEAH? TRY THIS!
LOOK--THINGS ARE CLEARLY OUTTA CONTROL HERE.
I CAN TELL YOU DON'T WANT TO HURT ANYONE, RIGHT? IF YOU JUST STOP NOW, I PROMISE--
WHOA!
I HAVE YOU!
SHURI, I THINK HE'S FREAKING OUT. I THINK HE NEEDS HELP.
KRRCH
J-JUST LEAVE ME ALONE!

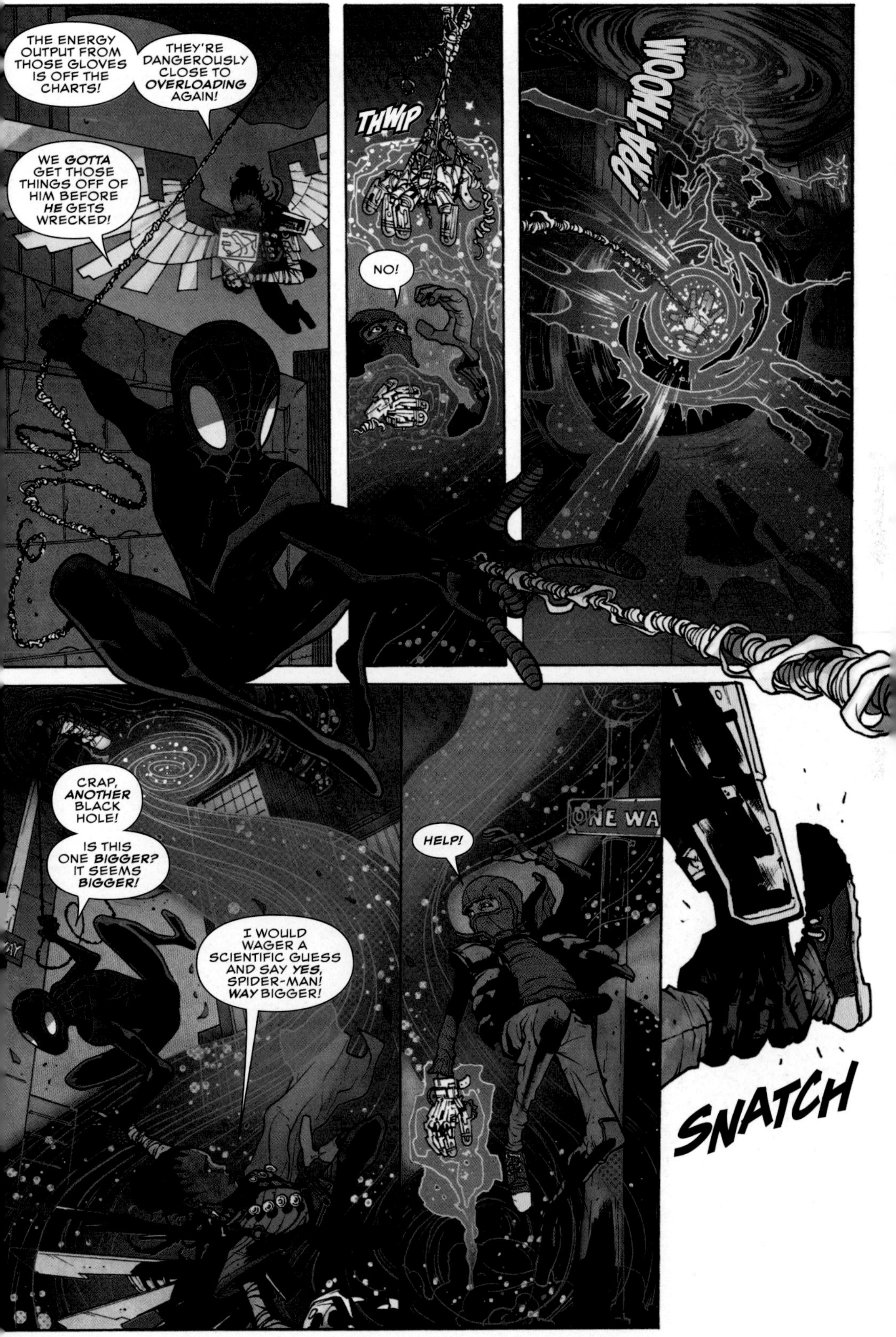
THE ENERGY OUTPUT FROM THOSE GLOVES IS OFF THE CHARTS!
THEY'RE DANGEROUSLY CLOSE TO OVERLOADING AGAIN!
WE GOTTA GET THOSE THINGS OFF OF HIM BEFORE HE GETS WRECKED!
THWIP
NO!
PRA-THOOM
CRAP, ANOTHER BLACK HOLE!
IS THIS ONE BIGGER? IT SEEMS BIGGER!
I WOULD WAGER A SCIENTIFIC GUESS AND SAY YES, SPIDER-MAN! WAY BIGGER!
ONE WA
HELP!
SNATCH

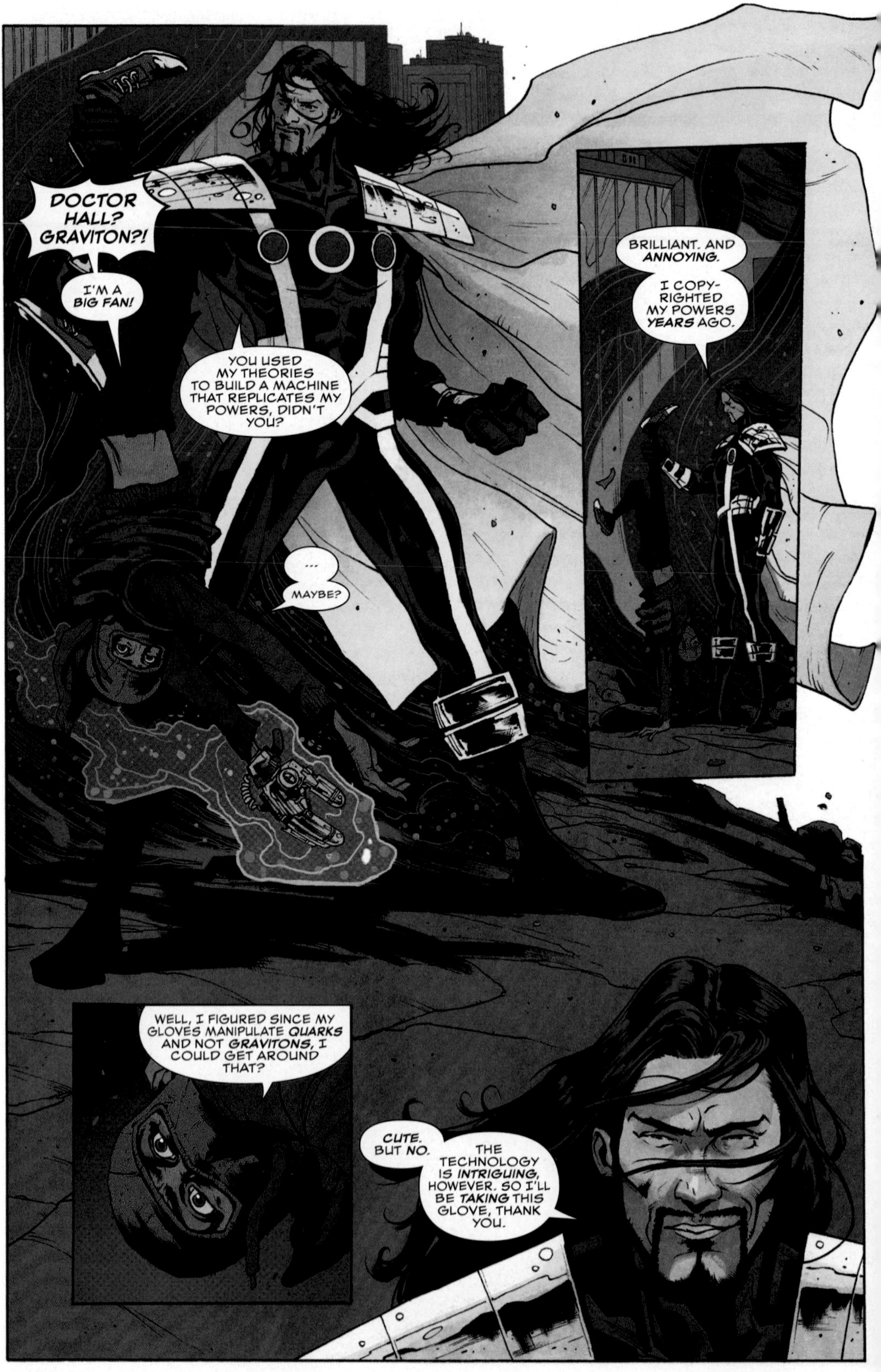
DOCTOR HALL? GRAVITON?!
I'M A BIG FAN!
YOU USED MY THEORIES TO BUILD A MACHINE THAT REPLICATES MY POWERS, DIDN'T YOU?
...
MAYBE?
BRILLIANT. AND ANNOYING.
I COPY-RIGHTED MY POWERS YEARS AGO.
WELL, I FIGURED SINCE MY GLOVES MANIPULATE QUARKS AND NOT GRAVITONS, I COULD GET AROUND THAT?
CUTE. BUT NO.
THE TECHNOLOGY IS INTRIGUING, HOWEVER. SO I'LL BE TAKING THIS GLOVE, THANK YOU.

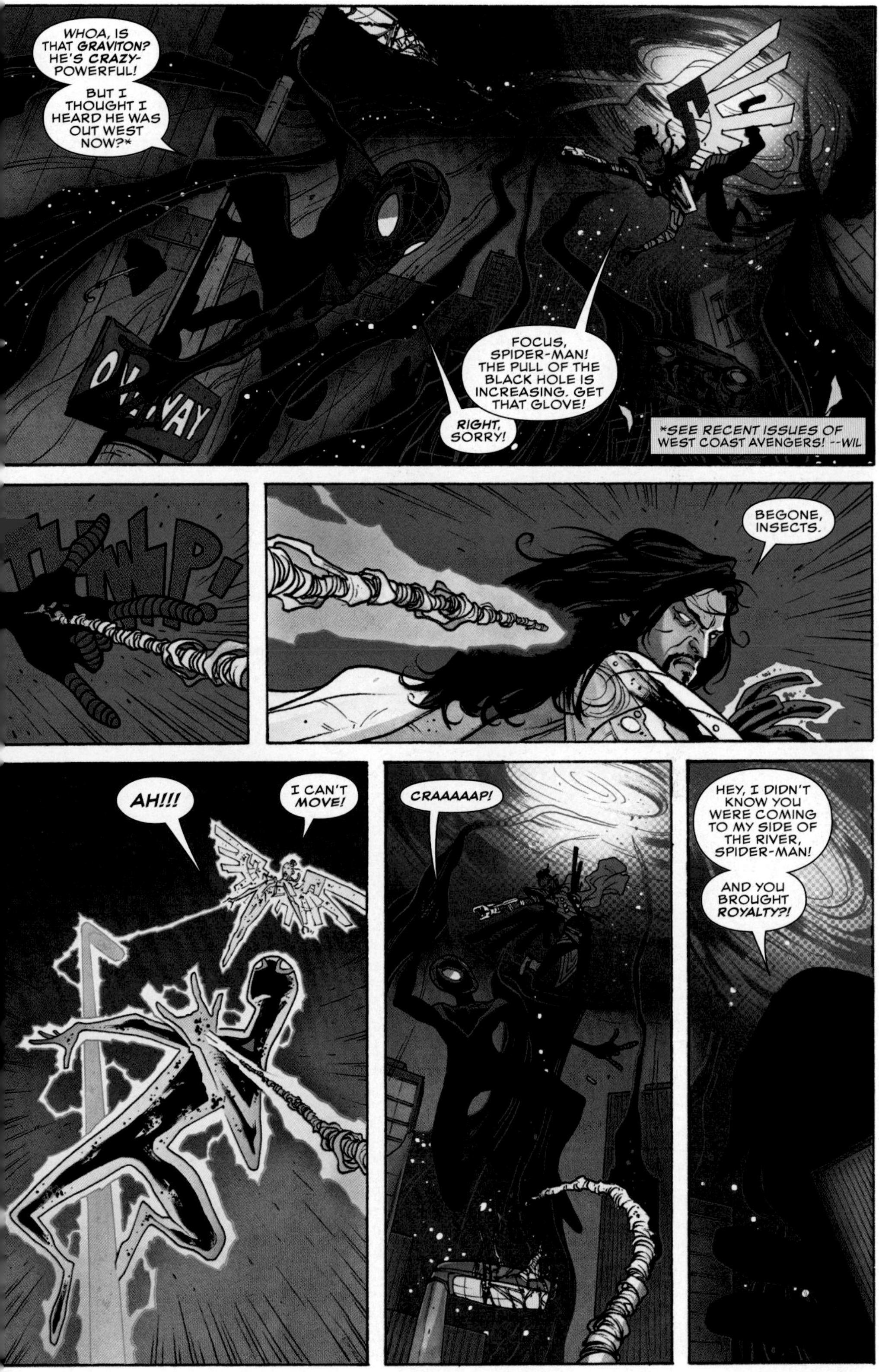
WHOA, IS THAT GRAVITON? HE'S CRAZY-POWERFUL!
BUT I THOUGHT I HEARD HE WAS OUT WEST NOW?*
FOCUS, SPIDER-MAN! THE PULL OF THE BLACK HOLE IS INCREASING. GET THAT GLOVE!
RIGHT, SORRY!
*SEE RECENT ISSUES OF WEST COAST AVENGERS! --WIL
THWIP!
BEGONE, INSECTS.
AH!!!
I CAN'T MOVE!
CRAAAAAP!
HEY, I DIDN'T KNOW YOU WERE COMING TO MY SIDE OF THE RIVER, SPIDER-MAN!
AND YOU BROUGHT ROYALTY?!

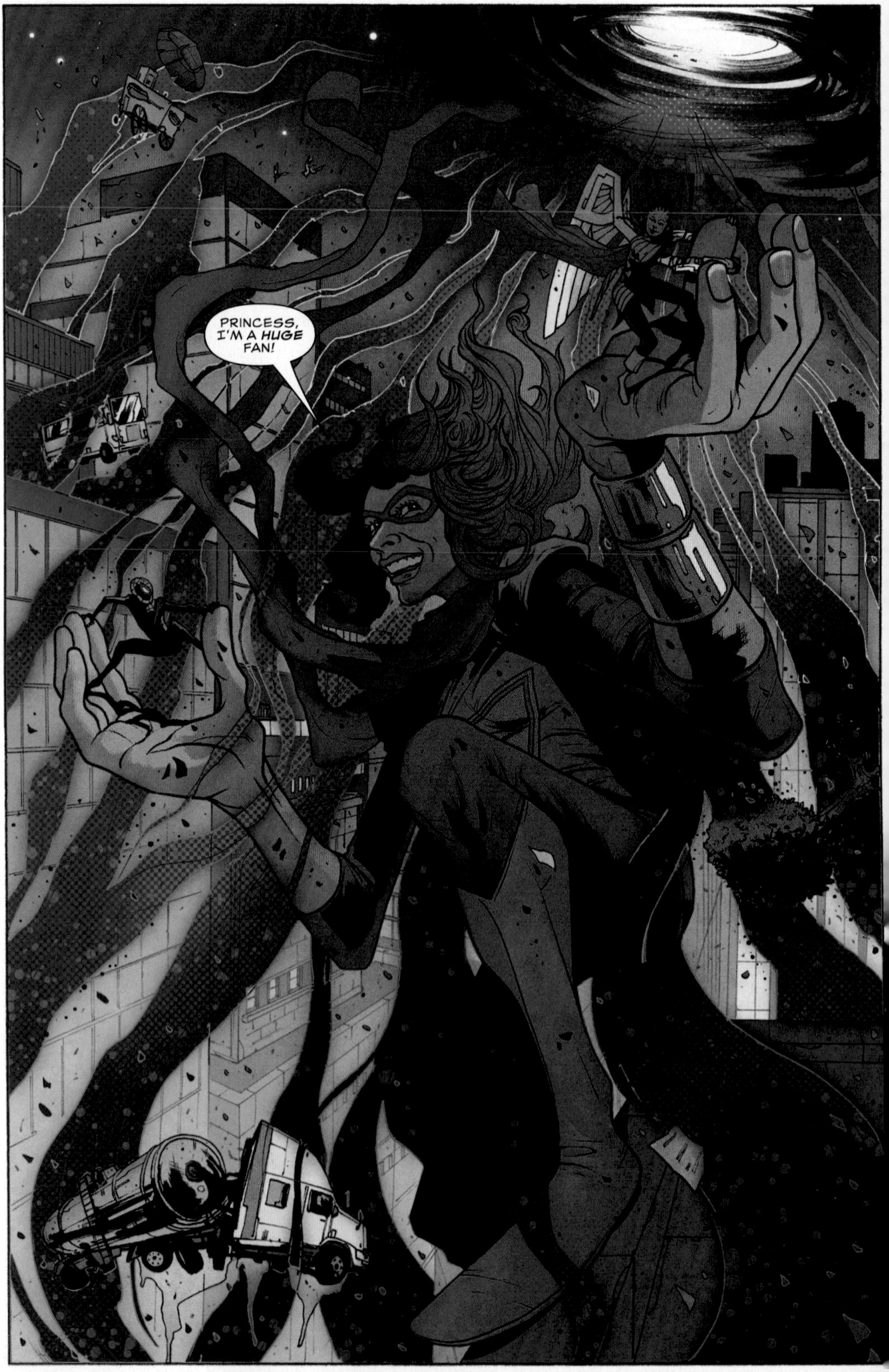
PRINCESS, I'M A *HUGE* FAN!

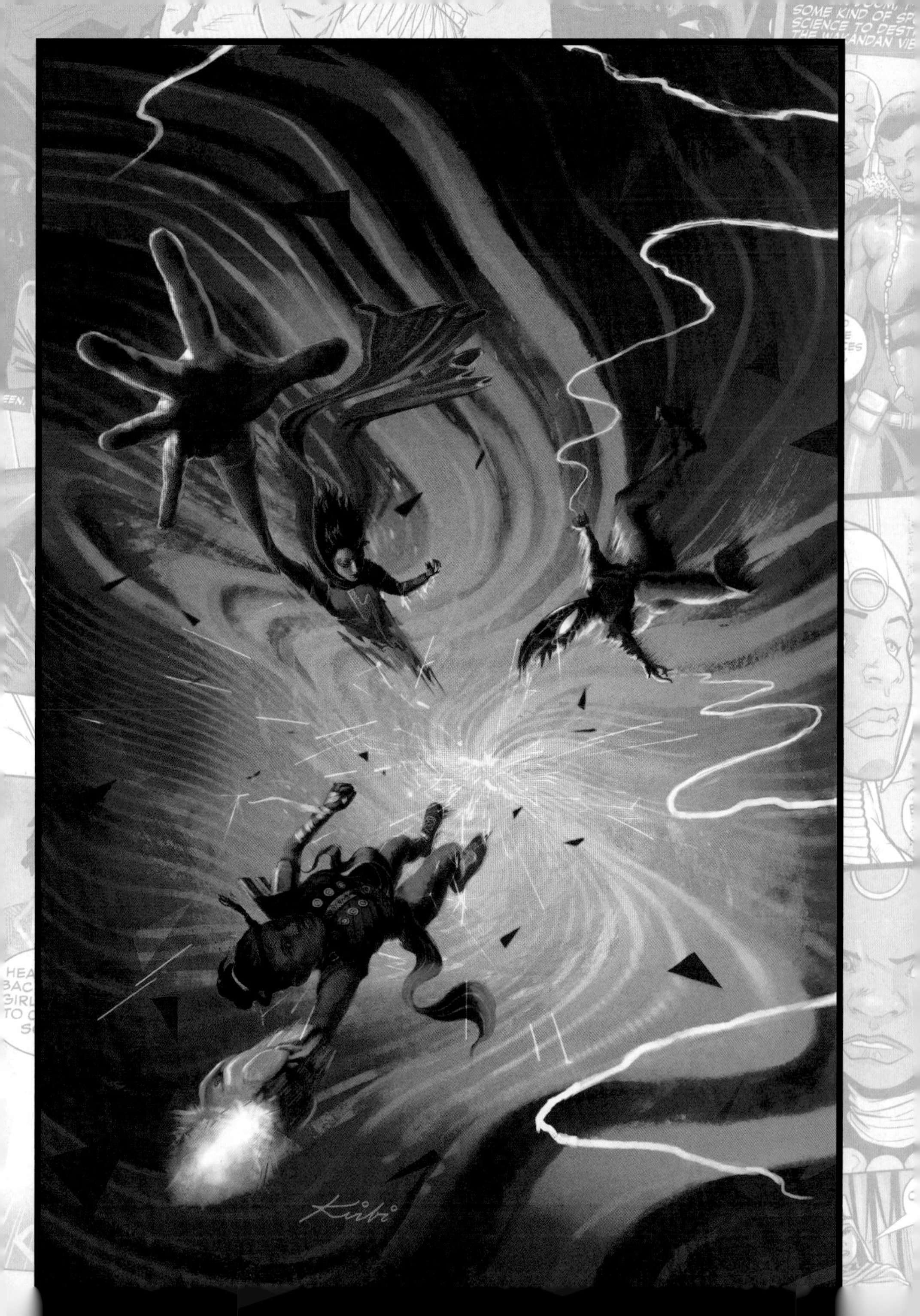

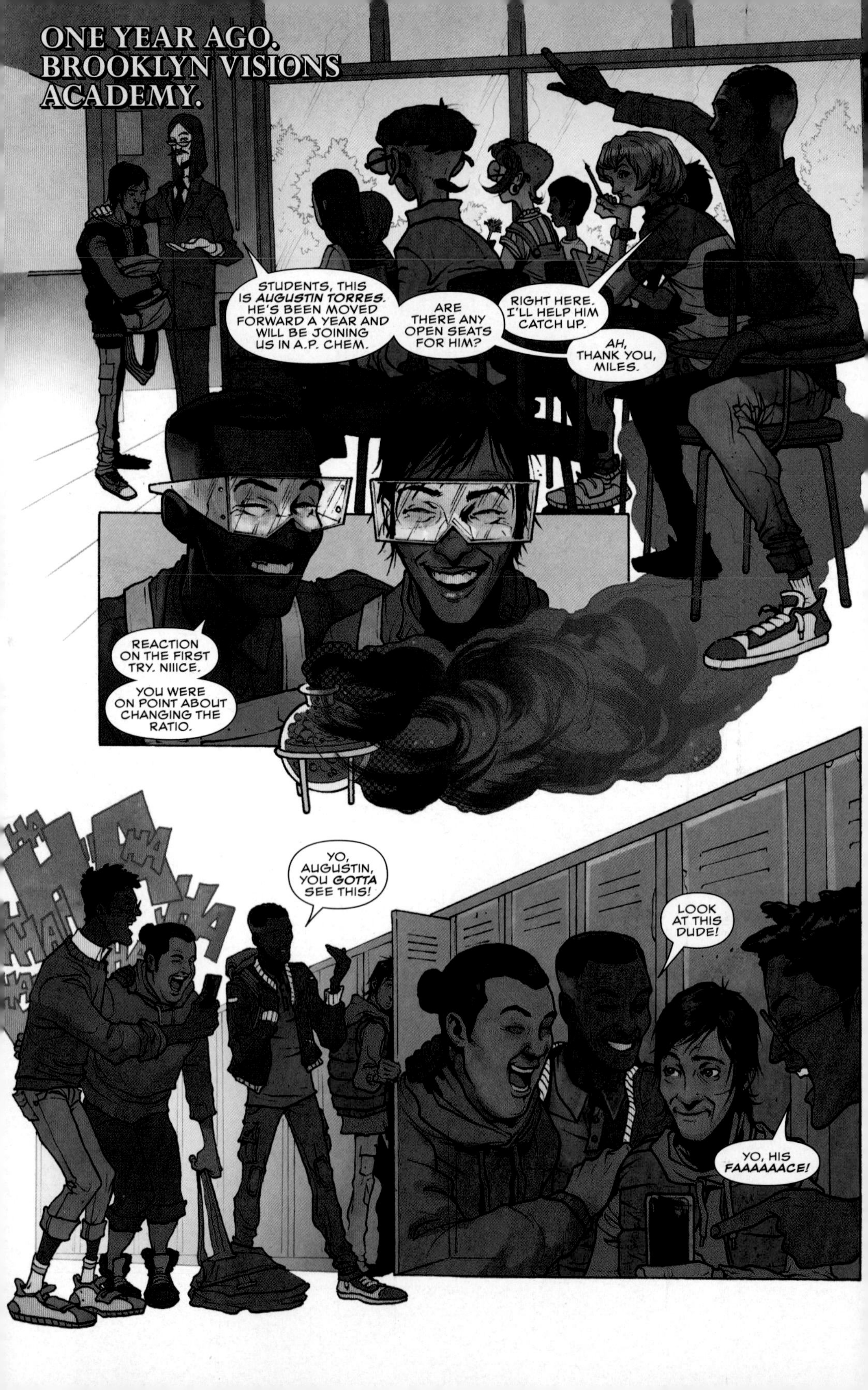
ONE YEAR AGO. BROOKLYN VISIONS ACADEMY.
STUDENTS, THIS IS AUGUSTIN TORRES. HE'S BEEN MOVED FORWARD A YEAR AND WILL BE JOINING US IN A.P. CHEM.
ARE THERE ANY OPEN SEATS FOR HIM?
RIGHT HERE. I'LL HELP HIM CATCH UP.
AH, THANK YOU, MILES.
REACTION ON THE FIRST TRY. NIIICE.
YOU WERE ON POINT ABOUT CHANGING THE RATIO.
YO, AUGUSTIN, YOU GOTTA SEE THIS!
LOOK AT THIS DUDE!
YO, HIS FAAAAAACE!

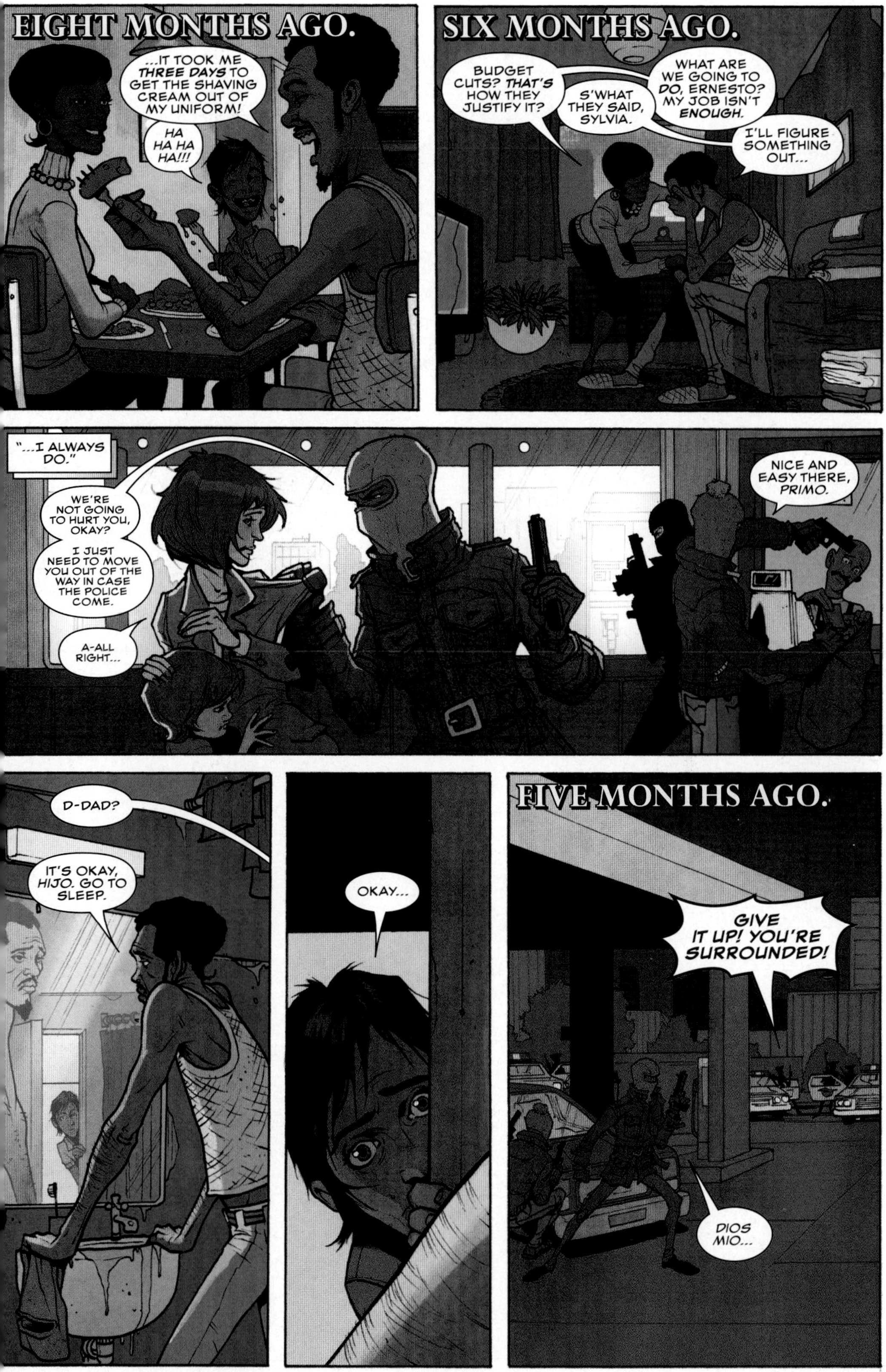
EIGHT MONTHS AGO.
...IT TOOK ME THREE DAYS TO GET THE SHAVING CREAM OUT OF MY UNIFORM!
HA HA HA HA!!!
SIX MONTHS AGO.
BUDGET CUTS? THAT'S HOW THEY JUSTIFY IT?
S'WHAT THEY SAID, SYLVIA.
WHAT ARE WE GOING TO DO, ERNESTO? MY JOB ISN'T ENOUGH.
I'LL FIGURE SOMETHING OUT...
"...I ALWAYS DO."
WE'RE NOT GOING TO HURT YOU, OKAY?
I JUST NEED TO MOVE YOU OUT OF THE WAY IN CASE THE POLICE COME.
A-ALL RIGHT...
NICE AND EASY THERE, PRIMO.
D-DAD?
IT'S OKAY, HIJO. GO TO SLEEP.
OKAY...
FIVE MONTHS AGO.
GIVE IT UP! YOU'RE SURROUNDED!
DIOS MIO...

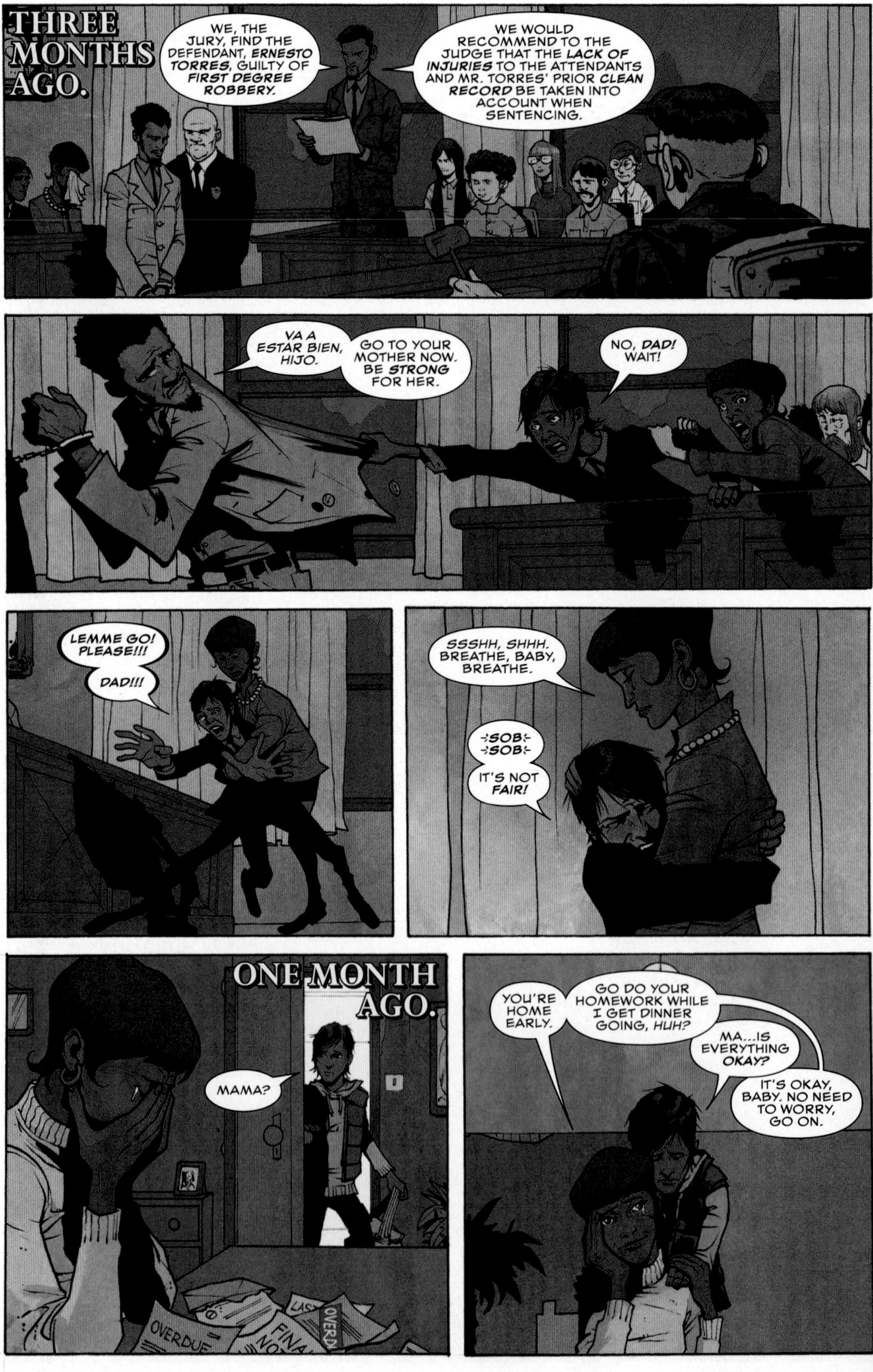
THREE MONTHS AGO.
WE, THE JURY, FIND THE DEFENDANT, ERNESTO TORRES, GUILTY OF FIRST DEGREE ROBBERY.
WE WOULD RECOMMEND TO THE JUDGE THAT THE LACK OF INJURIES TO THE ATTENDANTS AND MR. TORRES' PRIOR CLEAN RECORD BE TAKEN INTO ACCOUNT WHEN SENTENCING.
VA A ESTAR BIEN, HIJO.
GO TO YOUR MOTHER NOW. BE STRONG FOR HER.
NO, DAD! WAIT!
LEMME GO! PLEASE!!!
DAD!!!
SSSHH, SHHH. BREATHE, BABY, BREATHE.
SOB
SOB
IT'S NOT FAIR!
ONE MONTH AGO.
MAMA?
OVERDUE
FINAL NOTI
OVERD
LAST
YOU'RE HOME EARLY.
GO DO YOUR HOMEWORK WHILE I GET DINNER GOING, HUH?
MA...IS EVERYTHING OKAY?
IT'S OKAY, BABY. NO NEED TO WORRY, GO ON.

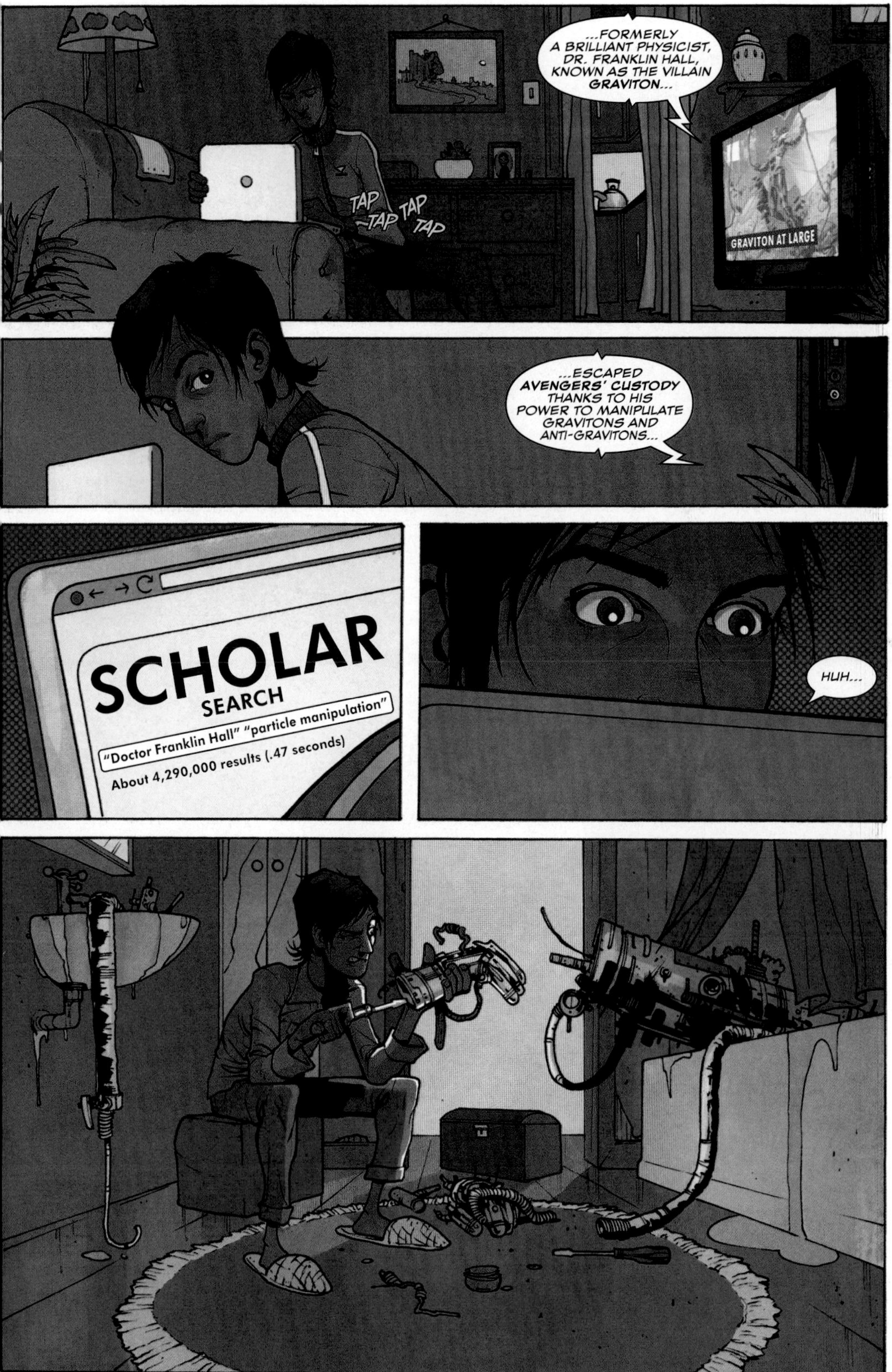
...FORMERLY A BRILLIANT PHYSICIST, DR. FRANKLIN HALL, KNOWN AS THE VILLAIN GRAVITON...
GRAVITON AT LARGE
TAP TAP TAP TAP
...ESCAPED AVENGERS' CUSTODY THANKS TO HIS POWER TO MANIPULATE GRAVITONS AND ANTI-GRAVITONS...
SCHOLAR
SEARCH
"Doctor Franklin Hall" "particle manipulation"
About 4,290,000 results (.47 seconds)
HUH...

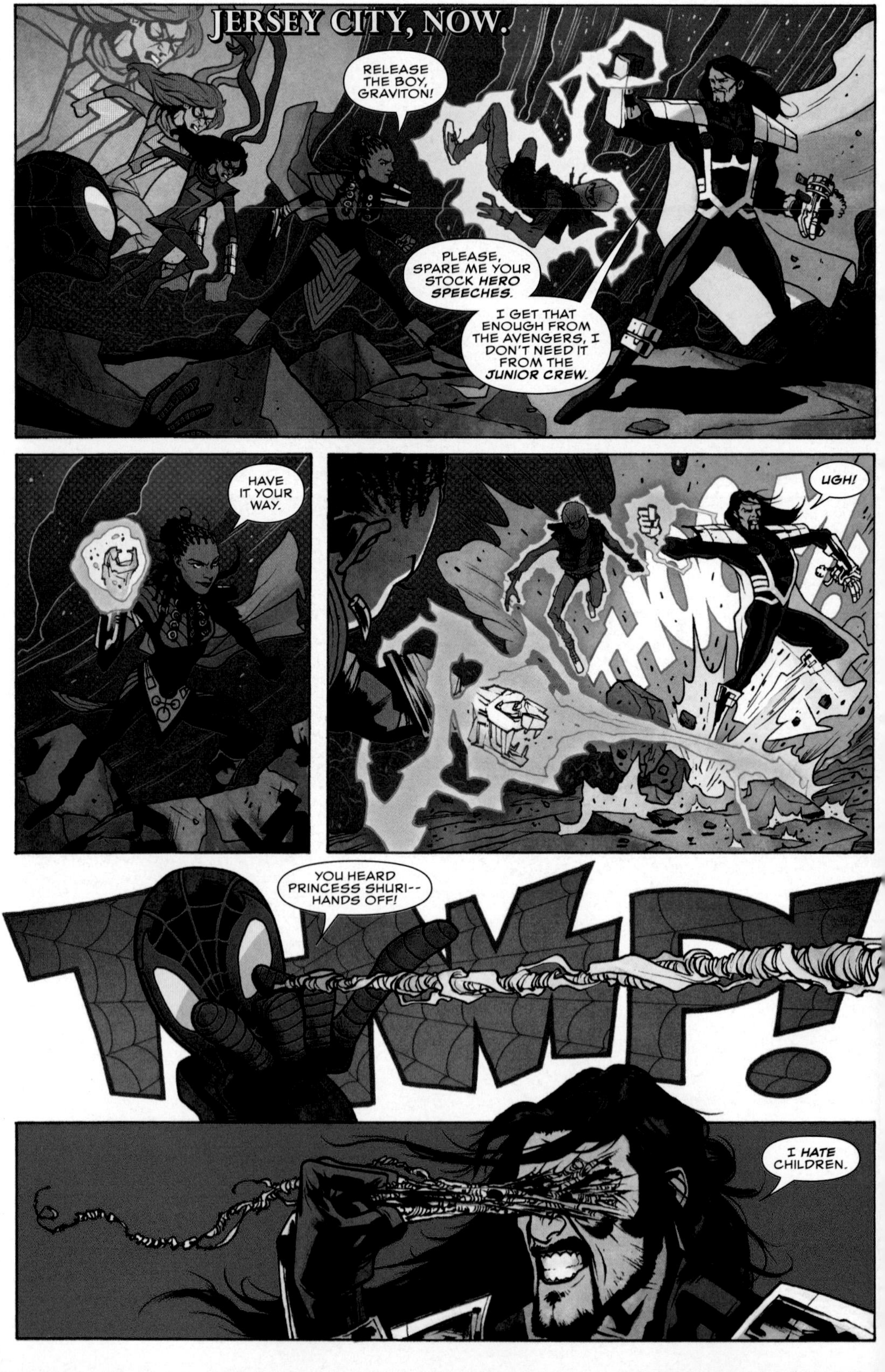
JERSEY CITY, NOW.
RELEASE THE BOY, GRAVITON!
PLEASE, SPARE ME YOUR STOCK HERO SPEECHES.
I GET THAT ENOUGH FROM THE AVENGERS, I DON'T NEED IT FROM THE JUNIOR CREW.
HAVE IT YOUR WAY.
UGH!
YOU HEARD PRINCESS SHURI-- HANDS OFF!
THWIP!
I HATE CHILDREN.

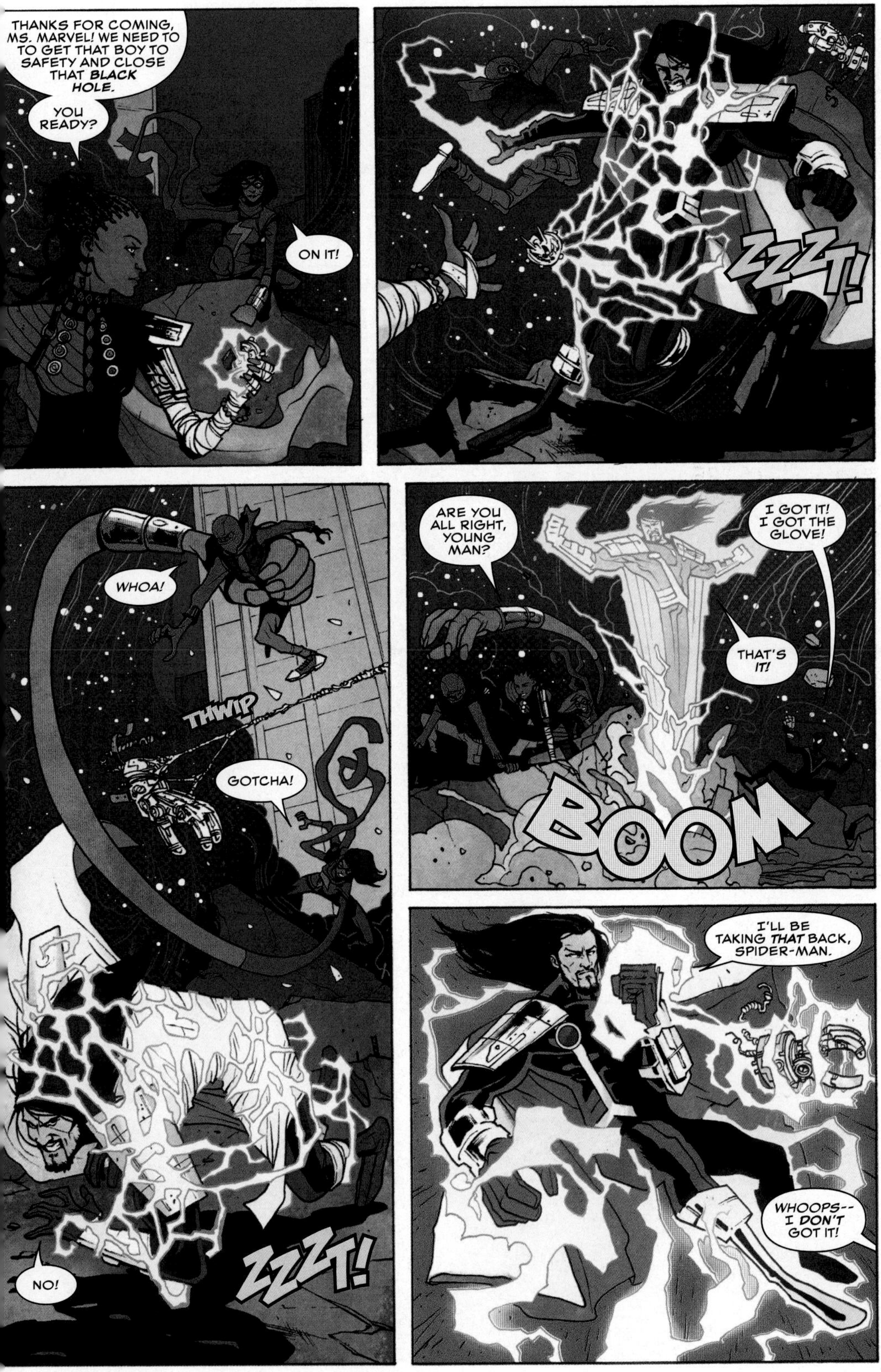
THANKS FOR COMING, MS. MARVEL! WE NEED TO TO GET THAT BOY TO SAFETY AND CLOSE THAT BLACK HOLE.
YOU READY?
ON IT!
ZZZT!
WHOA!
THWIP
GOTCHA!
NO!
ZZZT!
ARE YOU ALL RIGHT, YOUNG MAN?
I GOT IT! I GOT THE GLOVE!
THAT'S IT!
BOOM
I'LL BE TAKING THAT BACK, SPIDER-MAN.
WHOOPS-- I DON'T GOT IT!

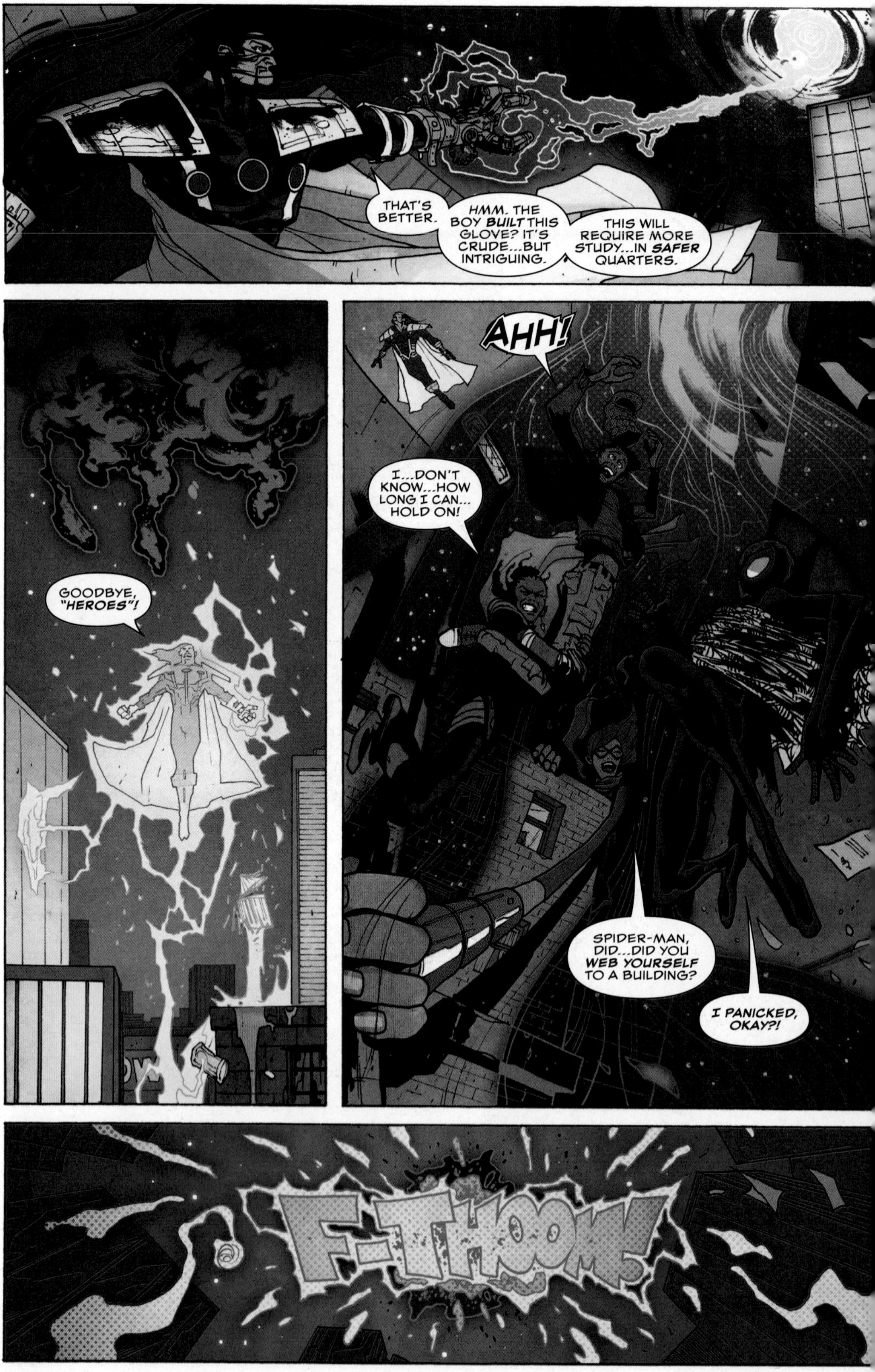
THAT'S BETTER.
HMM. THE BOY BUILT THIS GLOVE? IT'S CRUDE...BUT INTRIGUING.
THIS WILL REQUIRE MORE STUDY...IN SAFER QUARTERS.
GOODBYE, "HEROES"!
AHH!
I...DON'T KNOW...HOW LONG I CAN... HOLD ON!
SPIDER-MAN, DID...DID YOU WEB YOURSELF TO A BUILDING?
I PANICKED, OKAY?!
F-THOOM!

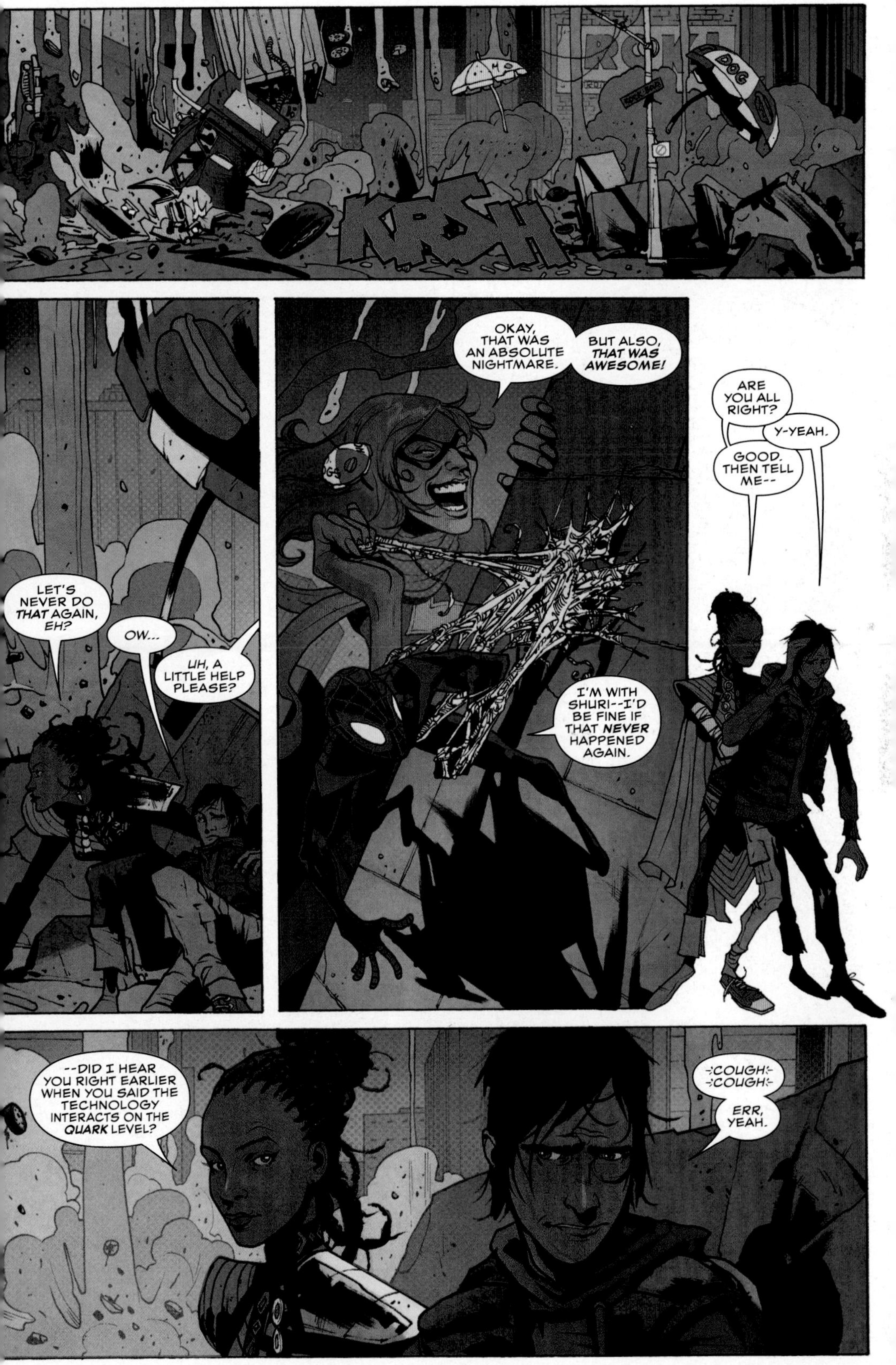
KRSH
LET'S NEVER DO THAT AGAIN, EH?
OW...
UH, A LITTLE HELP PLEASE?
OKAY, THAT WAS AN ABSOLUTE NIGHTMARE.
BUT ALSO, THAT WAS AWESOME!
I'M WITH SHURI--I'D BE FINE IF THAT NEVER HAPPENED AGAIN.
ARE YOU ALL RIGHT?
Y-YEAH.
GOOD. THEN TELL ME--
--DID I HEAR YOU RIGHT EARLIER WHEN YOU SAID THE TECHNOLOGY INTERACTS ON THE QUARK LEVEL?
COUGH COUGH
ERR, YEAH.

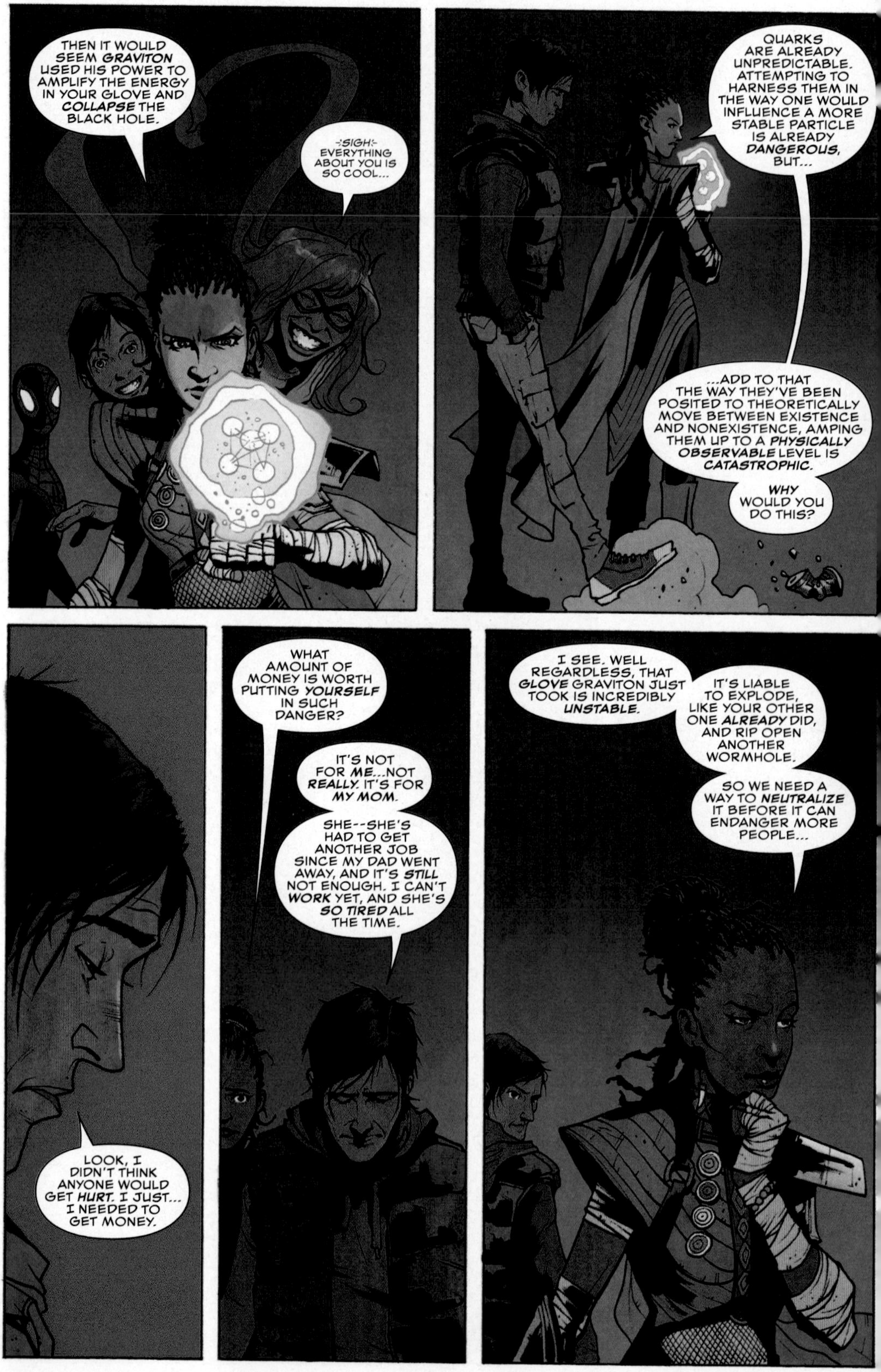
THEN IT WOULD SEEM GRAVITON USED HIS POWER TO AMPLIFY THE ENERGY IN YOUR GLOVE AND COLLAPSE THE BLACK HOLE.
-SIGH- EVERYTHING ABOUT YOU IS SO COOL...
QUARKS ARE ALREADY UNPREDICTABLE. ATTEMPTING TO HARNESS THEM IN THE WAY ONE WOULD INFLUENCE A MORE STABLE PARTICLE IS ALREADY DANGEROUS, BUT...
...ADD TO THAT THE WAY THEY'VE BEEN POSITED TO THEORETICALLY MOVE BETWEEN EXISTENCE AND NONEXISTENCE, AMPING THEM UP TO A PHYSICALLY OBSERVABLE LEVEL IS CATASTROPHIC.
WHY WOULD YOU DO THIS?
LOOK, I DIDN'T THINK ANYONE WOULD GET HURT. I JUST... I NEEDED TO GET MONEY.
WHAT AMOUNT OF MONEY IS WORTH PUTTING YOURSELF IN SUCH DANGER?
IT'S NOT FOR ME...NOT REALLY. IT'S FOR MY MOM.
SHE--SHE'S HAD TO GET ANOTHER JOB SINCE MY DAD WENT AWAY, AND IT'S STILL NOT ENOUGH. I CAN'T WORK YET, AND SHE'S SO TIRED ALL THE TIME.
I SEE. WELL REGARDLESS, THAT GLOVE GRAVITON JUST TOOK IS INCREDIBLY UNSTABLE.
IT'S LIABLE TO EXPLODE, LIKE YOUR OTHER ONE ALREADY DID, AND RIP OPEN ANOTHER WORMHOLE.
SO WE NEED A WAY TO NEUTRALIZE IT BEFORE IT CAN ENDANGER MORE PEOPLE...

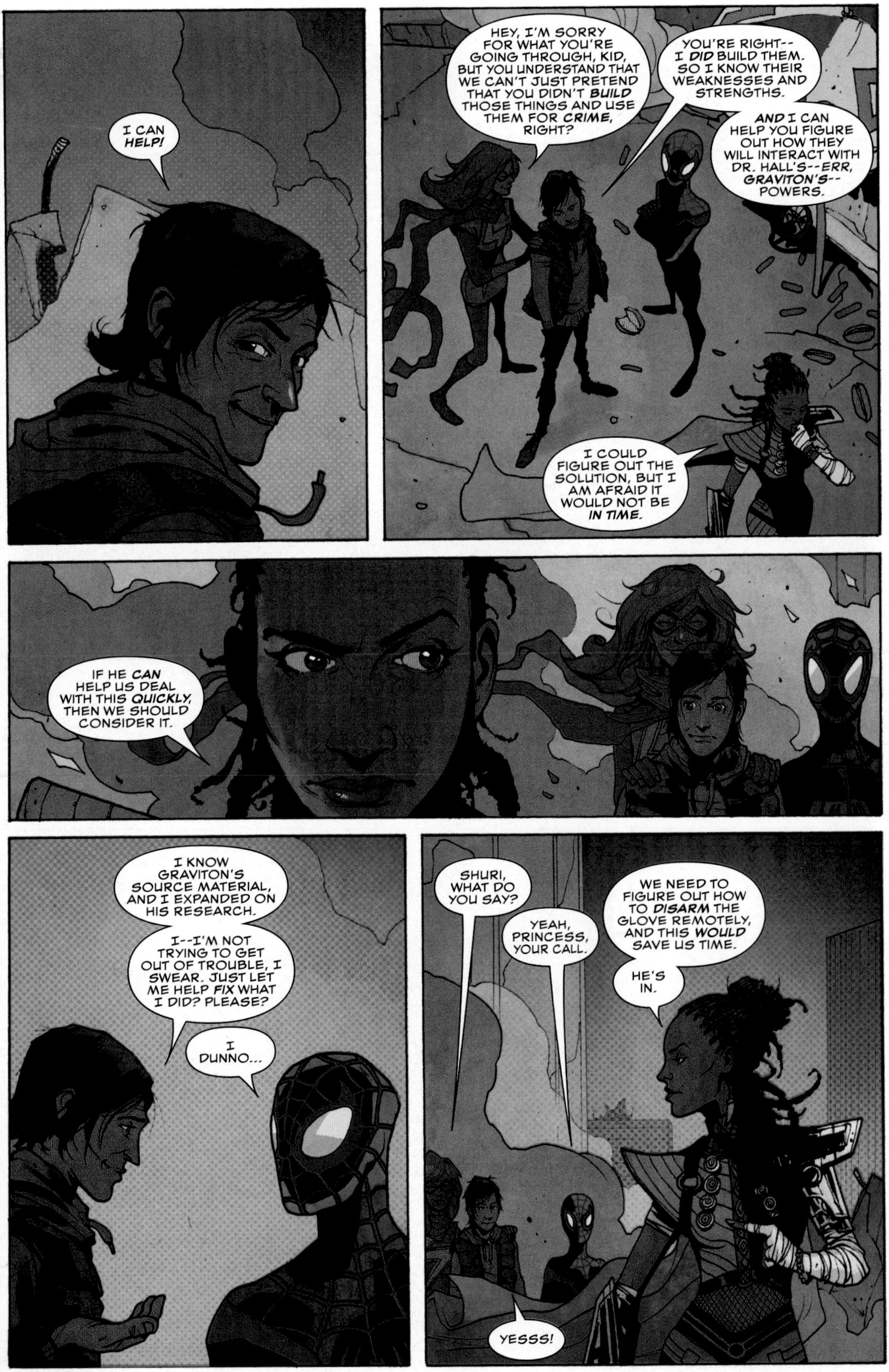
I CAN HELP!
HEY, I'M SORRY FOR WHAT YOU'RE GOING THROUGH, KID, BUT YOU UNDERSTAND THAT WE CAN'T JUST PRETEND THAT YOU DIDN'T BUILD THOSE THINGS AND USE THEM FOR CRIME, RIGHT?
YOU'RE RIGHT-- I DID BUILD THEM. SO I KNOW THEIR WEAKNESSES AND STRENGTHS.
AND I CAN HELP YOU FIGURE OUT HOW THEY WILL INTERACT WITH DR. HALL'S--ERR, GRAVITON'S-- POWERS.
I COULD FIGURE OUT THE SOLUTION, BUT I AM AFRAID IT WOULD NOT BE IN TIME.
IF HE CAN HELP US DEAL WITH THIS QUICKLY, THEN WE SHOULD CONSIDER IT.
I KNOW GRAVITON'S SOURCE MATERIAL, AND I EXPANDED ON HIS RESEARCH.
I--I'M NOT TRYING TO GET OUT OF TROUBLE, I SWEAR. JUST LET ME HELP FIX WHAT I DID? PLEASE?
I DUNNO...
SHURI, WHAT DO YOU SAY?
YEAH, PRINCESS, YOUR CALL.
WE NEED TO FIGURE OUT HOW TO DISARM THE GLOVE REMOTELY, AND THIS WOULD SAVE US TIME.
HE'S IN.
YESSS!

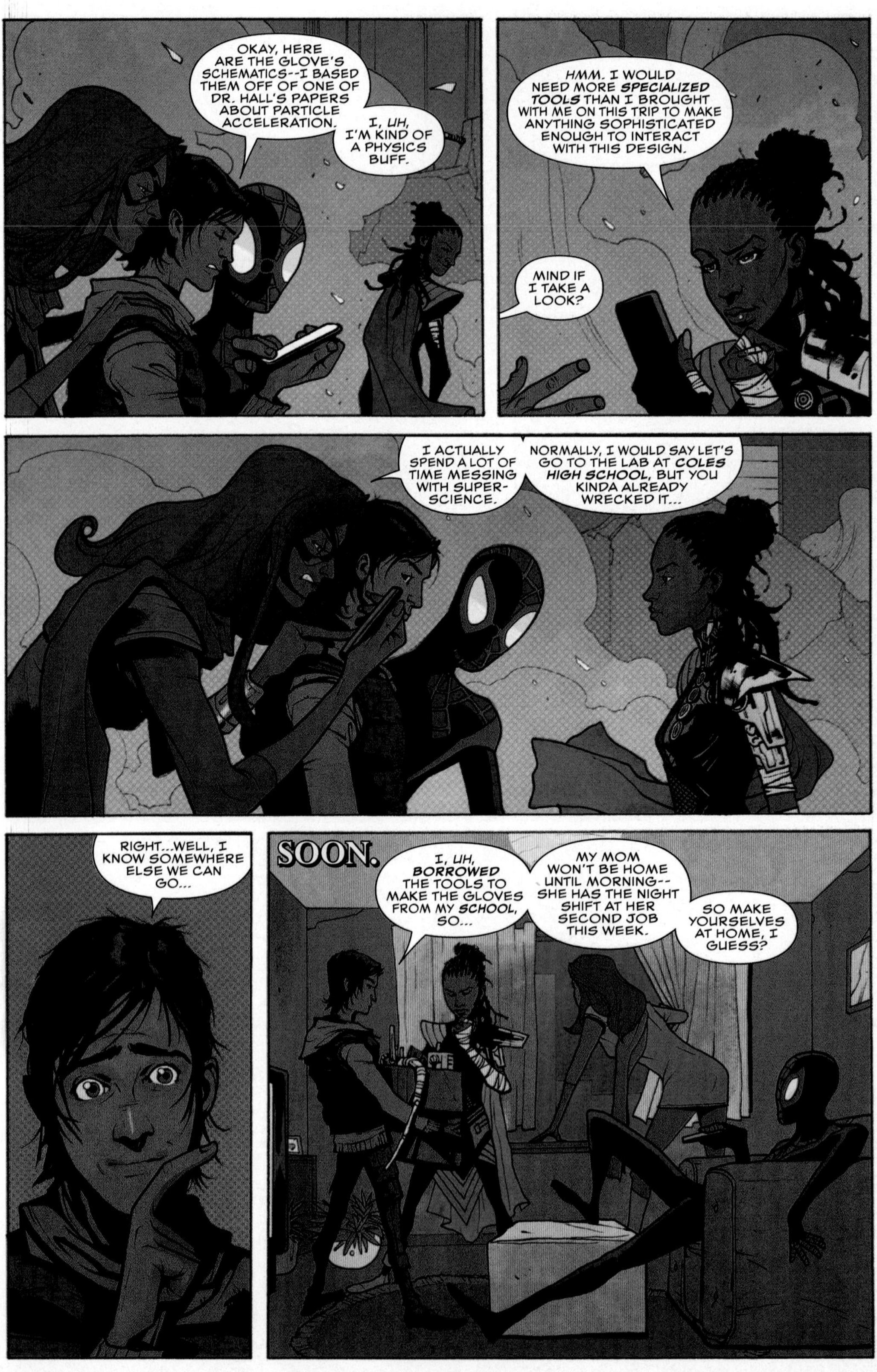
OKAY, HERE ARE THE GLOVE'S SCHEMATICS--I BASED THEM OFF OF ONE OF DR. HALL'S PAPERS ABOUT PARTICLE ACCELERATION.
I, UH, I'M KIND OF A PHYSICS BUFF.
HMM. I WOULD NEED MORE SPECIALIZED TOOLS THAN I BROUGHT WITH ME ON THIS TRIP TO MAKE ANYTHING SOPHISTICATED ENOUGH TO INTERACT WITH THIS DESIGN.
MIND IF I TAKE A LOOK?
I ACTUALLY SPEND A LOT OF TIME MESSING WITH SUPER-SCIENCE.
NORMALLY, I WOULD SAY LET'S GO TO THE LAB AT COLES HIGH SCHOOL, BUT YOU KINDA ALREADY WRECKED IT...
RIGHT...WELL, I KNOW SOMEWHERE ELSE WE CAN GO...
SOON.
I, UH, BORROWED THE TOOLS TO MAKE THE GLOVES FROM MY SCHOOL, SO...
MY MOM WON'T BE HOME UNTIL MORNING--SHE HAS THE NIGHT SHIFT AT HER SECOND JOB THIS WEEK.
SO MAKE YOURSELVES AT HOME, I GUESS?

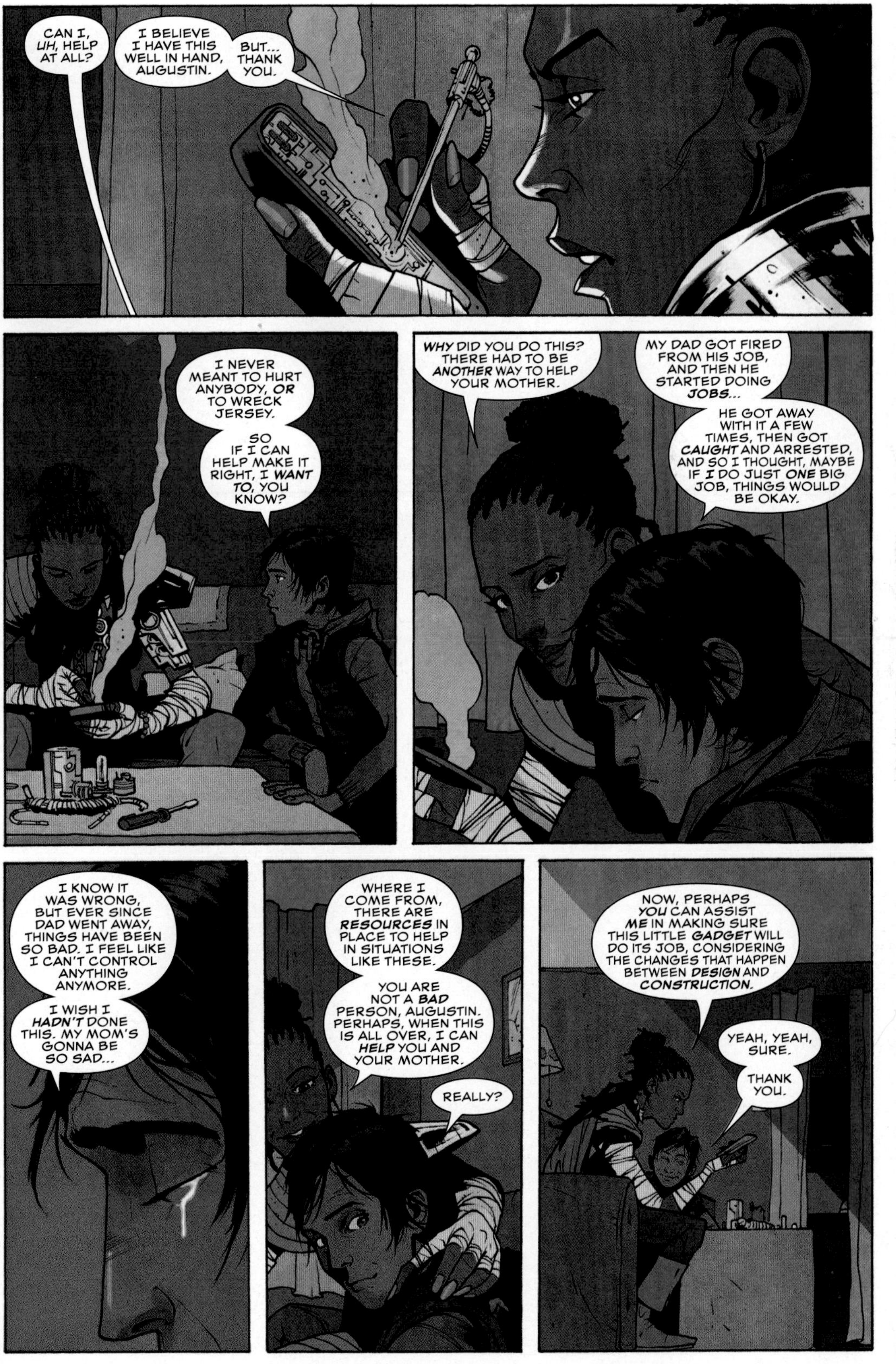
CAN I, UH, HELP AT ALL?
I BELIEVE I HAVE THIS WELL IN HAND, AUGUSTIN.
BUT... THANK YOU.
I NEVER MEANT TO HURT ANYBODY, OR TO WRECK JERSEY.
SO IF I CAN HELP MAKE IT RIGHT, I WANT TO, YOU KNOW?
WHY DID YOU DO THIS? THERE HAD TO BE ANOTHER WAY TO HELP YOUR MOTHER.
MY DAD GOT FIRED FROM HIS JOB, AND THEN HE STARTED DOING JOBS...
HE GOT AWAY WITH IT A FEW TIMES, THEN GOT CAUGHT AND ARRESTED, AND SO I THOUGHT, MAYBE IF I DO JUST ONE BIG JOB, THINGS WOULD BE OKAY.
I KNOW IT WAS WRONG, BUT EVER SINCE DAD WENT AWAY, THINGS HAVE BEEN SO BAD. I FEEL LIKE I CAN'T CONTROL ANYTHING ANYMORE.
I WISH I HADN'T DONE THIS. MY MOM'S GONNA BE SO SAD...
WHERE I COME FROM, THERE ARE RESOURCES IN PLACE TO HELP IN SITUATIONS LIKE THESE.
YOU ARE NOT A BAD PERSON, AUGUSTIN. PERHAPS, WHEN THIS IS ALL OVER, I CAN HELP YOU AND YOUR MOTHER.
REALLY?
NOW, PERHAPS YOU CAN ASSIST ME IN MAKING SURE THIS LITTLE GADGET WILL DO ITS JOB, CONSIDERING THE CHANGES THAT HAPPEN BETWEEN DESIGN AND CONSTRUCTION.
YEAH, YEAH, SURE.
THANK YOU.

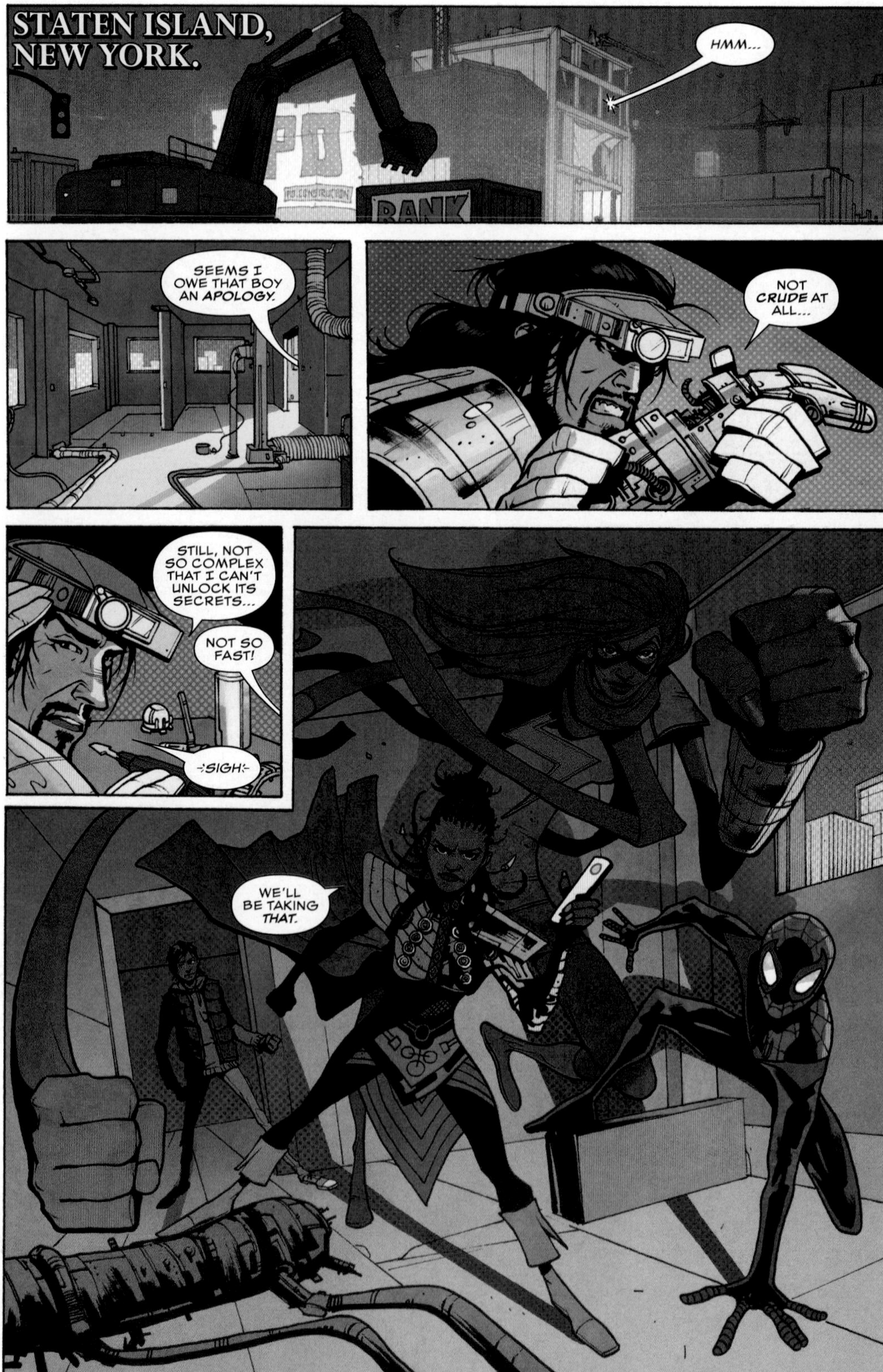
STATEN ISLAND, NEW YORK.
HMM...
SEEMS I OWE THAT BOY AN APOLOGY.
NOT CRUDE AT ALL...
STILL, NOT SO COMPLEX THAT I CAN'T UNLOCK ITS SECRETS...
NOT SO FAST!
-SIGH-
WE'LL BE TAKING THAT.

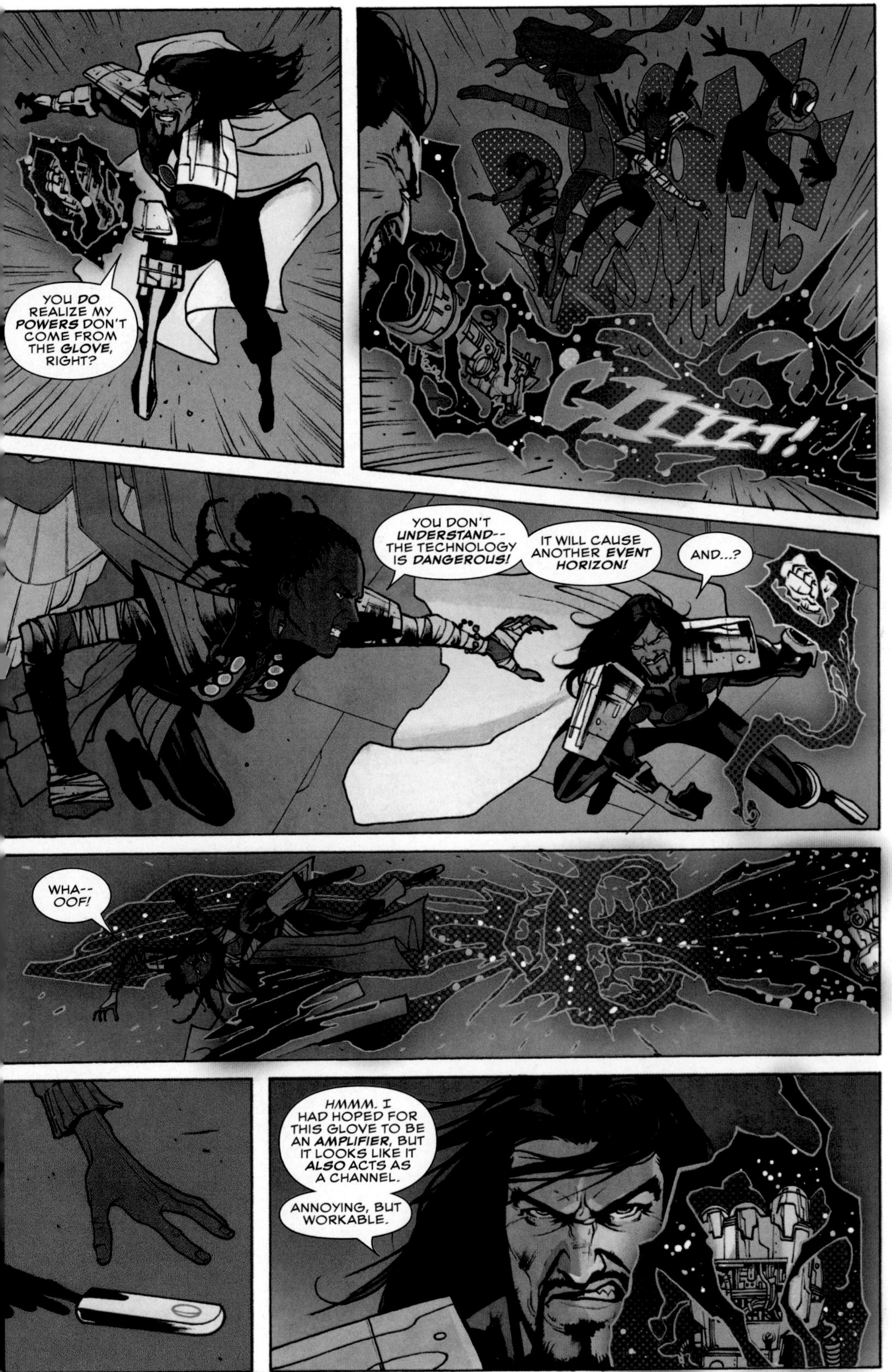

YOU *DO* REALIZE MY ***POWERS*** DON'T COME FROM THE ***GLOVE***, RIGHT?
GZZZT!
YOU DON'T ***UNDERSTAND***-- THE TECHNOLOGY IS ***DANGEROUS!***
IT WILL CAUSE ANOTHER ***EVENT HORIZON!***
AND...?
WHA-- OOF!
HMMM. I HAD HOPED FOR THIS GLOVE TO BE AN ***AMPLIFIER***, BUT IT LOOKS LIKE IT ***ALSO*** ACTS AS A CHANNEL.
ANNOYING, BUT WORKABLE.

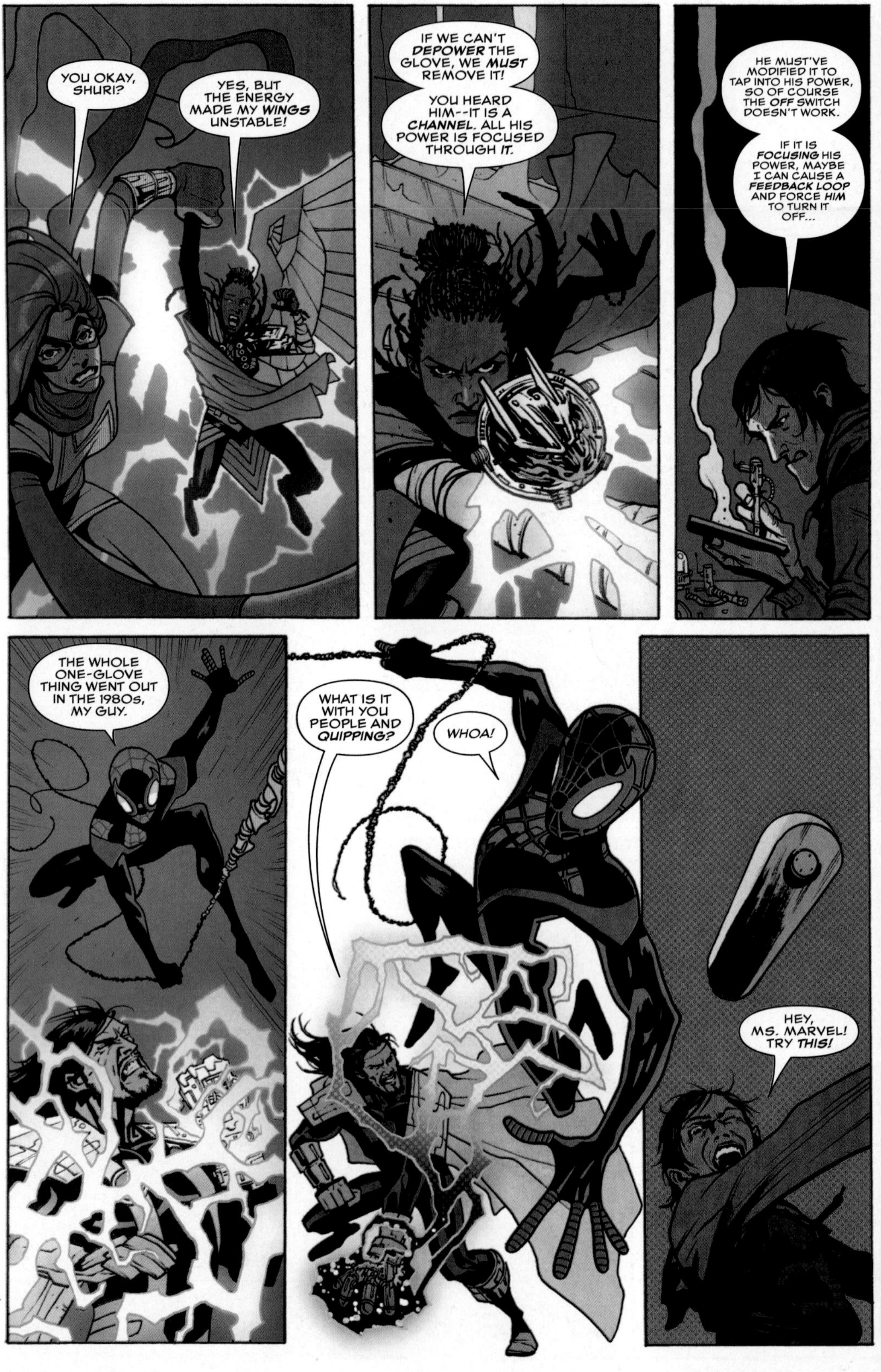
YOU OKAY, SHURI?
YES, BUT THE ENERGY MADE MY WINGS UNSTABLE!
IF WE CAN'T DEPOWER THE GLOVE, WE MUST REMOVE IT!
YOU HEARD HIM--IT IS A CHANNEL. ALL HIS POWER IS FOCUSED THROUGH IT.
HE MUST'VE MODIFIED IT TO TAP INTO HIS POWER, SO OF COURSE THE OFF SWITCH DOESN'T WORK.
IF IT IS FOCUSING HIS POWER, MAYBE I CAN CAUSE A FEEDBACK LOOP AND FORCE HIM TO TURN IT OFF...
THE WHOLE ONE-GLOVE THING WENT OUT IN THE 1980s, MY GUY.
WHAT IS IT WITH YOU PEOPLE AND QUIPPING?
WHOA!
HEY, MS. MARVEL! TRY THIS!

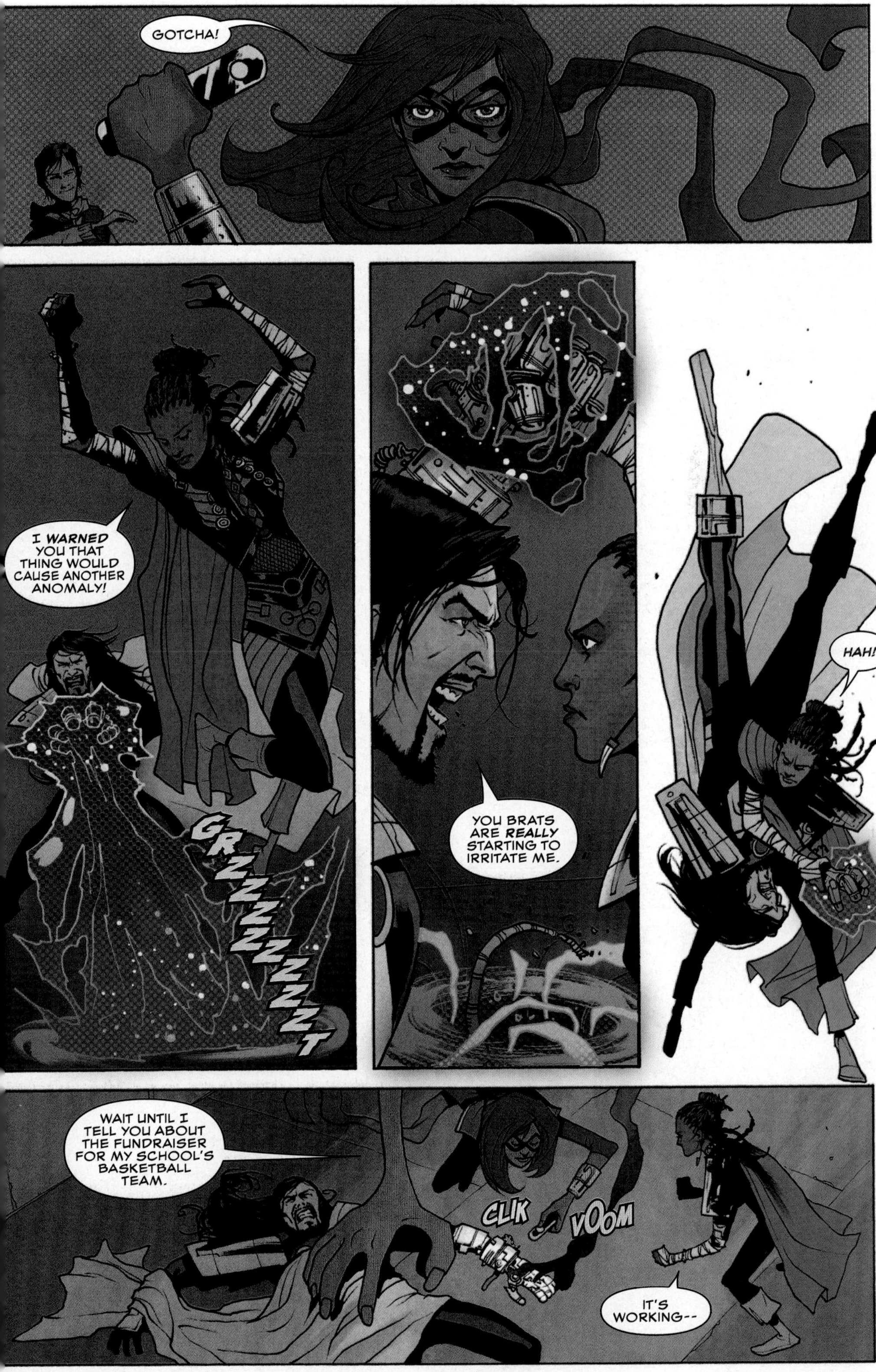
GOTCHA!
I WARNED YOU THAT THING WOULD CAUSE ANOTHER ANOMALY!
GRZZZZZZZT
YOU BRATS ARE REALLY STARTING TO IRRITATE ME.
HAH!
WAIT UNTIL I TELL YOU ABOUT THE FUNDRAISER FOR MY SCHOOL'S BASKETBALL TEAM.
CLIK
VOOM
IT'S WORKING--

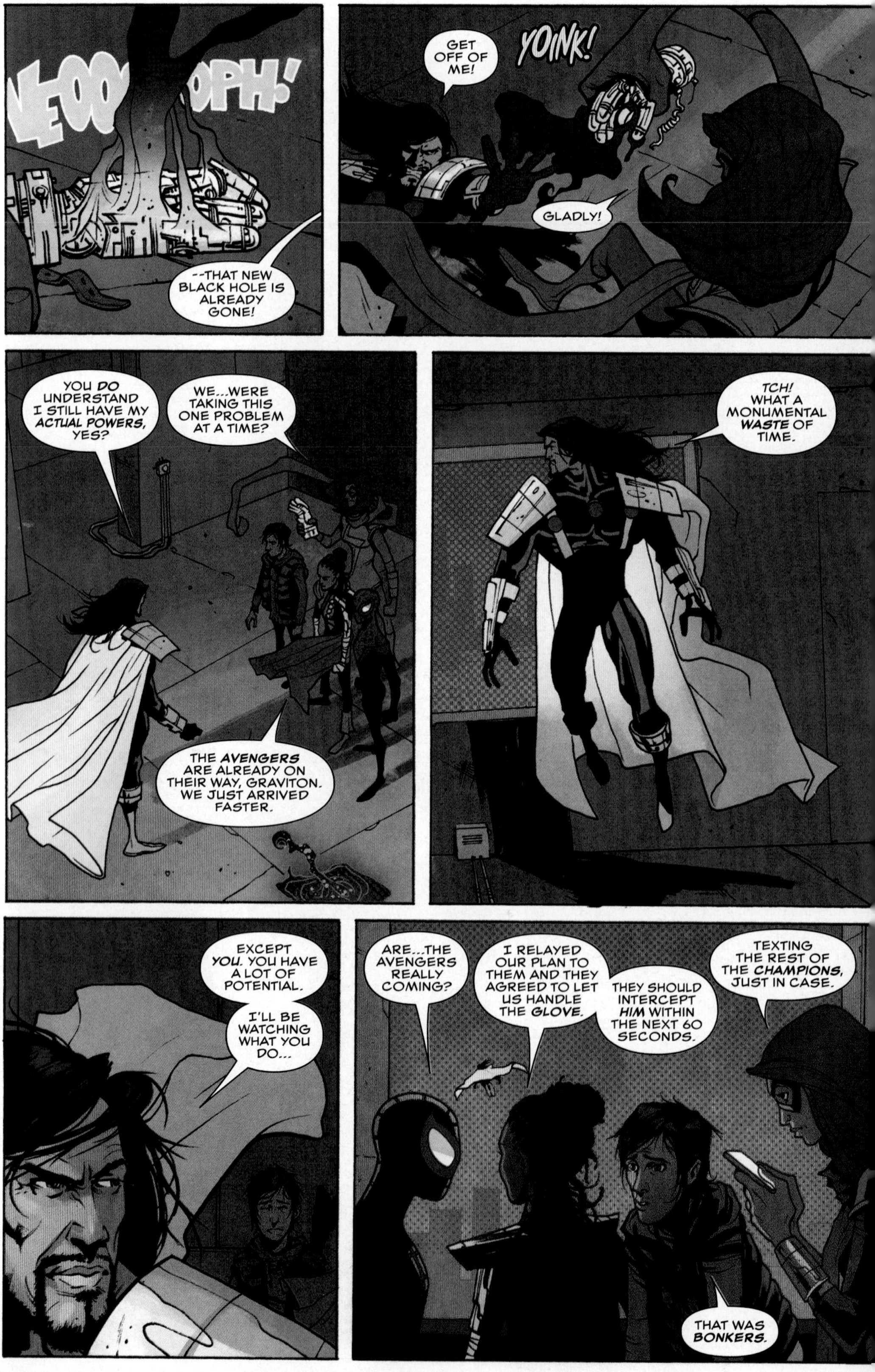
VEOOOOOPH!
--THAT NEW BLACK HOLE IS ALREADY GONE!
GET OFF OF ME!
YOINK!
GLADLY!
YOU *DO* UNDERSTAND I STILL HAVE MY *ACTUAL POWERS,* YES?
WE...WERE TAKING THIS ONE PROBLEM AT A TIME?
THE *AVENGERS* ARE ALREADY ON THEIR WAY, GRAVITON. WE JUST ARRIVED FASTER.
TCH! WHAT A MONUMENTAL *WASTE* OF TIME.
EXCEPT *YOU.* YOU HAVE A LOT OF POTENTIAL.
I'LL BE WATCHING WHAT YOU DO...
ARE...THE AVENGERS REALLY COMING?
I RELAYED OUR PLAN TO THEM AND THEY AGREED TO LET US HANDLE THE *GLOVE.*
THEY SHOULD INTERCEPT *HIM* WITHIN THE NEXT 60 SECONDS.
TEXTING THE REST OF THE *CHAMPIONS,* JUST IN CASE.
THAT WAS *BONKERS.*

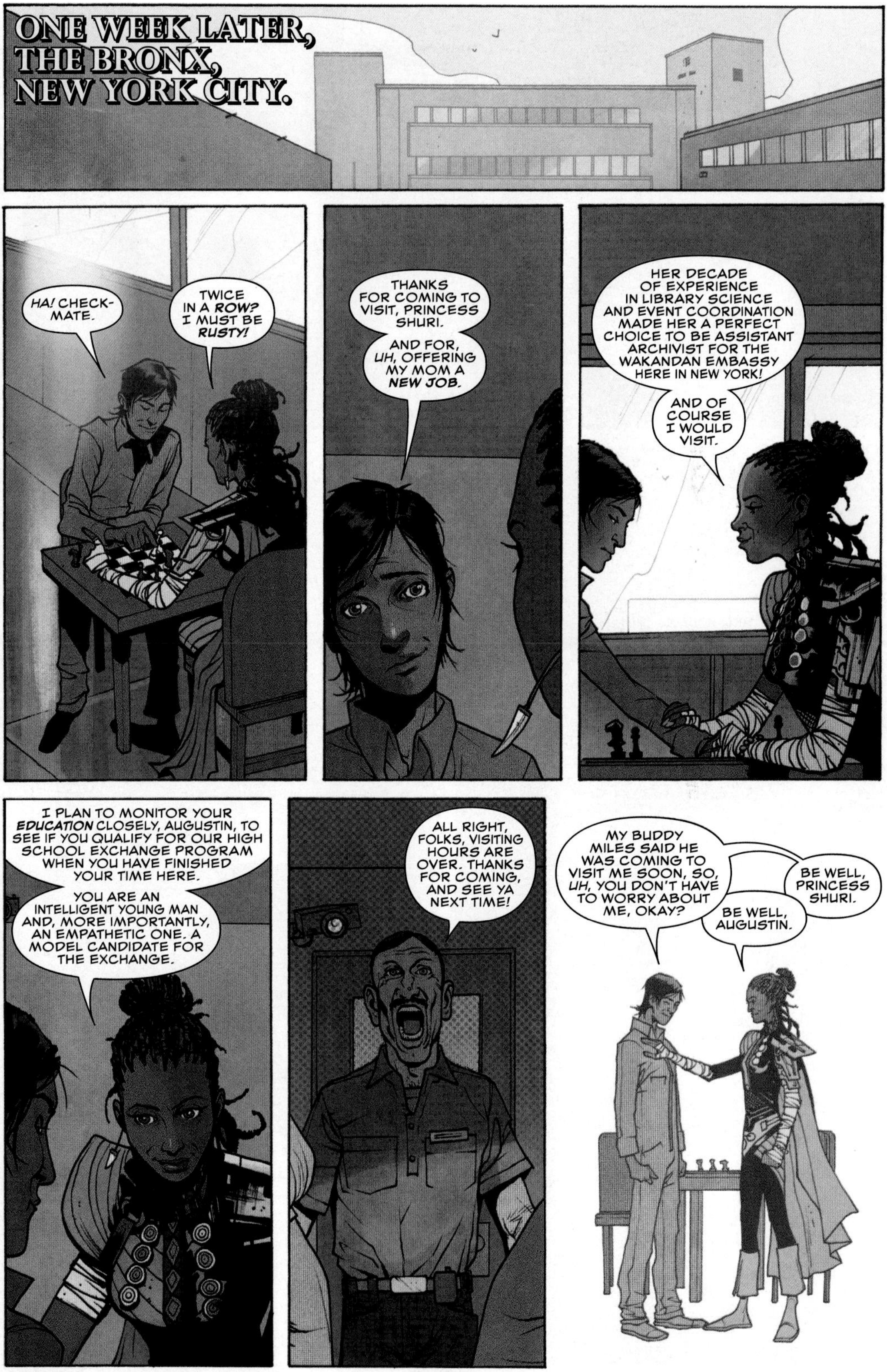
ONE WEEK LATER, THE BRONX, NEW YORK CITY.
HA! CHECK-MATE.
TWICE IN A ROW? I MUST BE RUSTY!
THANKS FOR COMING TO VISIT, PRINCESS SHURI.
AND FOR, UH, OFFERING MY MOM A NEW JOB.
HER DECADE OF EXPERIENCE IN LIBRARY SCIENCE AND EVENT COORDINATION MADE HER A PERFECT CHOICE TO BE ASSISTANT ARCHIVIST FOR THE WAKANDAN EMBASSY HERE IN NEW YORK!
AND OF COURSE I WOULD VISIT.
I PLAN TO MONITOR YOUR EDUCATION CLOSELY, AUGUSTIN, TO SEE IF YOU QUALIFY FOR OUR HIGH SCHOOL EXCHANGE PROGRAM WHEN YOU HAVE FINISHED YOUR TIME HERE.
YOU ARE AN INTELLIGENT YOUNG MAN AND, MORE IMPORTANTLY, AN EMPATHETIC ONE. A MODEL CANDIDATE FOR THE EXCHANGE.
ALL RIGHT, FOLKS, VISITING HOURS ARE OVER. THANKS FOR COMING, AND SEE YA NEXT TIME!
MY BUDDY MILES SAID HE WAS COMING TO VISIT ME SOON, SO, UH, YOU DON'T HAVE TO WORRY ABOUT ME, OKAY?
BE WELL, PRINCESS SHURI.
BE WELL, AUGUSTIN.

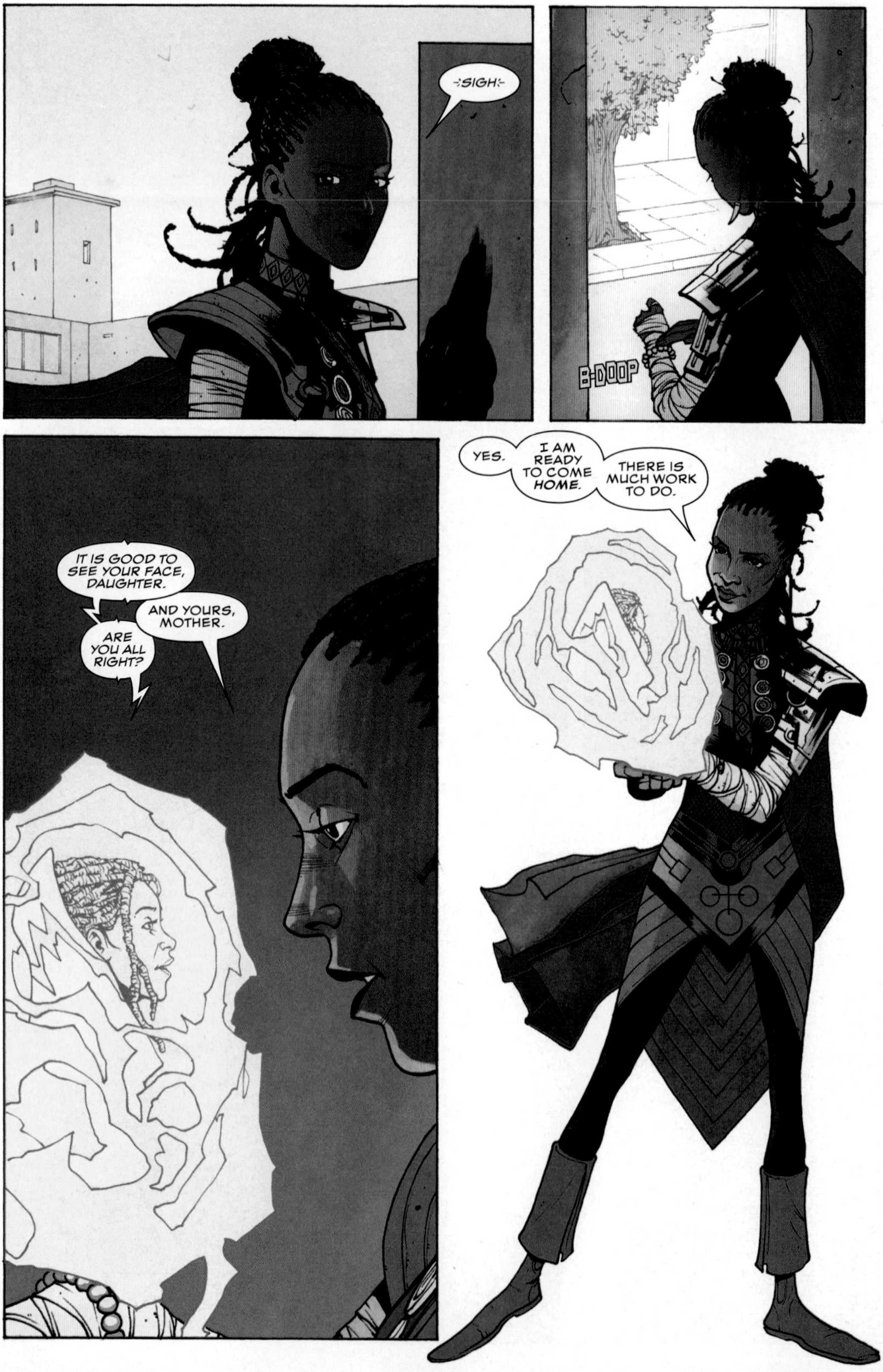
-SIGH-
B-DOOP
IT IS GOOD TO SEE YOUR FACE, DAUGHTER.
AND YOURS, MOTHER.
ARE YOU ALL RIGHT?
YES.
I AM READY TO COME HOME.
THERE IS MUCH WORK TO DO.

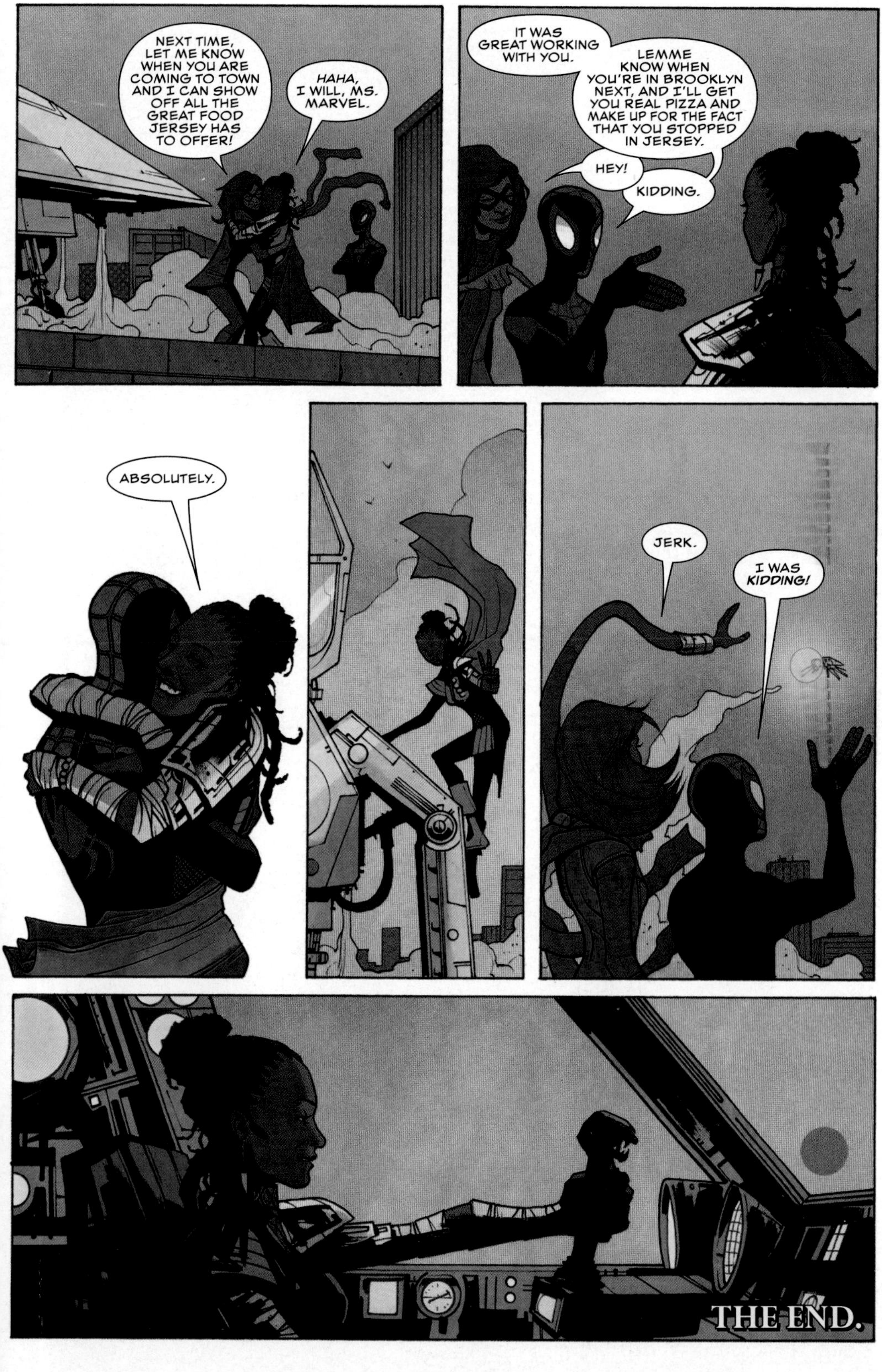
NEXT TIME, LET ME KNOW WHEN YOU ARE COMING TO TOWN AND I CAN SHOW OFF ALL THE GREAT FOOD JERSEY HAS TO OFFER!
HAHA, I WILL, MS. MARVEL.
IT WAS GREAT WORKING WITH YOU.
LEMME KNOW WHEN YOU'RE IN BROOKLYN NEXT, AND I'LL GET YOU REAL PIZZA AND MAKE UP FOR THE FACT THAT YOU STOPPED IN JERSEY.
HEY!
KIDDING.
ABSOLUTELY.
JERK.
I WAS KIDDING!
THE END.

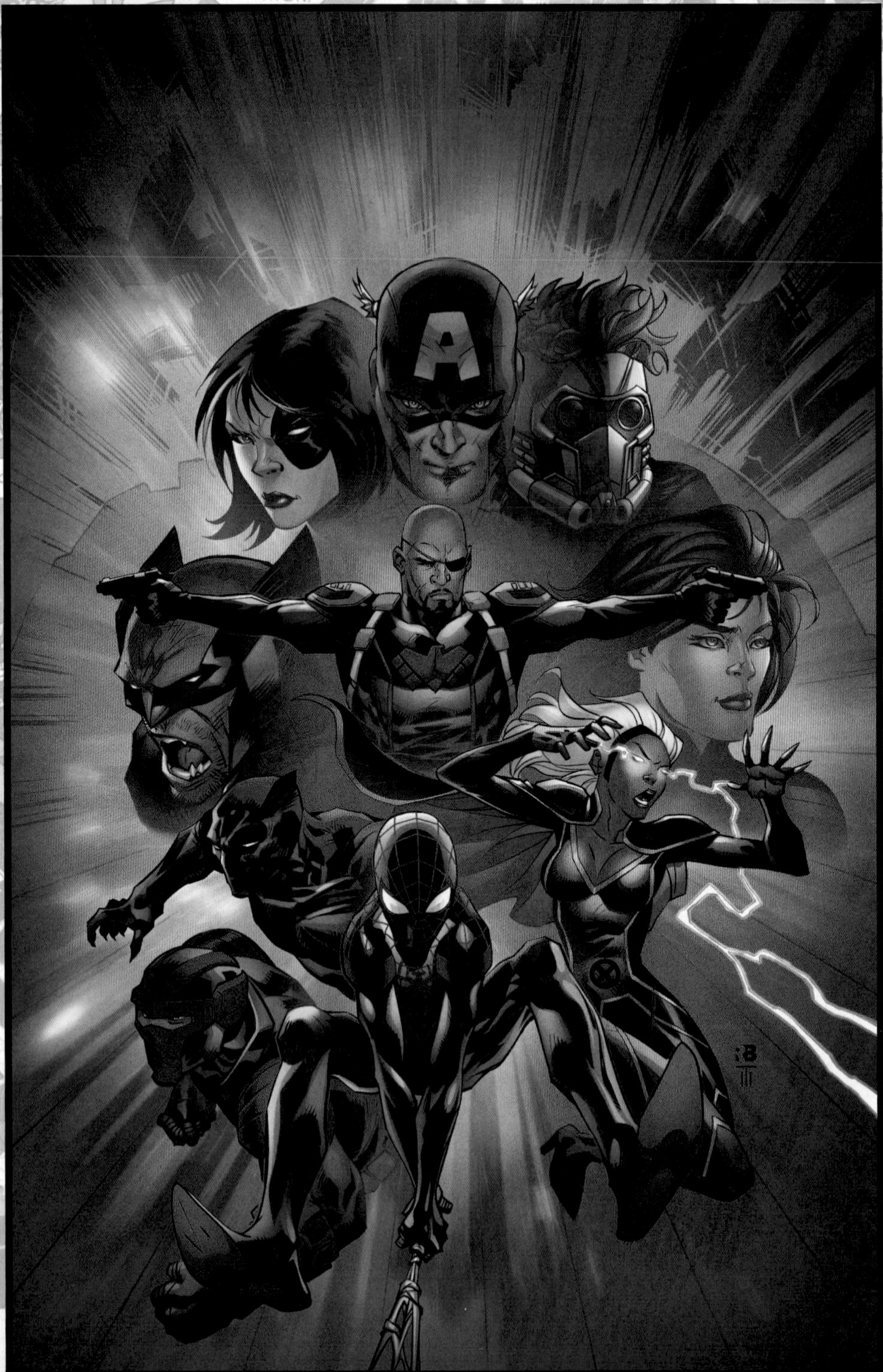

MARVEL'S VOICES #1

TIME FOR THE FIRST INTERNATIONAL SCIENCE RACE EXPO! THE BRIGHTEST SCIENTISTS HAVE COME OUT TO PARTICIPATE — INCLUDING SHURI AND THE

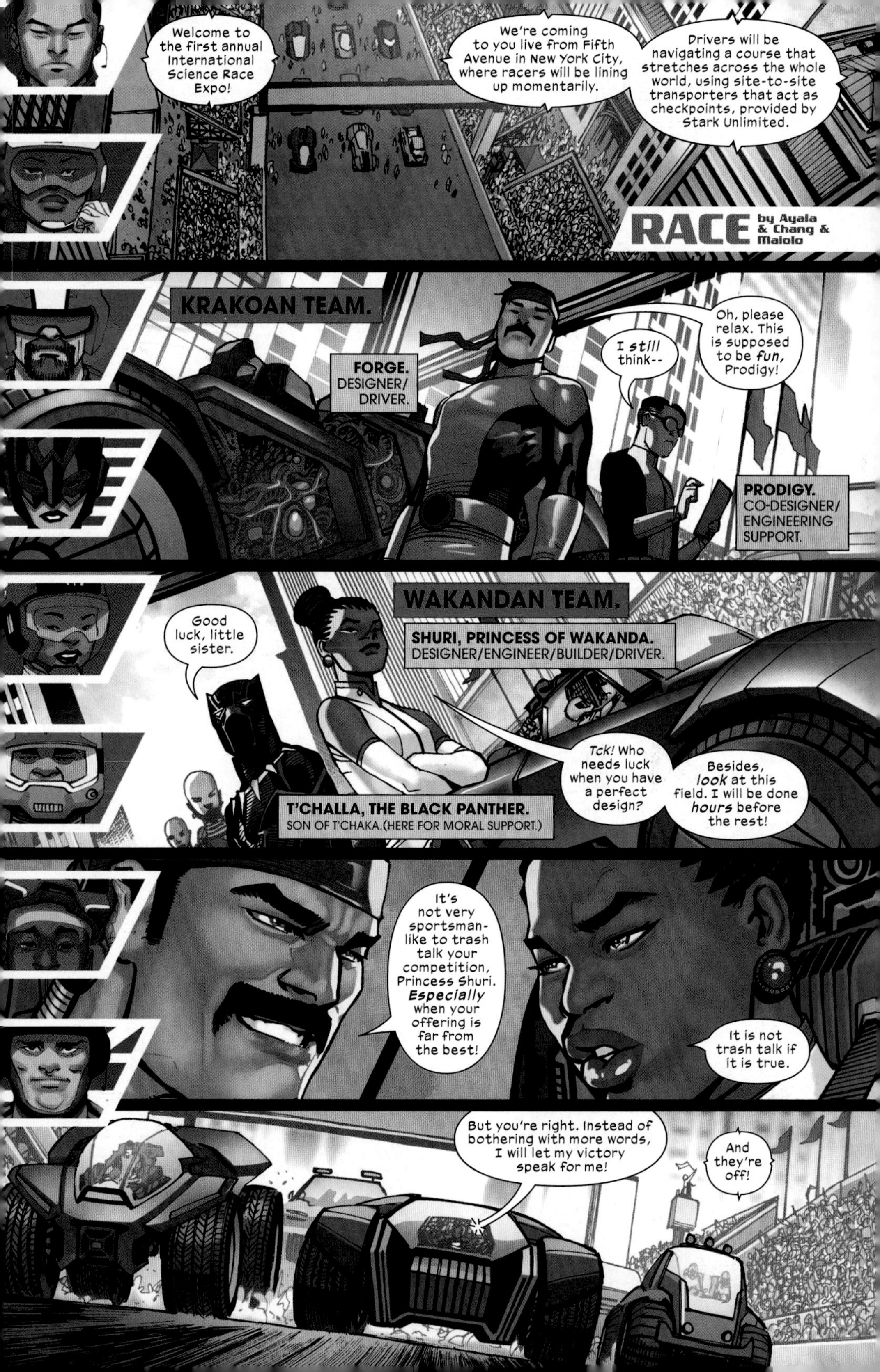

Welcome to the first annual International Science Race Expo!
We're coming to you live from Fifth Avenue in New York City, where racers will be lining up momentarily.
Drivers will be navigating a course that stretches across the whole world, using site-to-site transporters that act as checkpoints, provided by Stark Unlimited.
RACE by Ayala & Chang & Maiolo
KRAKOAN TEAM.
FORGE. DESIGNER/DRIVER.
I still think--
Oh, please relax. This is supposed to be fun, Prodigy!
PRODIGY. CO-DESIGNER/ENGINEERING SUPPORT.
WAKANDAN TEAM.
SHURI, PRINCESS OF WAKANDA. DESIGNER/ENGINEER/BUILDER/DRIVER.
Good luck, little sister.
T'CHALLA, THE BLACK PANTHER. SON OF T'CHAKA. (HERE FOR MORAL SUPPORT.)
Tck! Who needs luck when you have a perfect design?
Besides, look at this field. I will be done hours before the rest!
It's not very sportsman-like to trash talk your competition, Princess Shuri. Especially when your offering is far from the best!
It is not trash talk if it is true.
But you're right. Instead of bothering with more words, I will let my victory speak for me!
And they're off!

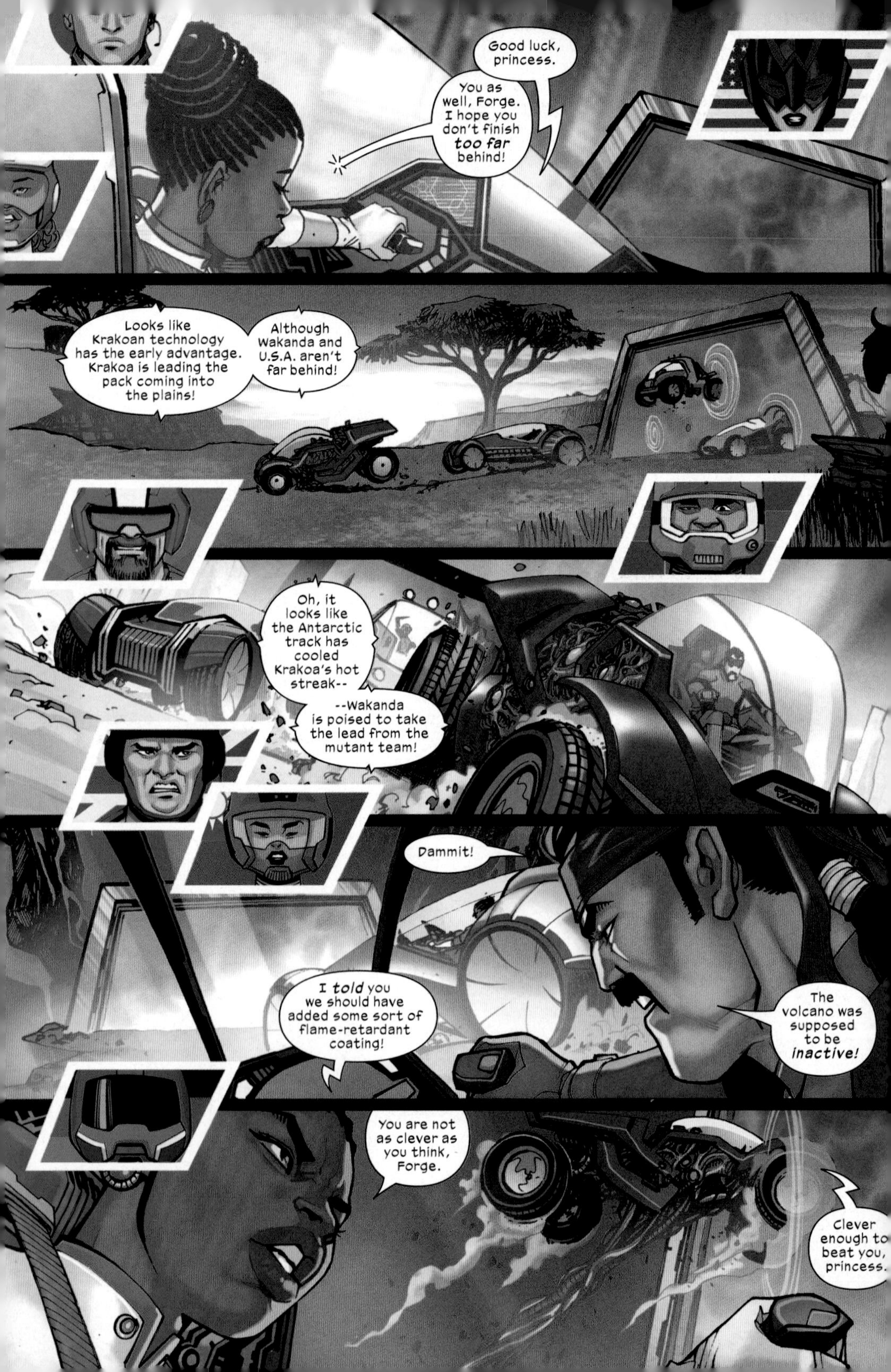

Good luck, princess.
You as well, Forge. I hope you don't finish *too far* behind!
Looks like Krakoan technology has the early advantage. Krakoa is leading the pack coming into the plains!
Although Wakanda and U.S.A. aren't far behind!
Oh, it looks like the Antarctic track has cooled Krakoa's hot streak--
--Wakanda is poised to take the lead from the mutant team!
Dammit!
I *told* you we should have added some sort of flame-retardant coating!
The volcano was supposed to be *inactive!*
You are not as clever as you think, Forge.
Clever enough to beat you, princess.

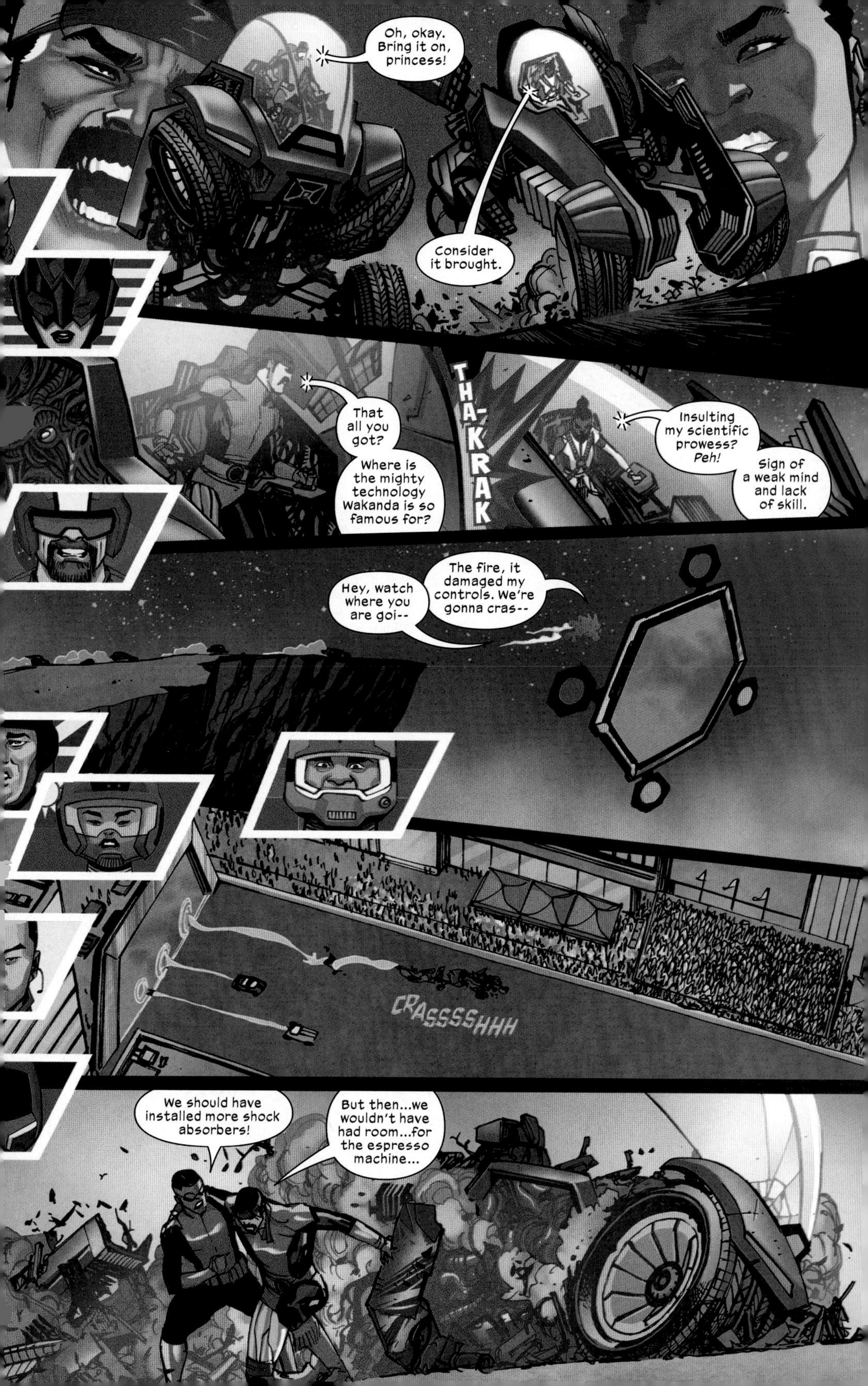

Oh, okay. Bring it on, princess!
Consider it brought.
That all you got?
Where is the mighty technology Wakanda is so famous for?
THA-KRAK
Insulting my scientific prowess? *Peh!*
Sign of a weak mind and lack of skill.
The fire, it damaged my controls. We're gonna cras--
Hey, watch where you are goi--
CRASSSSHHH
We should have installed more shock absorbers!
But then...we wouldn't have had room...for the espresso machine...

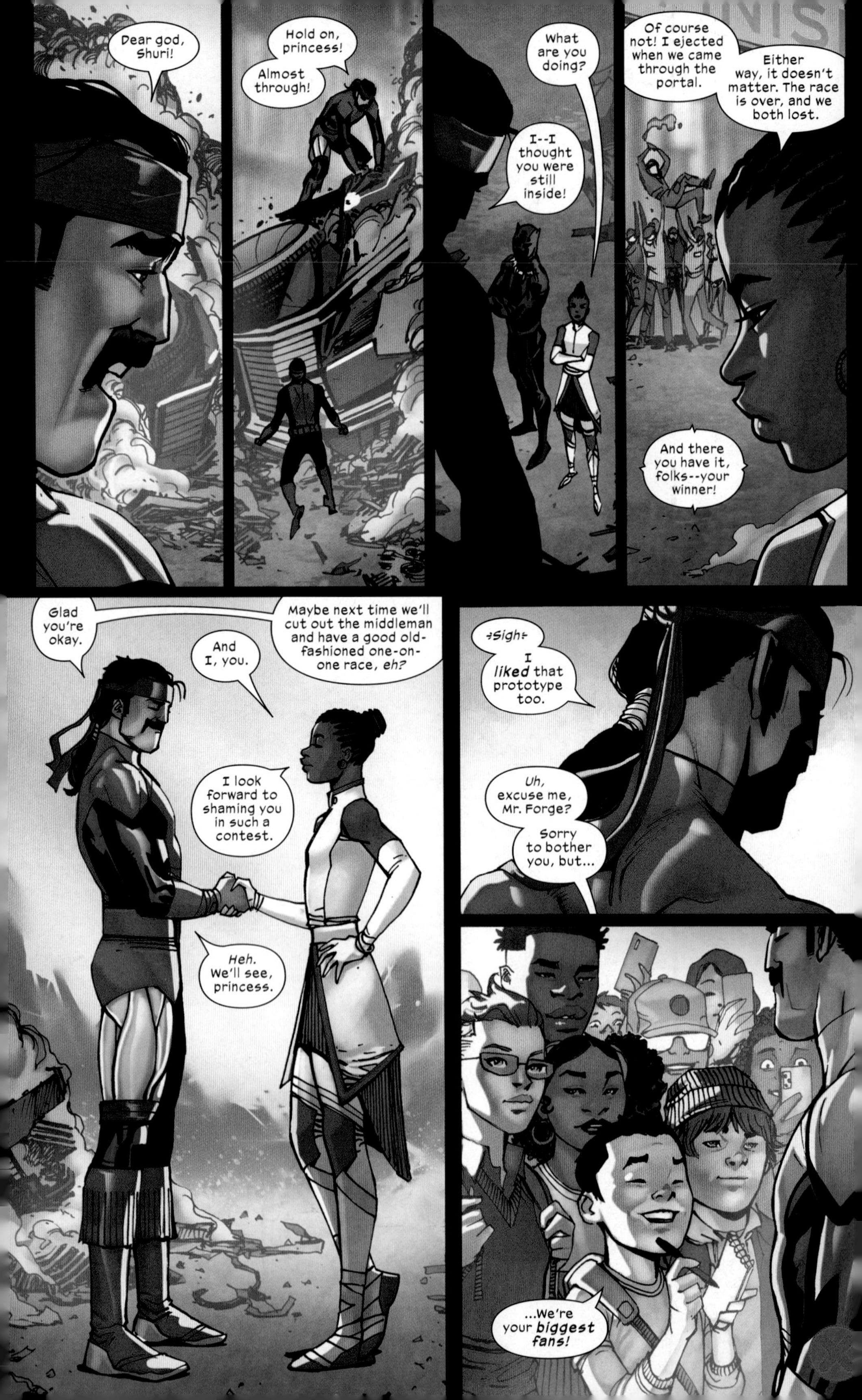
Dear god, Shuri!
Hold on, princess!
Almost through!
What are you doing?
I--I thought you were still inside!
Of course not! I ejected when we came through the portal.
Either way, it doesn't matter. The race is over, and we both lost.
And there you have it, folks--your winner!
Glad you're okay.
And I, you.
Maybe next time we'll cut out the middleman and have a good old-fashioned one-on-one race, *eh?*
I look forward to shaming you in such a contest.
Heh. We'll see, princess.
Sigh
I *liked* that prototype too.
Uh, excuse me, Mr. Forge?
Sorry to bother you, but...
...We're your **biggest** *fans!*

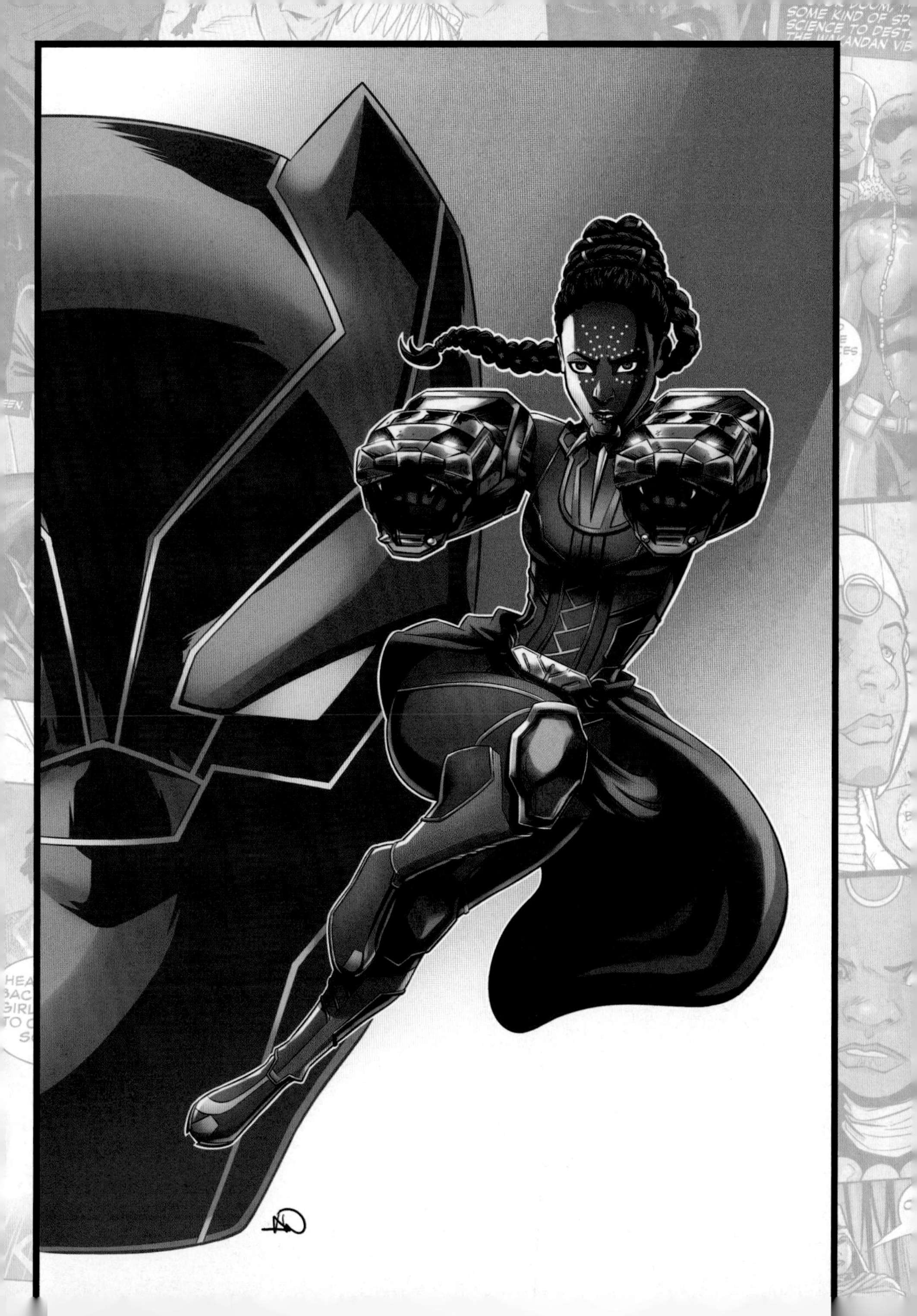

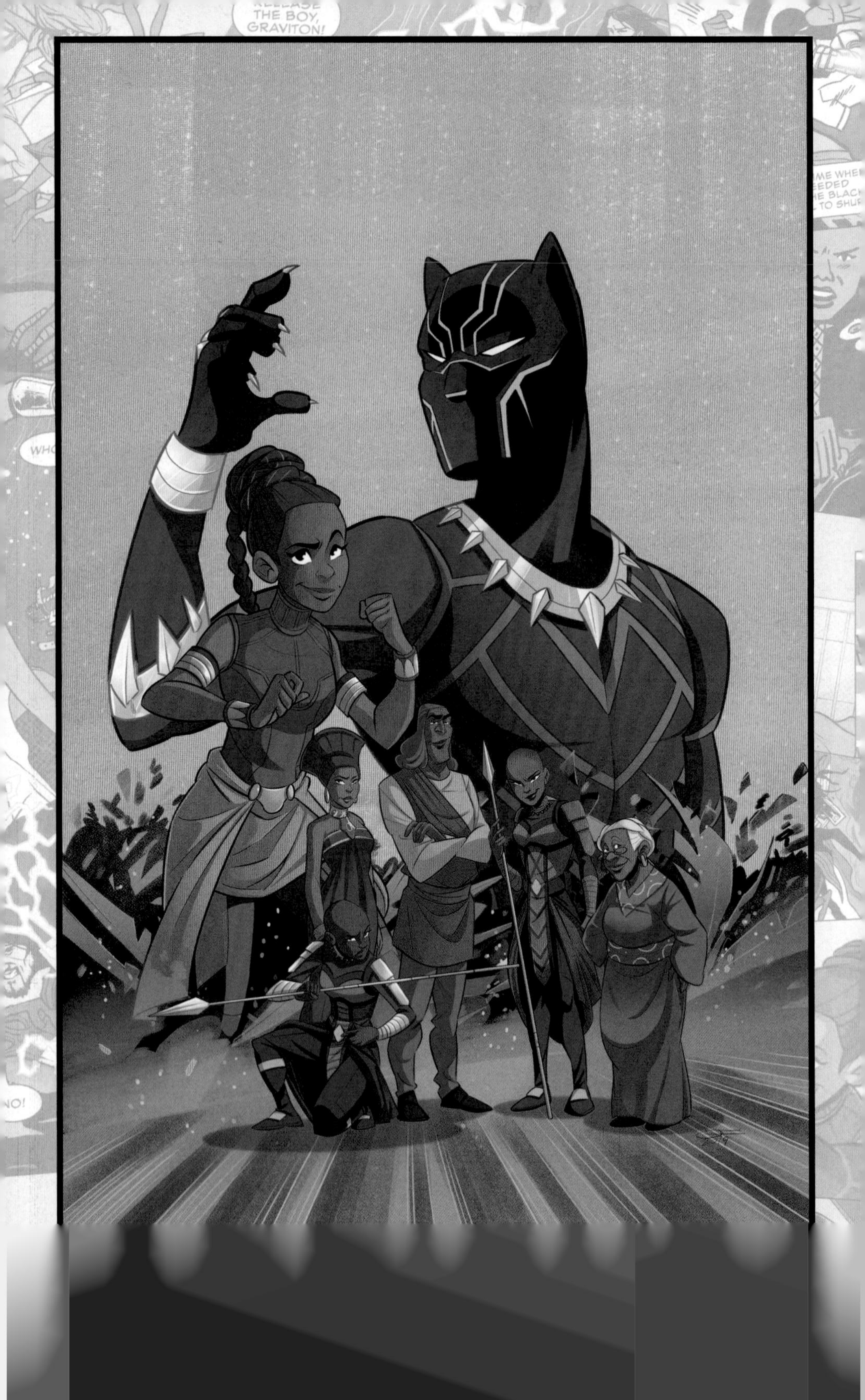
THE BOY,
GRAVITON!
NO!

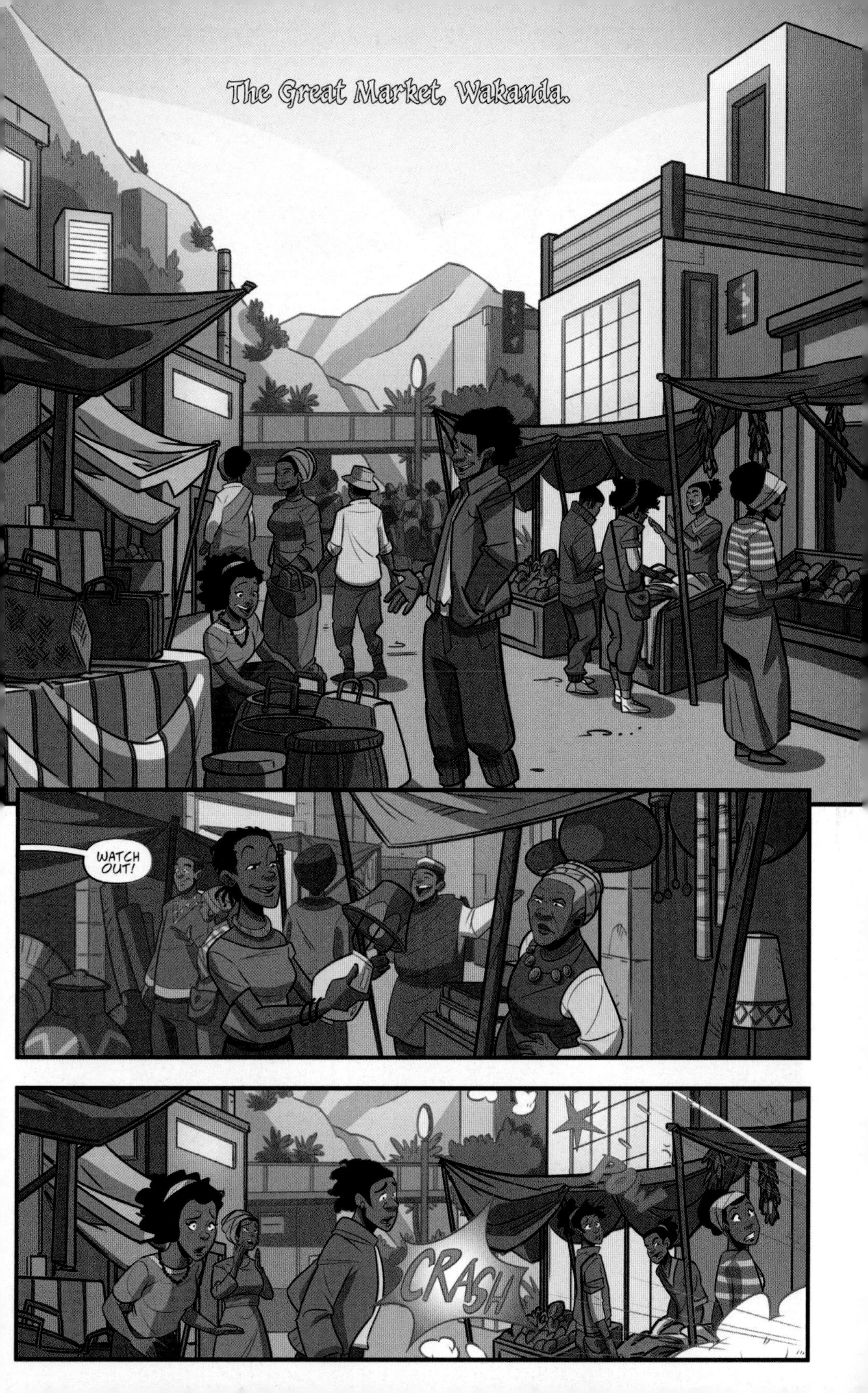
The Great Market, Wakanda.
WATCH OUT!
CRASH

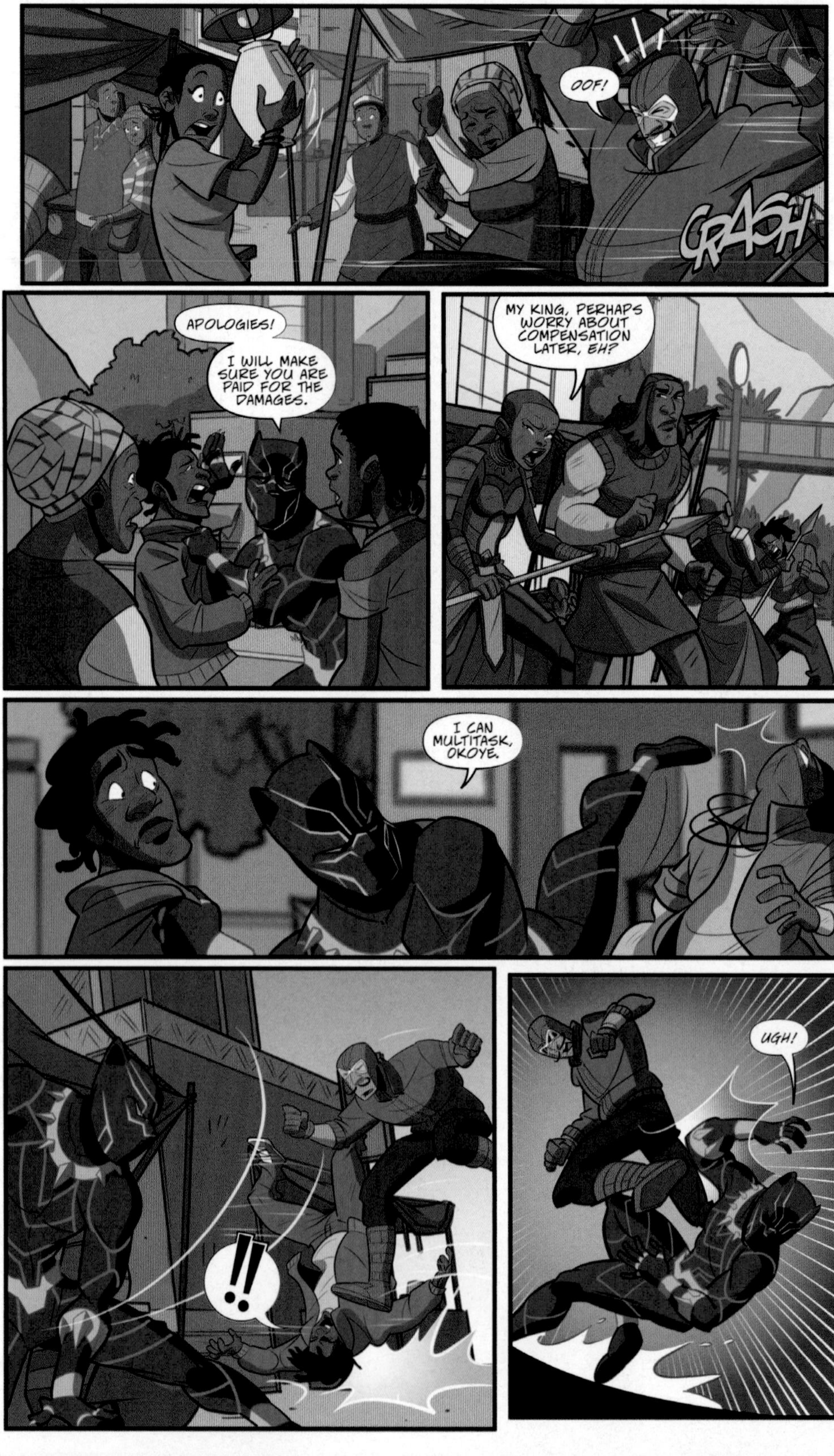
OOF!
CRASH
APOLOGIES!
I WILL MAKE SURE YOU ARE PAID FOR THE DAMAGES.
MY KING, PERHAPS WORRY ABOUT COMPENSATION LATER, EH?
I CAN MULTITASK, OKOYE.
!!
UGH!

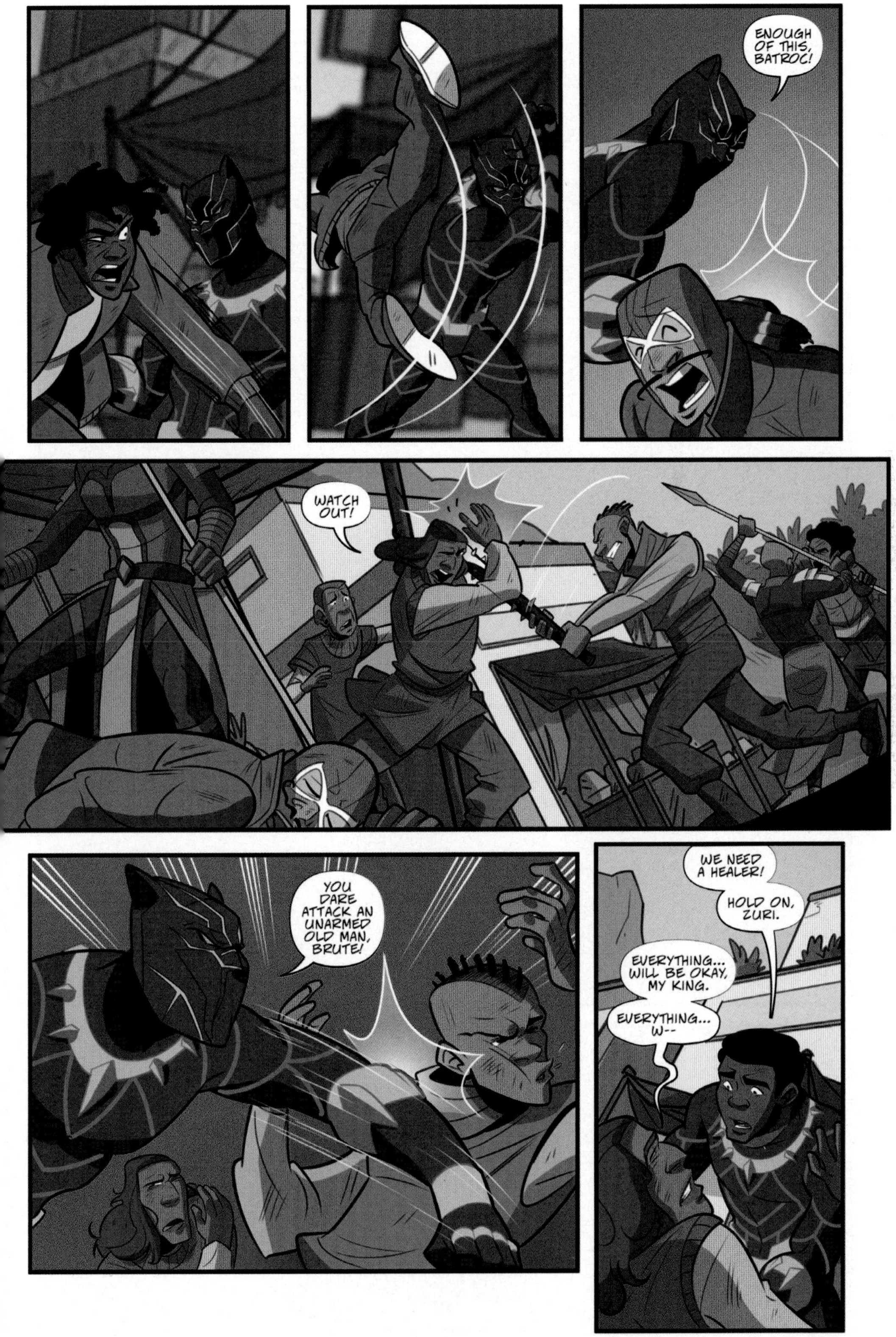
ENOUGH OF THIS, BATROC!
WATCH OUT!
YOU DARE ATTACK AN UNARMED OLD MAN, BRUTE!
WE NEED A HEALER!
HOLD ON, ZURI.
EVERYTHING... WILL BE OKAY, MY KING.
EVERYTHING... W--

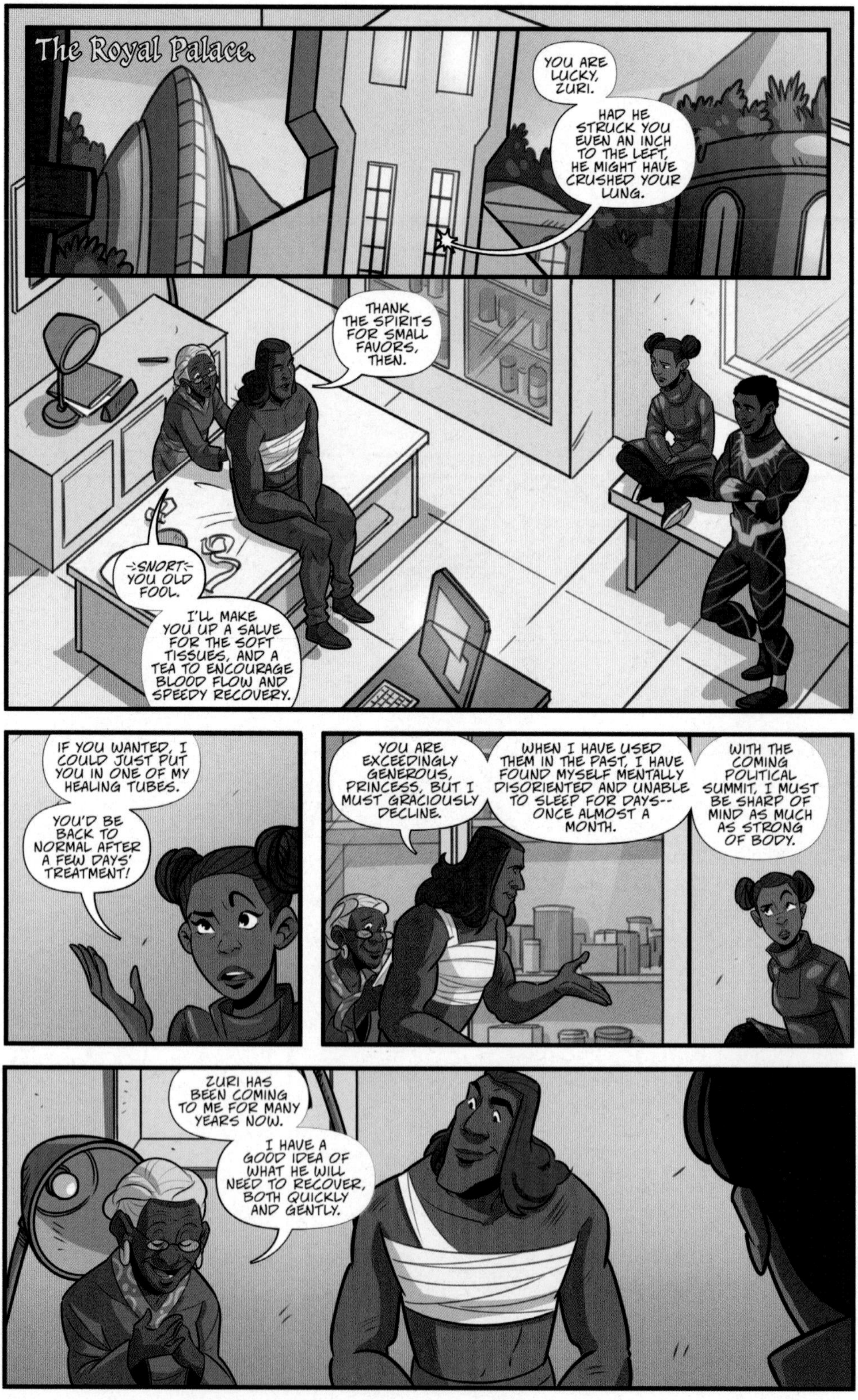
The Royal Palace.
YOU ARE LUCKY, ZURI.
HAD HE STRUCK YOU EVEN AN INCH TO THE LEFT, HE MIGHT HAVE CRUSHED YOUR LUNG.
THANK THE SPIRITS FOR SMALL FAVORS, THEN.
-SNORT- YOU OLD FOOL.
I'LL MAKE YOU UP A SALVE FOR THE SOFT TISSUES, AND A TEA TO ENCOURAGE BLOOD FLOW AND SPEEDY RECOVERY.
IF YOU WANTED, I COULD JUST PUT YOU IN ONE OF MY HEALING TUBES.
YOU'D BE BACK TO NORMAL AFTER A FEW DAYS' TREATMENT!
YOU ARE EXCEEDINGLY GENEROUS, PRINCESS, BUT I MUST GRACIOUSLY DECLINE.
WHEN I HAVE USED THEM IN THE PAST, I HAVE FOUND MYSELF MENTALLY DISORIENTED AND UNABLE TO SLEEP FOR DAYS-- ONCE ALMOST A MONTH.
WITH THE COMING POLITICAL SUMMIT, I MUST BE SHARP OF MIND AS MUCH AS STRONG OF BODY.
ZURI HAS BEEN COMING TO ME FOR MANY YEARS NOW.
I HAVE A GOOD IDEA OF WHAT HE WILL NEED TO RECOVER, BOTH QUICKLY AND GENTLY.

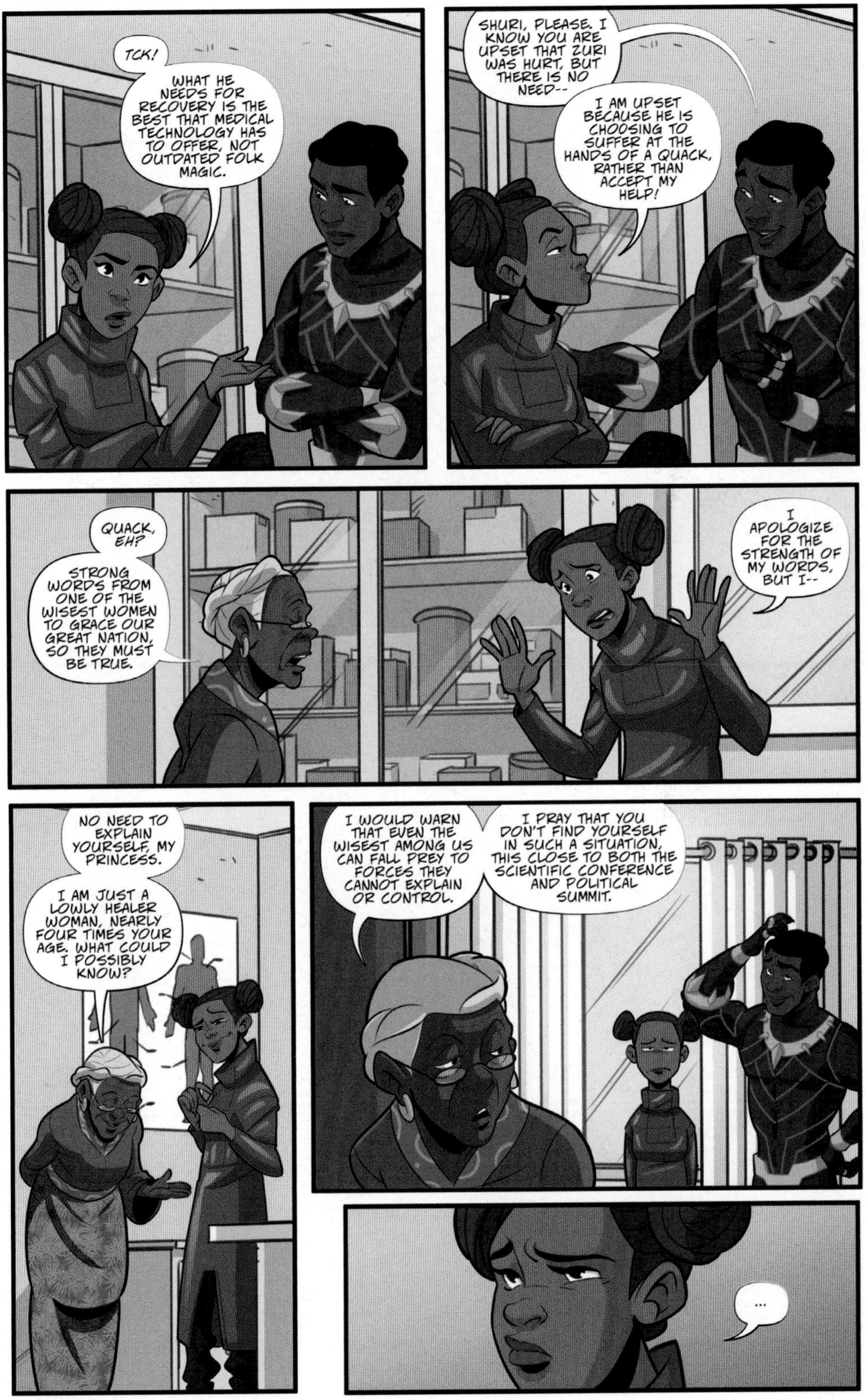
TCK!
WHAT HE NEEDS FOR RECOVERY IS THE BEST THAT MEDICAL TECHNOLOGY HAS TO OFFER, NOT OUTDATED FOLK MAGIC.
SHURI, PLEASE. I KNOW YOU ARE UPSET THAT ZURI WAS HURT, BUT THERE IS NO NEED--
I AM UPSET BECAUSE HE IS CHOOSING TO SUFFER AT THE HANDS OF A QUACK, RATHER THAN ACCEPT MY HELP!
QUACK, EH?
STRONG WORDS FROM ONE OF THE WISEST WOMEN TO GRACE OUR GREAT NATION, SO THEY MUST BE TRUE.
I APOLOGIZE FOR THE STRENGTH OF MY WORDS, BUT I--
NO NEED TO EXPLAIN YOURSELF, MY PRINCESS.
I AM JUST A LOWLY HEALER WOMAN, NEARLY FOUR TIMES YOUR AGE. WHAT COULD I POSSIBLY KNOW?
I WOULD WARN THAT EVEN THE WISEST AMONG US CAN FALL PREY TO FORCES THEY CANNOT EXPLAIN OR CONTROL.
I PRAY THAT YOU DON'T FIND YOURSELF IN SUCH A SITUATION, THIS CLOSE TO BOTH THE SCIENTIFIC CONFERENCE AND POLITICAL SUMMIT.
...

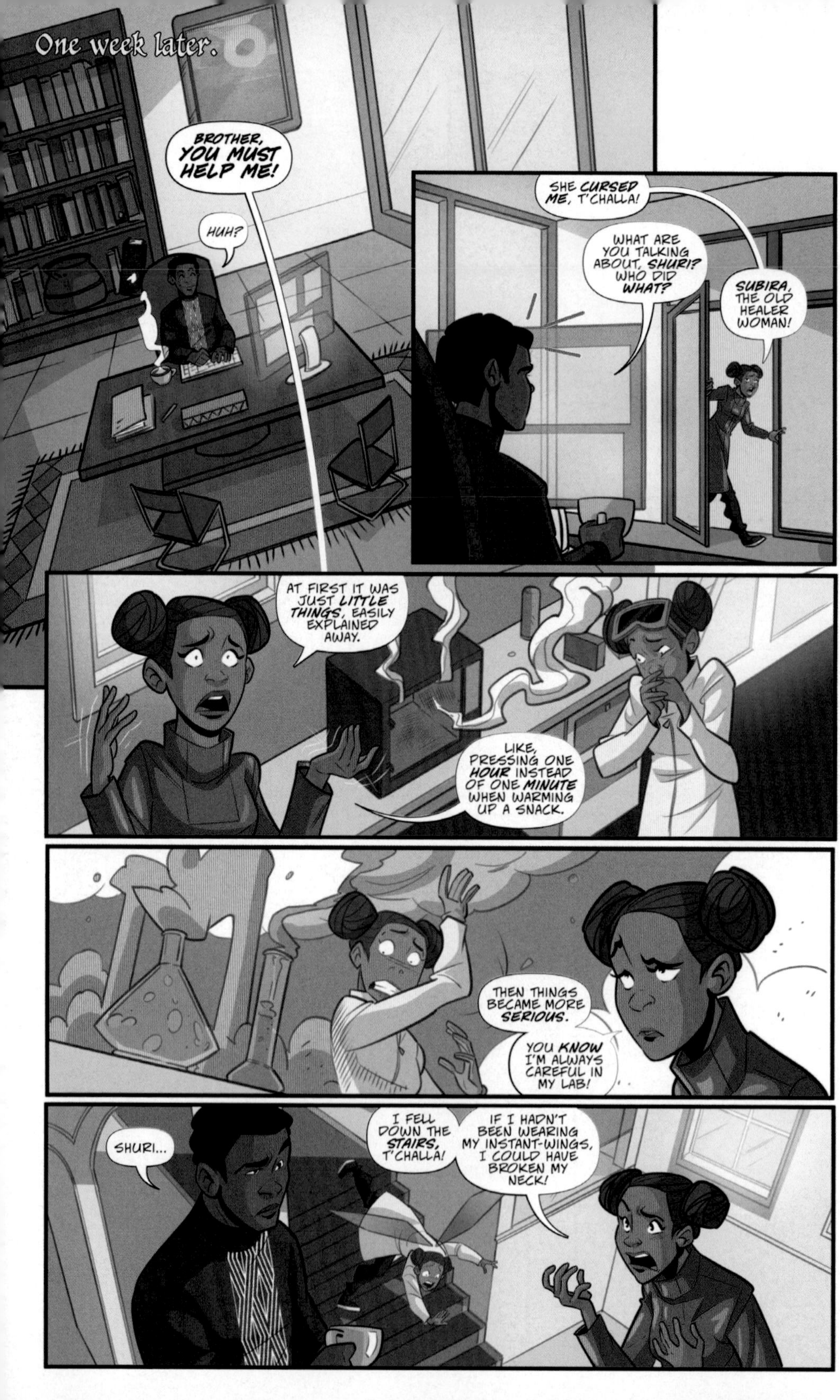
One week later.
BROTHER, YOU MUST HELP ME!
HUH?
SHE CURSED ME, T'CHALLA!
WHAT ARE YOU TALKING ABOUT, SHURI? WHO DID WHAT?
SUBIRA, THE OLD HEALER WOMAN!
AT FIRST IT WAS JUST LITTLE THINGS, EASILY EXPLAINED AWAY.
LIKE, PRESSING ONE HOUR INSTEAD OF ONE MINUTE WHEN WARMING UP A SNACK.
THEN THINGS BECAME MORE SERIOUS.
YOU KNOW I'M ALWAYS CAREFUL IN MY LAB!
SHURI...
I FELL DOWN THE STAIRS, T'CHALLA!
IF I HADN'T BEEN WEARING MY INSTANT-WINGS, I COULD HAVE BROKEN MY NECK!

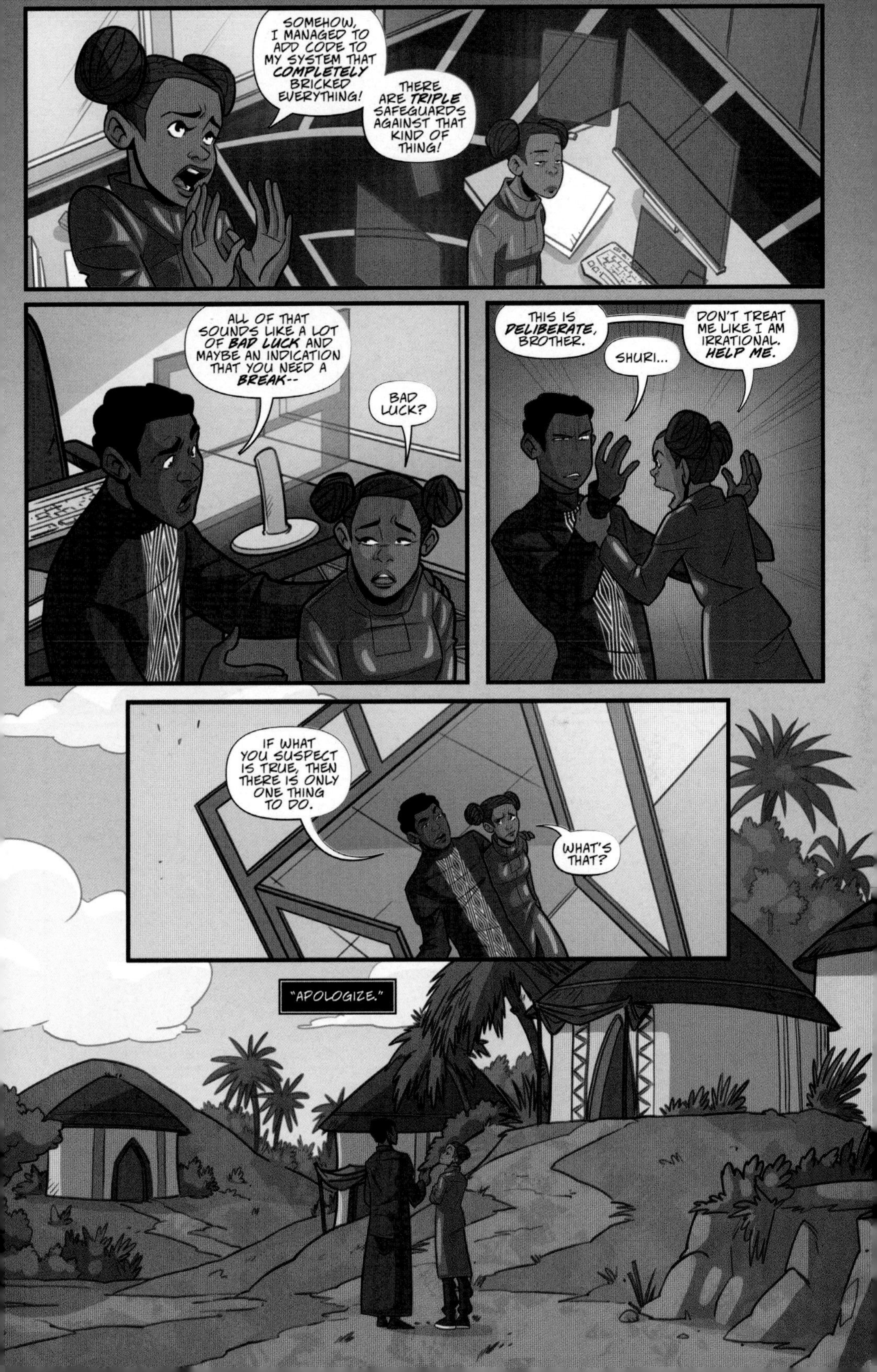
SOMEHOW, I MANAGED TO ADD CODE TO MY SYSTEM THAT COMPLETELY BRICKED EVERYTHING!
THERE ARE TRIPLE SAFEGUARDS AGAINST THAT KIND OF THING!
ALL OF THAT SOUNDS LIKE A LOT OF BAD LUCK AND MAYBE AN INDICATION THAT YOU NEED A BREAK--
BAD LUCK?
THIS IS DELIBERATE, BROTHER.
SHURI...
DON'T TREAT ME LIKE I AM IRRATIONAL. HELP ME.
IF WHAT YOU SUSPECT IS TRUE, THEN THERE IS ONLY ONE THING TO DO.
WHAT'S THAT?
"APOLOGIZE."

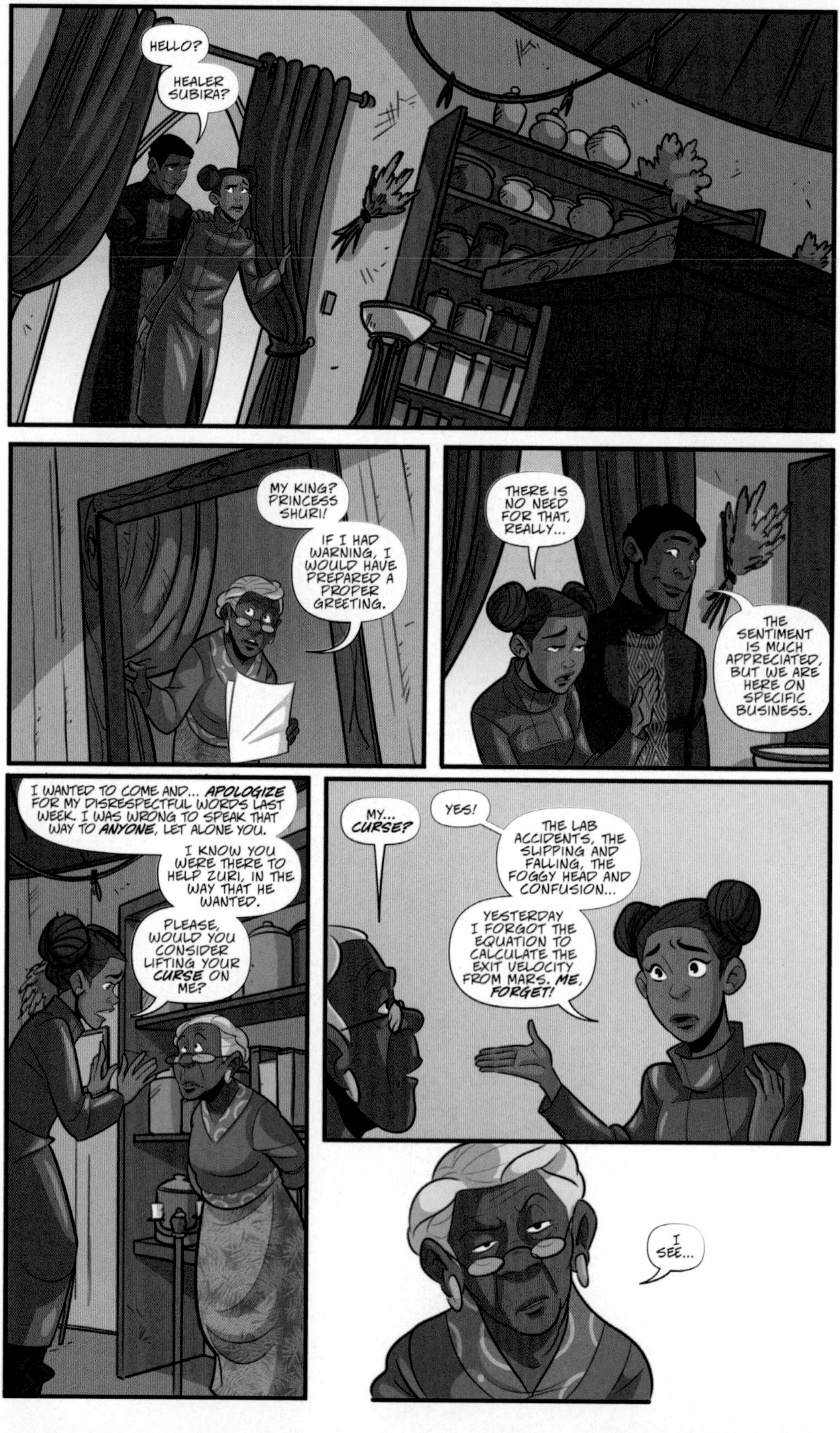
HELLO?
HEALER SUBIRA?
MY KING? PRINCESS SHURI!
IF I HAD WARNING, I WOULD HAVE PREPARED A PROPER GREETING.
THERE IS NO NEED FOR THAT, REALLY...
THE SENTIMENT IS MUCH APPRECIATED, BUT WE ARE HERE ON SPECIFIC BUSINESS.
I WANTED TO COME AND... APOLOGIZE FOR MY DISRESPECTFUL WORDS LAST WEEK. I WAS WRONG TO SPEAK THAT WAY TO ANYONE, LET ALONE YOU.
I KNOW YOU WERE THERE TO HELP ZURI, IN THE WAY THAT HE WANTED.
PLEASE, WOULD YOU CONSIDER LIFTING YOUR CURSE ON ME?
MY... CURSE?
YES!
THE LAB ACCIDENTS, THE SLIPPING AND FALLING, THE FOGGY HEAD AND CONFUSION...
YESTERDAY I FORGOT THE EQUATION TO CALCULATE THE EXIT VELOCITY FROM MARS. ME, FORGET!
I SEE...

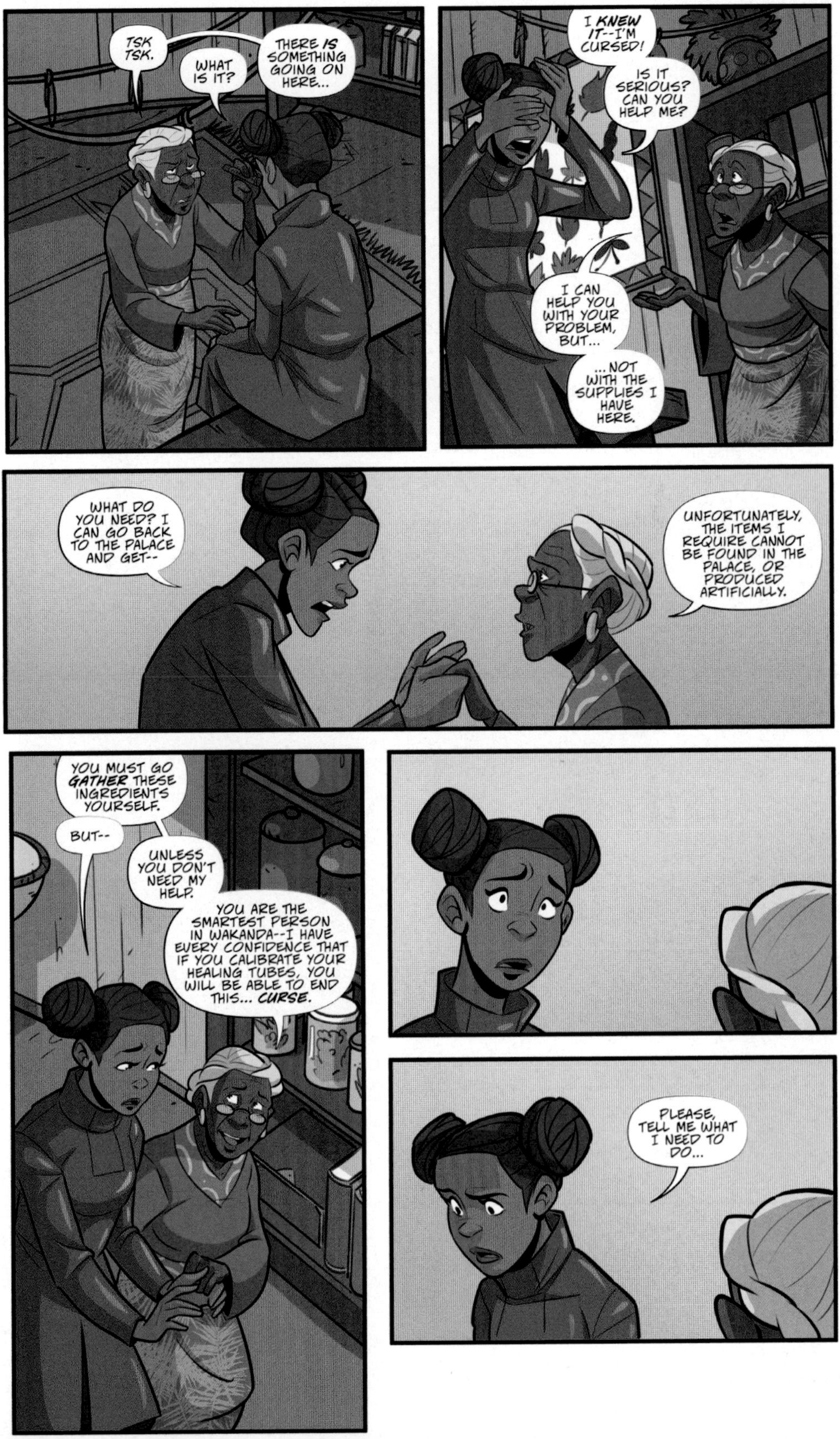
TSK TSK.
WHAT IS IT?
THERE IS SOMETHING GOING ON HERE...
I KNEW IT--I'M CURSED!
IS IT SERIOUS? CAN YOU HELP ME?
I CAN HELP YOU WITH YOUR PROBLEM, BUT...
...NOT WITH THE SUPPLIES I HAVE HERE.
WHAT DO YOU NEED? I CAN GO BACK TO THE PALACE AND GET--
UNFORTUNATELY, THE ITEMS I REQUIRE CANNOT BE FOUND IN THE PALACE, OR PRODUCED ARTIFICIALLY.
YOU MUST GO GATHER THESE INGREDIENTS YOURSELF.
BUT--
UNLESS YOU DON'T NEED MY HELP.
YOU ARE THE SMARTEST PERSON IN WAKANDA--I HAVE EVERY CONFIDENCE THAT IF YOU CALIBRATE YOUR HEALING TUBES, YOU WILL BE ABLE TO END THIS... CURSE.
PLEASE, TELL ME WHAT I NEED TO DO...

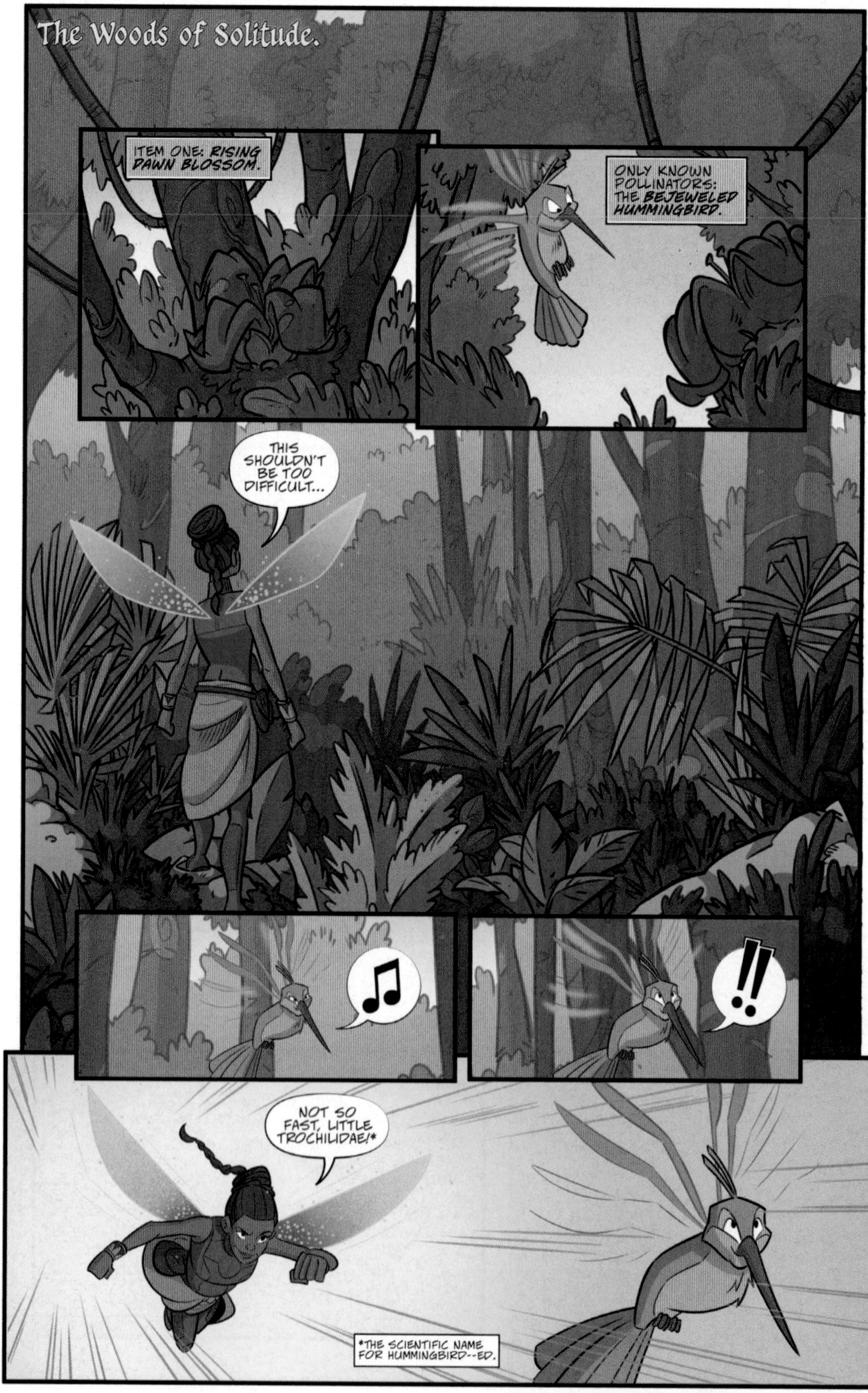
The Woods of Solitude.
ITEM ONE: RISING DAWN BLOSSOM.
ONLY KNOWN POLLINATORS: THE BEJEWELED HUMMINGBIRD.
THIS SHOULDN'T BE TOO DIFFICULT...
♫
!!
NOT SO FAST, LITTLE TROCHILIDAE!*
*THE SCIENTIFIC NAME FOR HUMMINGBIRD--ED.

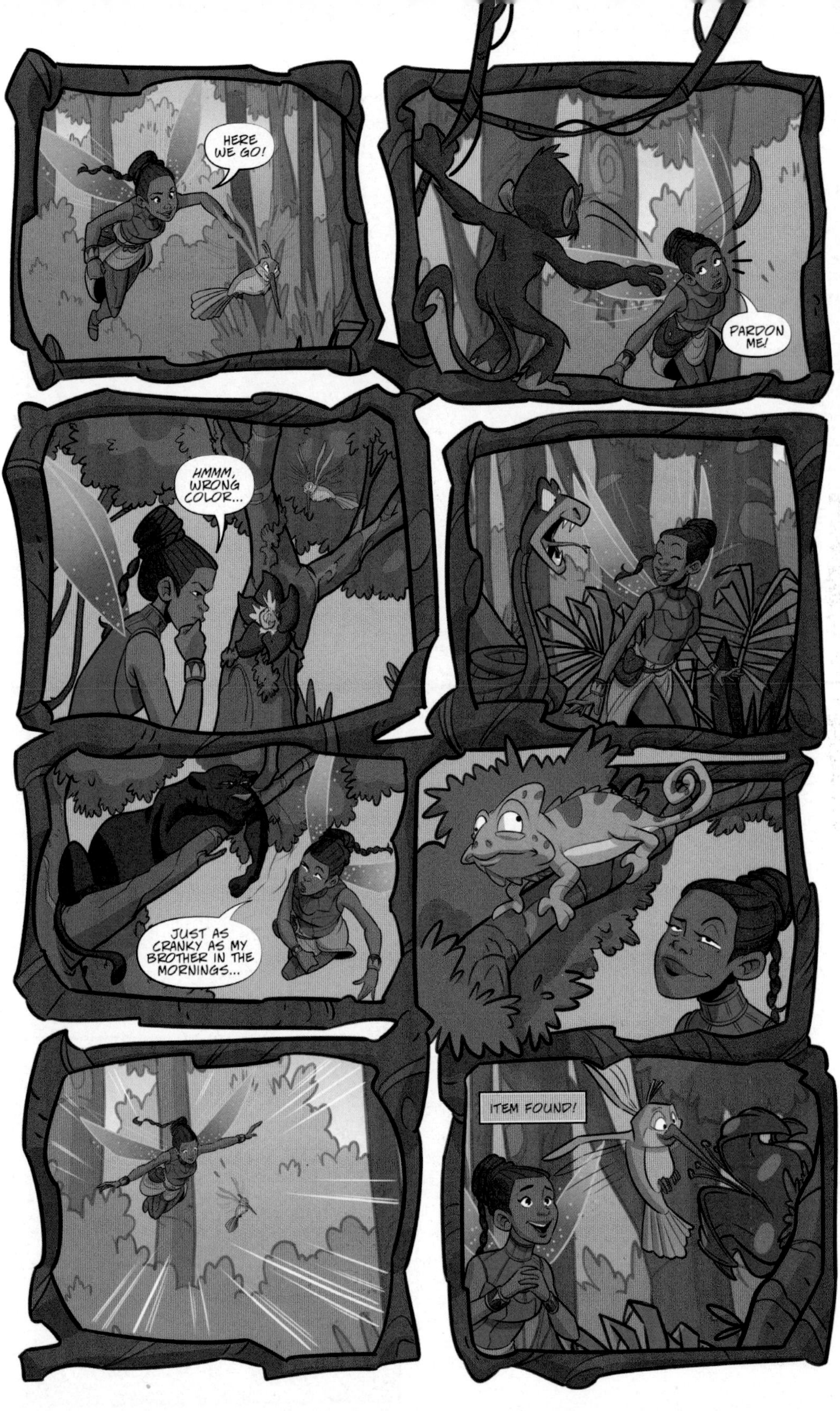
HERE WE GO!
PARDON ME!
HMMM, WRONG COLOR...
JUST AS CRANKY AS MY BROTHER IN THE MORNINGS...
ITEM FOUND!

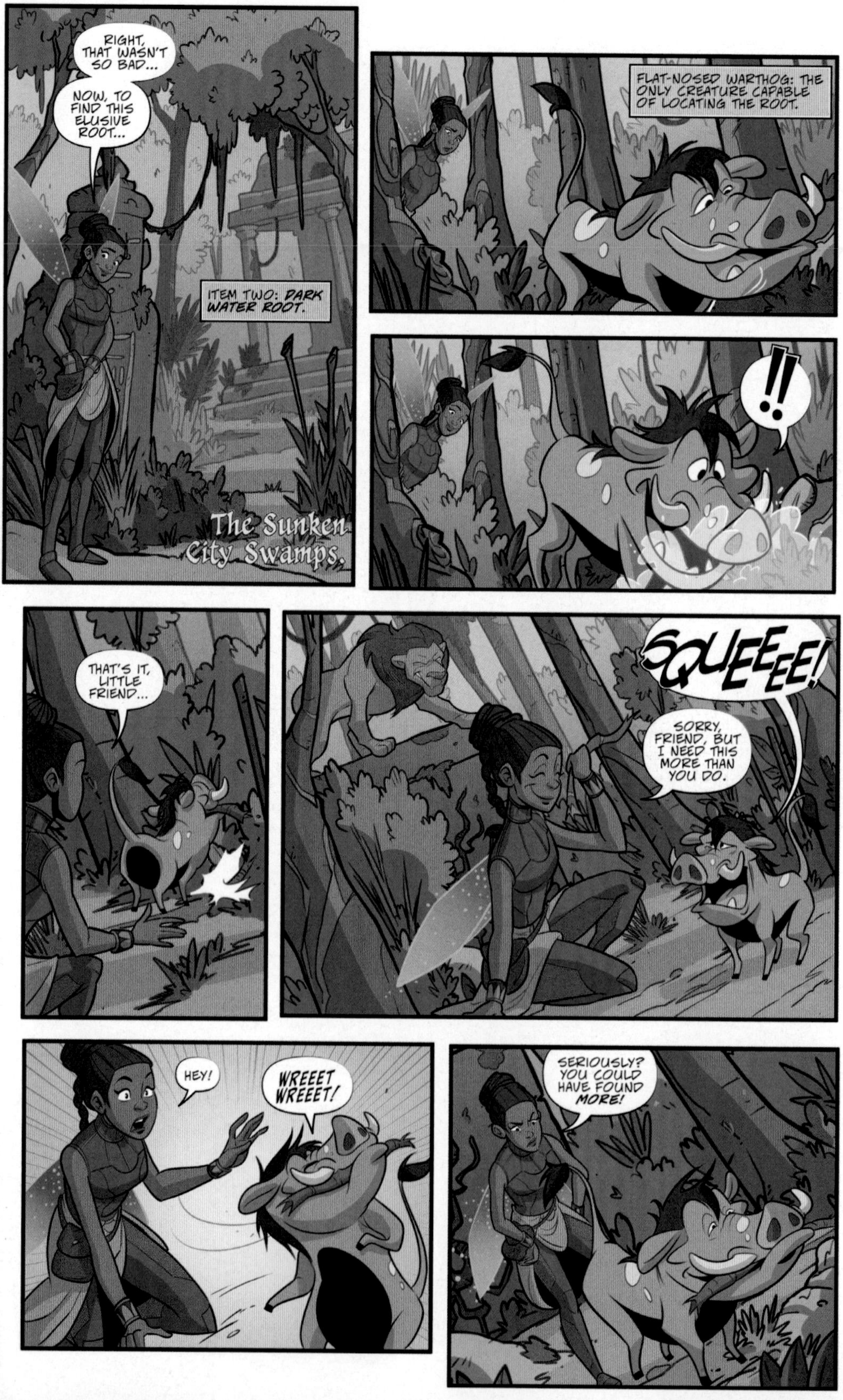
RIGHT, THAT WASN'T SO BAD...
NOW, TO FIND THIS ELUSIVE ROOT...
ITEM TWO: DARK WATER ROOT.
The Sunken City Swamps.
FLAT-NOSED WARTHOG: THE ONLY CREATURE CAPABLE OF LOCATING THE ROOT.
!!
THAT'S IT, LITTLE FRIEND...
SQUEEEEE!
SORRY, FRIEND, BUT I NEED THIS MORE THAN YOU DO.
HEY!
WREEET WREEET!
SERIOUSLY? YOU COULD HAVE FOUND MORE!

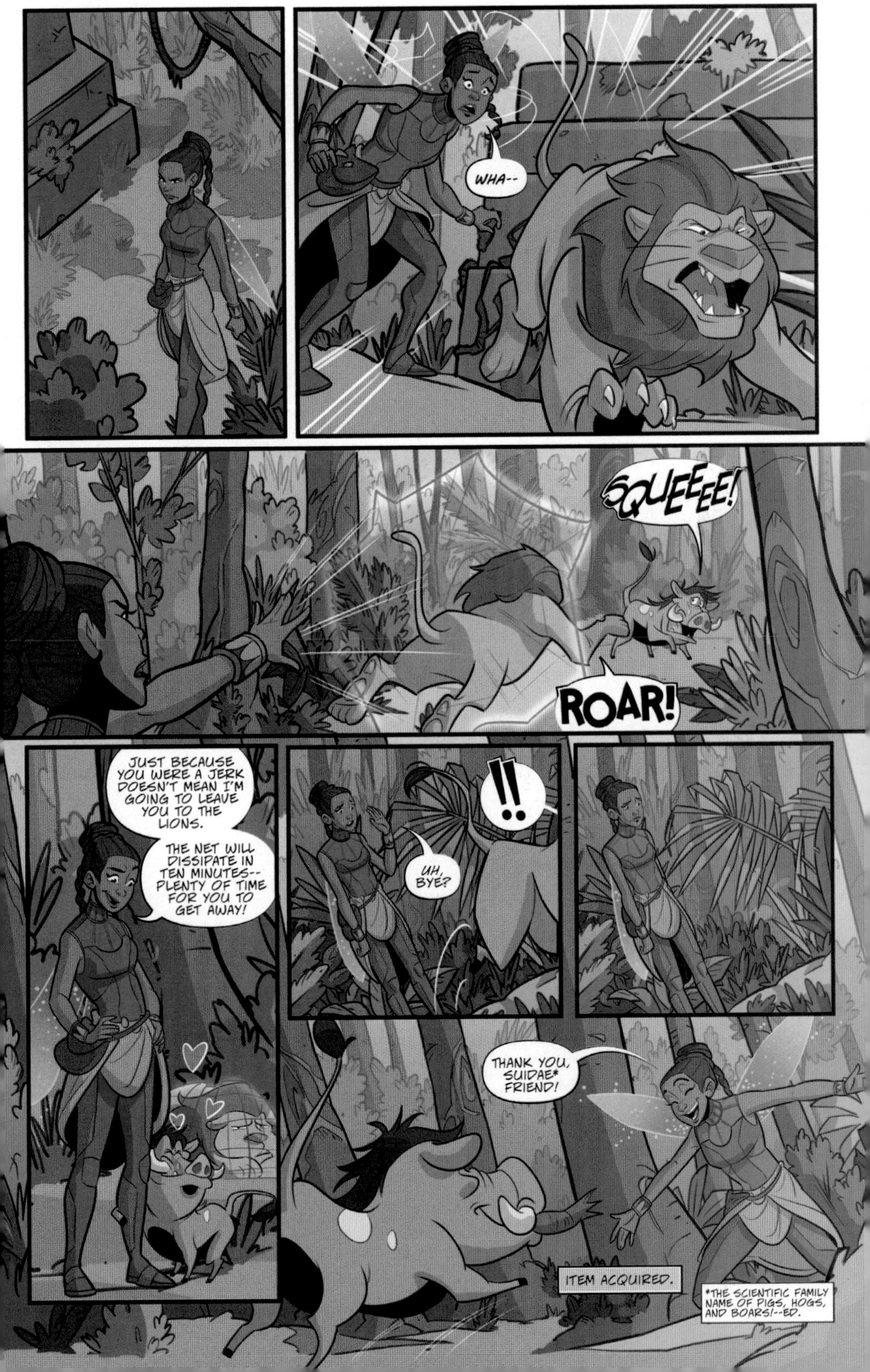
WHA--
SQUEEEEE!
ROAR!
JUST BECAUSE YOU WERE A JERK DOESN'T MEAN I'M GOING TO LEAVE YOU TO THE LIONS.
THE NET WILL DISSIPATE IN TEN MINUTES--PLENTY OF TIME FOR YOU TO GET AWAY!
!!
UH, BYE?
THANK YOU, SUIDAE* FRIEND!
ITEM ACQUIRED.
*THE SCIENTIFIC FAMILY NAME OF PIGS, HOGS, AND BOARS!--ED.

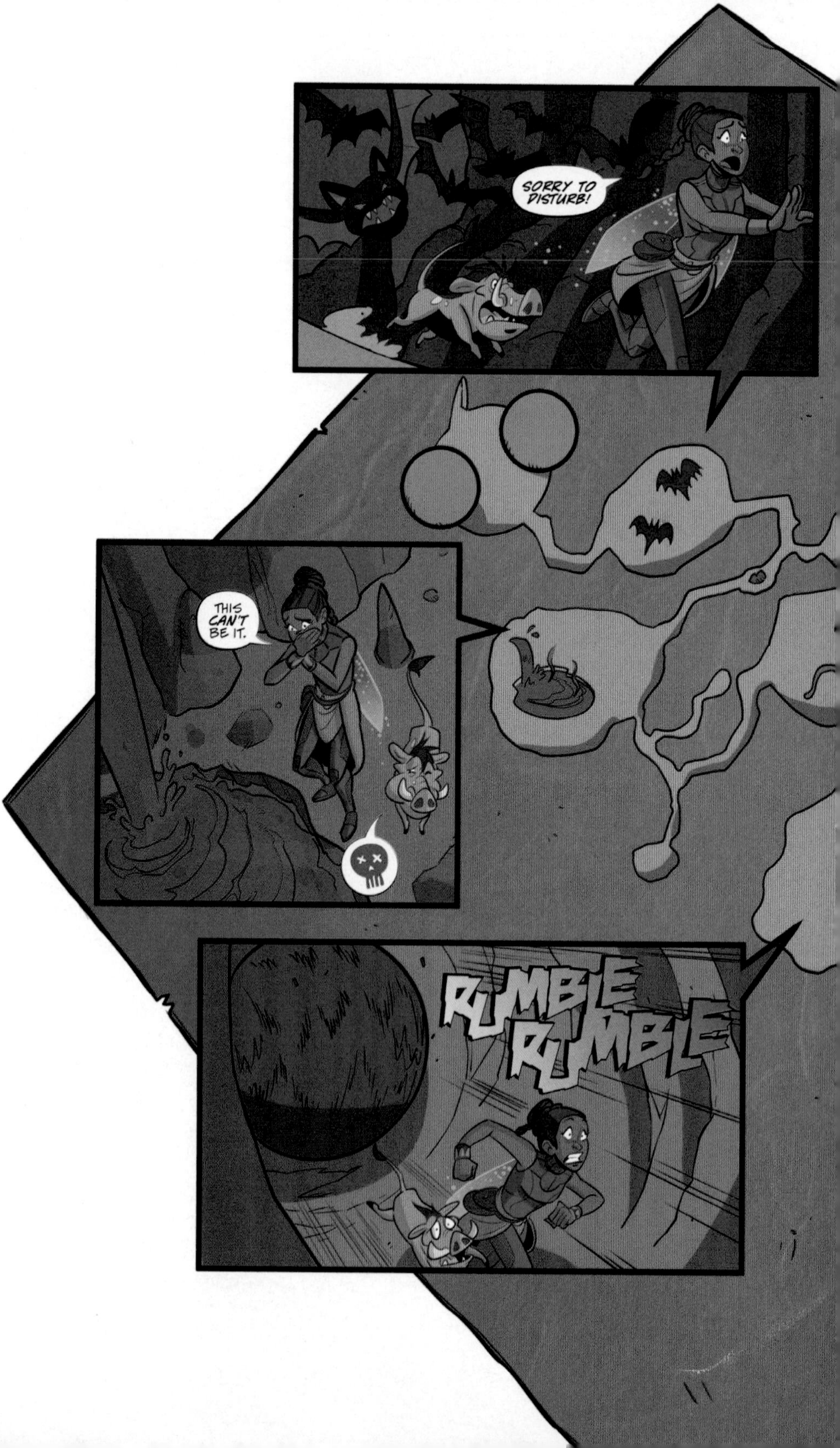
SORRY TO DISTURB!
THIS CAN'T BE IT.
RUMBLE RUMBLE

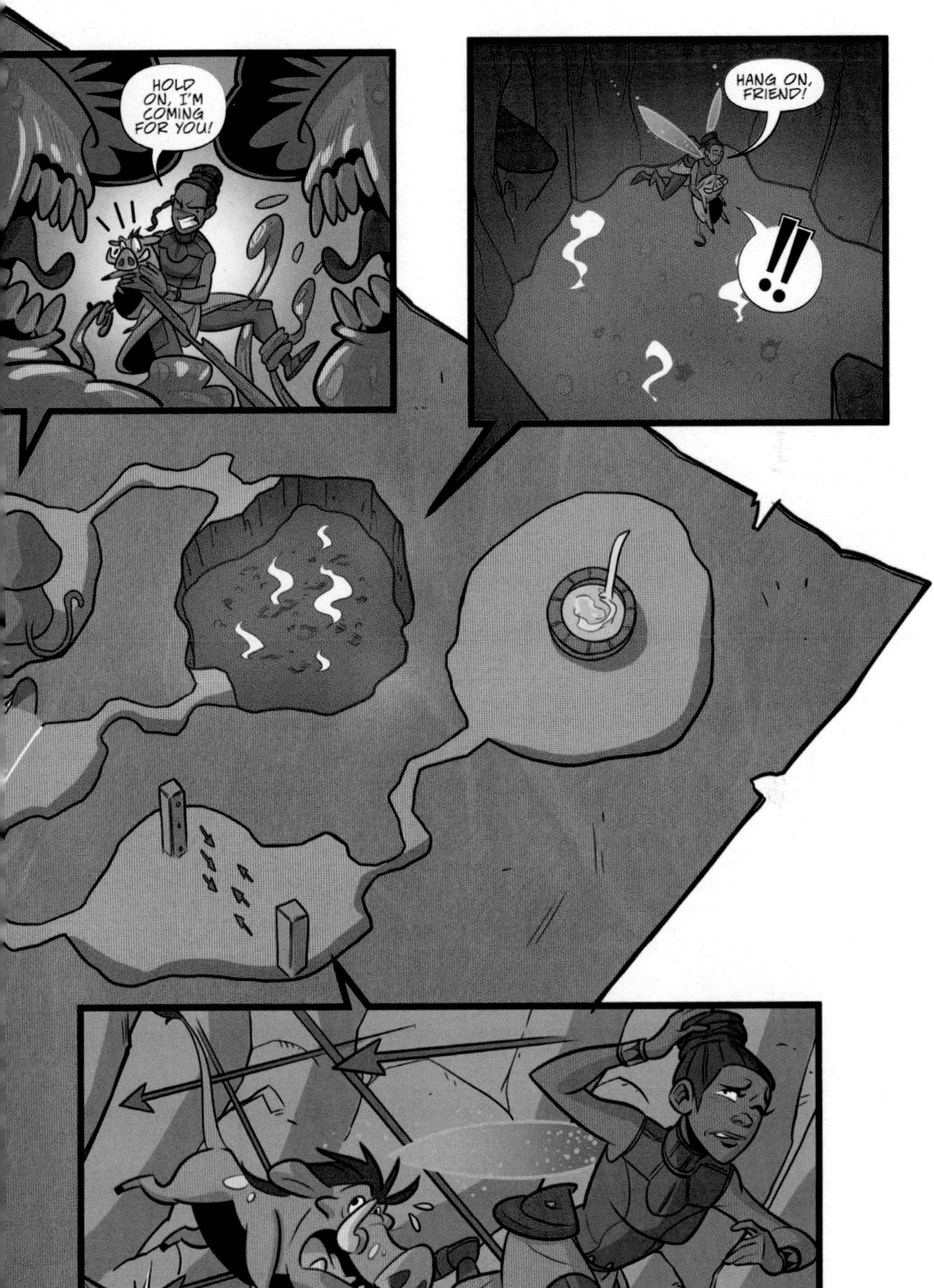
HOLD ON, I'M COMING FOR YOU!
HANG ON, FRIEND!
!!
?

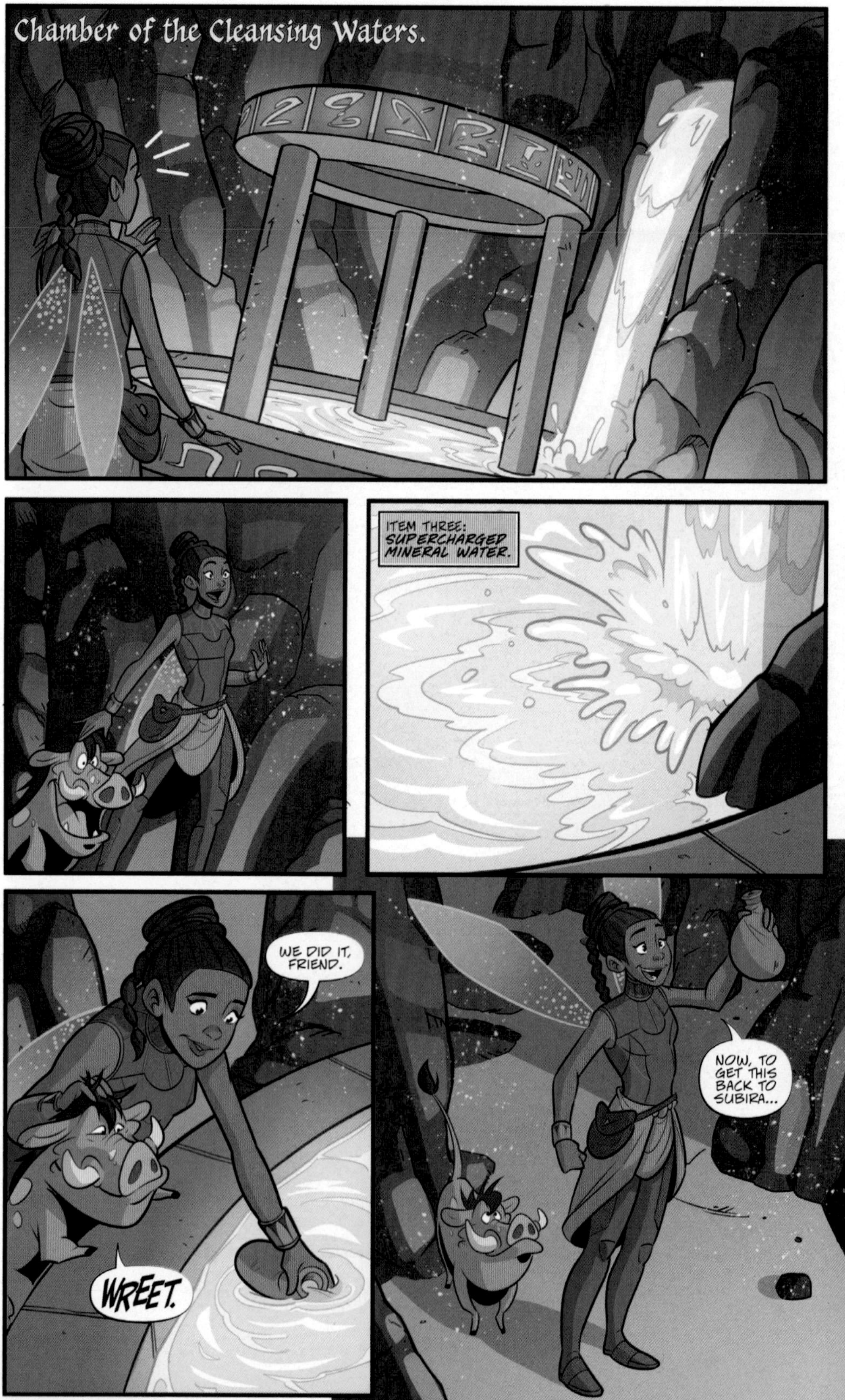
Chamber of the Cleansing Waters.
ITEM THREE: SUPERCHARGED MINERAL WATER.
WE DID IT, FRIEND.
WREET.
NOW, TO GET THIS BACK TO SUBIRA...

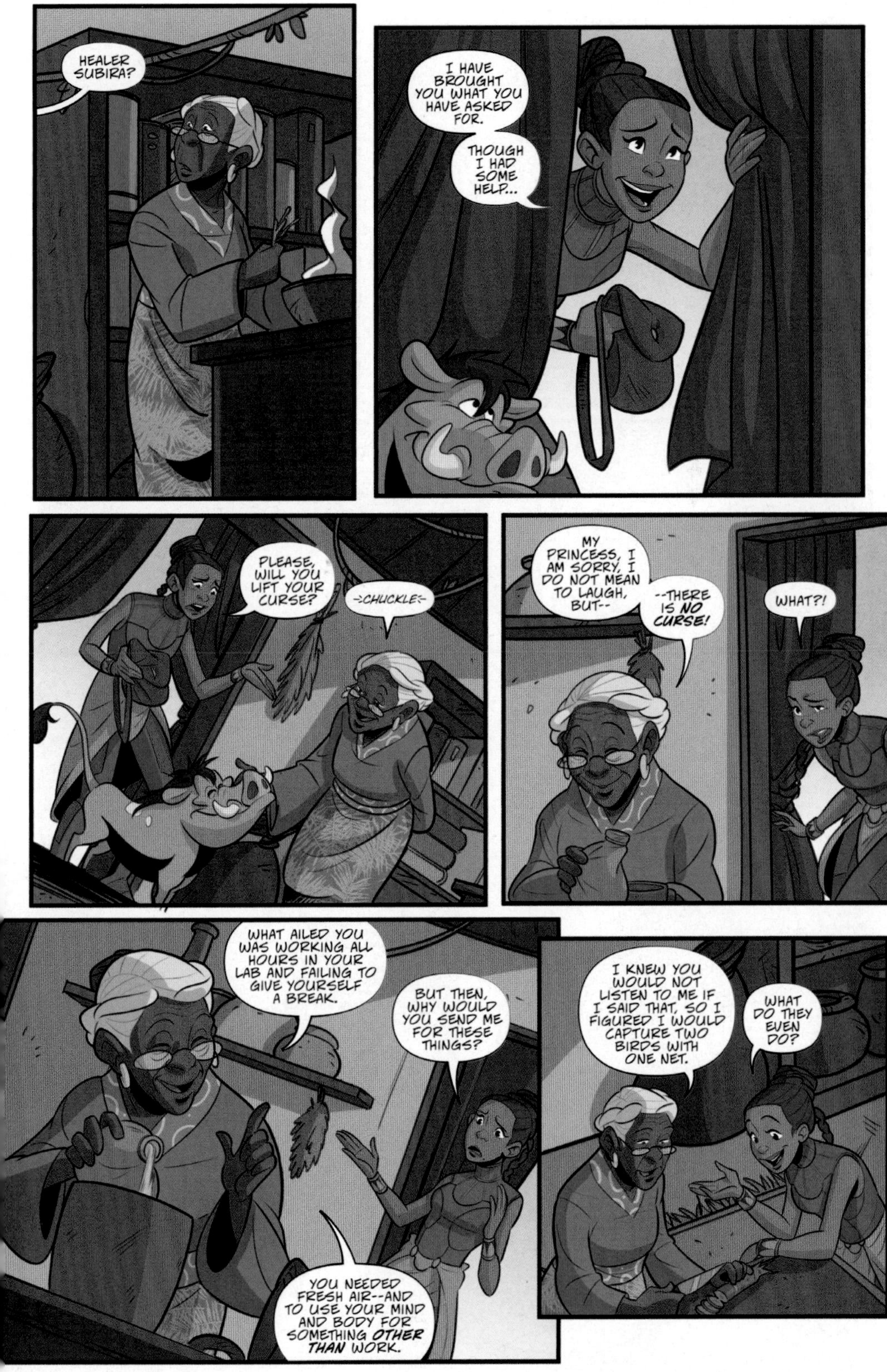
HEALER SUBIRA?
I HAVE BROUGHT YOU WHAT YOU HAVE ASKED FOR.
THOUGH I HAD SOME HELP...
PLEASE, WILL YOU LIFT YOUR CURSE?
CHUCKLE
MY PRINCESS, I AM SORRY, I DO NOT MEAN TO LAUGH, BUT--
--THERE IS **NO CURSE!**
WHAT?!
WHAT AILED YOU WAS WORKING ALL HOURS IN YOUR LAB AND FAILING TO GIVE YOURSELF A BREAK.
BUT THEN, WHY WOULD YOU SEND ME FOR THESE THINGS?
YOU NEEDED FRESH AIR--AND TO USE YOUR MIND AND BODY FOR SOMETHING **OTHER THAN** WORK.
I KNEW YOU WOULD NOT LISTEN TO ME IF I SAID THAT, SO I FIGURED I WOULD CAPTURE TWO BIRDS WITH ONE NET.
WHAT DO THEY EVEN DO?

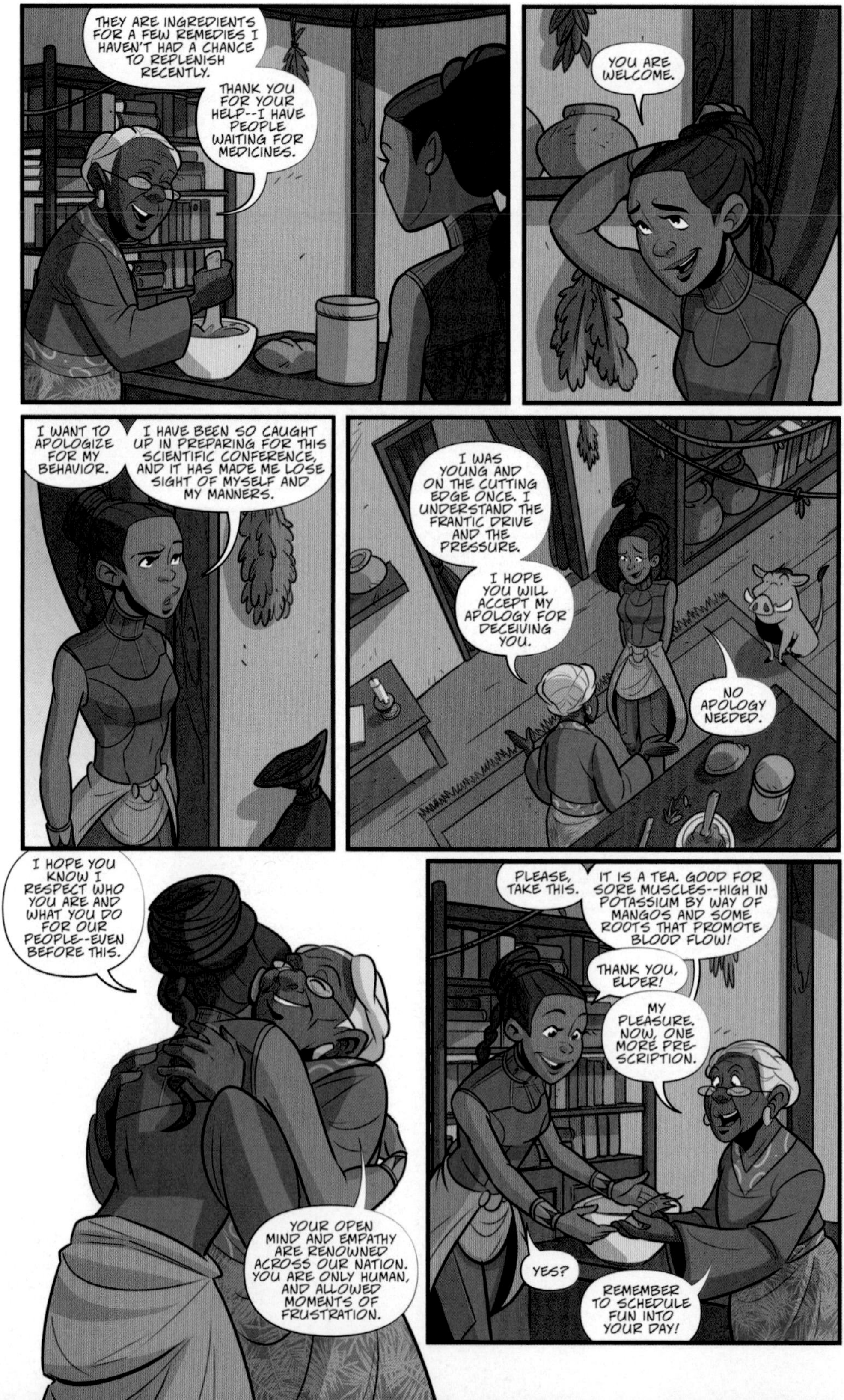
THEY ARE INGREDIENTS FOR A FEW REMEDIES I HAVEN'T HAD A CHANCE TO REPLENISH RECENTLY.
THANK YOU FOR YOUR HELP--I HAVE PEOPLE WAITING FOR MEDICINES.
YOU ARE WELCOME.
I WANT TO APOLOGIZE FOR MY BEHAVIOR.
I HAVE BEEN SO CAUGHT UP IN PREPARING FOR THIS SCIENTIFIC CONFERENCE, AND IT HAS MADE ME LOSE SIGHT OF MYSELF AND MY MANNERS.
I WAS YOUNG AND ON THE CUTTING EDGE ONCE. I UNDERSTAND THE FRANTIC DRIVE AND THE PRESSURE.
I HOPE YOU WILL ACCEPT MY APOLOGY FOR DECEIVING YOU.
NO APOLOGY NEEDED.
I HOPE YOU KNOW I RESPECT WHO YOU ARE AND WHAT YOU DO FOR OUR PEOPLE--EVEN BEFORE THIS.
YOUR OPEN MIND AND EMPATHY ARE RENOWNED ACROSS OUR NATION. YOU ARE ONLY HUMAN, AND ALLOWED MOMENTS OF FRUSTRATION.
PLEASE, TAKE THIS.
IT IS A TEA. GOOD FOR SORE MUSCLES--HIGH IN POTASSIUM BY WAY OF MANGOS AND SOME ROOTS THAT PROMOTE BLOOD FLOW!
THANK YOU, ELDER!
MY PLEASURE. NOW, ONE MORE PRESCRIPTION.
YES?
REMEMBER TO SCHEDULE FUN INTO YOUR DAY!

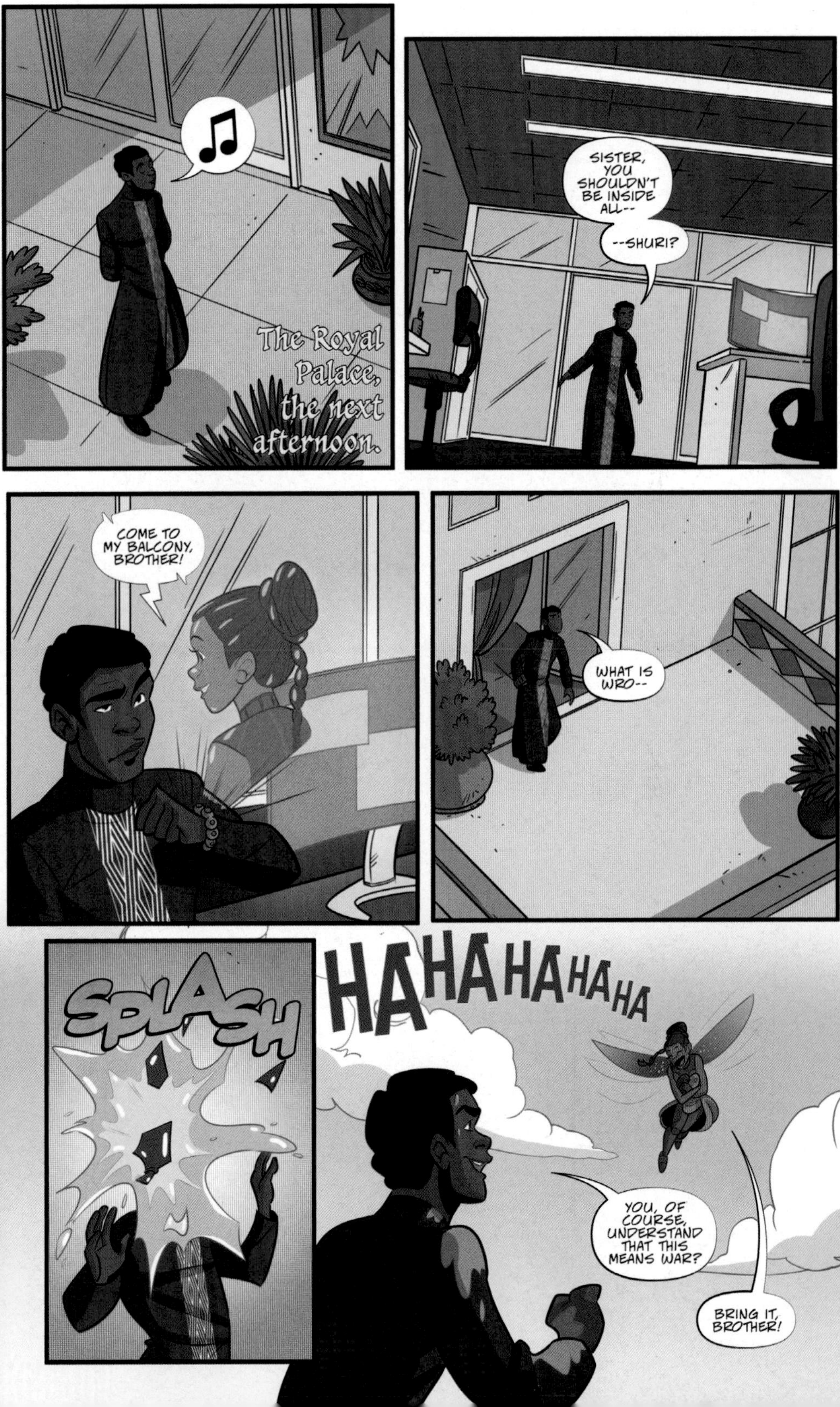
♫
The Royal Palace, the next afternoon.
SISTER, YOU SHOULDN'T BE INSIDE ALL--
--SHURI?
COME TO MY BALCONY, BROTHER!
WHAT IS WRO--
SPLASH
HAHAHAHAHAHA
YOU, OF COURSE, UNDERSTAND THAT THIS MEANS WAR?
BRING IT, BROTHER!

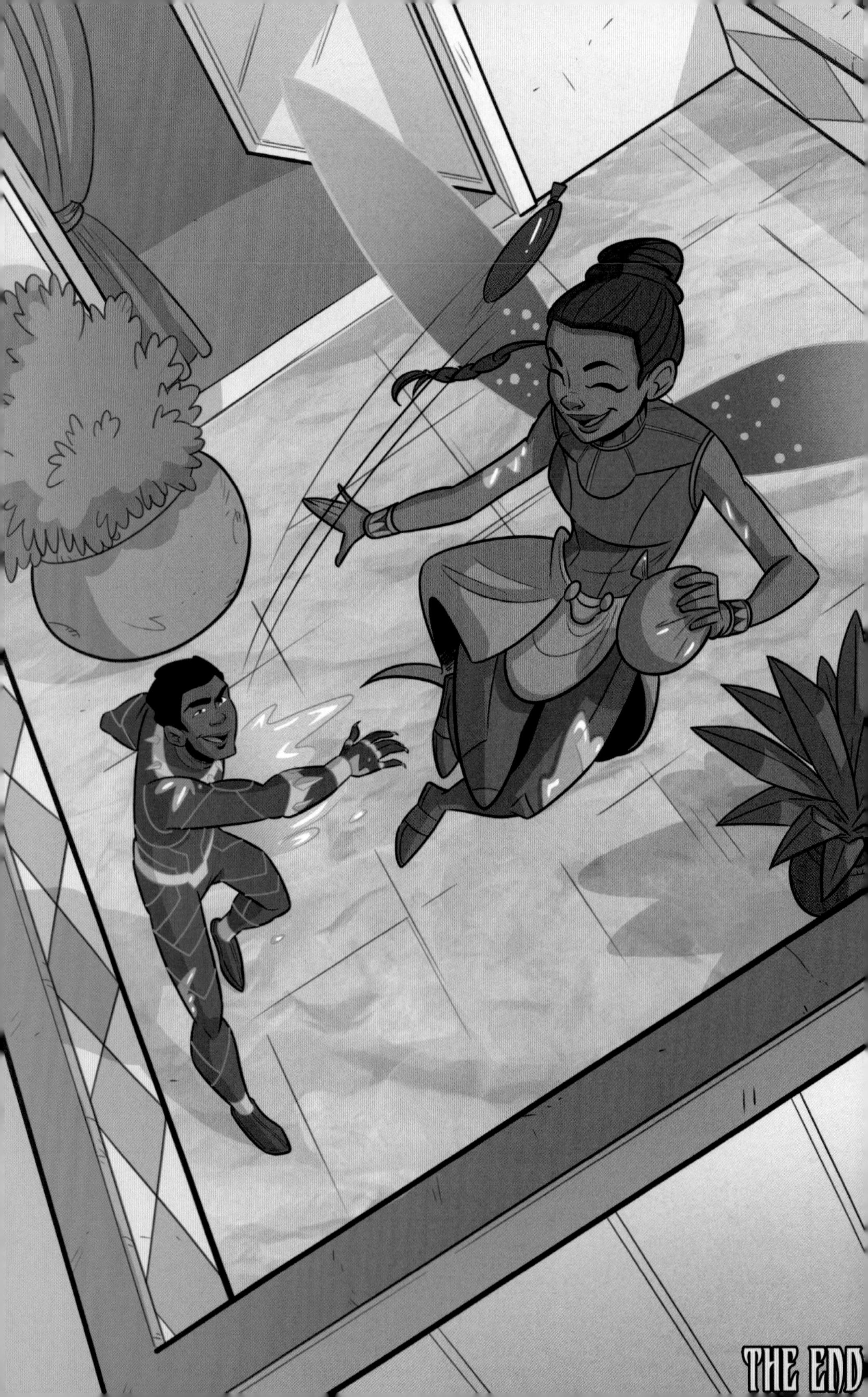
THE END

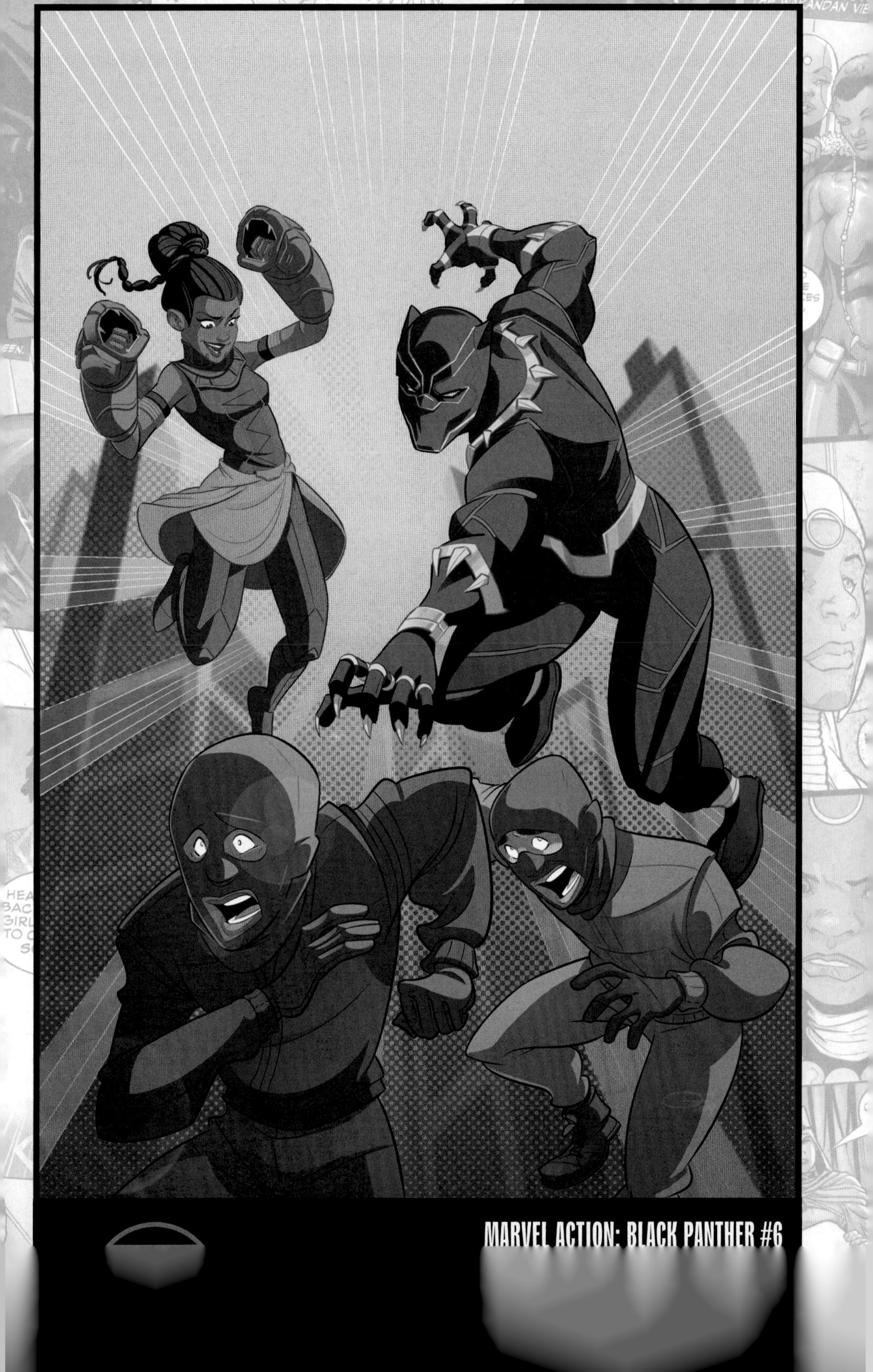

MARVEL ACTION: BLACK PANTHER #6

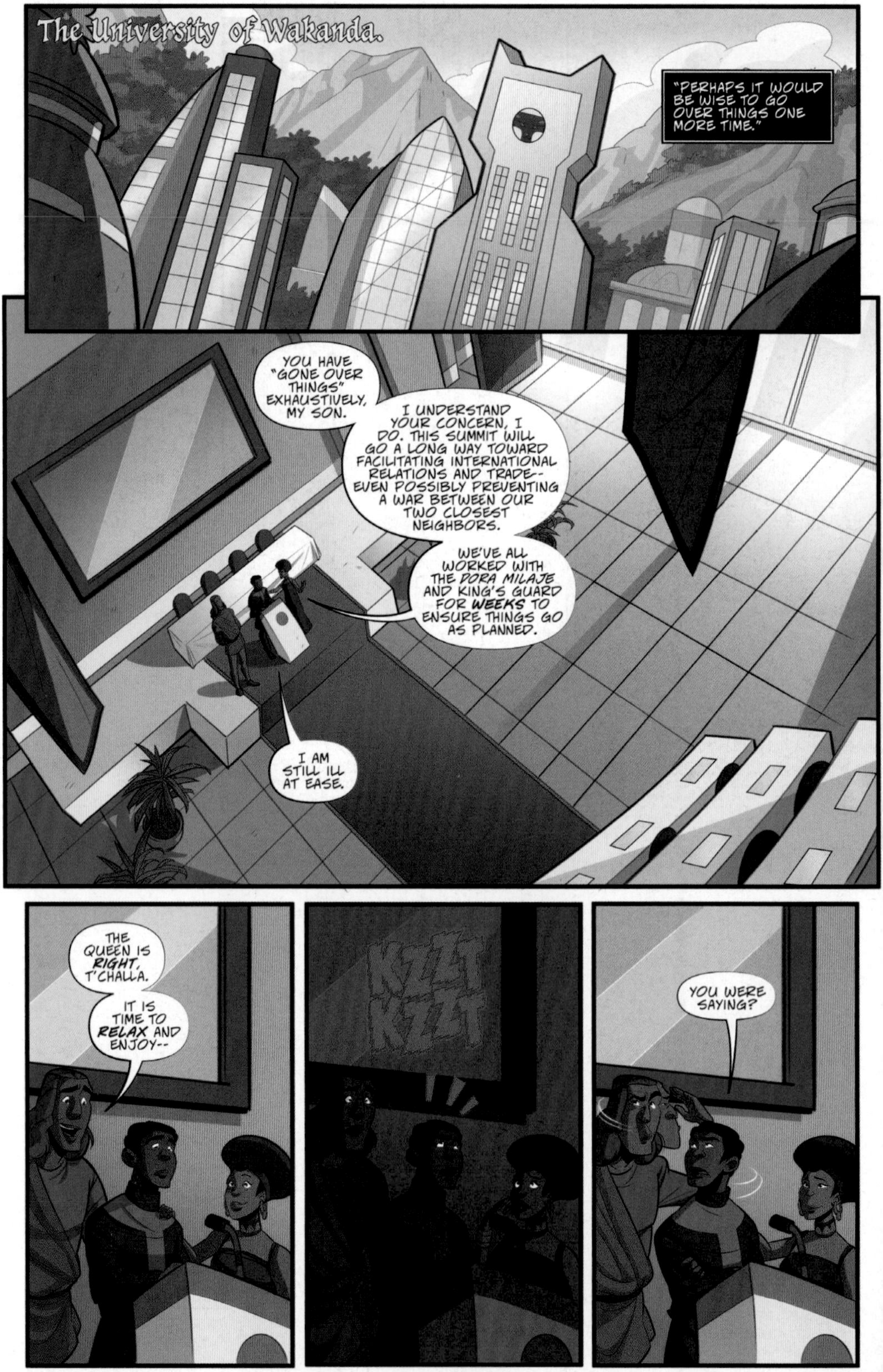
The University of Wakanda.
"PERHAPS IT WOULD BE WISE TO GO OVER THINGS ONE MORE TIME."
YOU HAVE "GONE OVER THINGS" EXHAUSTIVELY, MY SON.
I UNDERSTAND YOUR CONCERN, I DO. THIS SUMMIT WILL GO A LONG WAY TOWARD FACILITATING INTERNATIONAL RELATIONS AND TRADE-- EVEN POSSIBLY PREVENTING A WAR BETWEEN OUR TWO CLOSEST NEIGHBORS.
WE'VE ALL WORKED WITH THE DORA MILAJE AND KING'S GUARD FOR WEEKS TO ENSURE THINGS GO AS PLANNED.
I AM STILL ILL AT EASE.
THE QUEEN IS RIGHT, T'CHALLA.
IT IS TIME TO RELAX AND ENJOY--
KZZZT KZZZT
YOU WERE SAYING?

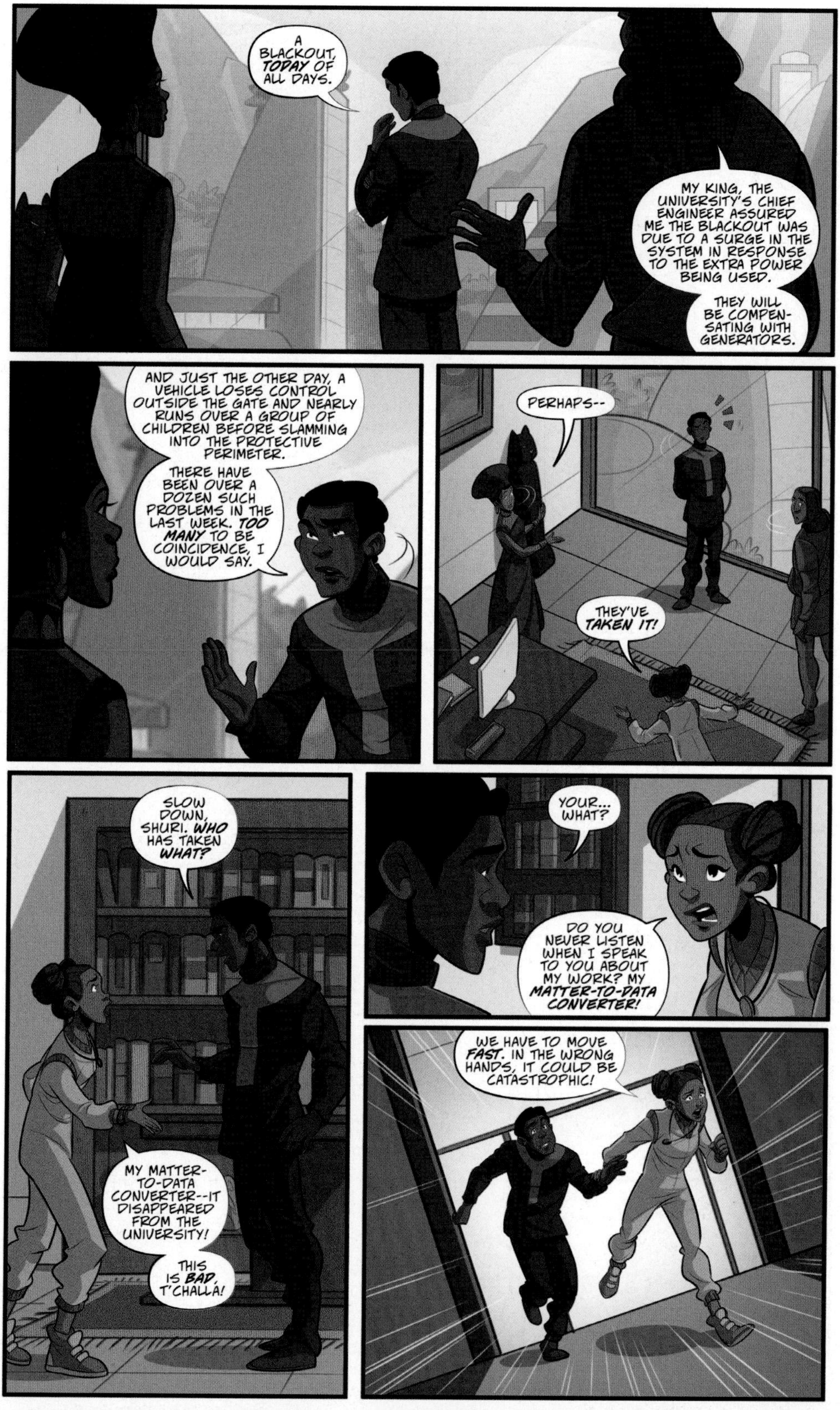
A BLACKOUT, TODAY OF ALL DAYS.
MY KING, THE UNIVERSITY'S CHIEF ENGINEER ASSURED ME THE BLACKOUT WAS DUE TO A SURGE IN THE SYSTEM IN RESPONSE TO THE EXTRA POWER BEING USED.
THEY WILL BE COMPENSATING WITH GENERATORS.
AND JUST THE OTHER DAY, A VEHICLE LOSES CONTROL OUTSIDE THE GATE AND NEARLY RUNS OVER A GROUP OF CHILDREN BEFORE SLAMMING INTO THE PROTECTIVE PERIMETER.
THERE HAVE BEEN OVER A DOZEN SUCH PROBLEMS IN THE LAST WEEK. TOO MANY TO BE COINCIDENCE, I WOULD SAY.
PERHAPS--
THEY'VE TAKEN IT!
SLOW DOWN, SHURI. WHO HAS TAKEN WHAT?
MY MATTER-TO-DATA CONVERTER--IT DISAPPEARED FROM THE UNIVERSITY!
THIS IS BAD, T'CHALLA!
YOUR... WHAT?
DO YOU NEVER LISTEN WHEN I SPEAK TO YOU ABOUT MY WORK? MY MATTER-TO-DATA CONVERTER!
WE HAVE TO MOVE FAST. IN THE WRONG HANDS, IT COULD BE CATASTROPHIC!

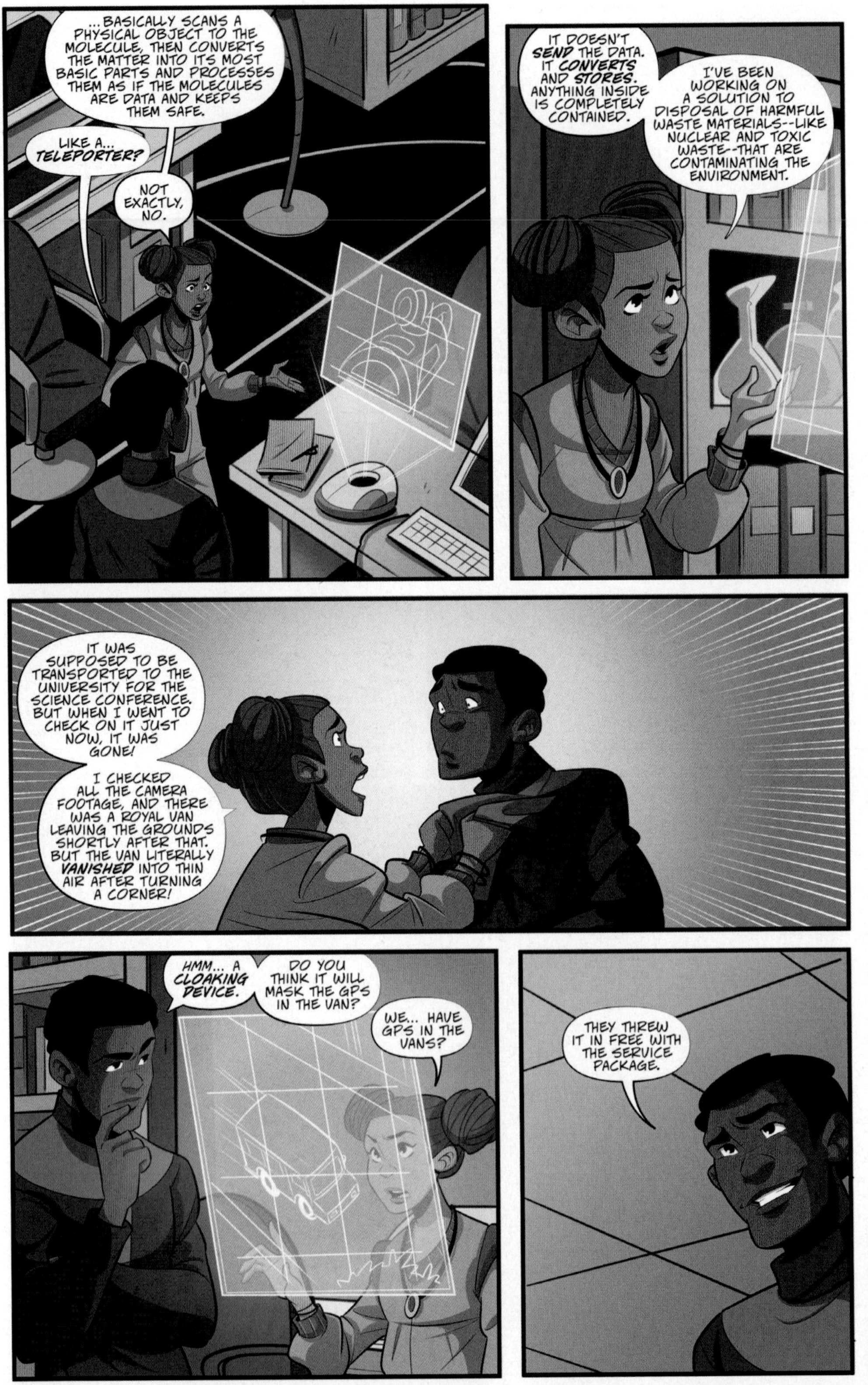
...BASICALLY SCANS A PHYSICAL OBJECT TO THE MOLECULE, THEN CONVERTS THE MATTER INTO ITS MOST BASIC PARTS AND PROCESSES THEM AS IF THE MOLECULES ARE DATA AND KEEPS THEM SAFE.
LIKE A... TELEPORTER?
NOT EXACTLY, NO.
IT DOESN'T SEND THE DATA. IT CONVERTS AND STORES. ANYTHING INSIDE IS COMPLETELY CONTAINED.
I'VE BEEN WORKING ON A SOLUTION TO DISPOSAL OF HARMFUL WASTE MATERIALS--LIKE NUCLEAR AND TOXIC WASTE--THAT ARE CONTAMINATING THE ENVIRONMENT.
IT WAS SUPPOSED TO BE TRANSPORTED TO THE UNIVERSITY FOR THE SCIENCE CONFERENCE. BUT WHEN I WENT TO CHECK ON IT JUST NOW, IT WAS GONE!
I CHECKED ALL THE CAMERA FOOTAGE, AND THERE WAS A ROYAL VAN LEAVING THE GROUNDS SHORTLY AFTER THAT. BUT THE VAN LITERALLY VANISHED INTO THIN AIR AFTER TURNING A CORNER!
HMM... A CLOAKING DEVICE.
DO YOU THINK IT WILL MASK THE GPS IN THE VAN?
WE... HAVE GPS IN THE VANS?
THEY THREW IT IN FREE WITH THE SERVICE PACKAGE.

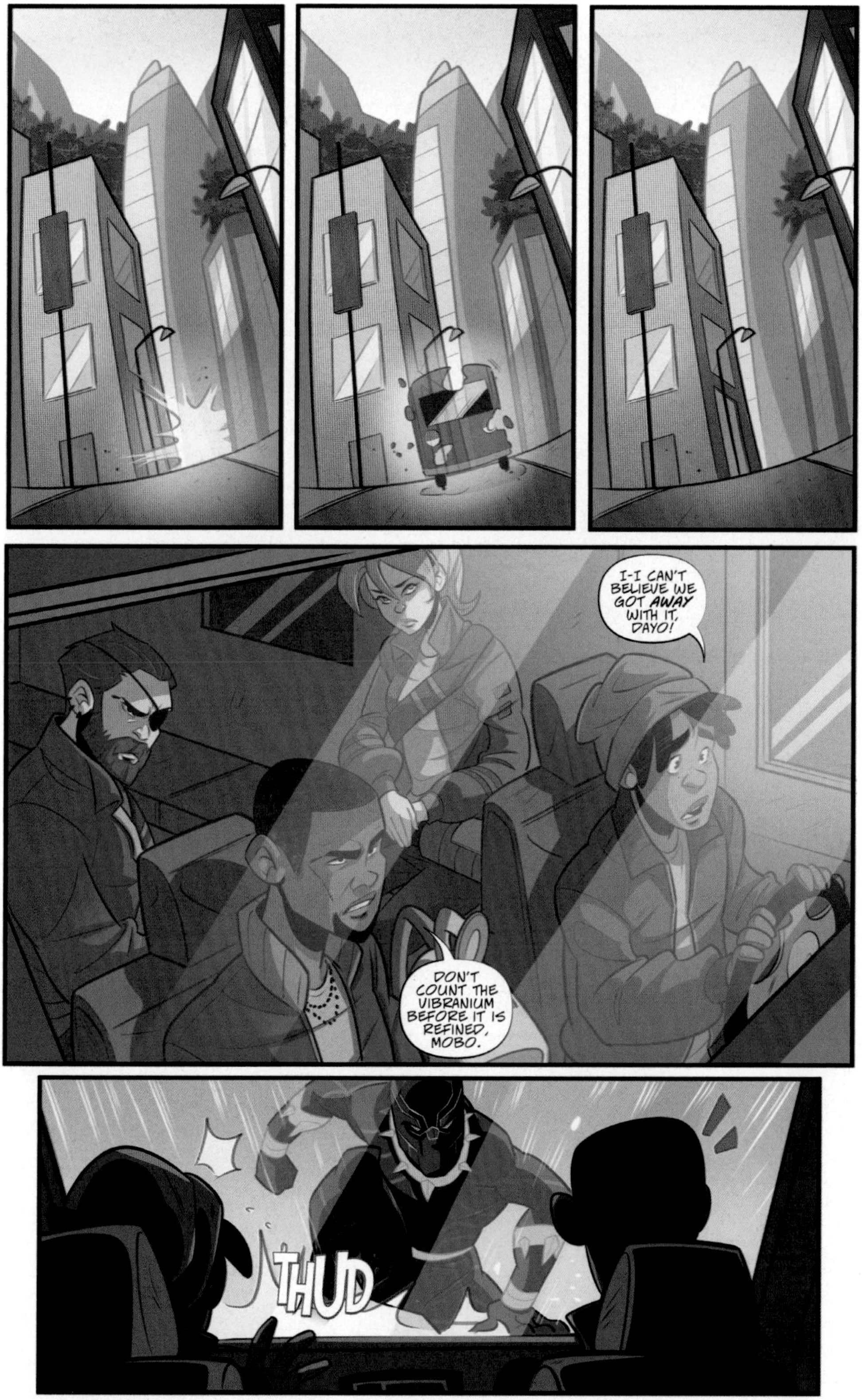
I-I CAN'T BELIEVE WE GOT AWAY WITH IT, DAYO!
DON'T COUNT THE VIBRANIUM BEFORE IT IS REFINED, MOBO.
THUD

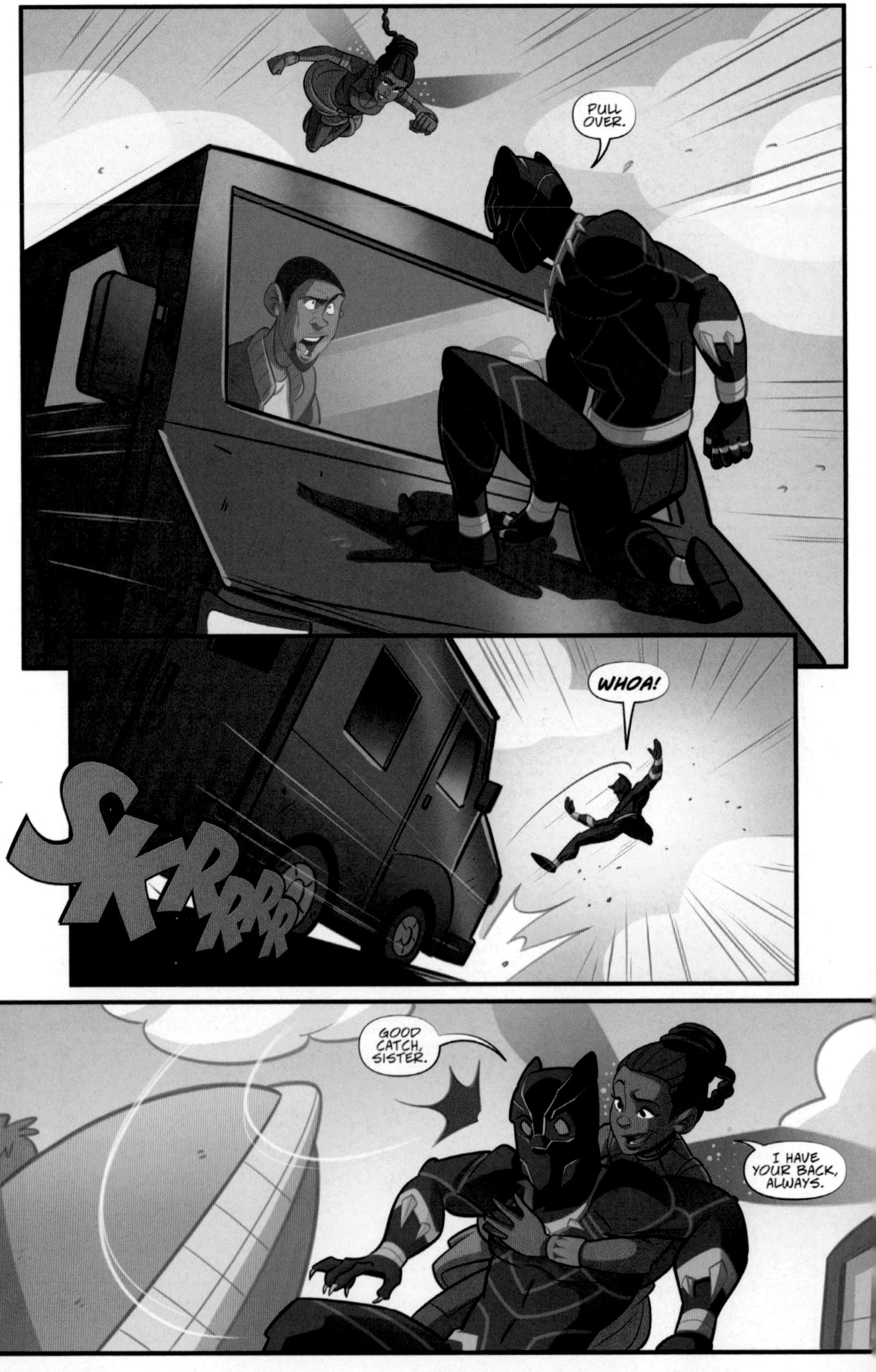
PULL OVER.
WHOA!
SKRRRRR
GOOD CATCH, SISTER.
I HAVE YOUR BACK, ALWAYS.

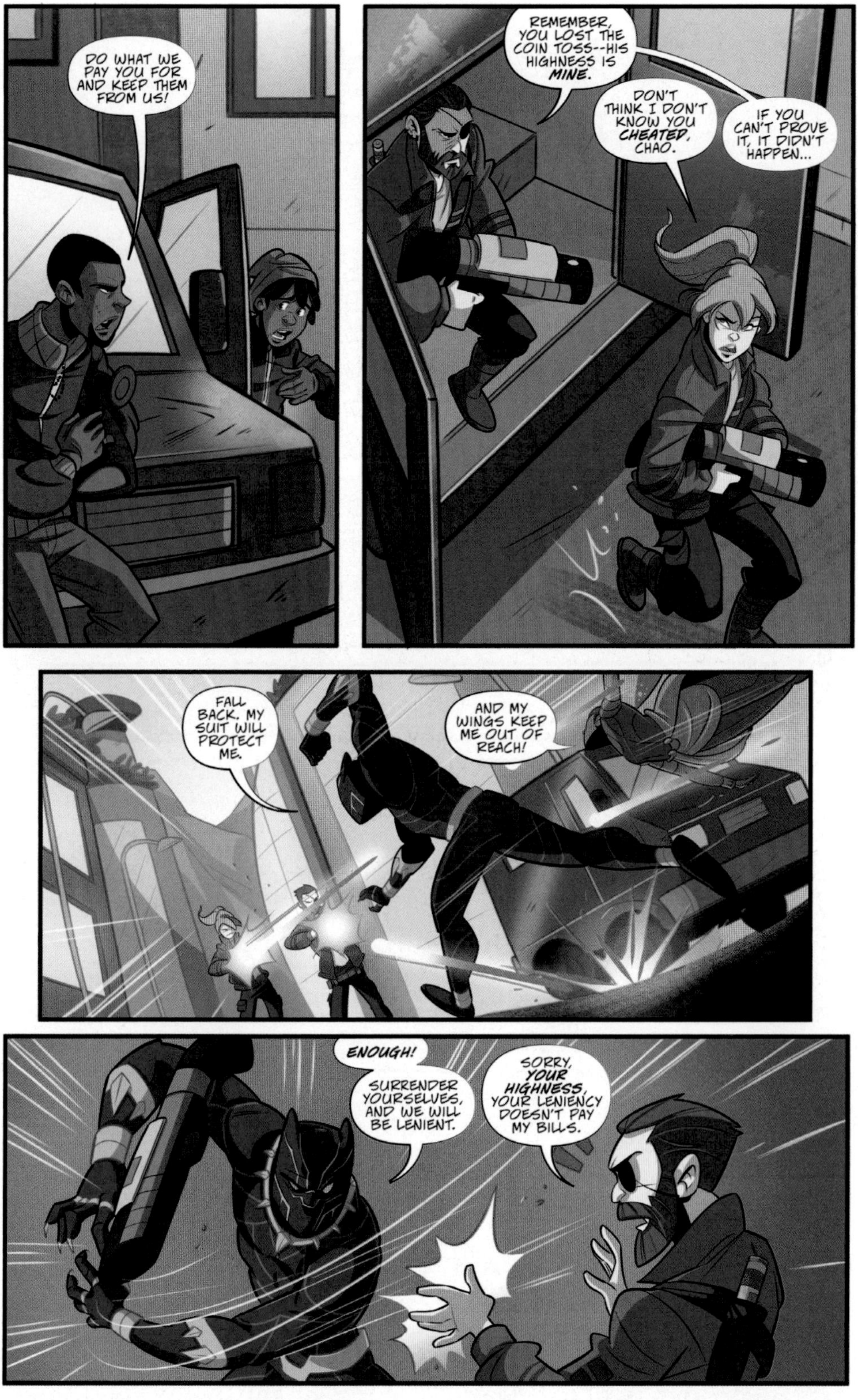

DO WHAT WE PAY YOU FOR AND KEEP THEM FROM US!
REMEMBER, YOU LOST THE COIN TOSS--HIS HIGHNESS IS **MINE**.
DON'T THINK I DON'T KNOW YOU **CHEATED**, CHAO.
IF YOU CAN'T PROVE IT, IT DIDN'T HAPPEN...
FALL BACK. MY SUIT WILL PROTECT ME.
AND MY WINGS KEEP ME OUT OF REACH!
ENOUGH!
SURRENDER YOURSELVES, AND WE WILL BE LENIENT.
SORRY, **YOUR HIGHNESS**, YOUR LENIENCY DOESN'T PAY MY BILLS.

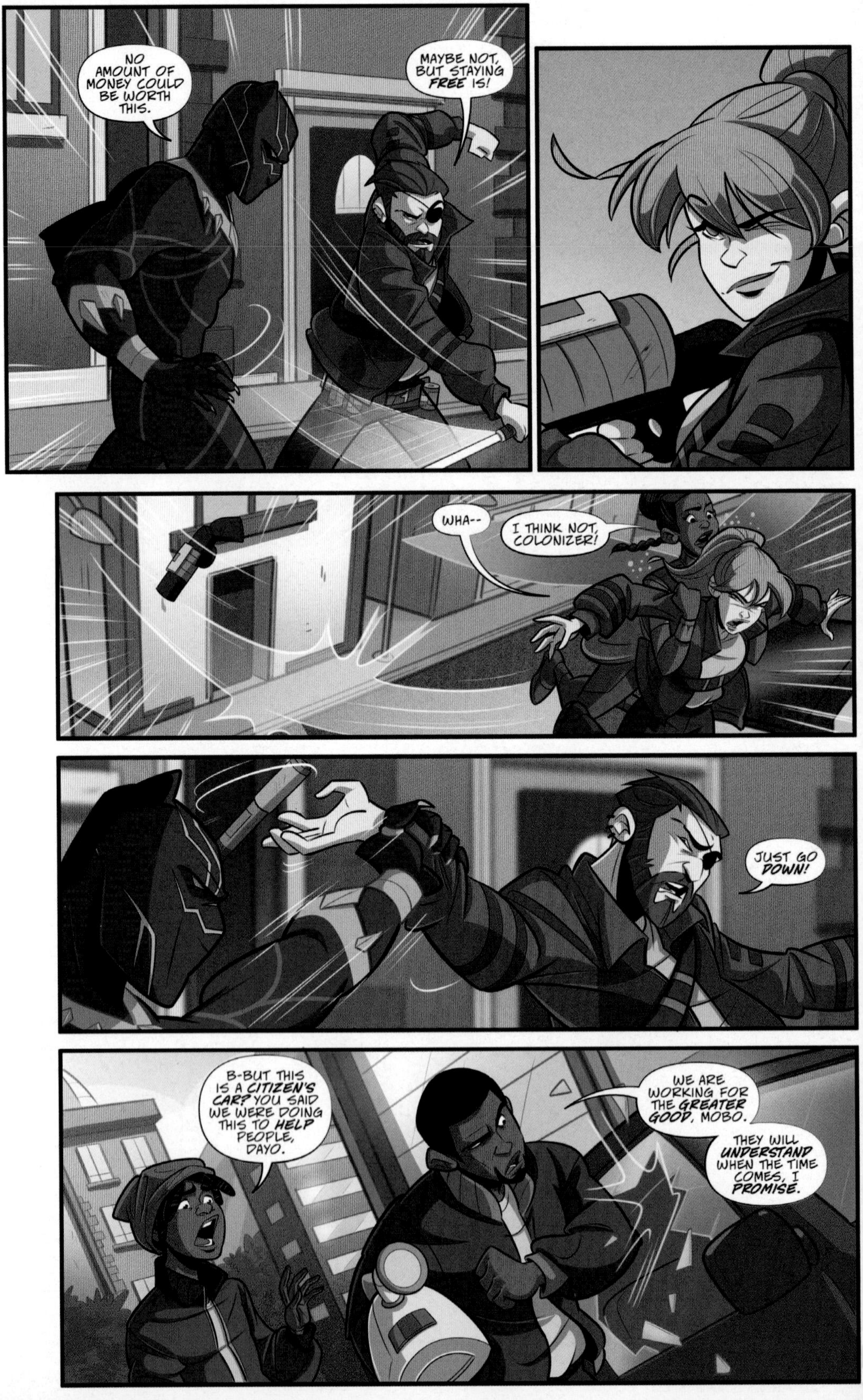
NO AMOUNT OF MONEY COULD BE WORTH THIS.
MAYBE NOT, BUT STAYING ***FREE*** IS!
WHA--
I THINK NOT, COLONIZER!
JUST GO ***DOWN!***
B-BUT THIS IS A ***CITIZEN'S CAR?*** YOU SAID WE WERE DOING THIS TO ***HELP*** PEOPLE, DAYO.
WE ARE WORKING FOR THE ***GREATER GOOD***, MOBO.
THEY WILL ***UNDERSTAND*** WHEN THE TIME COMES, I ***PROMISE***.

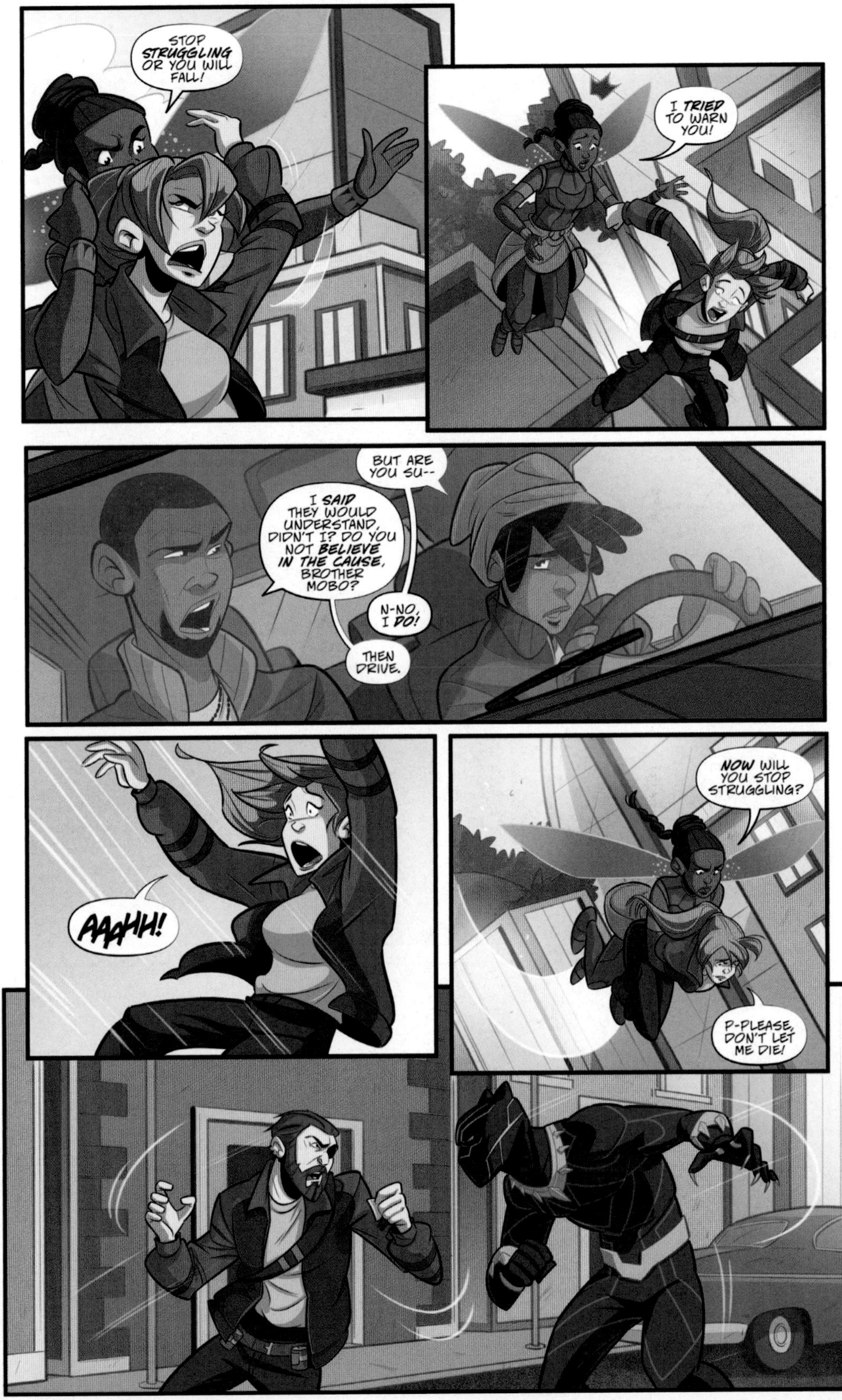
STOP STRUGGLING OR YOU WILL FALL!
I TRIED TO WARN YOU!
BUT ARE YOU SU--
I SAID THEY WOULD UNDERSTAND, DIDN'T I? DO YOU NOT BELIEVE IN THE CAUSE, BROTHER MOBO?
N-NO, I DO!
THEN DRIVE.
AAAHH!
NOW WILL YOU STOP STRUGGLING?
P-PLEASE, DON'T LET ME DIE!

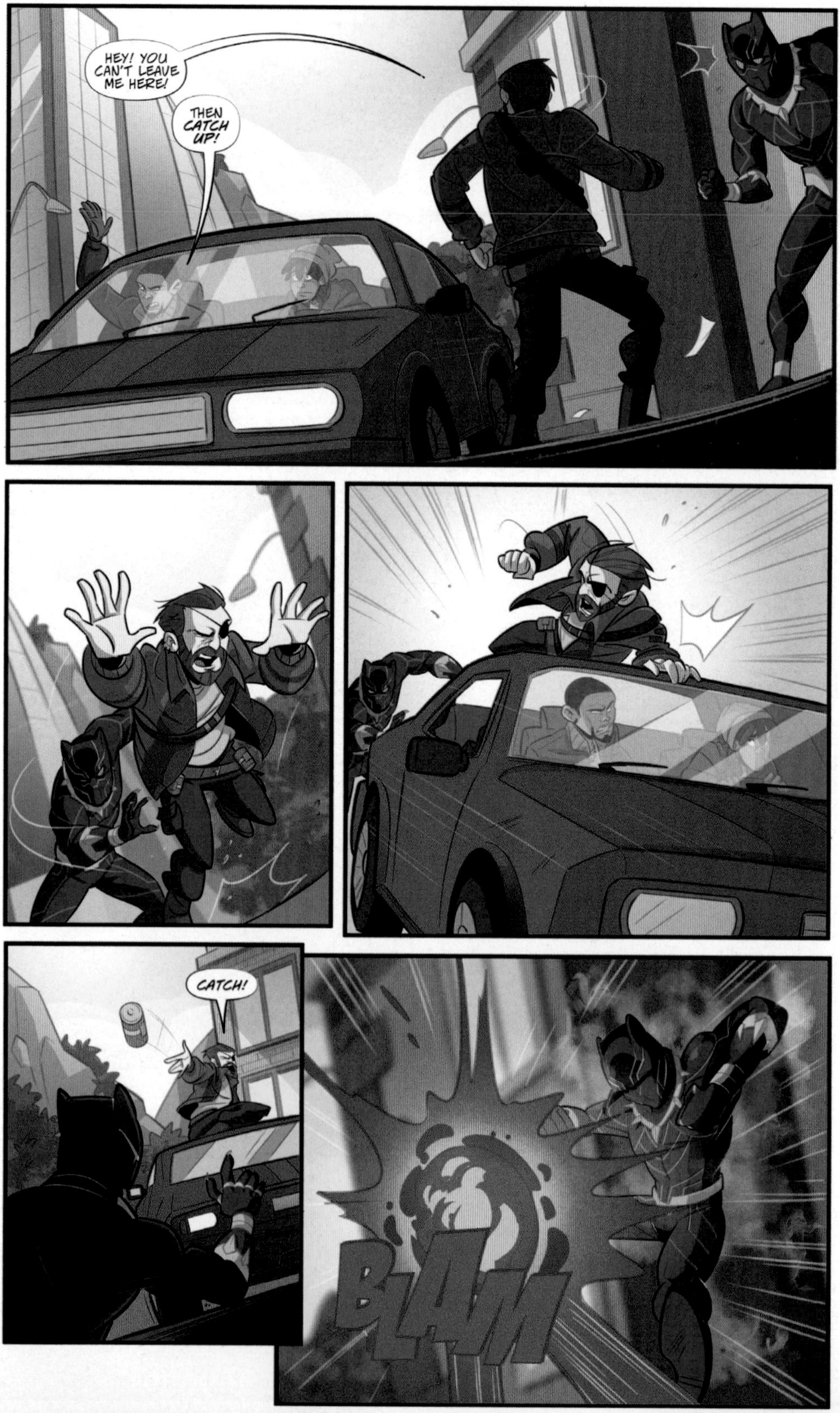
HEY! YOU CAN'T LEAVE ME HERE!
THEN CATCH UP!
CATCH!
BLAM

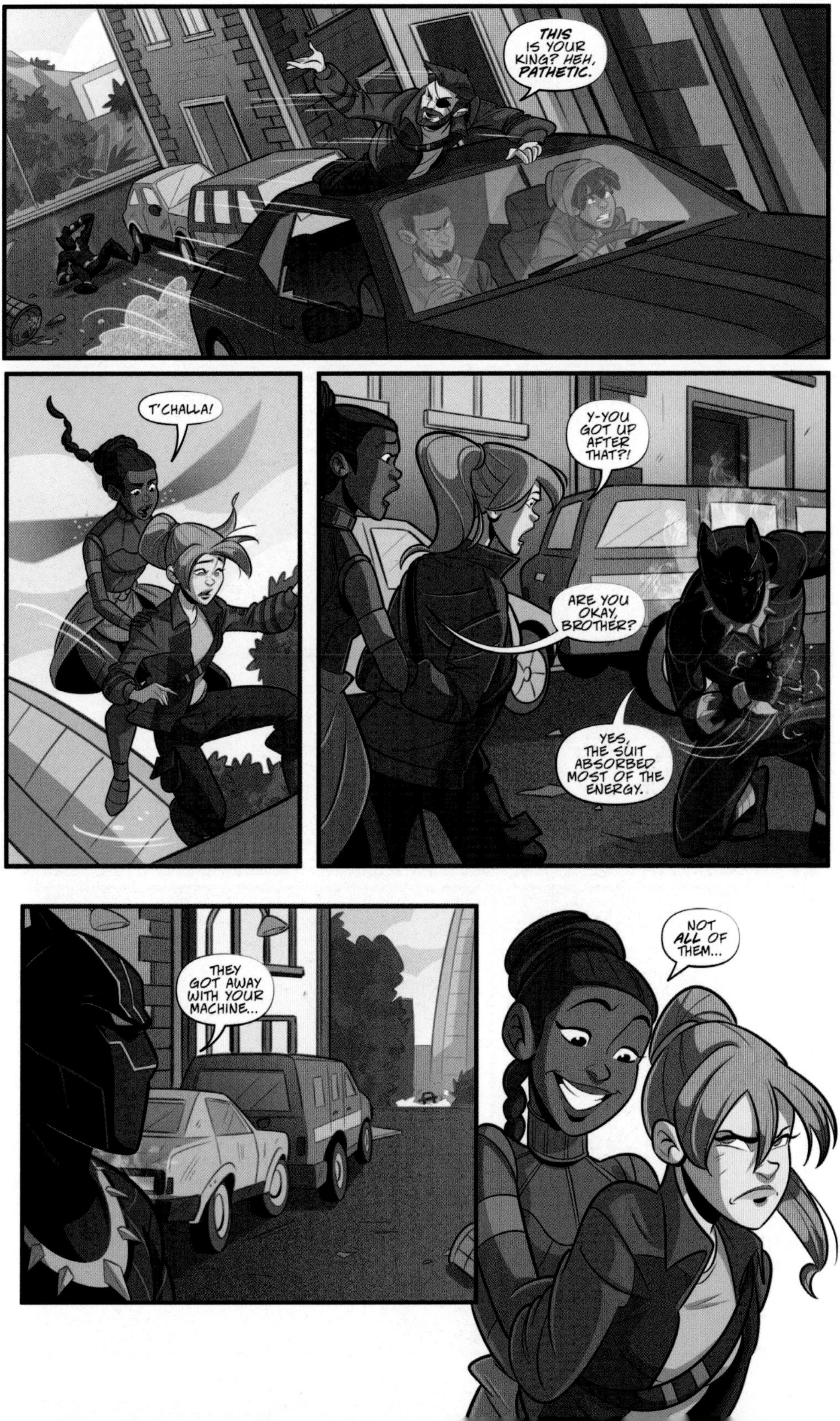
THIS IS YOUR KING? HEH, PATHETIC.
T'CHALLA!
Y-YOU GOT UP AFTER THAT?!
ARE YOU OKAY, BROTHER?
YES, THE SUIT ABSORBED MOST OF THE ENERGY.
THEY GOT AWAY WITH YOUR MACHINE...
NOT ALL OF THEM...

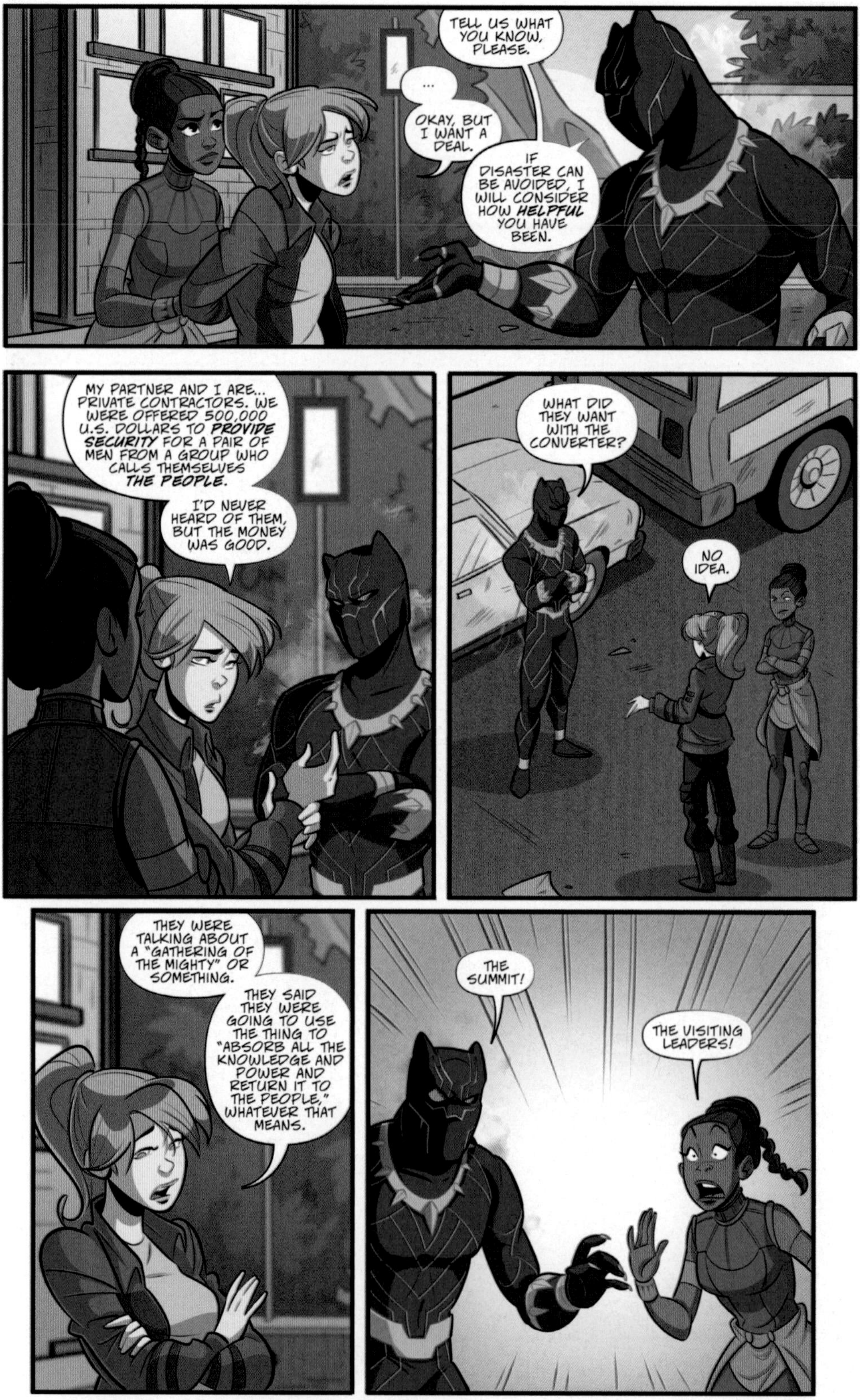
TELL US WHAT YOU KNOW, PLEASE.
...
OKAY, BUT I WANT A DEAL.
IF DISASTER CAN BE AVOIDED, I WILL CONSIDER HOW **HELPFUL** YOU HAVE BEEN.
MY PARTNER AND I ARE... PRIVATE CONTRACTORS. WE WERE OFFERED 500,000 U.S. DOLLARS TO **PROVIDE SECURITY** FOR A PAIR OF MEN FROM A GROUP WHO CALLS THEMSELVES **THE PEOPLE**.
I'D NEVER HEARD OF THEM, BUT THE MONEY WAS GOOD.
WHAT DID THEY WANT WITH THE CONVERTER?
NO IDEA.
THEY WERE TALKING ABOUT A "GATHERING OF THE MIGHTY" OR SOMETHING.
THEY SAID THEY WERE GOING TO USE THE THING TO "ABSORB ALL THE KNOWLEDGE AND POWER AND RETURN IT TO THE PEOPLE," WHATEVER THAT MEANS.
THE SUMMIT!
THE VISITING LEADERS!

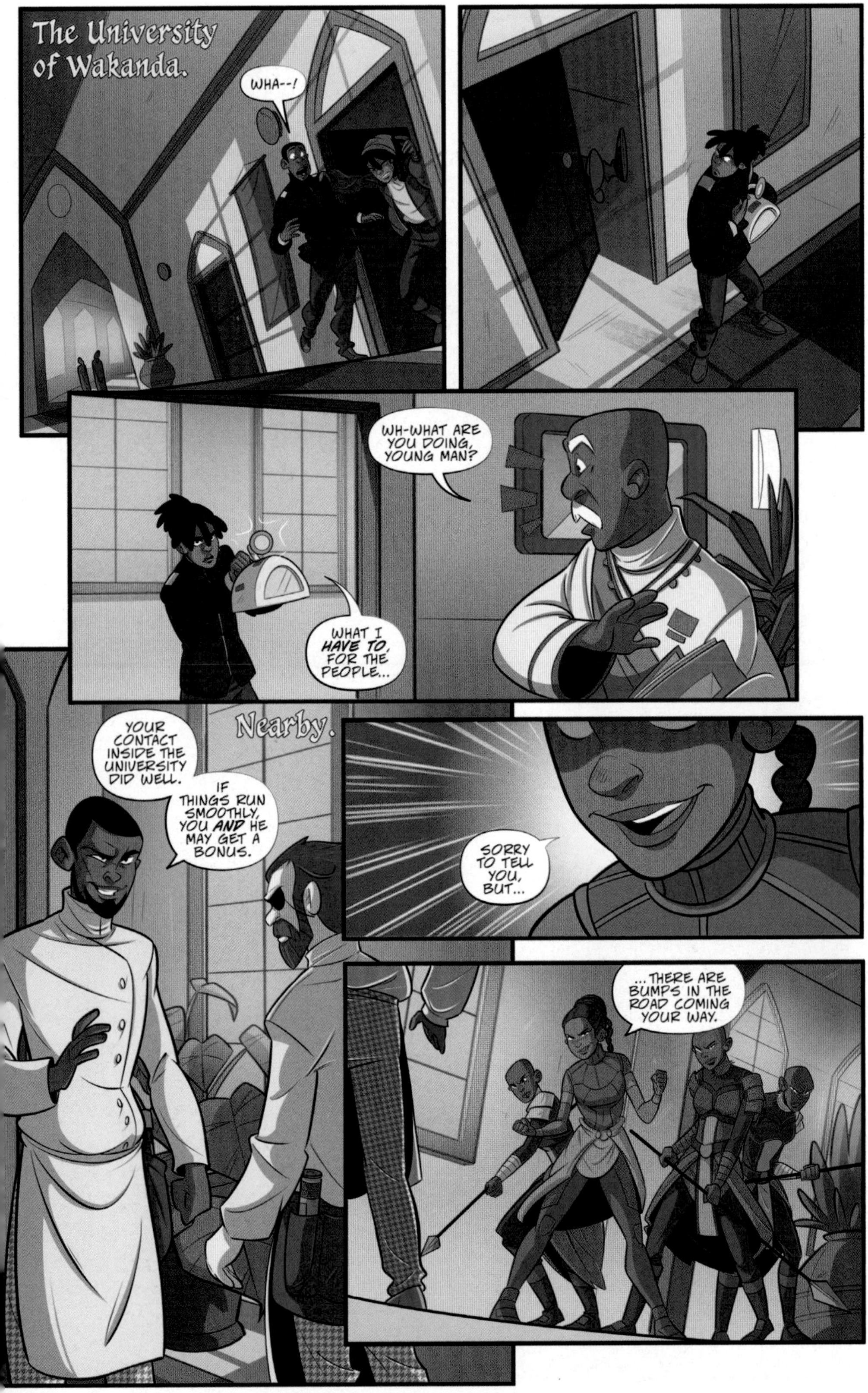
The University of Wakanda.
WHA--!
WH-WHAT ARE YOU DOING, YOUNG MAN?
WHAT I HAVE TO, FOR THE PEOPLE...
Nearby.
YOUR CONTACT INSIDE THE UNIVERSITY DID WELL.
IF THINGS RUN SMOOTHLY, YOU AND HE MAY GET A BONUS.
SORRY TO TELL YOU, BUT...
...THERE ARE BUMPS IN THE ROAD COMING YOUR WAY.

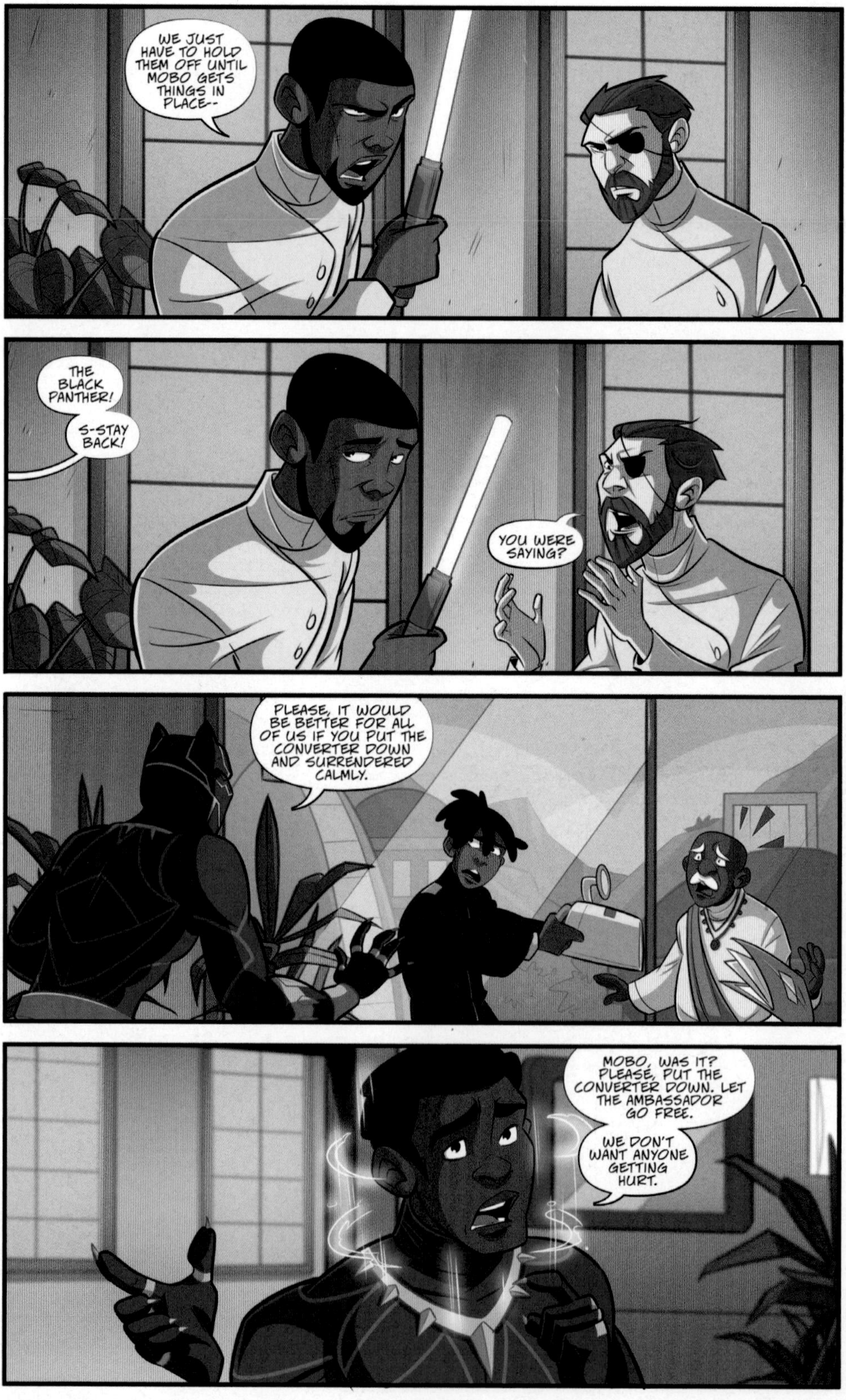
WE JUST HAVE TO HOLD THEM OFF UNTIL MOBO GETS THINGS IN PLACE--
THE BLACK PANTHER!
S-STAY BACK!
YOU WERE SAYING?
PLEASE, IT WOULD BE BETTER FOR ALL OF US IF YOU PUT THE CONVERTER DOWN AND SURRENDERED CALMLY.
MOBO, WAS IT? PLEASE, PUT THE CONVERTER DOWN. LET THE AMBASSADOR GO FREE.
WE DON'T WANT ANYONE GETTING HURT.

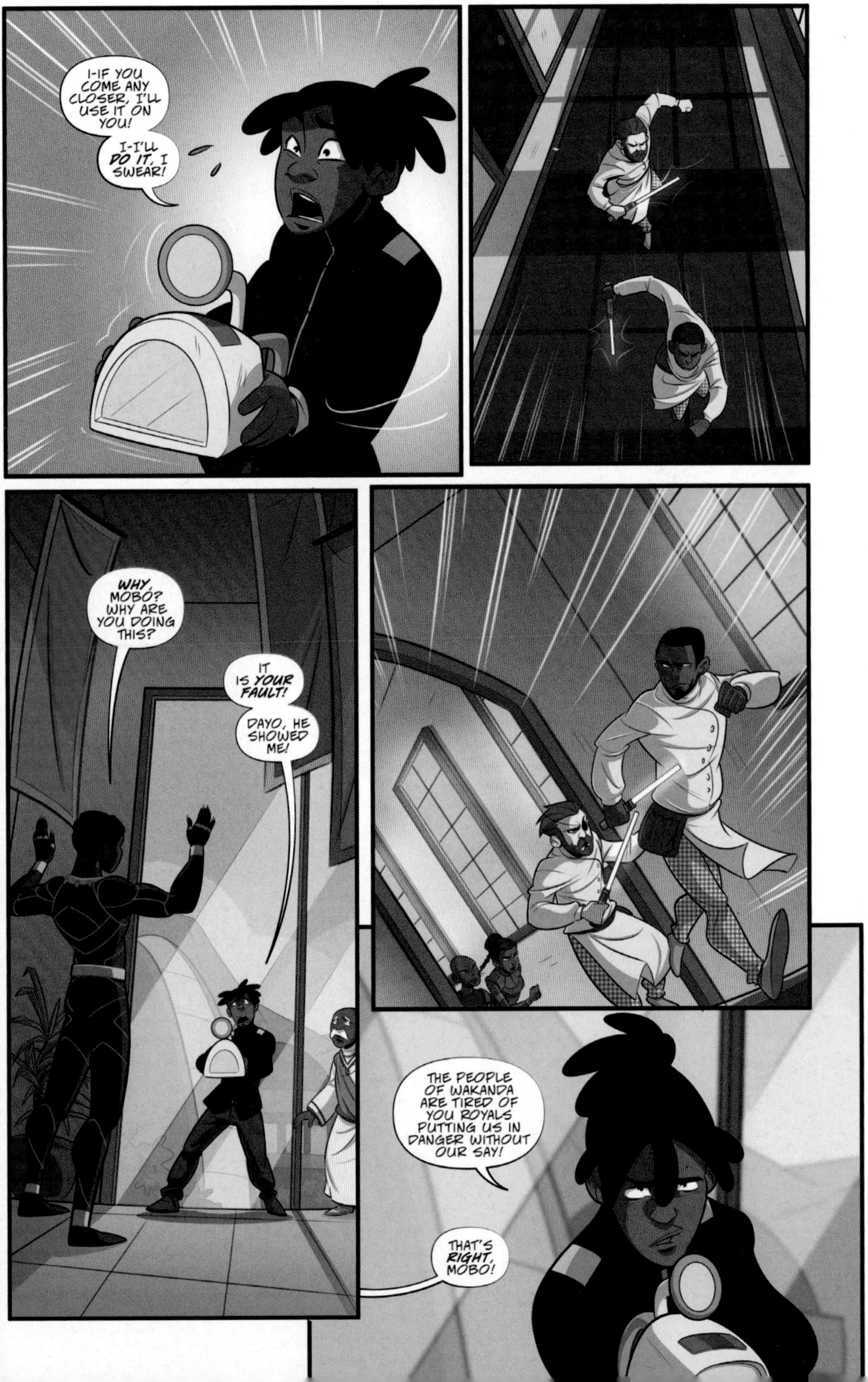
I-IF YOU COME ANY CLOSER, I'LL USE IT ON YOU!
I-I'LL ***DO IT***, I SWEAR!
WHY, MOBO? WHY ARE YOU DOING THIS?
IT IS ***YOUR FAULT!***
DAYO, HE SHOWED ME!
THE PEOPLE OF WAKANDA ARE TIRED OF YOU ROYALS PUTTING US IN DANGER WITHOUT OUR SAY!
THAT'S ***RIGHT***, MOBO!

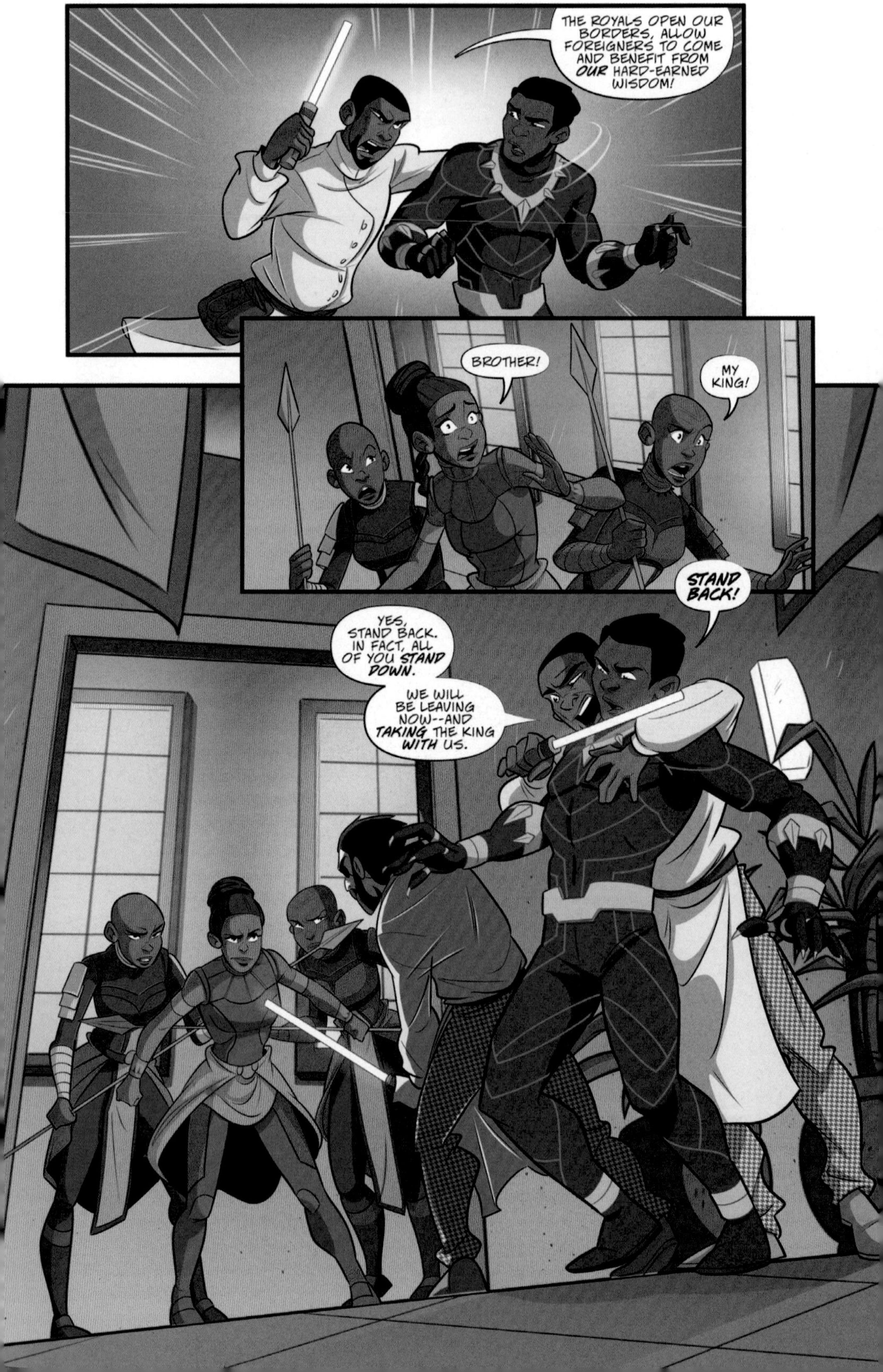
THE ROYALS OPEN OUR BORDERS, ALLOW FOREIGNERS TO COME AND BENEFIT FROM OUR HARD-EARNED WISDOM!
BROTHER!
MY KING!
STAND BACK!
YES, STAND BACK. IN FACT, ALL OF YOU STAND DOWN.
WE WILL BE LEAVING NOW--AND TAKING THE KING WITH US.

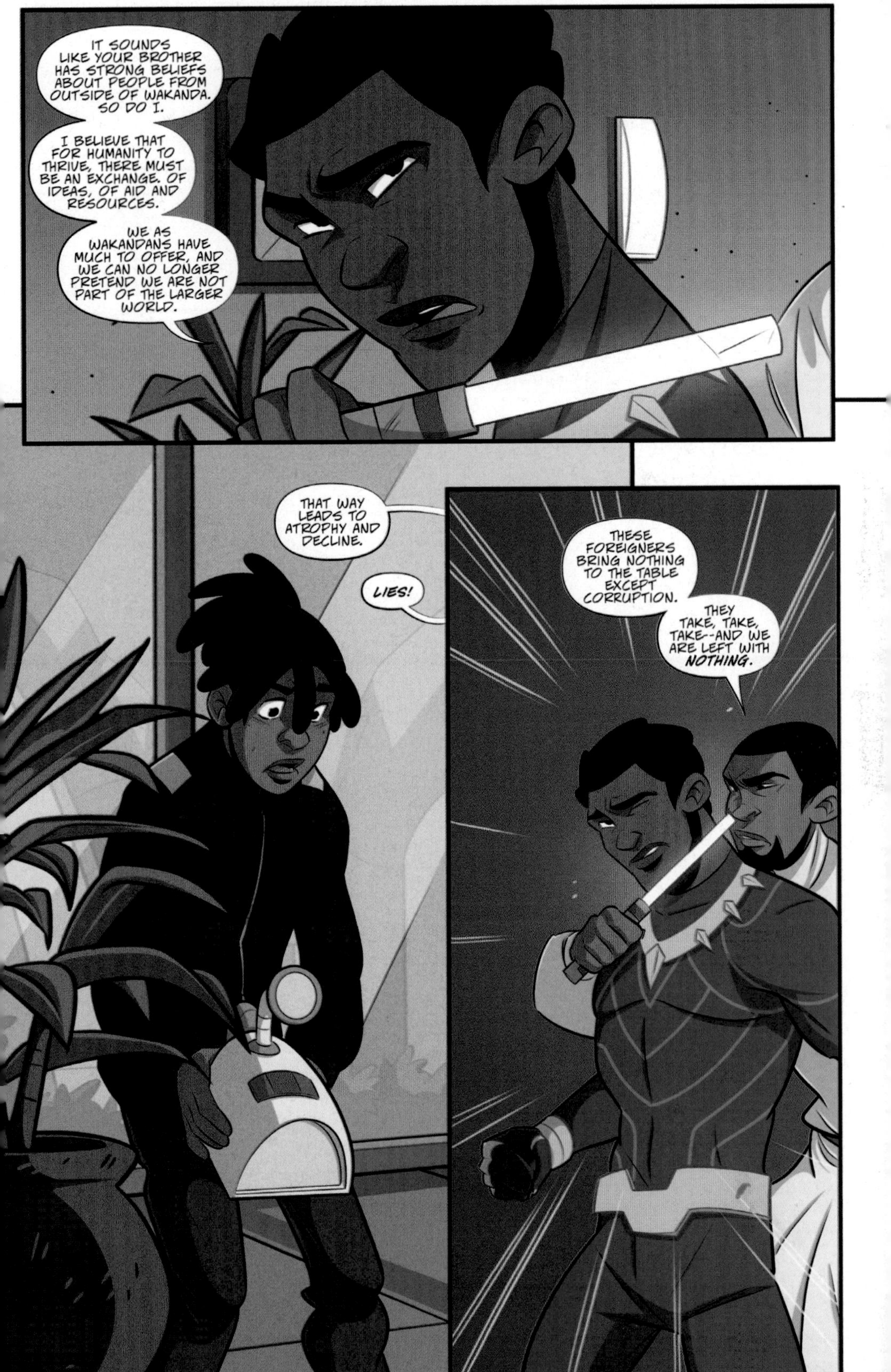
IT SOUNDS LIKE YOUR BROTHER HAS STRONG BELIEFS ABOUT PEOPLE FROM OUTSIDE OF WAKANDA. SO DO I.
I BELIEVE THAT FOR HUMANITY TO THRIVE, THERE MUST BE AN EXCHANGE. OF IDEAS, OF AID AND RESOURCES.
WE AS WAKANDANS HAVE MUCH TO OFFER, AND WE CAN NO LONGER PRETEND WE ARE NOT PART OF THE LARGER WORLD.
THAT WAY LEADS TO ATROPHY AND DECLINE.
LIES!
THESE FOREIGNERS BRING NOTHING TO THE TABLE EXCEPT CORRUPTION.
THEY TAKE, TAKE, TAKE--AND WE ARE LEFT WITH *NOTHING*.

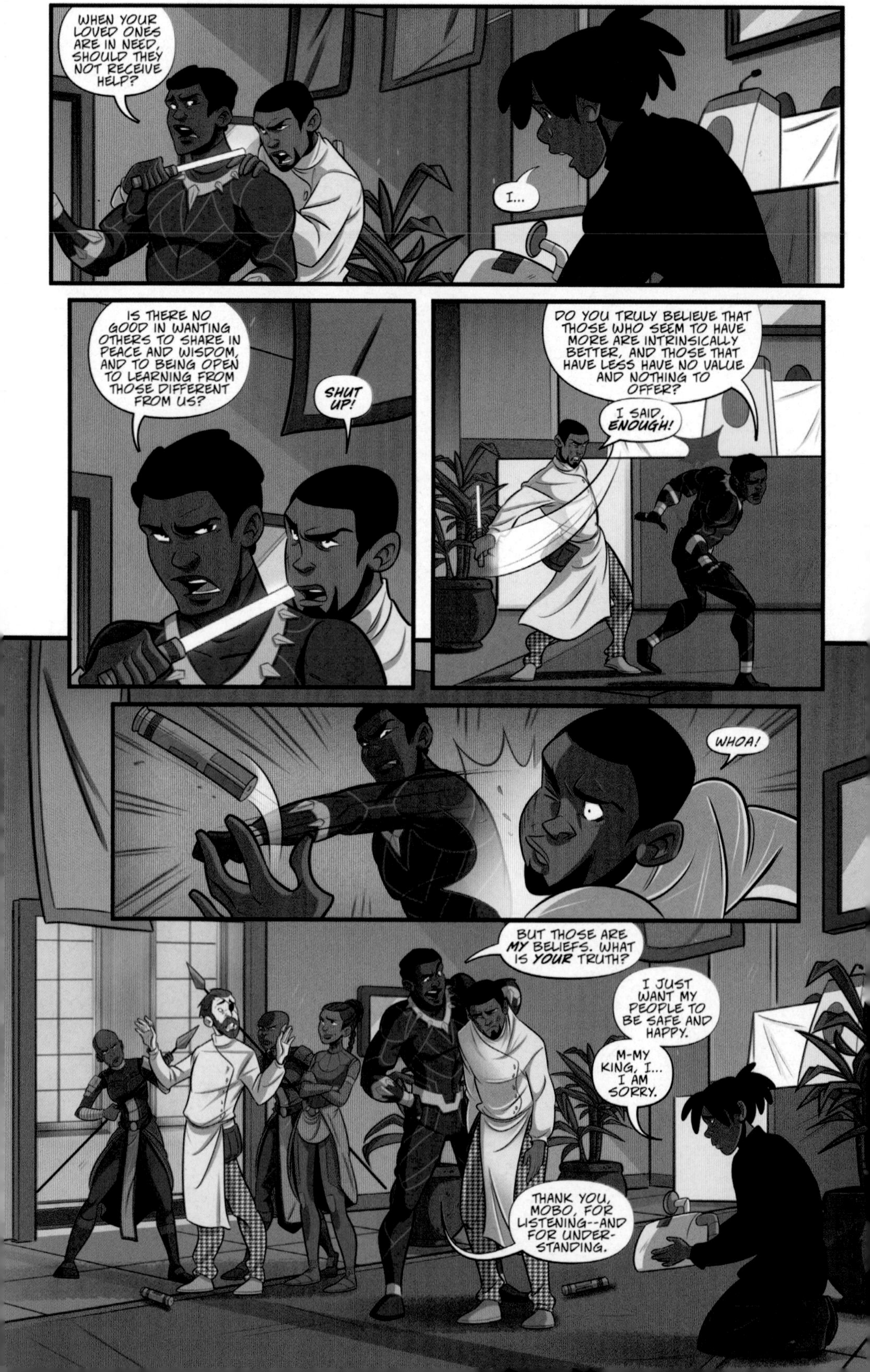
WHEN YOUR LOVED ONES ARE IN NEED, SHOULD THEY NOT RECEIVE HELP?
I...
IS THERE NO GOOD IN WANTING OTHERS TO SHARE IN PEACE AND WISDOM, AND TO BEING OPEN TO LEARNING FROM THOSE DIFFERENT FROM US?
SHUT UP!
DO YOU TRULY BELIEVE THAT THOSE WHO SEEM TO HAVE MORE ARE INTRINSICALLY BETTER, AND THOSE THAT HAVE LESS HAVE NO VALUE AND NOTHING TO OFFER?
I SAID, ENOUGH!
WHOA!
BUT THOSE ARE MY BELIEFS. WHAT IS YOUR TRUTH?
I JUST WANT MY PEOPLE TO BE SAFE AND HAPPY.
M-MY KING, I... I AM SORRY.
THANK YOU, MOBO, FOR LISTENING--AND FOR UNDER-STANDING.

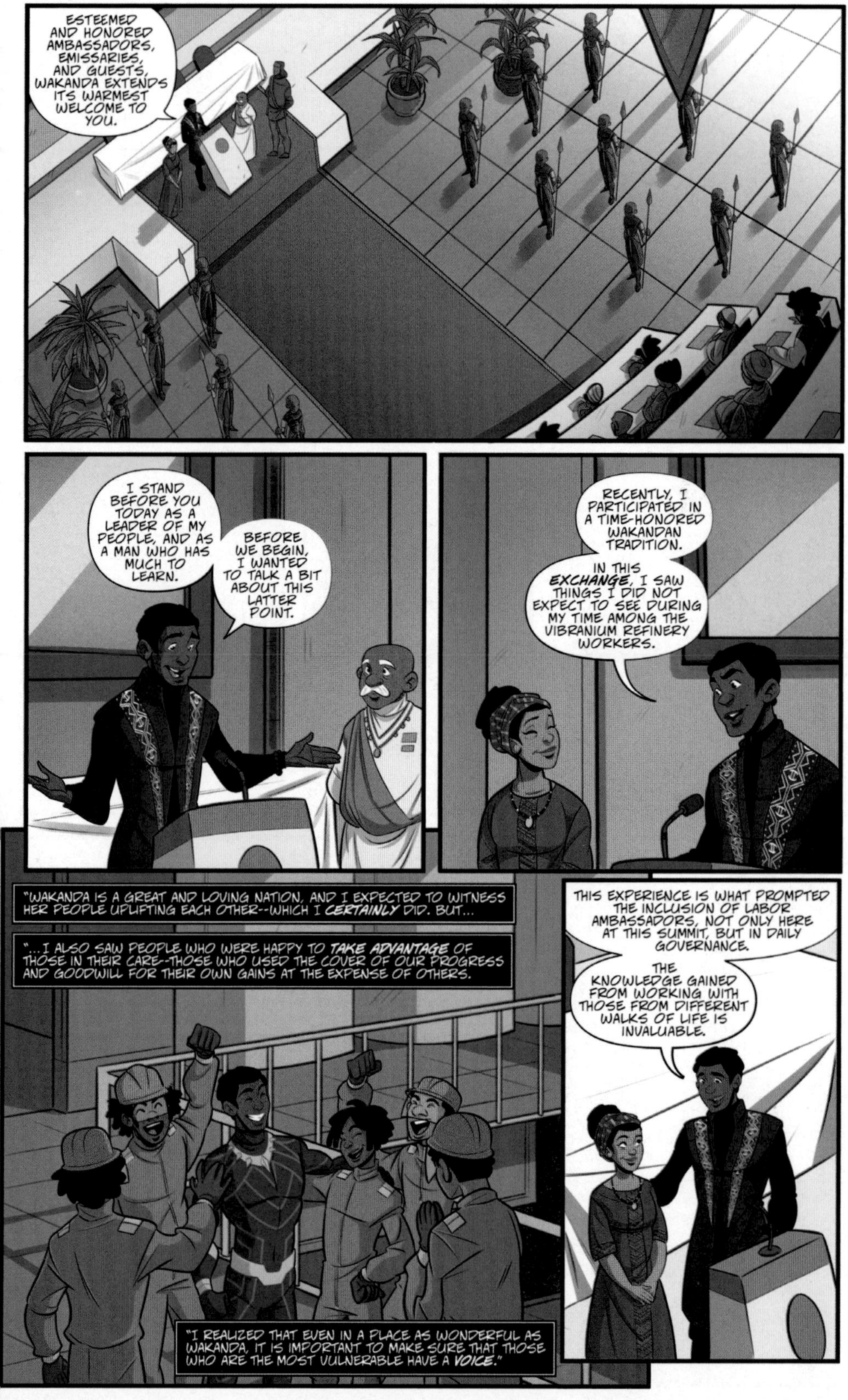

ESTEEMED AND HONORED AMBASSADORS, EMISSARIES, AND GUESTS, WAKANDA EXTENDS ITS WARMEST WELCOME TO YOU.
I STAND BEFORE YOU TODAY AS A LEADER OF MY PEOPLE, AND AS A MAN WHO HAS MUCH TO LEARN.
BEFORE WE BEGIN, I WANTED TO TALK A BIT ABOUT THIS LATTER POINT.
RECENTLY, I PARTICIPATED IN A TIME-HONORED WAKANDAN TRADITION.
IN THIS EXCHANGE, I SAW THINGS I DID NOT EXPECT TO SEE DURING MY TIME AMONG THE VIBRANIUM REFINERY WORKERS.
"WAKANDA IS A GREAT AND LOVING NATION, AND I EXPECTED TO WITNESS HER PEOPLE UPLIFTING EACH OTHER--WHICH I CERTAINLY DID. BUT...
"...I ALSO SAW PEOPLE WHO WERE HAPPY TO TAKE ADVANTAGE OF THOSE IN THEIR CARE--THOSE WHO USED THE COVER OF OUR PROGRESS AND GOODWILL FOR THEIR OWN GAINS AT THE EXPENSE OF OTHERS.
"I REALIZED THAT EVEN IN A PLACE AS WONDERFUL AS WAKANDA, IT IS IMPORTANT TO MAKE SURE THAT THOSE WHO ARE THE MOST VULNERABLE HAVE A VOICE."
THIS EXPERIENCE IS WHAT PROMPTED THE INCLUSION OF LABOR AMBASSADORS, NOT ONLY HERE AT THIS SUMMIT, BUT IN DAILY GOVERNANCE.
THE KNOWLEDGE GAINED FROM WORKING WITH THOSE FROM DIFFERENT WALKS OF LIFE IS INVALUABLE.

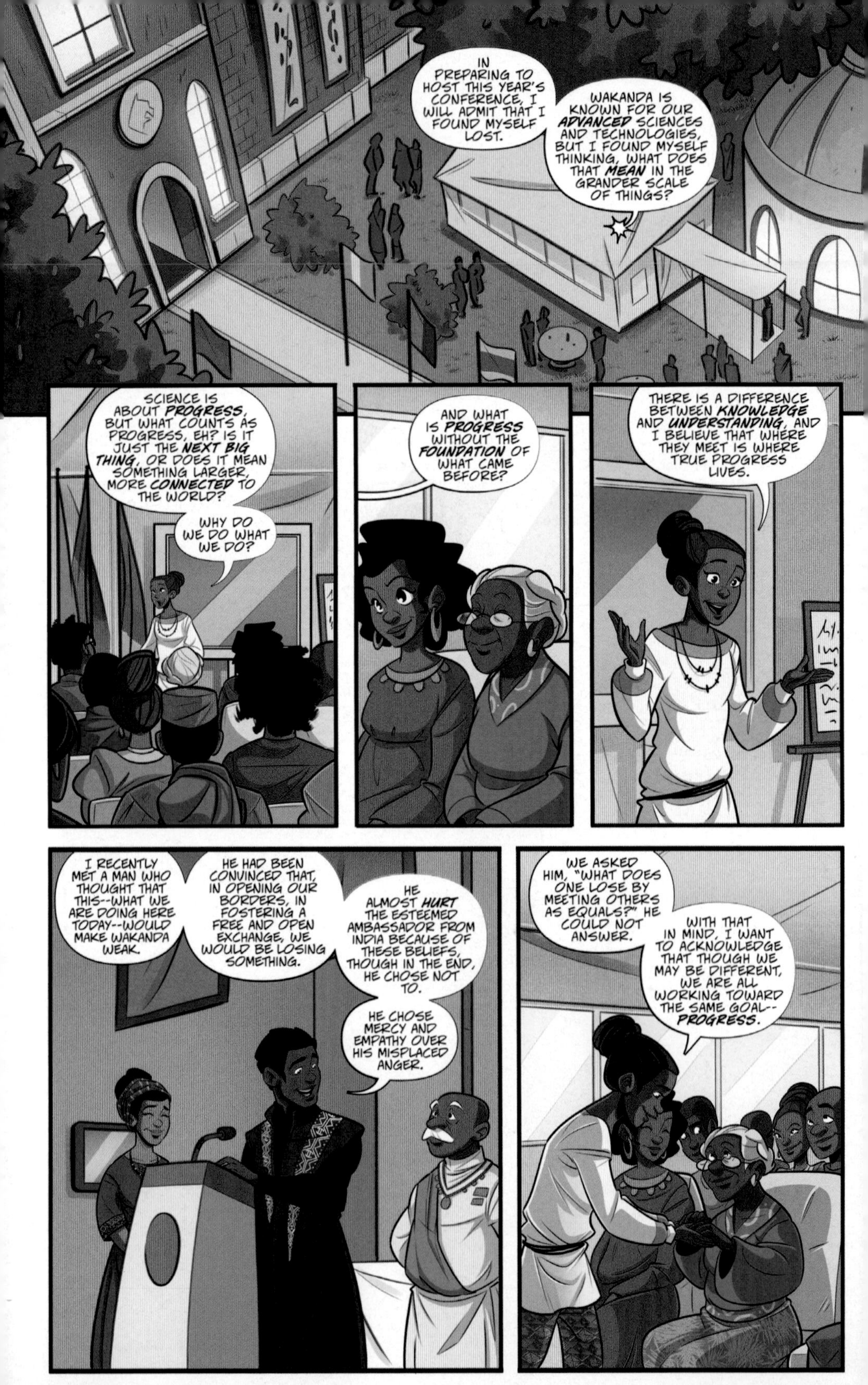
IN PREPARING TO HOST THIS YEAR'S CONFERENCE, I WILL ADMIT THAT I FOUND MYSELF LOST.
WAKANDA IS KNOWN FOR OUR ADVANCED SCIENCES AND TECHNOLOGIES, BUT I FOUND MYSELF THINKING, WHAT DOES THAT MEAN IN THE GRANDER SCALE OF THINGS?
SCIENCE IS ABOUT PROGRESS, BUT WHAT COUNTS AS PROGRESS, EH? IS IT JUST THE NEXT BIG THING, OR DOES IT MEAN SOMETHING LARGER, MORE CONNECTED TO THE WORLD?
WHY DO WE DO WHAT WE DO?
AND WHAT IS PROGRESS WITHOUT THE FOUNDATION OF WHAT CAME BEFORE?
THERE IS A DIFFERENCE BETWEEN KNOWLEDGE AND UNDERSTANDING, AND I BELIEVE THAT WHERE THEY MEET IS WHERE TRUE PROGRESS LIVES.
I RECENTLY MET A MAN WHO THOUGHT THAT THIS--WHAT WE ARE DOING HERE TODAY--WOULD MAKE WAKANDA WEAK.
HE HAD BEEN CONVINCED THAT, IN OPENING OUR BORDERS, IN FOSTERING A FREE AND OPEN EXCHANGE, WE WOULD BE LOSING SOMETHING.
HE ALMOST HURT THE ESTEEMED AMBASSADOR FROM INDIA BECAUSE OF THESE BELIEFS, THOUGH IN THE END, HE CHOSE NOT TO.
HE CHOSE MERCY AND EMPATHY OVER HIS MISPLACED ANGER.
WE ASKED HIM, "WHAT DOES ONE LOSE BY MEETING OTHERS AS EQUALS?" HE COULD NOT ANSWER.
WITH THAT IN MIND, I WANT TO ACKNOWLEDGE THAT THOUGH WE MAY BE DIFFERENT, WE ARE ALL WORKING TOWARD THE SAME GOAL-- PROGRESS.

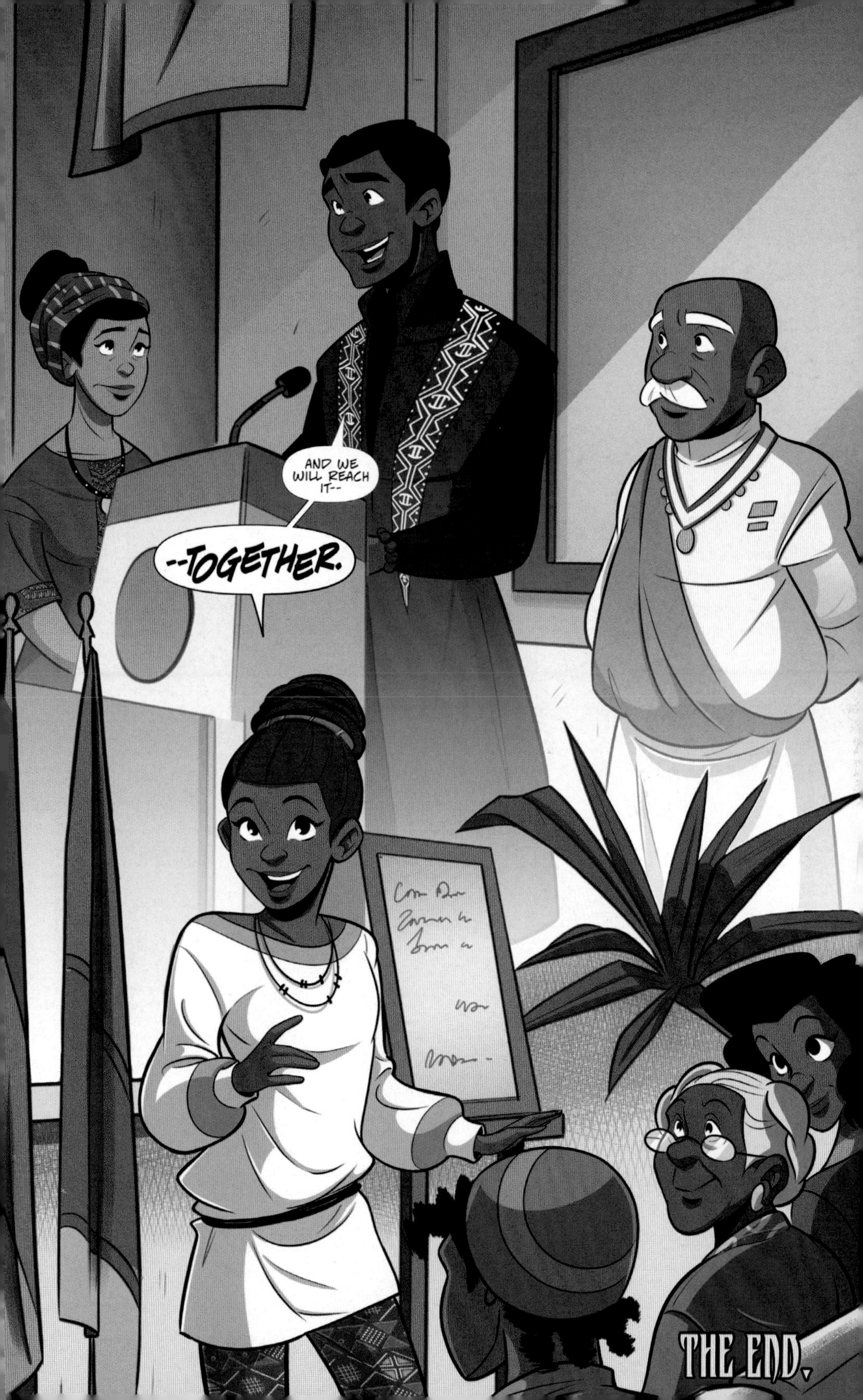
AND WE WILL REACH IT--
--TOGETHER.
THE END.

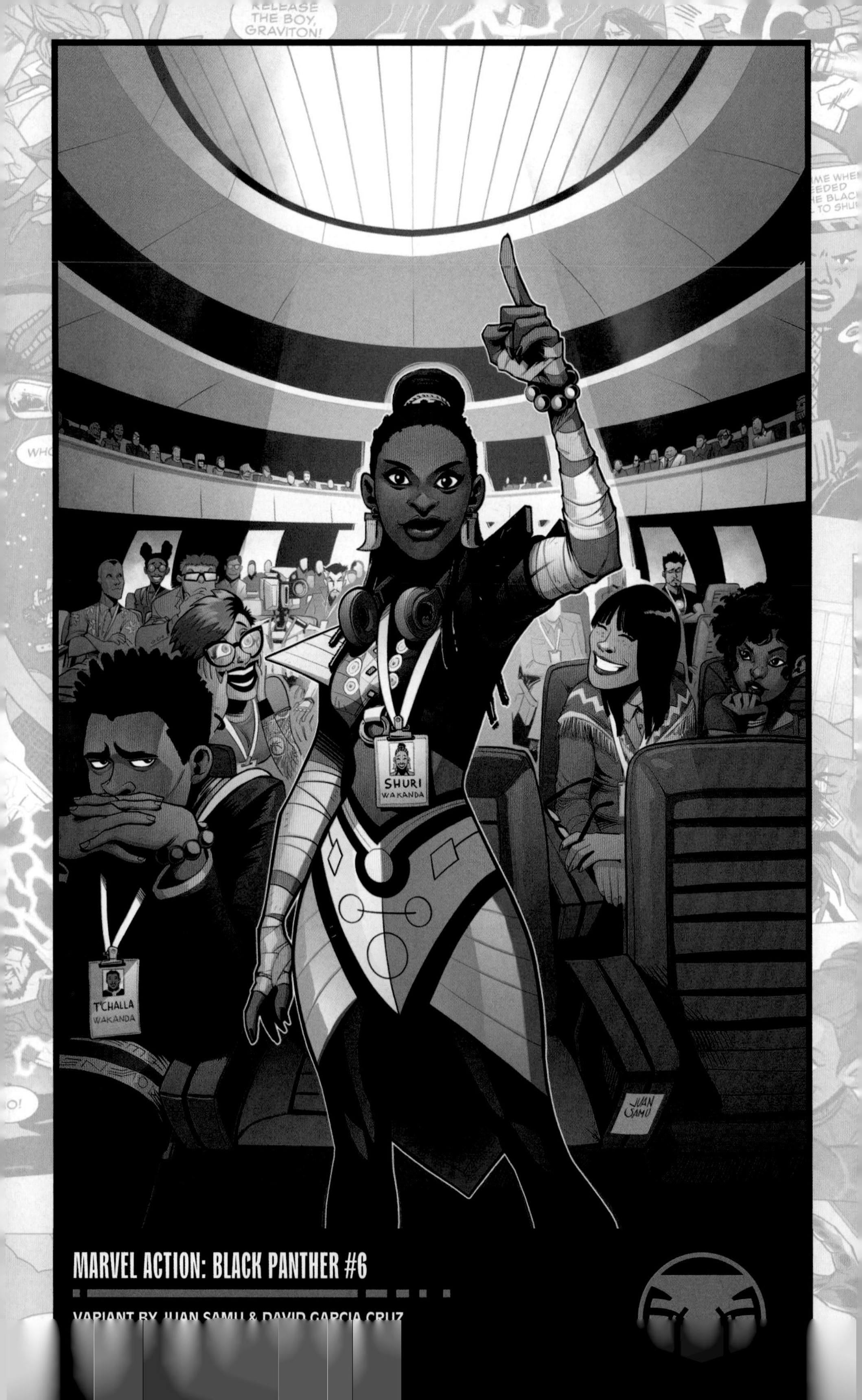
RELEASE THE BOY, GRAVITON!
SHURI
WAKANDA
T'CHALLA
WAKANDA
JUAN SAMU

MARVEL ACTION: BLACK PANTHER #6

VARIANT BY JUAN SAMU & DAVID GARCIA CRUZ

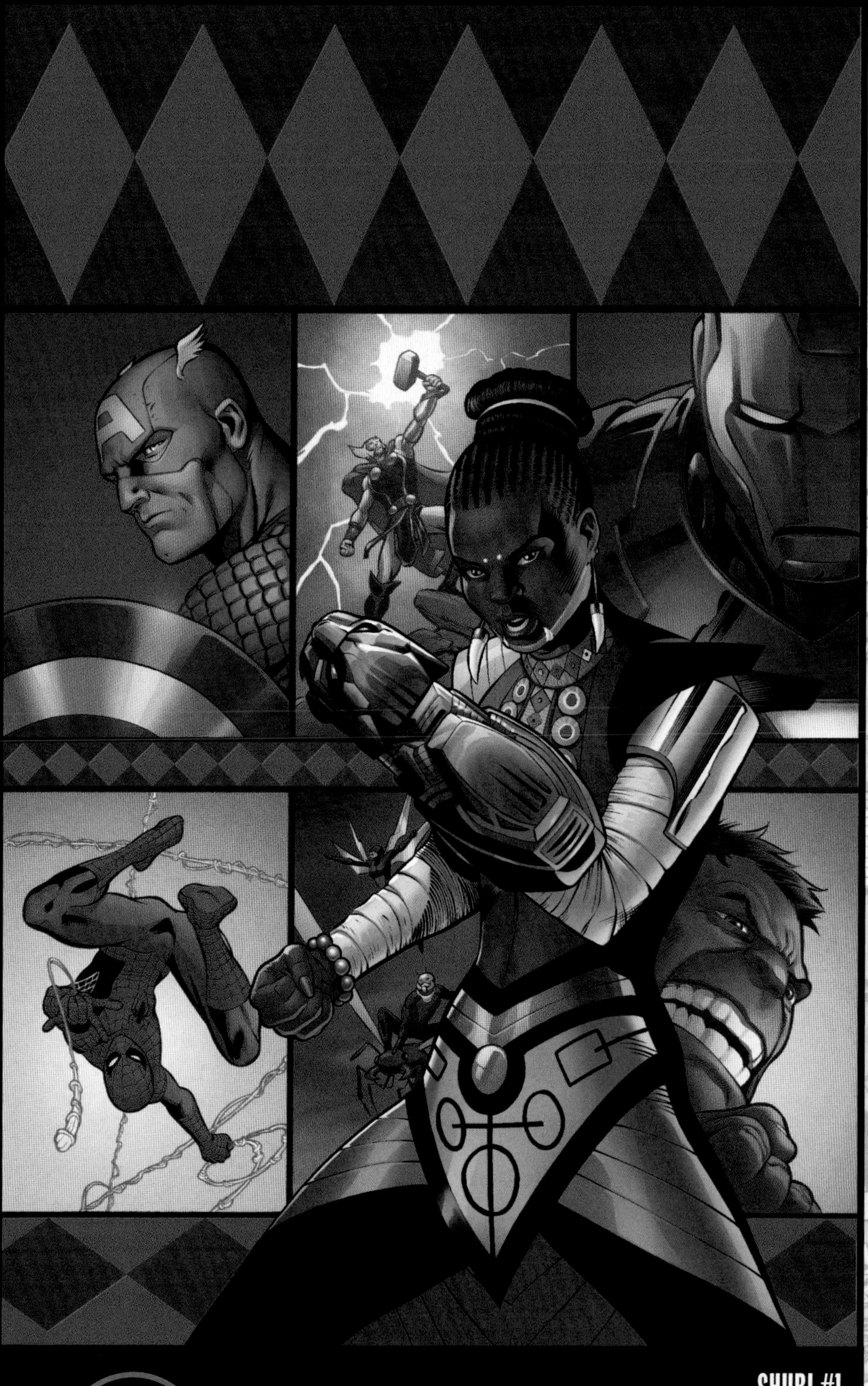

SHURI #1

VARIANT BY CARLOS PACHECO,
RAFAEL FONTERIZ & LAURA MARTIN

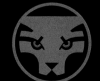

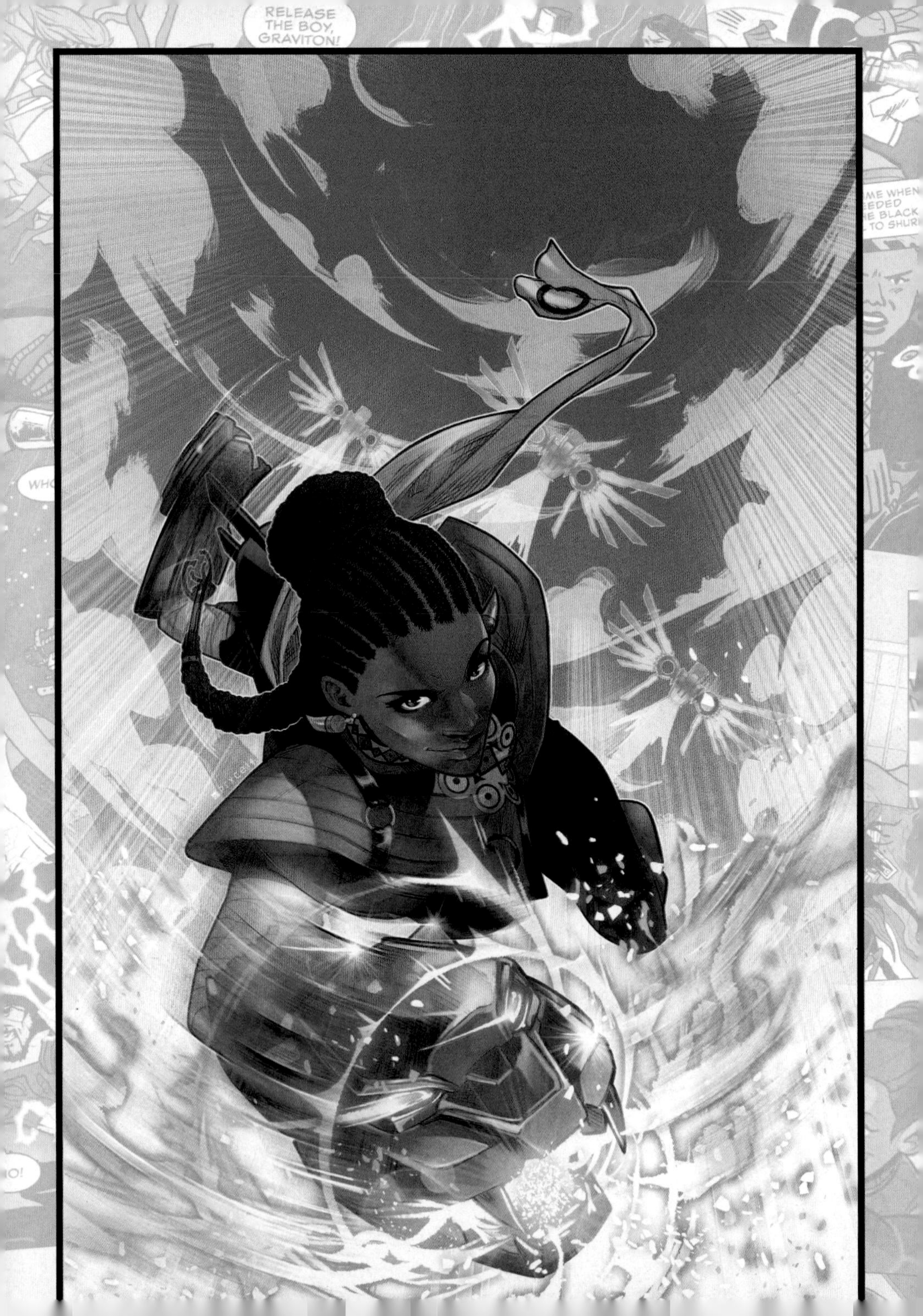
RELEASE THE BOY, GRAVITON!

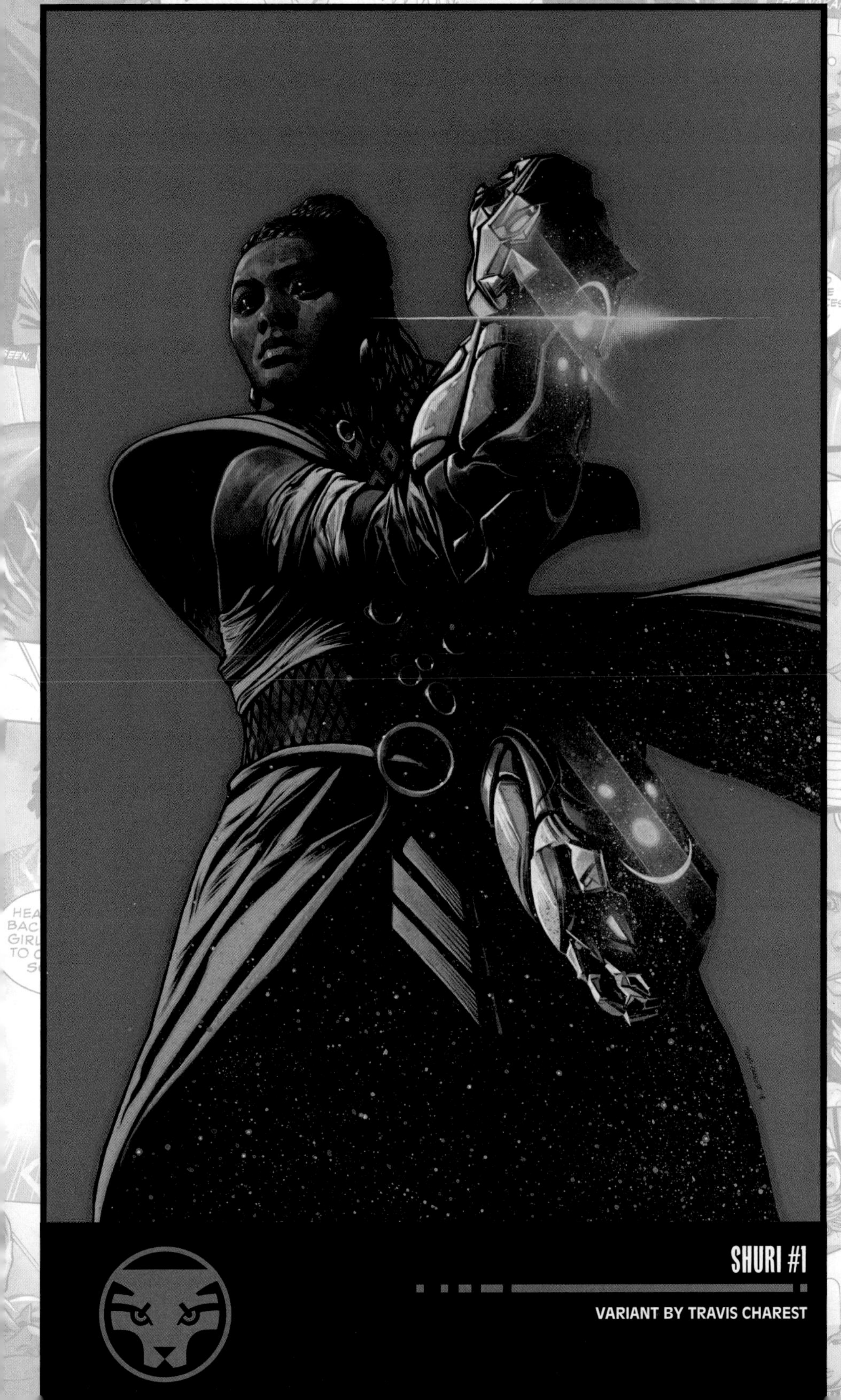

SHURI #1

VARIANT BY TRAVIS CHAREST

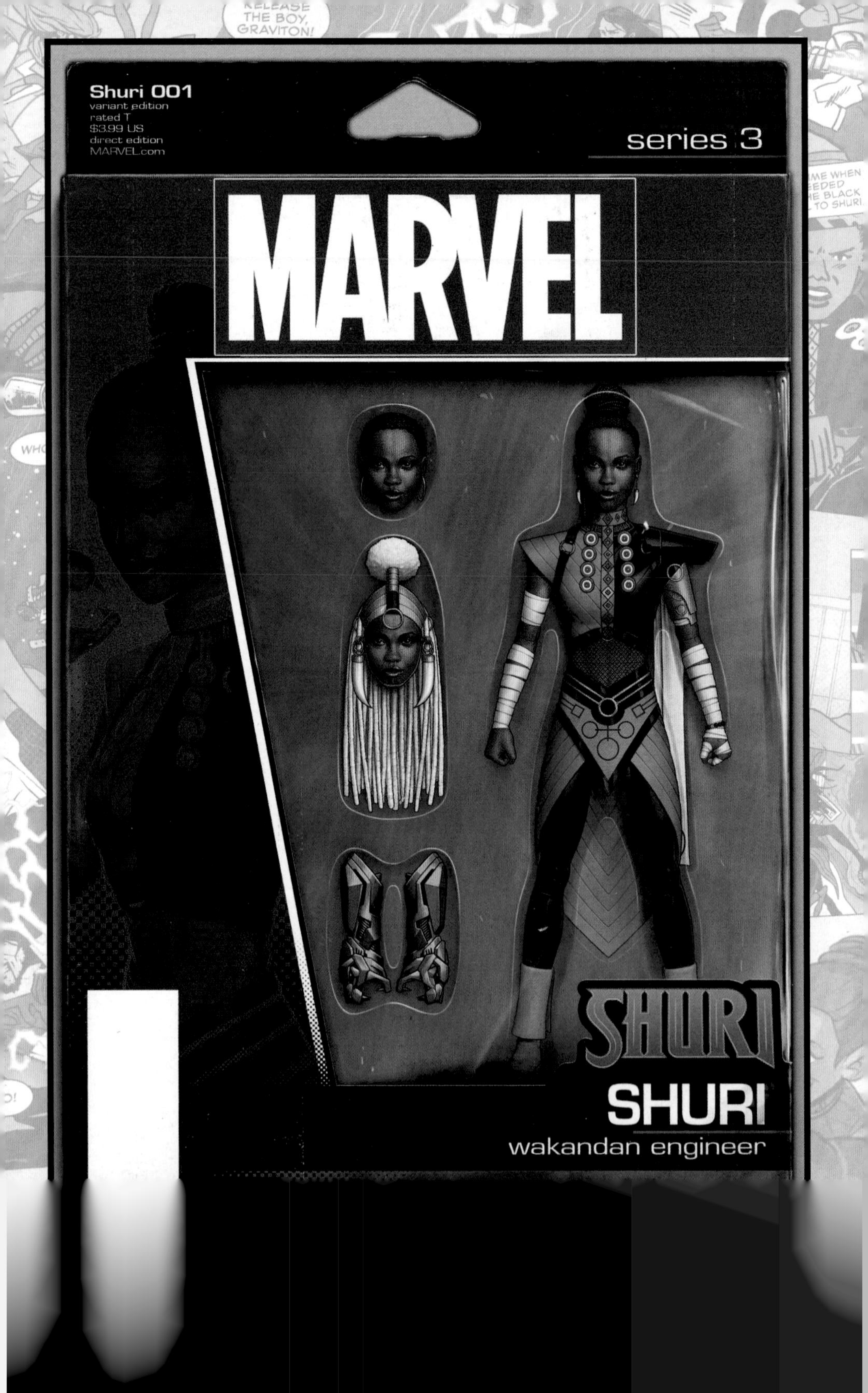
THE BOY, GRAVITON!
Shuri 001
variant edition
rated T
$3.99 US
direct edition
MARVEL.com
series 3
MARVEL
SHURI
SHURI
wakandan engineer